SIGN OF THE TIMES ANTHOLOGY

A Chronicle of Decadence in the Atomic Age

10 YEARS

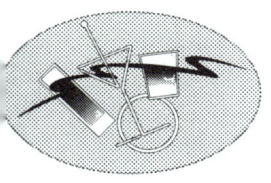 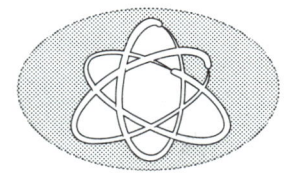 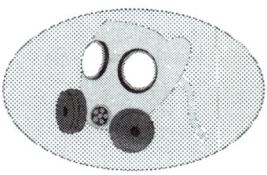

© Studio 403, 1992

All rights reserved. No part of this publication may be reproduced, transmitted, transcribed, stored in a retrieval system, or translated into any language in any form by any means without the written permission of Studio 403.

In the near future, an electronic version of this anthology edition will be available. The electronic edition will include the complete text of all ten years of *Sign of the Times—Chronicle of Decadence in the Atomic Age*.

Published by:
Studio 403
221 Boylston Avenue East
Seattle, Washington 98102

First/Last Edition—Summer 1992

ISBN 0-9633943-0-4

Body text is 10 point Palton on 12 points lead, with Palton Bold headlines in 24 point. The entire book was composed using Microsoft Word for Windows 2.0 and Aldus Pagemaker 4.0, with cover art produced using Aldus Freehand 3.1. All pages were imaged on the LaserMaster1000 courtesy of manna from heaven.

Special Thanks:
Kent Asmussen, Sally Brunsman, Laurie Lindsay, Wallis Bolz, Eric Nygren, and Judith Bloch

Front Cover Design:
Darcie Furlan

Back Cover Design:
Studio 403

For my brother, Karl.
You would have enjoyed this book.

Preface

From the first issue, published in the fall of 1981

On this 24th day of October I write these grave words about the state of our beloved union. As we know, our destiny is in the hands of a two bit actor playing in a four star ballgame. We cannot continue in this suicidal direction without going to war with another strain of our own genetic make-up. In the constant fight to maintain a decadent lifestyle, it gives me great pleasure to unveil a new publication: *Sign of the Times—A Chronicle of Decadence in the Atomic Age. Sign of the Times* is to be a biannual publication with the first issue consisting of eight pages and with a press run of 1,000. The content will be a varied bill of fiction, political satire, photography and graphics. Just plain black on white, there is no color in these desperate times.

People say that nothing is free anymore. I heard it myself at the local convenience store. I don't believe it. I won't believe it...and will commit financial suicide to prove my point. What I want is free—they call it *freedom*. As Ronnie brings us closer to our own demise, I find a bit of narcissistic journalism is called for. Success out of defiance of proven economics...to prove that life does not exist solely by and for the flow of money...the belief in the fairy tales of truth, justice and the American way is why I choose to take the plunge.

Would you care to take the plunge with me? *Sign of the Times—A Chronicle of Decadence in the Atomic Age* will be emotionally and/or financially supported by its readership; it shall go on. Want to help?

We change trains here.

It is my philosophy that life is for the living. One should live the singularly proven life we are given with the maximum amount of humor possible. For if we cannot snicker at the antics of oneself, how can we be expected to laugh at our government's suicidal direction? This brings us to fanatics, be they religious, political or economic. What these people lost when they acquired *fanaticism* is the ability to take two steps back and see the situation in the light of day.

My last comments deal with things heard on the street. Street gossip is the barometer by which I judge the quality of life. When a woman was asked her opinion of hairy upper torsos on males, she calmly replied, "I don't like trees on my playground." So my question is: "Ronnie, why rain on my parade?"

Ten years later

During the year that it has taken to produce this anthology issue, I have been forced to think about the magazine in the grand scheme of the world. The print run remains at 1,000, including the anthology—mostly for reasons of economy. It still remains a labor of love . What started as a reaction to the first Reagan administration carried over through the second and on through the Bush White House. With this fall's election, I know not the outcome of either the nation or the magazine. Maybe it's just time to get off this continent for a while.

All of the biographies are from the original stories and don't really reflect what is happening in the authors' lives today. Some are alive, others dead, many just lost.

Mark Stephen Souder
Publisher & Editor
Sign of the Times — Chronicle of Decadence in the Atomic Age

Table of Contents

Story	Author	Story	Original Printing	Page
1	Steve Anderson	Where Water Buffalo Fly	Volume 4, Number 2	1
2	Susan Bergman	Hunger in the Hours Before Morning	Volume 3, Number 1	6
3	Captain Rat	Joey	Volume 1, Number 3	12
4	Todd M. Cobb	Linus Iscariot	Volume 5, Number 1	19
5	Jeff Cochran	Speed, After All, Is Important	Volume 1, Number 2	24
6	Patricia Flinn	Reflections in a Hoboken Tenement…	Volume 3, Number 4	26
7	Scott Haugaard & Mark Whitaker	Some Enchanted Evening	Volume 2, Number 4	32
8	Kearin Sandwick	You Hardly Believed It Yourself	Volume 2, Number 1	37
9	Jacob Levich	Out in the Cold	Volume 1, Number 3	43
10	Laurie Lindsay	The Flight of Ms. Harriet Peacock	Volume 4, Number 3	50
11	R.A. Lindsey	Young Impression	Volume 3, Number 2	59
12	Terence A. Loose	Eyes of Despair	Volume 5, Number 2	65
13	T. Jackson Lyons	Between Love and Lust	Volume 2, Number 1	68
14	James Maloney	Artichoke Art	Volume 1, Number 2	77
15	James Maloney	The Bar	Volume 3, Number 1	79
16	Jay Marvin	The Rag Picker	Volume 3, Number 1	81
17	F.J. Matozzo	The Golden Fleece	Volume 4, Number 1	87
18	Andrew McCormick	Compassion	Volume 1, Number 1	93
19	Ralph Robert Moore	Sex on Sheets	Volume 3, Number 3	98
20	Brenda Munroe	Lyle's Dream	Volume 5, Number 1	110
21	Kim Pearson	Weirdos Sleep Till Noon	Volume 3, Number 2	115

Table of Contents

Story	Author	Story	Original Printing	Page
22	Patrick Quinn	The Hitchhiker and the Doctor	Volume 2, Number 4	120
23	Patrick Quinn	The Secret	Volume 5, Number 2	129
24	Richard Rabicoff	The Chair of Privilege	Volume 2, Number 3	135
25	Diane M. Rebel	The Hunt	Volume 2, Number 2	148
26	Red Onion	Beating the TV	Volume 3, Number 4	152
27	Ben Satterfield	Everybody Talks About Reality...	Volume 3, Number 4	161
28	Ben Satterfield	The Naked Facts	Volume 4, Number 4	169
29	Gary Smith	A Lady Not Quite of Quality	Volume 3, Number 1	179
30	Gary Smith	Fergus' Closet	Volume 3, Number 3	188
31	Willie Smith	The Wild West	Volume 3, Number 4	199
32	Willie Smith	Essay on the Vacuum	Volume 4, Number 1	203
33	Dale L. Sproule	On the Punko Beat, Beat, Beat	Volume 2, Number 3	206
34	C. P. Stancich	The Heterosexualization of a Catamite	Volume 1, Number 4	216
35	C. P. Stancich	The Belch of Midge Besselman's Husband	Volume 4, Number 2	224
36	Dave Swartout	Tutelary Angels	Volume 5, Number 1	228
37	Dave Swarto&ut	Lupine	Volume 5, Number 2	245
38	Uncle River	The Drunk	Volume 4, Number 3	254
39	Vava Pussy	Vavadoo	Volume 4, Number 3	256
40	Gary Wiener	Six Inches Up	Volume 3, Number 4	259

1

Steve Anderson
Where Water Buffalo Fly

At the end of highway #4, me and Snowball were about as deep into the Nam Bo as you get. Less than forty more miles down and we'd be in Rach Tau, the southmost point in Vietnam that had a name. Of course, we weren't headed that way.

At Hong My village, we turned our jeep over to some ARVN rangers, just like we had been ordered. We could've sold it back there at Can Tho and nobody would've known the difference, but we didn't. So instead, the ARVNs will sell it, and nobody still won't know the difference.

Since we had some slack in the schedule we decided to sack out and rest for a day or so, because in the Army it isn't smart to finish anything early. But a helicopter was beating around the area, and with that thump-thump-thump bouncing off the bamboo we didn't have much luck getting to sleep. Anyway, we heard other noise—cheering, maybe—on the other side of the village.

"Sounds like a party," said Snowball. "We gotta check that out." So he was fast to get his green bandana on his head, the one that made him look like Aunt Jemima in camouflage. That was a joke he told, not me.

Just half a klick from where we had tried to camp out, we found the celebration. Half the people in the village were standing around a drained rice paddy, watching four American GIs slipping and sliding in the mud while strapping a harness on a water buffalo. The buffalo just stood there, its head twisted back, its eye rolled sideways to see what was going on. They have eyes, these buffalo, about the size of your fist.

On its back sat a little kid wearing one of those flat cone-shaped hats, his grin bigger than his face.

"Aw, shit, man, look at that!" said Snowball.

If you've seen one kid on a water buffalo you've seen them all, but you didn't say that to Snowball.

We eased through the crowd, Snowball speaking a lot of Vietnamese with the kids and the mamasans, who couldn't help but smile with him. Vietnamese just seem to naturally like spades. But I kept Snowball moving, because he didn't need much excuse to stop and haul out that bag of candy. The kids followed us anyway, and by the time we got up front, there were enough to make up a little gang. They kept at arm's length, but hung around close enough to be first in line for whatever we had to give.

We walked over to where a couple of NCOs stood off by themselves, overlooking the job, their arms folded and resting on their big stomachs. One was a first-sergeant, the other a staff sergeant, and neither much more than glanced our way, which kind of surprised me. For one thing, we had these noise suppressors on our '16s that made them look more like small bazookas than rifles. For another, we wore face paint that gave us the look of people who hadn't made it home for a couple of nights—and wouldn't make it tonight, either. Up around Long Binh, they looked at us like we were from the zoo. But not here.

"How y'all doin' ?" I asked in a cracker voice that usually went down alright with most white boys.

The first-sergeant wouldn't turn, but the other one spared us some time. "Where you headed?" he asked.

"Just passing through," I said. It seemed like he didn't much care where we were headed, so I went on. "We thought we heard a chopper. Is that what the party's about?"

"We're doing some public *re*lations work. Soon as we get this buff trussed up, a chopper's going to lift it over to Song Doc. It's been rented out."

Snowball didn't look happy about these plans. "I seen artillery moved around this way. Not no buffalo though," he said.

Somehow his words pulled the first-sergeant's chain, and his voice filled the space around us.

"At Can Tho, we lifted body bags this way after Tet. We couldn't truck them out fast enough to beat the maggots. So we just airlifted them. Choppers didn't even have to land. They'd just drop a line and we'd hook them on."

He still hadn't so much as looked our way.

But before anybody had time to get down to hard feelings, one of the GIs who'd been working on the buffalo popped smoke, and we all stood and waited. When you think a helicopter is coming you don't think about much else.

In a couple of minutes a Huey seemed to jump up from behind a stand of palm trees. It probably had been out hot-rodding, because it was loaded down with guys just sitting up there, like they were only along for the ride.

This Huey wasn't one of those beefed up models, and it was carrying a pretty heavy load already, so I thought it was a little small to do an air-lift job. Of course, I don't know how much a water buffalo weighs.

The GIs on the ground got the kid off the buffalo, and they all cleared away. The chopper moved over the buffalo and hovered about thirty to thirty-five feet above. A guy up there who looked like he was laughing threw out a line. A GI on the ground ran back to the buffalo, all stooped over like the prop was beating away no more than six inches above his head. He attached the line to the harness, and ran back out of the way, now acting like something was going to blow up.

The chopper rose gradually to take up the slack in the line, then the big blades started slapping the air hard, trying to get that buffalo off the ground. That chopper pulled and pulled, but it couldn't bring that water buffalo straight up.

To get enough lift, the chopper had to start forward. That maneuver brought the buffalo off the ground, barely, but it had him swinging back and forth in about a twenty foot arc. The chopper itself started swinging in the opposite direction of the buffalo, and this double pendulum didn't look like something that the pilot was going to be able to handle.

He powered up in a spiral for maybe a couple of hundred feet, trying to get the load under control. Now the buffalo was bellowing like hell and was swinging all over the place, worse than before. The pilot knew not to go any higher, but the problem was he couldn't land the buff either with it swinging like that—not without snapping its legs off.

There was no going up and there was no going down. The joy ride was over.

The problem had to solve itself, and it did pretty soon. Something broke or came loose in all that harnessing, and the buffalo fell—turning over and over and not bellowing anymore. At least I didn't hear anything. After the ground caught the buffalo, the most noise you could hear was from that chopper. It had gone shooting up in the air real fast after losing its load, and the pilot still wasn't in control.

In a few seconds, though, all them Vietnamese broke loose. They were crying and laughing and making just about any other kind of noise. I don't think they knew what to do, but they stayed away from us.

The bunch of kids who'd been waiting for Snowball had disappeared. In fact, all the Vietnamese were disappearing from this place, slipping away into the hedges, and it was getting quiet.

"Well I'll be dipped in shit," said the first-sergeant.

"Oh, Lordy, Lordy," said the staff sergeant in the country twang of some back home grandad, like normal cussing couldn't handle the occasion.

"These folks gotta have a buffalo," said Snowball. "What they gonna do?"

"Guess there'll be one hell of a barbecue tonight," the first-sergeant said.

"These people don' need no dead buffalo. It's gotta be alive."

"Shit, son," said the first-sergeant, turning our way for the first time. "The U.S. Army bought them this one. Now we'll buy them another one—probably a better one. Why do you care?"

From our back angle, I had thought I had pretty much put together what the first-sergeant looked like. But when I finally saw him face on, I was mainly surprised at what I didn't see. He was just a middle-aged man who was overweight and who had a pasty-face with nothing in it to remember. He was as plain and ordinary a looking human as you'd ever see. That's all there was to it.

We got on our way before the big cookout. Too much attention to this spot didn't help us, so we were off. I didn't want to think too much more about that buffalo. We had to do recon through at least two places where unfriendly gooks would try to blow our asses off if they saw us, and I like to have my mind clear for that sort of thing.

Snowball, though, just couldn't let it go.

"That was a awful thing to do. We always fuckin' over them people."

"But if they'd got the buff over to whatever village that was, everybody would've come out ahead. Maybe there ain't much more than a little luck separating something that's real good and something that's real bad."

"Seems to me bad and good ain't much alike. So what you talking about?"

"Okay, I don't know what I'm talking about. But it was still just an accident."

"Shit. It was a accident and it wasn't a accident. That's all I got to say about it."

But it wasn't all he had to say, because he hounded my ass for the next fifty miles that we walked and crawled through swamps and mangrove forests. It was the injustice of it that bothered Snowball, but since he was used to injustice, I figured that maybe he'd soon get over the buffalo.

On the other hand, though, I don't know how either one of us is ever going to forget watching something that big—something that didn't know what to do with its legs—fall so far for no good reason.

Steve Anderson has published one other short story, "American Expedition." It too has a Vietnam setting.

2

Susan Bergman
Hunger in the Hours Before Morning

It was in the Speed Queen that I met my first lover, the only man who ever really understood me and my wild ways. Probably I fell for his enormous nose, which somehow instinctively I knew to be a sign of virility, jutting from his face like a challenge, an easy target for bums and gentlemen alike. The Speed Queen was on M Street, which was just down from where I lived in a cold yellow room over a record store, where punks hung out and sometimes managed, by breaking the lock on a door labeled 'Private,' to get up to my place and spray paint and beat on my door. I lived just outside Georgetown, down the street from the brick shopping gallery, and even I sometimes felt like a rat in a mansion, a little carrier of filth and disease.

My first lover was quite mad and not very clean, but he managed to survive by sleeping under the bridge and by always keeping a thick knife where he could easily reach it (this knife was also a symbol of virility, which I must admit I prize, though a bit less these days, now that my metabolism has slowed and I have come to despise most everyone I meet).

He came to the Speed Queen to get warm and clean himself up a little, which he did by stripping to the waist and plunging his arms into a washing machine that was in the wash cycle. His timing had to be perfect so that no one guarding their clothing would catch him—the germ-encrusted arms of a wild-eyed man are undesirable—and stop him.

On this particular day I had slid for a moment into the coffee shop next door to buy hot chocolate and a donut from the huge woman behind the counter. The place was called 'D.C. Eats,' or something. The chocolate in the hot chocolate never dissolved, but stuck in a thick ooze of grainy sweetness at the bottom of the styrofoam cup. (I don't even like donuts but I ordered them for the pleasure of watching her fingers, each of them the size and seeming consistency of candles which are left out in the sun too long, twitter above the donuts, then grab one with the speed of a frog's tongue.) I think she hated me, that donut woman, because my hair was a strange dead blonde color, spattered by orange in places and just beginning to heap into dreadlocks (the spatters weren't on purpose, I'd got into a fight with the woman in the flat above me, and she'd booby-trapped my front door, so actually quite a lot of my body was orange as well). But anyway, about Joe.

I walked back into the Speed Queen just as he was doing the deed—up to his shoulders in my belching and sudsing machine (his hair too—the soap stuck like lace on the tattered ends)—and I said, with a greasy wad of dough in my mouth, "What the fuck are you doing, mister," and he said, "Well, honey, your machine seems to be on the blink, you see this long tie-dyed garment has wrapped its way around the agitator and made a horrible noise and being the manager here I felt it was my duty to intercede." And then I said, "Bullshit," and he said, "Will you marry me," to which I replied, "No, but if you get your arms out of my laundry I will crawl with you behind the dryers and fuck you until you bleed." "I am already bleeding," he said, raising his arms for inspection, and indeed, beneath his right ribcage the blood surged out. "But you are most kind," he said. And so he closed the lid of the machine and we crawled into the space behind the dryers; and it was there that I came to understand that the ways of love are best pursued in rage—which is why I call him my first lover because the two before him were more like brother puppies, to nuzzle for warmth. With Joe I felt the kind of molten heat from which life is formed. And, though it may just have been insanity, the nursing of purple-blue bruises was thrilling to me: I was more of an animal then and could lose myself in the glory of rut.

When we finished, the washing machine was done as well. I told him to come back to my room with me where we would continue if he would help me carry my clothes (seeing as they were wet and I had no money to use the dryers) and not drop any. He came with me, and we hung the clothes on the hooks on the walls or over furniture. He told me I ought never to put my clothes away since they made the place look bright and almost cheery. I opened a can of stewed tomatoes, in preparation of eating them, and said, "What is your name, mister."

"Joseph Cavanaugh Wrigley the Third and what are you doing with those tomatoes?"

"I need vitamin C," I said, and dropped a whole one in my mouth, like the wraith of a jawbreaker.

"I am the son of the largest canned vegetable baron in the country and if you let me eat those with you I will tell you my story."

"Save it for later, mister," I said. "Come take a shower with me and we'll screw on the tiles, but hurry because Kenneth will be here soon and we don't want to make him angry—besides, I thought you said you are the manager of the Speed Queen."

"And who is Kenneth," he asked, stripping once more to the waist and swinging his long hair around to swish heavy over his spine. "Oh, it's not important, only take off your pants please and oh, my you do have a large nose, don't you."

"Take off your clothes," he said.

When we got into the bathroom I said, "It's thrilling and all, but do you really need to keep that knife slung around your waist the whole time," and he said, "Yes. This knife is my woman. I keep her with me always, wrapping her arms around me." And I said sarcastically, "Yeah, what's her name, Betty?" He said nothing, grabbed my hair (which was like a carpet) and dragged me to the shower, turned the water on and pulled me inside. I wasn't nervous at all, only excited and in love.

Jammed against the wall, I heard myself growl, "Kill me, kill me." And he almost did when I grabbed at his knife for the hell of it because I was jealous of the fucker. Joe, water rivulets of grime running down his torso, looked into my eyes and drawled, "Don't you ever, ever, my lamb." Just to prove he meant it, he pulled the blade out and before I could think, flicked me on my hip. I screamed and jumped but the water ran red down my leg. Thinking my scalp would be ripped off, I grabbed for his knees; his other hand was still jammed in my hair.

"You are a fucking maniac," I shrieked, my arms flailing. I sunk my teeth into his thigh, which tasted of hair and water and dirt and soap and a little of blood because he nicked himself too.

He snarled at me, "You animal, my lamb, come up here, I love you."

I stopped and he lifted me up and our two wounds joined and our two bloods ran twisting together down the drain. Then the bitch upstairs pounded on her floor, my ceiling, in objection to the racket we were making. He held me and I pushed slowly away and knelt. The water streaming down made it hard to breathe. I put my mouth to his hip and sucked the blood and his hands clenched at my head, wrapped with my hair, and then someone started pounding on the front door.

"That's Kenneth." I stood up.

"Doesn't he have a key," he said, then he kneeled down in the warm torrent and sucked the blood from my hip.

"Of course not, he always forgets it." But he was yelling now, we could hear him as we turned off the water.

"Why don't you stay with me," I said.

"Hey, let me in, I know you're in there!" Kenneth yelled on the other side of the door, or rather, Dove did, as they called him on the streets because of his grey clothes and the way he seemed to fly on his skateboard. I could not call him Dove, though, since he was from the suburbs of Northern Virginia and had a thick hard ass and spiked hair and was staying with me because he got the best drugs.

"Sorry, baby, your time is up," I said, dripping and naked at the door. "This is Joseph Cavanaugh Wrigley the Third and he's my lover now." I slammed the door quickly in his face and locked it, then pranced to the window and threw out some things that fluttered to the street; little grey clothes gently winged down.

Kenneth pounded but eventually went away. In the hush beneath the damp and gaudy clothes of my exile, Joseph told me his story: it wasn't very interesting, and I didn't believe him anyway because of the way his eyes gleamed when he told it. But I loved him like a savage, like a bloody brutal beast, and he loved me that way too, hard and fierce and full of lust and sorrow. His face with its huge wedge of nose made him like like a horse to me. When he looked into my face it was always with sorrow, as if he knew what was coming, and was sorry for it. That was years ago before I gave up lust. I don't know, I guess I was a true beast then or perhaps we became something altogether different from other animals and people. (There in the room we called the hovel of love and fucking, he would tell me stories I did not believe; and I would twist my hair while watching and listening to him until it was a heap of mangy, floating gauze. Our limbs entwined, I stared in awe of his festering tattoos and of the words that poured from his lips.)

He would never sleep there but had to return to the bridge at night. On the floor, I would writhe and plead and beg, but no, no, grab his ankles, no. I grew thinner and thinner, my bones jutting from the shoulders (he liked to call my feet the fans of famine). My cheekbones stuck out too, and he liked them.

"They're like bows," he would say.

"Please don't leave," I'd reply.

Finally I got used to it, except that I would lie in a ball on my mattress, growling his name over and over, gnawing my own arm. Sometimes in my frenzy I would go out and find some horny little spike-haired boy, but Joe always came back. At first, I was jealous of the knife but he kept it with him and soon I didn't care; I loved it as freely as I loved him.

Then one week he didn't come back. I knew he was dead but I couldn't bear to find out. I felt it like a wire had snapped in my head. Suddenly there was less voltage.

I went down to the bridge around sunset when the hoboes gathered. Trying to look tough, I took along a tire iron left over from the days of Kenneth, as if it would protect me. I went up to one of the older, thinner men and said, "Where is Joe?"

"Oh, he got into a fight one night, a bunch of punks came looking for him with pipes and such and they finally drug him off and kicked him into the canal." The scream started to rise in me. I knew it because I felt dead.

"No," I said. "No." It took me over and I screamed. The scream wrenched from my body and hammered echoes off the bridge like the savagery of the two of us exploding in me out of me. I pounded at the hobo and then I went to find Kenneth.

I found him and said, "Honey, come back to me." I kissed the new long scar that ran down his face—it was oozing and hadn't healed. When we got home I found another slice around the back of his shoulder over his thick little rock of a bicep. We never said anything about it. I was filled with death and didn't have the energy for revenge. I stayed with him, quietly drinking in (for a week or so) the smell of his slippery sweat, until one night when he was drunk and passed out on the twisted sheets: Suddenly I hated him with the ugly oily wrath of a snake. I slid my tongue over his body for the last time. I got myself drunk and I dug out the knife from where I knew he'd been hiding it. In the shower, alone, I sliced open my old wound again. The hot water made it run red, and I caught the blood in a cup with the water and drank it.

"Here's to you, my dead lover."

I went back into the room. Kenneth didn't even wake up when I walked out to get a bus to take me back home. I walked up to the front door, one morning, knocked, and said, "Mama, Daddy, I'm home and I'm beat and I need you to take me back."

They sent me to a sanitarium for a few weeks, to sit in the sun and bake and let the flesh grow back on my bones. Then they sent me to a nice college where I studied English literature, which I now teach. But I still keep the knife under my pillow. Whenever a new lover comes and wonders about the knife, I say, "Oh, honey, now never you mind. A girl's got to have some kind of protection." Sometimes I think he didn't really die, my first lover, but instead lives inside me. And I think he did that, jumped inside me, because he knew his days were numbered. So when that feeling gets too big, like he's growing too big in there, I just slit the scar again, let the blood run out, catch it in a cup, and raise it in a toast. I raise it and drink it, still warm, down, because even though I need to get on with my own life, I just can't stand to lose him. I can't let him go.

Susan Bergman, though described by some as a "manic-depressive," is really quite docile and, in fact, behaves more like a four year old than a psychopath. Her cooking is not exceptional. She is afraid of heights.

3

Captain Rat
Joey

It started with a whore on the way to Oklahoma. I provided the car; Steve the whore provided the drugs. From Kansas City it is six hours each direction.

Leaving Friday night on the freeway Steve said "Stick this under your tongue." We were headed to OK City to see a punk—new wave band that had crashed at my house the weekend before.

After thirty miles I was wondering exactly what was melting under the heat of my tongue. At eighty in the fast lane everything seemed a blur of white lines. Images were moving along with the scenery. All Steve could manage was giggles. Giggles from what was normally a staid business professional. Anything for a price. He was a friend; this wasn't business.

By the time sixty miles had lapsed, I no longer felt in control of the car. From my adolescence I still had understanding friends strung out across the western states. By understanding, I mean that there was usually a bottle of whiskey to be found. It was a tough trip up the stairs to Mal's second floor six-room complex of tiny rooms. A drink is what I needed, something to bring me to a familiar plane.

Mal was a true host, even clean glasses. The rest of the evening was spent in bliss. The conversation was engaging; the eventual sleep was needed. Reports from the morning told of several broken glasses and a beer-stained sleeping bag. Somehow I missed most of the exciting parts even though I was present.

The sun was high in the sky by the time Steve and I arose. It was the kind of clear Kansas morning you read about in serial novels. Mal had gone to work but left coffee on the stove. Somehow I needed it. After several cups the car was loaded and ready. For the day's travel Steve wanted the top stowed in the trunk. It was still summer; hot and sunny in excess of ninety degrees. As far as I was concerned, there was no better reason to own a Porsche. Given my druthers, I'd own a vehicle from the three classes: luxury, sports convertible and a motorcycle.

Several miles outside town, Steve managed to soak the dashboard in Budweiser foam. Noting the fact that he was drinking warm beer for breakfast, I suggested that we stop for some cold ones. Pulling into small town Kansas in a foreign sports car for beer at noon tends to garner some stares. Looking hungover didn't help much.

Back on the road with cold Bud in the crotch, the warm sun gave us both refreshing warmth. I was restraining myself from using heavy drugs for the daylight hours. We were staying with the bass player's mother while in OK City. I thought it might be nice if I could pronounce the words, "Hello Mom."

We hit the Kansas-Oklahoma border doing ninety and didn't slow till we hit the outskirts of OK City. What a flat town.

From the sketchy directions I found the house. He was home; brother was home; mother was home. Such a change from what I had expected. I assumed that the bass player from the Slow Voids would live in a ramshackle place, not gentrified inner city. So much for assumptions.

Dinner and off to the show. Arriving early we got the privilege and boredom of watching the Voids set up. The only challenge was not falling over from the free drinks and ludes. The ludes were a present from Steve the whore to the band and groupies. The bassist's girlfriend was more than happy to take several.

Meanwhile the bar was filling with people. Steve and I sat near the back at a small table by the john. The whole place was filled with heteros. It's a weird feeling being the only two gay guys in a straight country western bar listening to new wave-punk music; not to mention the fact that it's Oklahoma City in the summertime.

As our pockets empty, our bellies fill with beer and the whiskey smuggled in. I know that I'm drunk. Steve is one step removed from reality. His mouth is running over with obscenities toward the bassist's girlfriend. After verbal threats Steve slows down to the point of slumping over in his seat next to the stage where we had moved after the first set. I had taken up cruising the bar for something a little livelier than Steve. I returned to the table to find Steve being brought to by the club's bouncers. That got him as far as the parking lot, where he collapsed in the exit lane. Did you ever watch one drunk try and move another drunk out of the road? Had I just been watching I'm sure it would have been funnier.

How we made it home that evening I'm not sure. I don't think I drove. I do remember getting breakfast in bed served by the bassist. After what I remembered of the evening before I was surprised by his generosity. Maybe this sort of thing is a regular occurrence in OK City. His reaction to us curled up in bed did surprise me since he had told of his brother's "affliction." "As long as I don't have to look at it" was his attitude. He didn't go for it much when we were playing grabass on the couch. I can't really see why. Did I throw up when he was sucking on his girlfriend's tits?

After the night before, we decided it was prudent to leave soon. Maybe that's why we got breakfast in bed; it's quicker. Burnt out but well fed, we hit the road for the capital of the Midwest, Kansas City. The only stops along the way were for beer, cigarettes and gas.

Steve had left his lover at home for this weekend journey. He was never able to explain to me how you can be a prostitute and have a lover too. He said it was human nature. I couldn't swallow it.

Benny was waiting for us. He had the look of a man who had been waiting all weekend. The apartment was a studio, the kind with a Murphy bed that folds from the wall. The kitchen was literally covered in Budweiser cans. Steve was a Bud fan, it was hard to miss. Benny had a friend visiting to kill the time till Steve and I showed up.

Joey had fiery red hair hanging neatly to the sides. It was nice to be around gay men again. A weekend in the straight world had left me rather burnt out. My body was still pulsing with the amphetamines, pot and alcohol of the day's drive. I sat spread over the width of the overstuffed chair. The conversation was low-keyed and relaxed; my body could stand no more.

Time drug on. My mind was frazzled. I offered Joey the chance to split this pop stand and he agreed. I guess he was as tired of hearing of the weekend's revelry as I was. He left his truck at Steve's and we took the Porsche to my place.

He was as impressed as the rest of my tricks were at the inside of the 914. It was, after all, a nice car. Joey had the class not to drool, however. Although it was three miles between Steve's place and mine, the journey through city traffic was swift.

The house where I rented my room was a sight to behold. If you like flamingos, it was heaven. There were flamingos of every variety: stone, plastic, oil painted, ceramic. That, in combination with my collection of neon signs, made the place be known as the Neon Flamingo Palace. My room was over the living room; the Boom Boom Room as it was known to weekend guests. Three of us made our home there: the rotund woman who owned the place, the cocaine salesman's woman friend and myself.

When Joey and I arrived, no one was about. The place was never crowded during the day, but did begin to fill up around the midnight hour. On rare occasions we would have a sit-down family style dinner. Out of the upstairs bedroom I pulled a bottle of whiskey for Joey and me. I never left any alcohol downstairs— it would never last. The whiskey helped make the transition from newly acquainted to lover easier.

We spent that evening in each other's arms. It was wonderful to have six feet of free-spirited redhead in my bed. To say the least I was smitten. Both he and I had work in the morning. It made me wish I had spent the weekend with him instead of Steve.

Work seemed to go slowly. I longed to be in Joey's grasp again. It seems that when I find a man who measures up to my standards of intellect, cuteness, and street sense...I want to be around him all the time. This desire has killed off a good many relationships that I've started. My friends call it "burning itself out before it has a chance to start," sort of like a campfire without enough kindling.

That evening we were together again. It seemed as wonderful as the night before. Eating dinner, drinking, smoking, it was all of a dream. The time together had the spark of magic that neither of us wanted to end. It seemed as if the rest of the world were standing still just to let us go on. We made love upstairs, downstairs, outside, in the car, wherever and whenever.

Things were not going as well at my workplace. I think that it paled in comparison to my love life in the off hours. Joey was working in a mall and just as frustrated as I was. It was my idea to load up both our vehicles and head west. It sounded like a positive step at the time. I gave notice to my landlady—Joey gave notice to the friend he was living with. Both of us told our employers. Life and its commitments were changing fast and furious. Soon we would have only ourselves to depend on.

In the process of settling accounts with my landlady I found myself sleeping behind my best friend's couch for three weeks. It got a little crowded with both Joey and me back there. Both of us learned the art of humping quietly. Raul, my friend, was very understanding about the arrangement. He knows I would do the same for him in a minute if the need was there.

The day finally came for us to leave. The Porsche was loaded to the gills, Joey's pickup truck was full, including the trailer filled with my neon and other oddities. Juan had decided to join us on the trip, splitting his time between Joey and me. It would be nice to have company for both of us, I thought. Of course the weather had to be shitty; the rain was coming down lightly over grey skies.

Trouble started less than thirty miles out of town on the freeway. The right front end of the Porsche dropped as I heard a loud snap under the hood. I pulled to the side, Joey following, to find what I had expected. Another tie-rod had snapped. The same one had snapped six months before.

I really love making split-minute decisions on the edge of the roadway. Back we went.

We nursed the car back to my mechanic in North Kansas City. It being the weekend, no one was there. The only thing to do was to leave a note. "Please replace tie-rod and sell. Will send pink slip." After a quick phone call to my father explaining the details, we loaded the truck with more stuff and headed out again.

By the middle of the night we had reached the house of a friend on the outskirts of Denver. It was a well-deserved stopping point. With three of us crowded into the front seat of Joey's pickup, we were glad for the breathing room. Out host made us feel welcome with glasses of sweet mulberry wine. Sleep was what we needed with an early day facing us.

The day's goal was Yellowstone and the Old Lodge. I thought it would be nice to stay in something old and wooden. As it turned out, the old lodge was closed for the winter. And what with the snow, half the roads in Yellowstone were closed. We felt lucky to have made it through with the trailer.

With the rangers wishing us good luck, we headed out of Yellowstone. In West Yellowstone we found a cheap motel. Eighteen dollars for the three of us, which included a hot tub, sauna and two beds. Such a deal—it was the off-season. That was fine with us; Juan in one bed with Joey and me in the other.

It being the off-season, half the businesses were boarded up. We found a locals' cafe for a quick breakfast and the purchase of some tacky postcards. The city of Olympia in Washington was the destination for this day's travel.

The plan from here was that Joey and I would start looking for work in both Seattle and Portland. We would then settle in whichever city one of us found work in first. I had friends in Olympia so we would have a place to stay for a couple of weeks.

As it turned out Joey had a friend in Portland who was an old teacher of his. After calling her up, we decided to settle in Portland since it looked as if she could get him some kind of job with her firm. The next chore was to find a place to live.

On a Sunday journey south with the want-ads in hand we started making calls. A duplex in the Northwest part of town sounded promising enough to drive by and see. From my friends who had lived in Portland before I had learned that the Northwest was "the" area of town for the young white professionals and students.

The landlord described the place as the upstairs of an older home. She warned of a drunk lady who lived downstairs. Along with everything else she said that the shower would hold one comfortably, but probably not two or three. Why she thought we were interested in this I do not know. Before she would give us a tour, she gave me the address so we could go by and look to make sure it was up to our "standards." At that point my only standard was a cheap roof over my head.

We rented the place on the spot. There went any money for food. It was time to call daddy for more money.

Somewhere along the line things between Joey and me got more tense. With a base of friends in Olympia to feed my ego, I tended to let Joey fend for himself. That, coupled with my money worries, job worries and doubt, was working a wedge into our relationship. The world was once again present.

The amount of furniture we brought with us looked bare in the two-bedroom apartment. Both of us were busy looking for work so it didn't much matter that we had little to sit on in the living room. The bed worked and that was what was supposed to count.

With all the job hunting, our conversations tended to be business communication. No longer were there walks in the park holding hands. Work, work, lack of work.

In a couple of weeks I had found a job. Joey still was looking hard, but I could tell he was running out of determination. He had doubts as to why he was 2,000 miles from home looking for a job in an economically depressed area when he had no trouble finding work in Kansas City.

After many a tearful session, Joey decided to pack it all in and head for the security of home. I guess it had been too many months with no security, no firm base from which to operate. With no secure base, I was more tense and tended to take it out on Joey. For Joey there was no support base of friends a few hours away. His base was thousands of miles away.

A year or so later I still think fondly of Joey. He was a special force in my life, although I doubt if I ever told him so. In the family I come from, love is taken for granted, though rarely expressed. This is not to say that we were not a loving family, only that we never verbalized it. In retrospect I should have been more vocal with my support. Maybe next time around I will remember the past while adapting it to the future.

Captain Rat has three pastimes—Buggery, Business and Booze. Business pays the bills—buggery and booze provide the entertainment.

4

Todd M. Cobb
Linus Iscariot

Linus looked at Charlie Brown's big round head, the lone curly hair spiraling from his brow, the half crescent ears jutting from the sides, and loved him like never before. He took in a deep breath and tried to fight off the tears, it seemed like all he wanted to do anymore was cry; ever since Bethany. At Bethany, Charlie Brown had gathered them all around him and, in a hushed, somber tone, said that soon he would be betrayed — by one of this number.

They'd all been shocked, thrown out their chests and proclaimed it would never be them, each with as much conviction as the next. Who could betray one so precious as Charlie? What could make a man turn on his leader, his master? Nothing on Earth.

Or so Linus had thought.

Satan had come to him in a dream, as he often did, in the guise of a lean, white beagle with a long nose and black ears. Linus stirred in his sleep and gathered his blanket more tightly around him. The beagle perched itself atop a rock and glared at him. He could feel the frigid eyes of coal bearing down on him, boring through his very soul. The beagle didn't speak, Linus simple understood.

"How can you say such a thing?" Linus had said in his dream, "How can you?"

The beagle did not move, but continued to stare.

"But why me? No one loves Charlie Brown more than I. I am part of him. Betraying him would be betraying myself."

The beagle did not blink.

"I will not! I will not betray him! There is nothing you can do, nothing you can say!"

The beagle grinned. Like a serpent it crawled on its belly leaving a trail in the dust and moved from the rock. It stopped next to him and he could smell it, foul and fetid; reeking of darkness and sorrow and fear.

Linus wailed and gnashed his teeth. "NO! NO! Say it isn't so! Anything but that, anything — just don't take *that* from me!"

Why? Why had he been forsaken so? Of all the things in the world, there was only one he believed he could not do without, could not *live* without.

The beagle's paw snaked out like lightning and tore the blanket from Linus's shoulders. Even in the dream, Linus shivered at the cold.

Wrapping itself in Linus's blue security blanket, the beagle sang a song in its strange nasal voice. Then it danced. Then it became night, mingled with the dust at its feet and was gone.

That night in Bethany, Linus had jolted from sleep still shaking from his dream. On the ground next to him was the trail left by the beagle as it had crawled on its stomach, the footprints where it had danced and its awful smell. Linus wept and prayed but found no comfort in it. Eventually he slept again, but fitfully — he was cold, so cold, for he no longer had his beloved blanket.

Time from that point on had become a blur. He'd gone to Jerusalem in a frenzied search for this blanket. Believing he glimpsed it hanging from the window of a ship he went inside. He found only soldiers waiting. When he asked for his blanket he was told he knew what he had to do and Linus relented. He wept as he broke faith with Charlie Brown, but all he wanted was his blanket. Please, could he have it back? The soldiers promised it would be in his hands once Charlie Brown was in theirs. Somewhere in the back, Linus heard a beagle laugh.

The next day Linus had lead the soldiers to where Charlie Brown was eating a peanut butter sandwich with the remaining eleven. Linus, dizzy and sickened with grief, approached Charlie Brown. "You are the one that I love the most," he told his master, "You ...," but he could not continue. He threw his arms around

Linus Iscariot

Charlie Brown and kissed him. His gesture was full of the admiration and love that could not be expressed by words, but it was also the signal to the soldiers. This is the one, the embrace had said, this is the one you are after.

Charlie Brown placed a gentle hand on Linus's tear stained shoulder. "I knew it would be you, Linus," he said, his voice low and even, "I knew it would be you and I love you for it."

The soldiers, ridiculously armed to apprehend such a man of peace, led Charlie Brown away.

* * *

The memory of all that had transpired burned Linus's eyes like acid tears as he watched Charlie Brown, naked and beaten, standing in court before Lucy.

"You say you are the truth, Charlie Brown, son of the barber," Lucy intoned.

With slow, almost indiscernible motion, Charlie Brown nodded.

"So speak. Tell us this truth and I will set you free. That simple, barber's son, the truth for freedom."

Linus leaned forward in the crowd. He had made a terrible mistake, he'd sold out his dearest friend for his blanket — which he still did not possess — but now he was faced with the opportunity for absolution. Charlie Brown need only answer Lucy's question and he would be free. Linus had kept up his end of the bargain, he'd given them Charlie Brown, now if Charlie would only give them what they wanted he could go free and Linus would get his blanket.

"So, Charlie Brown — answer my question."

Yes, thought Linus, answer her question, please. Answer her question and we can leave ... please let us leave.

Charlie remained silent and spoke no truth.

"You missed the football again, Charlie Brown." Lucy, leaning back and crossing her arms, frowned. "So be it. Your fate was in your own hands. Your disposal was your own choice."

With that Lucy changed the sign over her head to read: "The Judge Is Out" and left. Linus fell to his knees, stricken with grief, and pounded his head on the ground. The crowd cheered Lucy's verdict. How quickly Charlie Brown had fallen from their favor. It was simply not stylish to follow the funny looking boy anymore, so they chose not to.

Their conviction as weak as their hypocrisy strong, the crowd had begun to stone the little boy with the round head as the soldiers took him away. They shouted and spat and cursed him; why had he not answered, why? Linus continued to dash his head upon the rocks. The crowd's anger and frustration boiled over and Linus felt it, too. Finally he stopped and, from between bloodied lips, whispered, "Good grief, Charlie Brown."

Women and children fought over stones to throw as the crowd kept up its constant barrage. Linus loved Charlie Brown, why had he ignored his chance to save himself? It infuriated Linus, it was like Charlie Brown wanted to die. WHY WHY WHY!! Linus demanded it of heaven, but there was no answer. His fury increased, blinded him and took control. HE rose from his knees clutching a large stone in his left hand. Emotion rolled through his body as all the anger he felt at himself was directed at Charlie Brown. And Linus, too, threw stones.

Even though they weren't the hardest to hit, Linus's stones caused Charlie Brown the most pain.

* * *

The sun had painted the sky the color of blood as the soldiers drove the nails through Charlie Brown's outstretched hands. The world shuddered with his screams. Prostrated on the crossbeam, it was almost impossible for him to breath. For each breath Charlie had to raise up on his impaled feet and snatch at the air while the shock waves of pain racked his body. Blood puddled at the base of the center beam. Charlie's sister Sally and Peppermint Patty were among the faithful who waited with Charlie trying to offer words of comfort and secretly hoping it would end soon and he could escape his torment.

Linus, his face hidden by a heavy hood in spite of the heat, watched from a distance. He watched as the sky turned black and Charlie Brown spoke and suffered and wept. As droplets of sweat rolled off the end of his nose, Linus watched flies and other pests light on Charlie's wounds, crawling over his eyes and tongue.

Then, as the world seemed to buckle and fold, Charlie Brown died — helpless and alone.

Linus remained motionless for hours, long after the crowd had left, until the solders took down the body. They wrapped the lifeless form in a funeral shroud and handed it to the grinning beagle who stood waiting. The beagle turned and faced the distant Linus, looking directly under this hood and into his eyes. It began walking, slowly, with deliberate steps, toward him. The single-member funeral procession seemed to take forever before the beagle reached Linus.

It stood before him for a moment, the remains of Charlie Brown in its paws, before it raised the cloth-covered body so Linus could see. Spots of blood has seeped through the blue material in places. Then, for the first and last time ever, the beagle spoke. "Here's your precious blanket, Linus, here's your precious blanket."

Todd M. Cobb is twenty-one years old and lives in Austin, Texas where he scrapes out a meager living pushing fish in the seafood department of a grocery store. He is also terrified of being locked naked in a room full of nuns.

5

Jeff Cochran
Speed, After All, Is Important

Kamchan spreads a towel on the bed before we fuck. His apartment is clean, neat and he wants to keep it that way. It's better for business. He wants me to fuck him.

"Oh, Jeff," he says. "So good, so good."

Kamchan's ass is always filled with some kind of lubricant. When he's on the streets, in the park, at home, always. Speed, after all, is important. I enter easily.

"Oh, Jeff, so good, so good."

Kamchan speaks little English. His understanding of the dynamics of U.S. money—supply and demand capitalism—is quite adroit. I enter easily. Speed, after all, is important.

Kamchan is twenty. When he was twelve, Kamchan crossed the Chinese border in Laos. He has always been a hustler; played fuck-boy for the aristocracy of Laos first, then Cambodia. When Kamchan was eighteen, Americans, thinking he was a Hmong tribesman, found him a sponsor family in the U.S. From Amarillo, Texas, Kamchan migrated to Seattle.

I ran into Kamchan on the streets in September, 1981. It's the last I've seen of him. He'd run into hard times. His welfare was cut off. He'd been robbed on Seattle's First Avenue, the local meat market. Kamchan, neat, pressed despite misfortune, bore one

Jeff Cochran

addition. A long belt carefully tied beyond the buckle, provided protection for the last valuable.

"I go to San Francisco, Jeff."

"Kamchan, you fuck me."

"Oh, Jeff, I love you. I love you."

We jay-walked across Howell Street. Red light crossing in Seattle can get you a twenty dollar ticket. I grab Kamchan before he walks into the street.

"It's O.K.," he explains. "I no speak English. I don't know lights."

We laugh. Clutch each other's ass. Walk arm-in-arm to the hostel where Kamchan lives.

"Jeff, I love you. I love you."

"Harder, Kamchan, harder."

Kamchan must register guests at the manager's desk of the hostel.

"He knows I play men. He knows I play you." ("Play men" is Kamchan's term for queer sex; hustling.)

"He don't like me. He say nothing." The last statement says, "He can fuck himself."

We climbed over a doper on the bottom step, and four flights up. There are three locks on his door; two work. Kamchan's room is mirrors, white lace curtains, red light bulbs. Service for two is set on a low side bar. A stereo. Low music.

The towel.

"Jeff, I love you. I love you."

"Harder, Kamchan, harder."

After sex we talk, about how his ass looked in the mirrors, about the robbery, about the streets, about friends, about lovers, about tricks. He's never asked, so I don't pay him.

Jeff Cochran is a jack of all trades—writer, software programmer, printer, chef, and all around nice guy.

6

Patricia Flinn
Reflections in a Hoboken Tenement with a Dead Dog

Early this morning my dog died and so all day long I've been trying to figure out what to do with the body.

I don't want to call the super because I know he'll just dump the poor thing in the garbage, and I don't want to call some vet because I heard vets give dead dogs to soap factories.

Also I'm reluctant to call the cops because most of the cops I know are bastards and wouldn't think twice about shoving some dead dog into a body bag, and when nobody was watching, tossing him into the city's incinerator.

I mean, maybe I'm being silly and all, but as far as I'm concerned, my dog deserves better than that.

If I had the dough I'd probably call up some fancy kennel and ask them to recommend a good pet cemetery, but right at the moment, considering what I got in the bank, I couldn't even afford the price of a cardboard box.

I suppose if he wasn't so big, I'd try putting him in the refrigerator for a while. At least that would give me time to try and figure out what to do with him, but since Sam is so broad, I'd doubt if he'd fit through the door. Besides, I wouldn't know what to do with all the food and stuff. Rotten eggs and sour milk can smell pretty bad, I've heard.

The freezer would probably be better if I had a nice big one, but since my freezer just about holds my two small ice-trays and a package or two of frozen stringbeans, even thinking of putting Sam in there is out of the question.

Naturally, if I had my own house with a nice big backyard I'd bury Sam out there, and think nothing of it. I'd put him under an old tree or something, or alongside one of the flower gardens. That way he'd always be around, so to speak.

I know lots of people with houses who do that. Why, I would even bet that in backyards all across America there are more dogs and cats under the ground than over it. They may not all have headstones and stuff, but what difference does that make? At least they're on familiar territory. At least they're not sitting in some trash can somewhere.

I guess it would be tough if you sell your house and all, but who knows, maybe someday they'll even have a law that says you have the right to come back and visit. Probably that will happen in some place like California someday. They're pretty sophisticated out there, I think.

Right now, though, poor Sam's just lying in the middle of the kitchen floor, stiff as a board.

If he were only a little smaller, I'd pick him up and carry him into my bedroom or off into some place where I wouldn't have to keep stepping over him, but being part Collie and part Shepherd, he's much too big for me to lift.

I suppose I could drag him by the paws or get down on my knees and push him across the floor, but somehow that doesn't strike me as the nice thing to do.

I mean, who'd think of dragging a person out of the way just because he happened to die in the middle of somebody's floor? Why should a dog be any different?

Still, it upsets me to have to keep stepping over him like that. In a sense it's like walking across somebody's grave fifty times a day.

Which is, come to think about it, what my goddamn uncle did to my father's grave on the day we were burying my mother.

I felt like punching him, the son of a bitch. I mean, the guy doesn't come once to see his own sister in the nursing home where she's cooped up for three years, but as soon as she dies, he's rushing off to the funeral parlor in his black suit and tie to shake hands with everyone and take his little peek at the corpse. For spite, I insisted we put her in a closed coffin, so nobody could see a thing.

But anyway, all the while he's at the cemetery, my uncle's stepping all over my father's grave. I'm the only one who notices because everybody else is looking off at my mother's casket being lowered into the ground while some priest is saying the "Our Father."

"Hey, have a little respect, will *ya?*" I whisper. "That's my pop under there."

The bastard looked at me like I had three heads. "What?" he says to me.

"That's my old man you're walking across," I tell him again.

"Don't worry," he says to me. "He don't feel nothing."

"You won't either if you don't get the f... off his grave," I said without blinking an eye.

Even though I'm his niece, I still refuse to put up with that kind of crap from anybody.

I mean, people just don't have any regard for the dead anymore. You see it all the time. Even among people who should know better. For example, going back to my mother again, her doctor, the one who pronounced her dead, was chewing bubble gum at the time. Can you imagine?

Oh, I guess for some people that's no big deal I mean, hey, he didn't actually blow any bubbles or anything — but Christ, come on, be honest. How would you feel if you just died and some clown started snapping gum a few inches away from your nose?

Anyway, that's why I'm not taking any chances with Sam. I mean, after all, if they treat people like that what the hell are they going to do with dogs?

So that's why I got to think of something to do with Sam's body. Something decent and respectable. Something that would let him know that I really liked having him for my dog and that I'm not just going to forget him all of a sudden just because he's dead and all.

If only I had more of an imagination. Or even somebody to talk to, some smart friend or something, but everyone I know is just about as boring as I am.

Take Rickie, for instance. I could call him and ask him to come over and give me a hand, but since he never liked Sam when Sam was alive, it just doesn't seem right. Besides, he'd probably just start cracking a bunch of dumb jokes about dead dogs and dead cats and then I'd get all mad and tell him to shove it. Rickie's pretty hard to take sometimes.

Or I suppose I could call Tony, but Tony would be so damn worried about messing up his brand new car that he'd probably give me some song and dance about disease and germs or something and then hang up the phone as fast as he could.

It's funny how you find out who your real friends are in situations like these. It's really interesting, as they say.

I'm sure if my mother and father weren't dead they'd think of something. They always did. My father especially was a really smart guy. Once when he was trying to stall off some loan sharks until he could get hold of a few bucks, he dressed up like a woman for a couple of days and went all over town in stockings and a pair of high heels. Even my mother didn't recognize him. Especially since he had shaved his legs and all.

I remember everybody at his funeral laughing and saying he was a really funny guy and that it was a shame he had to die so suddenly. But in the long run I suppose he was a lot better off than my mother who wound up in that nursing home with nobody coming to see her for months on end. At least he died fast without knowing what hit him. Which is the best way you can go, I guess, if you gotta go in the first place. Right?

I mean, look at poor Sam. It took him almost three days to die. He couldn't eat. He couldn't drink. He couldn't even move. He just lay there in his own mess, staring up at me. In a way he sort of reminded me of my mother. The way they both looked at me, I mean, just before they died. Like they were seeing something nobody else could see.

It was pretty scary, if you know what I mean, but as my father used to say, I guess it's no good dwelling on things like that for too long. Kind of makes you nuts. But anyway getting back to the issue at hand, I still have to think of something to do with Sam's body. Pretty soon it's gonna start to stink and then I'll really be in a fix. So I either got to get him out of here, or get him embalmed in some way.

It's a shame I don't know any honest undertakers.

I guess I could bring him down to the park when it gets dark and bury him there, but it would probably be just my luck to get arrested or mugged or something as I'm digging his grave.

If I had the guts I suppose I could call the local newspapers and invent some wild cock and bull story about him being a hero dog who got killed rescuing some blind kid from the path of an oncoming bus, but since I can't lie to save my life, I'd probably screw the whole thing up as soon as I opened my mouth. And besides, who's to say they'd even give Sam a decent burial after all? They could write him up in all the headlines, make him a hero, and still throw his body in a trash can when nobody was looking. In fact, sometimes at night when I can't sleep so well and I'm wandering around the apartment looking through old photographs and stuff of my parents when they were young way back in the thirties and forties, I get to thinking that maybe, just maybe, the funeral home might have done the same thing to my mother. You know, not put her body in the coffin and all. I mean, in the long run how would we know? How would anyone know? Who goes around checking closed coffins? They could put a Barbie Doll or a jar of roaches inside a closed coffin and nobody would be the wiser. Right?

Now I know some people may ask why would anyone do anything like that, but think about it for a minute. Maybe there's money involved. Maybe a crooked funeral director can make himself a big profit selling the corpse to some place that recycles it or something. An eye goes here, an ear goes there, maybe a couple of fingers and toes wind up in this or that place. Christ, after awhile, you're talking big bucks. And when it comes to big bucks, I don't trust anyone. Do you? Which is why I often have these horrible, horrible feelings that maybe, just maybe, my mother wasn't really in that coffin after all. And that the funeral home pulled an awful trick on us and somehow managed to ... to recycle her or something behind our backs. In my worse moments I have these nightmares, these terrible nightmares that bits and pieces of her are floating around all over the country with little 'For Sale' signs attached, and that sooner or later I'm going to run smack into someone who's already bought and wearing my mother's ears, or eyes, or lips, or what-have-you.

Sometimes it gets so bad I lie awake all night thinking that it's all my fault and that if I didn't insist on putting her into a closed coffin to spite all my nosy relatives, my mother would have had a really decent and proper burial.

Then just when I'm about to go stark raving nuts with guilt I start thinking that maybe I'm all wrong and that maybe she is really buried after all and resting quite comfortable, as they say.

So what it really all comes down to in the long run is this: I don't know what the hell to think.

I suppose if there were some way of looking into the coffin — that is, after having her dug up again I'd know for sure, but unless I did the digging and looking myself seeing everything with my own eyes this time I still would have a hard time accepting anybody else's word that she's really there.

I mean, as weird as it sounds, she is my mother and I have more right than anyone to dig her up again if I feel like it. I mean, it's not that I would be doing it for a lark or anything. I'd be doing it for her own good.

And I'd make absolutely certain that I'd put her back in again exactly as I found her, if I found her. I wouldn't disturb a thing, if I didn't have to.

And best of all, she'd know I was still thinking about her and caring enough about her to see to it that she was O.K. and all.

I'd even let her know about Sam.

She and my father both loved Sam.

In fact, if there were a way I could get Sam there in a little box or something, I could even... well ... maybe I could even consider burying him there.

With them, I mean.

Maybe not right in the same coffin, but you know, somewhere in the same hole and all.

There'd be plenty of dirt. And it's a nice clean place. Well kept, that's for sure.

It's really not a bad idea when you think about it.

As I said, they all really liked each other.

And I'd know once and for all that they'd all be together again.

Safe and sound.

I really can't see anything wrong with it.

Can you?

Patricia Flinn lives in Warren, New Jersey with her husband, Eugene, who is also a writer. Her short stories have been published in numerous literary magazines including Studia Mystica, Green Feather Magazine, Ripple's Poetry Magazine, The Crab Creek Review *and* The Rampant Guinea Pig. *She has also written plays, poems, theatre reviews, travel stories and literary essays, and she is one of the co-authors of* The Literary Guide To The United States, *published by Facts On File.*

7

Scott Haugaard and Mark Whitaker
Some Enchanted Evening

"It's alive," screamed the avocado as it driveled down the hallway into the crack at the end of the hall. It's not my fruit cried Loretta, a pudgy faced chick who never owned a dime in her life. Let's grab it. Well I don't know, what if it fights back. Right then Loretta digressed a bit.

"I was five years old when the plague came to town. It came in like a big avocado. It left people green. Yup, it left people green. We cleaned the bodies up. It took a long time but we managed to burn the corpses, bit by bit, into charred slime."

She came back to the present time. The air was warm. So was Tom. What do you think, right here. I don't know what about the plague and AIDS. We might die. What of it.

But then again, what if avocados themselves were the root of all evil? What if Satan himself was really a California avocado? One could walk into a Safeway anywhere in the world and take home the prince of darkness, and try to make guacamole out of the personification of evil. Then none of it would matter, for she loved guacamole so much, that even if she knew that it could spell eternal darkness, she would eat it anyway. As she lay there she suddenly felt a craving for the wretched green party dip. She got up and went into the kitchen...

"So my friend, you say that you love guacamole. Well I have got a deal for you...I will give you three wishes and a carload of the old Guaco baby...You know, the kind that gets you when you are just beginning to fall asleep at night, yea, late at night when the lights in the town—your town—that are on all the time. Yea, then, and only then will I come through with your wish...Your wish to eat the green Guacamole of youth. Yea, with a Capital G as in GGGGuacamole...You want to be young. You want to be able to fuck Tom yet one more time—the second wish, I am sure. You are so dumb, that I bet you will take me up on my wish. Do you listen to your soul, oh, no. I am in your deepest dreams. I crawl in your darkest thoughts. Fuck Tom. Fuck Tom, you say. But, I, the guacamole king with a Capital G still wins. Yea."

And she recoiled in terror. How, how could a simple avocado, and not a particularly ripe one at that, know her deepest thoughts? How indeed, answered the avocado, as it lay there on her kitchen counter.

"I know all, and you, without even knowing it, have stumbled across my secret...Yes, I am the prince of darkness. Actually, I could be any fruit or vegetable that would be appropriate, but for you, my dear, it was the California avocado."

Her mind was spinning. She hadn't eaten but two tabs of LSD, and that was hours and hours ago.

"No," said the avocado, seeping into the darkest corners of her soul, "I am not a mere hallucination...nothing as real as I am could be here simply as a side effect of that simplistic drug you worship so."

It was that moment that Tom, delicious Tom, came wandering into the kitchen...

"Ha!" exclaimed Loretta with swirling eyes, "You're there swinging your ego. What do you think, huh? I was told that we might be wanting to get something together. Get back. I dig black as in plague slime."

Loretta became one with the dirt at her feet. And it was good, she thought. If I could just go deeper, deeper into the bowels of what I abhor the most. In the dredges of my past...into the deep plagued slime with Tom and the Avocado god of my dreams. They went down the old, hardly used road, for days without water. After four days they dropped into one exhausted, fucked, humped and they were psyched and fucked up. The path was lost. They had no more water.

"What's that sound?"

Yup, you guessed right my friend, it was indeed the water from the prince of darkness himself—Avocado Man.

"I am water," he screamed.

They wandered down the path toward the sound, losing their way occasionally but always ending up on a path toward the water of their dark souls.

After another three days of walking they came upon the green blob who disappeared down the crack at the end of the hall a week ago. And a long and depressing hall it had been too. For Loretta had never understood what depression could be, until that hall, and the crack at the end into which crawled the thing that she despised the most. As much as she hated Tom, this was something worse, for years ago, this hall had been part of her. This hall, that she trod upon every day...fucked up. Junk, how many pounds?? No way to tell any more—acid sheet after sheet, day after day interrupted with week long drunken binges, and she had finally ended it all in that hallway. The lights on the ambulance had been beautiful, the last thing she would ever see in this deceased physical existence. She had come back to even brighter lights not nearly as beautiful as those that were to be her last. And the hall still stretched out before her. And now, now there was the green. The green that would not let her be, waiting...

Fucked up, yea, and worse than any other. Worse than that hall so many years ago. I saw the strip in front of her eyes the first time she snorted that shit in the hall. The Avocado Man with his evil intentions placed the mirror in front of her greedy face with a vengeance for things done in the past in Oregon. The hall, the hall, the hall was long. And if she traversed the whole length would she live to snort another day. Could she live till the end of it?

"I doubt it," thought the Avocado Man as he pondered the situation.

What, three more steps, the hardest steps? Back to the cave of lust for TOM, TOM, TOM. She fell deep deep into her clutch. Yes, she grabbed him, him in her arms. She was the Avocado man's, the man who kills all men. The woman who kills all souls. The man who kills all women. And I will watch you all with my three eyes. The roots of darkness which stare at your whitened eyes.

"You say yes, I say you're right. That is what you wish to have most of all. Fuck Tom you say. Grab him in your arms and you will know the sin of your deeds in my, and only my, tunnels of darkness. You say you need the water to servive. You say you seek the waters of your lust to survive. Wrong you are. It is the light of the Aboveground that you should be seeking. You ran out of water on the first day, and the Avocado Man showed you what. What did he show you my perverted friend? He showed you a way deeper than anything you have known before. He says that water runs ever downward. Ever downward until it is too late. But, I will tell you this, the sun shines from above.

Loretta looked up the tunnel where she had come down several days before and realized that there was indeed light there. A green sickly light, a light like no other, it was as if someone had taken an incandescent bulb and coated it with guacamole, that wonderfully weird party dip that she adored so. If only she had a chip, she could just hold it under the light and she would have guacamole forever...eternity. As she leaned toward it, the avocado that lay so normally on the kitchen counter, she became aware of Tom. He was there, with her. In the hall, in the tunnel, under the sickly green light, and, closest of all, in the kitchen. She could smell him, feel him, and she hated him. And yet...

"But wait," said the avocado, "could it be? Are you really that far gone, that fucked up that you would trade an eternity of green for that fucked up bastard?"

It had gone on forever. Tom...and the junk, she hated them both and yet they were so wonderful, the ambulance lights, Tom's face as he came inside of her, they were so beautiful. And the sickly green light grew greener, and she was confused...the avocado seemed to grow, but no, or was it. Tom sat down and lit a cigarette, and the blue smoke curled upward toward the green light...the result was awful.

Upward, upward as she rose in harmony with his pulsing spirit. They climbed higher than a man could travel alone. To the land of daisies they wandered with their spirit. Six feet high they rose, with stems of green, flowers of purple. They wandered around through the purple daisies. How bizarre, I will say. And Avocado Man with thoughts of dark, will you interfere with our young lovers. Will you interfere with the cigarette of their love. They are drifting; they are drifting farther than you will ever know.

They are drifting farther than you, with your mind in the gutter of darkness—it is beautiful. It is the purple of life. It is brighter than you will ever know Gutter Man. You worry about the junk and the hall. You worry about what Avocado-Gutter Man has told you. He will tell you anything to fuck up your mind. To fuck Tom. To fuck up your mind, to fuck up Tom. What is the difference, my friend with nothing in the head. What is the difference. The tunnel is dark. The hall was filled with junk and coke. Coke means life. Coke brings life. Coke kills life, and the man will be with you all the time. Fuck Tom, he tells you. Is that what you want, or do you just want your junk?

And if I was to tell you about the daisies, with purple at the outside and yellow at the inside, would you tell me that the tunnel was fucked. Coast over the sea of shit. Coast over the tunnel. Remember, when the weather gets rough you will try and think of Tom. Fuck Tom. Climb into the roots, my friend. They stare unendingly at your soul. The tendrils are reaching out at you as you ponder the three spots that you might wander to. Will you go there, or will you try to stay in the junk glow of the Talking Heads.

And her head spun like it had never spun before. All the junk in the world could never spin her head the way that it spun now. Tom sat patiently, and the blue smoke curled ever upward. As she drifted back into the avocado, she felt queasy. Was it really the truth? The hall, it reeked of...of what? Guacamole? Puke? She couldn't tell anymore. It was all too real, too true, it was here now in her kitchen, and she grabbed at the counter as her head spun with daisies, dime bags, the hall and parties with bowls of heavenly guacamole on coffee tables.

Much later, as the sun shone through the windows, as she wrapped her legs around Tom's hips, she wondered. She wondered if she would ever walk down her beloved hall again. Whether she would ever again go to a party with coffee tables laden with the weird party dip.

As they were fixing breakfast, she noticed that the avocado was gone.

Mark Whitaker and Scott Haugaard maintain that this piece is the fine product of a severe drunken binge of two sick and twisted youth. See what drugs will do to the minds of today's youth?

8

Kearin Sandwick
You Hardly Believed Yourself

At work that day, I remembered how you felt between my legs, and I could hardly wait to get back to you. I'd go along, running the bottle labeling machine, and have such a powerful sensation of memory—I ruined dozens of bottles that day. I was so happy I wanted to sing.

At morning break, the woman who drove the canteen truck noticed the hicky you'd left on my neck. Is it serious, she had asked. A late night at the bar, or an ongoing relationship? I don't know yet, I had answered, knowing full well what it was she wanted to know. I smiled, I'm trying, I added. I know that I was trying you, trying your patience with me, but to her I meant that I was trying to be serious.

I had been sleeping with you, in your bed, a few days a week, for months. Naked. The first night that you asked me over, you wanted to get me drunk and fuck me. Nothing serious, nothing to wrench your life around for, just fuck and that was all. No obligation. We drank, listened to jazz albums. The evening grew late, we went upstairs, took off our clothes, and went to bed. I talked you to sleep. The next day, a friend of yours came over and took us to the mountain. It was your first time there, and you were excited about the snow, and the height of it.

That weekend, your live-in lover was out of town, with her other lover. You were pissed. You didn't mention the details to me, in fact you didn't mention it much to me at all. After all, if she could do someone on the side, so could you. That I was to be your person on the side didn't mean I should know anything about her.

You didn't get to fuck me, but you enjoyed my company enough to try again. You called me again, as I had hoped you would. I came to spend the night with you, and again I talked you to sleep. I did that to you for a long time. At first, I didn't think that I wanted to do you. I liked you, I enjoyed your company, but I didn't want to fuck you.

I had gone through some pretty strange times in my head the year before that, had thoughts and feelings that I couldn't express to anyone enough to talk about, much less have anyone help me work them out. I was feeling very rejected from my last two love affairs. I was feeling inadequate both humanly and sexually. I was unhappy and lonely, and couldn't understand why someone should want to get to know me better, but you did want my body. That I could understand. Sex is a commodity, however bought. My body had been surveyed regularly at the bar...

Emotionally, you were high-strung. You were constantly having some sort of drama (dyke drama) with your lover, each pushing emotional buttons and playing head games on each other. The two of you had angry scenes whenever you went anywhere. I knew she existed; I had met her. You didn't hide what I saw as a disastrous relationship between the two of you. She hated me, and didn't believe you when you told her that we hadn't been fucking, had only been sleeping. You hardly believed it yourself. It certainly wasn't the way you wanted it.

* * *

Finally, I came to a point within myself. I had lain in bed with you for four, maybe five months, desperately wanting sex, but even more desperately being afraid of being physically and emotionally unable—inadequate. I decided I couldn't be afraid anymore, at least not to the point that it crippled me. I had to start somewhere, and that place seemed pretty obvious. I decided that I had to make a move. By this time, you had pretty much accepted that you weren't going to get into my cunt, and had stopped trying.

You accepted me on a different level, one with which you were totally unfamiliar. You'd never slept with someone you weren't fucking, and to be doing so on a fairly regular basis was almost too odd for you. If there was a first move to be made, it wasn't you who would make it. Intellectually, I contemplated this; intellectually, I attempted to sound out my emotions. How to make that move? I chickened out.

Life for you was rolling on. You took a vacation to the East Coast, a trip "home." Your mother and sister and brother were as they had always been. Your friends hadn't seen you for so long that a distance had grown up. You found out that you had asthma. You were sick, and glad to come home.

Homecoming was a shock to you. While you were gone, your house had been robbed. Kids. They took your answering machine, a car stereo that didn't work, a camera that didn't work. The rest of what they took wasn't worth money, but it meant a lot to you, the souvenirs of your lifetime. You cried, and for a week you didn't want to see anyone. Then you called a few friends, and one of them was me. I came to see you, be with you, hug you.

* * *

One night we'd gone to a bar. It was late when we got back, and you were tired. I was still pretty awake, but willing to go to bed. You crawled in, with me right behind you. We snuggled up, and you went to sleep, the kind of slow fade that I do to you now. I lay there, facing you, with my head just below yours. Timidly, I reached up and laid my lips on yours. A goodnight kiss was all I intended, but your sleeping mind made it into more. It was the move that I'd been waiting for. The sex that night wasn't anything astounding, but it led to another night, and another.

You didn't want to fall in love. I did. You had just been through a relationship that made you want to take a breather from anything resembling love. I was afraid of rejection, so I wasn't letting myself expect more than was stated. I hardly let myself expect anything at all.

My daily routine hadn't changed drastically. I was still getting up at your house at some ungodly hour of the morning, driving to my mother's house, picking up my carpoolers, and going to a dismal eight hour job. I'd get off work, drop my carpoolers at their respective homes, and drive up to your place.

My job was the same, get there, pack vitamins, take a breather around ten and buy something from the canteen truck, eat lunch around twelve, take another breather in the afternoon when I got bored or frustrated, and leave sometime around five.

The difference for me was that I had you on my mind, and I had the sensation of you with me all day. I longed for you, and was happy the day when the canteen woman noticed that hicky, so I could smile about you to someone else instead of holding you inside myself as I had all morning. It was the next day, or even a few days later that anyone noticed that mark you made on my neck. I smiled about you privately for a while before I said anything to anyone else.

I couldn't keep you a secret for long at all. I shared you first with my current co-worker and most recent ex-lover. I waxed eloquent, I spoke with stars in my eyes, I danced with joy, and she smiled that I was finally happy.

A week after that fatal kiss, I appeared at your house. It was Friday night, and we were going to do "something." Nothing in particular, just something. Saturday, you were going to a party, a costume Halloween party. I was trying to be nonchalant, too excited about you to try to expect to be a part of your life. I couldn't let myself be set up for the possibility that maybe it wouldn't be so. You hadn't formally asked me to go with you, though you'd talked around me to other friends about it. I think you had just assumed that I would go. I thought that when you finally got around to asking me to join you, I would turn you down. I had every intention of saying no, though my intent was not to snub you or to make you miss me. I thought that I would say no because I'm not much of a costume person, and more important, I couldn't allow myself the illusion of fitting so neatly into your life. You may not want me there at all, and I was so afraid of expecting too much.

Saturday morning was sunny and cheerful. I got up with you, and you were beautiful. Your friends called, and we went out to breakfast with them. One of them asked me if I was going to the party, and I shrugged. You still hadn't asked me to join you, and though I felt certain that you were expecting me to be with you, I really didn't want to find that I was wrong. I don't think that you ever did formally ask me to join you.

The party was wonderful. Your costume, the one that you had

to do drugs to allow yourself to wear, was outrageous, and it was a favorite of the party. We went to a friend's house, and he did your makeup. I didn't watch the transformation, and when you were done, I could hardly believe it was you. I spent the entire party in awe, looking at you, and hardly believing that it really was you.

At the party, another woman was flirting with me. It worried you, that I might go off with her, and leave you at the party, under the full influence of drugs, with no way home. When you realized, you asked my intent. You seemed somewhat panicked. Would I do this? You didn't want to stop me, you said, but you should know so that you could arrange a ride home. I was surprised. I had arrived with you, and would certainly leave with you. To do anything else had never occurred to me, would never occur to me. I told you this, and added that if I had wanted her, I could make arrangements to do it later. I was anxious that you understand that I was committed to you, that I would not do such a hurtful or rude thing.

Throughout the party, you kept thanking me for being such a good person. You thanked me for giving you a cigarette when you wanted one, for getting water when you were thirsty, for being at your side when you needed to touch security or reality. You even thanked me the next day numerous times. I woke up that next morning, and your arm was around me, holding me tight. When you woke up, you hugged me, and thanked me for taking care of you.

Later, we talked about what had happened at the party. You told me about your ex-lover, and how the two of you would go places, and she would pick up someone right in front of you. If you tried to object, she berated you for inhibiting her liberty. That I would not even think of doing such a thing was, to you, a new concept. You were so accustomed to her ways that you had forgotten that people usually consider the feelings of their lovers. You were astounded, and honored that I had that much respect for you.

Meanwhile, you were still trying to make the relationship with your ex-lover work. The two of you didn't think of yourselves as "ex-" yet. The two of you fought violently. You knew each other so well that you could each trigger the other's anger in an instant with a seemingly innocent comment. She'd call you in the middle of the night, and I'd lay next to you, listening to fights and reassurances, words of two people who both loved and hated each other. You couldn't and wouldn't get along, and wouldn't let go. Once, you left me to be with her, promising to be back soon. I laid in bed wondering whether you'd come back and tell me that you didn't want to see me again, that you wanted to see me always, wondering whether you'd be back at all. You came back that night, and I kept coming back.

Thanksgiving came, and you went out of town to be with friends. I stayed in town to be with my mother, but joined you the next day. I got to your friend's house where you were staying late in the day. You told me that you'd missed me. Suddenly, you realized that you wanted me in your life, more than you thought you would. That night, you told me that you loved me, and suddenly I could tell you what I had wanted to tell you for a while: I love you.

Although I didn't move in with you until months later, we slept together every night, most of them at your house, some at mine. That was a few years ago and we still sleep together every night.

Kearin is one of them two crazy white girls living in the ghetto. She writes in her spare time while managing the front desk of the Hotel Leslie.

9

Jacob Levich
Out in the Cold

Let's face it: after a while, international terrorism becomes a job just like any other.

I know my business is supposed to be glamourous. But try taking glamour to the bank. I mean to say, you can't just walk up to some girl in a bar and tell her you're the people's soldier. She'd either laugh her head off or call the FBI.

Don't get me wrong; terrorism has been good to me. I work with the People's Equalitarian Army (better known by its unfortunate acronym, PEA), a young but increasingly competitive terror firm based in the greater New York area. The job has its perquisites—flexible hours, travel opportunities, choice of salary or commission, that sort of thing.

But the PEA is like any business. Somebody gets to have all the fun, and somebody else has to do the paperwork.

I do the paperwork. After three years as the PEA's desk man in New Jersey, I still wouldn't know an AK-47 from a popgun. The world knows me as a certified public accountant with four polyester suits and an office in Bayonne. Not a hell of a lot of glamour about that, is there?

I hope you'll understand, anyway, that I'm basically an average guy. And if you understand that, maybe you'll also understand how it was that I managed to lose a gram of pure plutonium on a bus in Port Authority Terminal.

It happened, as these things invariably do, on a Monday. I had just fixed a morning cup of the instant mountain-grown, and was settling in at my desk for the usual quixotic stab at the "In" tray, when someone knocked at the door.

This kind of thing is a constant annoyance. Every few days, some idiot shows up at my office in search of a legitimate CPA. Since I know even less about accounting than I do about guerilla warfare, I have to politely refer him to a distinguished colleague, picked at random from the phone book. Simple enough, but it takes time.

Today's idiot proved to be a thin, nervous young man with the complexion of a nascent Richard Burton. The kind of kid who gives added meaning to the word "callow," if you know what I mean. I contrived a stage yawn and shot him the classic opening gambit.

"What can I do for you?"

He swallowed visibly and shuffled.

"Some friends of mine told me you're...political. Is that right?"

I didn't feel like spending forty minutes working around to the point. He obviously wasn't interested in having his books done, and he didn't look like an FBI agent. Even FBI agents don't wear white socks and penny loafers anymore. So I took the direct approach.

"That's right," I said.

"Then you are who I think you are?"

"I think I am."

"Well, then, I guess you are."

"What?"

"What I think you are."

This was beginning to sound like an absurdist drama. I felt it was time for a new tack, and pulled a line from an otherwise forgotten detective novel.

"Maybe I am and maybe I'm not. What's it to you?"

My visitor groaned.

"I didn't know I was going to have to deal with this Bogart shit," he said.

So much for playing detective. In my line of work, reality always seems to interfere with romance.

"Sorry," I said. Another painful pause. "So what's the problem?"

He drew a long breath.

"Well, I picked up something...at my job." Yet another pause. "I thought maybe you could use it."

"So what is it?" I asked with some agitation. I was getting bored.

"It's plutonium. A whole gram. One hundred percent pure."

In the tradition of Danny Thomas, I spewed a mouthful of coffee all over the desk blotter. I wasn't ready for plutonium at 9:30 on a Monday morning.

"I work for the power company, see?" he continued. "I've got these friends who work in the research lab. They're kind of political, too. Get the idea?"

I got the idea, and I told him so. I was ready to hear more, but he seemed to get spooked all of the sudden. Maybe he thought it unhealthy to hang around with the kind of dangerous loony who dribbles coffee down his shirt front. In any case, he slipped out the door without further word, leaving what appeared to be a lunch sack on my desk.

I looked inside. One cylindrical metal container, made presumably from lead, about the size of a pack of cigarettes. If my young friend was to be believed, there was plutonium inside that vial. I was sure of one thing—I wasn't going to be the one who found out.

Frankly, I had been about to tell him to get out and take his plutonium with him. I had no interest in handling that kind of contraband, regardless of its supposed political value. From what I understand about plutonium, you make one false move with the stuff and you've sterilized yourself and everyone else within a couple hundred miles downwind. Moreover, parts of you begin to fall off at unpredictable times, causing, I would imagine, considerable embarrassment at social gatherings.

The only thing to do, I reasoned, was to get rid of it as quickly as possible. But who would be willing to take it? The PEA already had more plutonium than it knew what to do with. Well-intentioned people had been stealing it and sending it our way for years.

Actually, though, there isn't much a political organization could do with plutonium. You've read in magazines, I know, that a six-year-old could make an atom bomb in his basement using dad's power tools. If you believe that, I suggest you get your own little vial of plutonium, or U-235, or something similarly potent. Give it a try. You'll be a smoldering pile of ash before you finish screwing the lid off.

The fact is, only two kinds of people have any use for a vial of pure plutonium: nuclear scientists and certifiable lunatics. I don't know any nuclear scientists, so I called Mongo.

Mongo (he seemed to have no last name) was a terrorist organization unto himself. He was at least six-eight and weighed about 290. Although he professed no political beliefs (as he was fond of saying, "Mongo just like to fuck things up"), he often made himself useful to the various branches of the terrorist underground. Whatever the job was, if it was too dangerous, too expensive, or too repulsive, you gave it to Mongo. He especially enjoyed the repulsive ones.

I told Mongo the story, using simple words where possible. Mongo had trouble with words of more than two syllables. He was, it seemed, only too happy to take the plutonium off my hands. I didn't ask why. For all I knew or cared, he gargled with the stuff.

I arranged to meet Mongo in a couple of hours in the classical sculpture gallery of the Metropolitan Museum. Not that he was some kind of connoisseur; he just got a thrill from snapping the limbs off priceless statues. The next bus to Manhattan was scheduled to come by in ten minutes. I slipped the lead vial, pretty gingerly, into an overcoat pocket, and headed for the nearest stop.

I arrived in the city with an hour or so to spare. I decided to kill some time checking out the marquees in Times Square, seeing which form of public perversion was top of the pops that week.

I was on the corner of 43rd and Eighth, wondering what "erotic Rolphing" might be, when I checked my pockets experimentally. I was quick to note 1) a conspicuous absence of anything resembling plutonium, and 2) the unmistakable presence of a gaping hole in the pocket of choice.

It is not easy to describe my feelings at that moment, but I'll try. Ever heard of shitting bricks? I was shitting monumental architecture.

After a minute or two, when my pulse rate had slowed to about 200, I realized that perhaps all was not lost. Indeed, I seemed to stand a pretty decent chance of recovering—that is, if I had lost my plutonium on the bus, and not on the street. Port Authority was the end of the line for my bus. Presumably, the driver was required to have at least a cursory look around for valuables before heading for the men's room to shoot up, or whatever it is bus drivers do on break. With luck, my little vial might already be burning a hole through the Lost and Found counter.

With a surge of hope, I located a pay phone, got Port Authority on the line, and, after several excruciating minutes of Muzak, was connected with the appropriate office.

"Lost and Found," said a voice on the other end. "What didja lose, asshole?" He was polite for a New Yorker.

"Well, it was a small, cylindrical metal vial—"

"What the fuck are you talking about, Mister College Degree?"

I tried a new approach.

"It was this weird little metal thing, kind of round like, about the size of your fist. You know?"

Comprehension.

"Oh, you mean the small, cylindrical metallic vial!"

"Right."

"Jesus Christ, why didn't you say so?"

The voice on the line suddenly assumed a confidential tone.

"Listen, buddy," it said. "We were kind of wondering what that thing is. Is there anything inside it?"

I didn't have to answer. There was no reason to answer. Only a fool would have felt compelled to answer. I answered.

"It's my...asthma medication." Glib, right?

An appropriate response was not long in coming.

"My grandmother's ass."

I figured I'd had enough abuse for one telephone call. I told him I would be down in about ten minutes to pick up the goods.

"Sure, asshole," said the voice. "Have a nice day."

I hung up and headed for the terminal.

I was feeling pretty cheerful by the time I reached the Lost and Found counter. Luck, it seemed, was with me again. For one thing, I had managed to find a working pay phone in central Manhattan, a small miracle in itself. For another, it looked as though I was certain to make good my loss, with no questions asked.

Well, as my friend on the telephone might have said, my grandmother's ass. I was striding toward the counter, displaying my practiced winning smile, when I caught a glimpse of something in the periphery of vision. It was only a brief glimpse, but years of paranoia have schooled me in rapid observation.

Behind the counter was a half-open door. I had seen, slipping through that door, a figure. A figure attired in the natty blue uniform of the New York City Transit Police. It could have been a coincidence,

I guess. Nobody—not even someone as demented as I—could have guessed what was in that vial. On the other hand, a guy who leaves a strange metallic object on the bus, afterwards insisting that it contains his asthma medication, is obviously up to some kind of no good. Ten to one, they figured I was smuggling drugs.

Get it? Some poor bastard spends twenty years behind the counter at Port Authority. Suddenly, he sees the chance to get his picture in the *Daily News*: "Bus Employee Cracks Drug Ring." So he hails the nearest transit cop, sticks him in the back room and waits.

Only a scenario, to be sure. But I was in no mood to take any chances. The thought of waiting at the counter, wearing a shit-eating grin while an imbecilic cop struggled to open a vial of stuff that would make Long Island glow in the dark, was too much for me.

I didn't have to write to Ann Landers to figure out what to do next. Take off. Split. Hit the trail. Make self scarce. And get Mongo.

It was the work of the moment to sashay outside and flag down a cab. I made it to the Met right on time.

Mongo was easy to find. He was removing the fingers from a Roman copy of Praxiteles' Hermes. Say what you will about him, Mongo has taste.

As I recounted the day's events, a disturbing gleam appeared in Mongo's eyes. He wasn't angry. Mongo likes a challenge.

He handed me a couple of marble fingers—a token, I suppose, of his esteem—and lumbered off toward the exit. I didn't follow him. I still have some instinct for self-preservation, and I had a feeling it was going to be a pretty blue Monday down at Port Authority.

To judge by the next morning's headlines, I was right.

Times: "Three Die, 17 Injured in Bus Station Incident."

Daily News: "Monster at Large After Port Authority Bloodbath."

Post: "Kill! Human Juggernaut Screamed."

I figured Mongo had had himself a pretty good old time. I gave him a call a few days later. It wasn't really my business any more, but I must confess to a certain curiosity, especially after headlines like those.

Unfortunately, Mongo was taciturn as always.

"Mongo get mad. Real mad," was the most he would tell me.

On a whim, I asked him what he planned to do with the plutonium. For a moment he was confused. Then the light dawned, and he told me his story in Mondo-fashion, relying heavily on onomatopoeia and the present indicative.

I was able to piece it together with a little effort. After wreaking considerable mayhem, Mongo, I gathered, had left the station with the vial in hand. He had tried to open it as soon as he hit the street. Fortunately for the tri-state area, the thing was equipped with a Mongo-proof cap. He tried squeezing it, biting it, and smashing it against the hoods of passing taxicabs. Nothing worked. Finally, he got frustrated and threw it in a trash can.

I gave Mongo a cheerful goodbye and rang off.

God only knows where that plutonium is now. The way I see it, it's only a matter of time before someone gets curious or the container corrodes. I don't like to contemplate what will happen then.

Not that I care much about the fate of countless millions up and down the Eastern Seaboard. I hear people are nicer in California, anyway.

It's just that when the worst happens, the PEA will be left out in the cold. Everybody from the PLO to the DAR will claim the credit, and we'll have no way of proving our responsibility.

That irks me. The PEA is in competition with a lot of other organizations, after all. You might say we're vying for the top spot on the terrorists' Fortune 500. A coup on the order of several million deaths would have been bound to put us in control of the market.

We blew it, I guess. You see, it's a business. Just like any other.

Jacob Levich is a Yale dropout working for a Southeast Portland weekly scandal rag. He is married and the proud father of no children.

10

Laurie Lindsay
The Flight of Ms. Harriet Peacock

Really, no kidding, that was her name. We never did actually introduce ourselves in the hours we spent together, but I caught a glimpse of her itinerary as we landed: Peacock, Harriet, Ms. It's a name that should belong to a dear friend of Miss Jane Marple, or a character in a board game.

I wasn't in the mood to meet or talk or listen to or be around anyone. I was sulking about being given a seat over the wing—I mean, if they're going to bother asking whether you want a window or an aisle seat, mightn't they figure you want to look at something other than the wing? I didn't want to be on this plane at all; I'd rather have covered the two thousand miles from Seattle to Wisconsin on the road, as was my tradition, but time didn't permit.

I've always liked driving across the continent. It is a form of meditation for me, an emptying of the mind I need to help ease me from one context to the next, from where I start to where I end up. The process, in fact, is much of why I travel. I like to know each inch of distance traveled. I like knowing that nobody in the world knows where I am, that at any exit I could pull off and start a new life. This revelation, which generally occurs at about 3am on any given road trip, reminds me that at any juncture, I am living the life I've chosen. On the road, suspended out of any context, the reality of choice leaps up in high relief against the terrain. Sometimes this jolts me into making major changes; sometimes it reaffirms my pleasure in my life. Always this line of contemplation is instructive, if not consistently comfortable. I relish every moment of desolation and exhilaration in a 36-hour drive.

There's something very unreal about going into a big crowded flying room in one city and shortly thereafter getting out into a distant city without having really covered any ground. The addition of an airport at either end lends air travel a surreal quality I don't like. But I compromise when necessary. When I fly, I take a window seat and a couple Bloody Marys, disengage myself as much as possible from the plane's interior, train my eyes on the terrain below, and simply space out. While it's impossible to telescope a three-day rapture into a three-hour flight, at least I can watch the topography and get a quiet time between social lives.

But this time even this much would be impossible. The plane turned out to be a jumbo jet, fully booked and chock full of small children and a contingent of Marine recruits. Worse, I was stuck with a view of the wing. I had been settled in my seat for half an hour, the air was stifling, and passengers were still boarding, wandering the aisles in confusion, tickets in hand, trying to sort sections, rows, and seats. I resented them for not rushing to their seats more efficiently. I resented them for being there at all. I was praying to the goddess of boarding passes that no one would come and occupy the seat next to mine, one of the last remaining. I was resenting the fact that there wasn't a chance in hell that would happen.

That's when Harriet Peacock appeared before me: a pale woman in her early forties, wearing a polyester double-knit leisure suit in horizontal stripes of white, mint green and menopause pink. A beam of sunlight forced its way through the window, illuminating her and glinting off the monofilament fibers. This, I thought, is a bad omen.

"Youseetay."

"Huh?" I couldn't make out what she'd said, but it was definitely aimed at me. It hadn't the inflection of a question, but she was waiting for a response. Had I seen Tay? Who the hell was Tay?

"Are-you-sit-ting-in-seat-A?" She enunciated it like some people address the blind—like I must be either deaf or stupid.

"Oh. Oh. Yah. I guess so."

She sat down next to me. My bad mood was now fully entrenched.

I inspected her as she settled in. Coke-bottle glasses made her eyes look tiny and sunken. Facial features neither unattractive nor compelling, unremarkable dark hair in a grown-out seventies shag. I decided she must be from the hinterlands, an agricultural culture where back-to-the-land nostalgia had never taken root, where polyester is still the easy-care miracle fabric of choice. She was, in fact, from somewhere outside Spokane.

She seemed harmless enough. Yet something about her alarmed me; all my sirens and yellow lights were engaged: Warning. Caution. Danger. Stayaway, Stayaway, Stayaway. Something in my head kept repeating: Something's wrong. I thought it was just my resentment at the intrusion and told myself to shut up, but the alarms were insistent: Something's wrong, stay away.

"You don't need to worry," she said, still arranging her things under her seat, on her lap, in her purse. She was moving slowly, listlessly. "Once I get settled in, I'm really very well behaved."

Now where the hell did that come from? I looked down at myself, trying to figure out from whence she'd gotten the notion that I wasn't comfortable, that she wasn't welcome. It wasn't too difficult to ascertain: my body had rolled itself up and away from her in a slow recoil; I was sitting up on one hip, pressed toward the wall. My forehead had been pressed to the window and it must have looked as though I was trying to use the window as an exit. I suppose I was. I sat up straight. There'd be no convincing her that the plane's wing and the tarmac beyond held such urgent fascination for me that I just *had* to climb out through the window to investigate *right now*. I was utterly embarrassed and ashamed.

As I worked to regain my composure she was saying something, but again her words were difficult to decipher. Her voice had a heavy, plodding sound lacking inflection or animation, without grace or finesse. It sounded for all the world like an onomatopoeic English translation of fresh manure hitting the ground: Plop. Plop thud. It lent her a distinct air of dull-wittedness.

But dull-wittedness wasn't cause for me to cringe away from her; nor would it set off my alarms like an encounter in a dark alley. Sitting next to her was like perching at the opening of a great, black void, a vacuum. For all the polyester and mousy hair, the woman had something going on that belonged to the Twilight Zone. Whatever it was, I was certain it didn't belong next to me. Swell, I thought. My own personal travel-size black hole.

All the passengers were seated but the plane still stood at the gate. My alarms droned on, Danger, Stayaway. One of the stewardesses was moving a service cart down the aisle. As the cart passed Harriet, a half-dozen packets of peanuts fell to the floor; she leaned over to pick them up and tried to hand them to the stewardess. The stewardess, however, was having a bad day. Somehow she misunderstood Harriet's intent and, rather than accepting the peanuts, grabbed another handful from the cart and threw them unceremoniously onto Harriet's lap. She shot Harriet a look so venomous I couldn't believe it was inspired by the distribution of peanuts. I wondered if Harriet had this sort of effect on everyone.

Harriet, crestfallen and misunderstood, gazed helplessly down at her lapful of peanuts. "But I was only trying to help," she said. It sounded like the last and final words of someone who, following one calamity too many, has given up on the world and will now simply wander away from it into oblivion. The poor dear was *really* forlorn. This was enough to start changing my attitude toward her. I mean, Harriet might be a black hole, but for the moment she was *my* black hole and I'll thank you not to mess with her. I sent the offending stewardess a glare that should have iced over her wings, but it only glanced off her as she aimed her parting shot at me, one of those evil eyes usually reserved for mothers whose children are wreaking havoc in a restaurant: Can't you keep that thing under control?!

As Harriet stowed the troublesome peanuts, I looked at her more closely. She was alarmingly pale; the black of the hairs on her forearms and the fringeling of a moustache above her lip accentuated her bloodless pallor. She appeared never to have met the elements, a creature of the indoors. Her skin had the translucence of a baby's or an ancient person's; it appeared the embodiment of fragility and vulnerability. She reminded me of the sickly kid in everybody's fourth grade class—the one who suffered asthma and all manner of allergies, who needed such thick glasses at such an early age, not what one would describe as "robust". She looked insubstantial, as though she were dissolving into the ether, right before my eyes.

The plane took off and I craned my neck to watch the receding planet, but the only sliver of a view beyond the wing was warped by the waves of heat coming off the engine. Harriet had started talking again and reluctantly I sat up straight, scowling at the prospect of commercial flight chit-chat.

"Are you on a business trip, or just pleasure? Or both?"

"I'm visiting my sister." I was determined not to encourage any further talk with detailed response or anything that could be construed as interest in her, her travel, or her life. I felt positively prickly.

"Are you just going to Minneapolis, or do you get a connecting flight?" I thought this was an odd way to ask where I was going.

"I'm going on to Madison, Wisconsin."

She paused, searching for a segue into what she had to tell me. And, I later understood, she really *did* need to tell me. "I don't want to alarm you," she offered, "but you might be on the same flight as my husband."

Clearly she was going to be difficult to ignore; her statement was designed to beget further inquiry. It worked. I was annoyed with her cryptic approach, but I went ahead anyway. Why, pray tell, ought I to be alarmed at the thought of sharing a 747 with her husband? Was he a pilot, but a very bad one? Why, if they were both traveling in the same direction at the same time, weren't they traveling together? Was she embarrassed to be seen with him? Was he an ax-murderer? *Should* I be alarmed? Was I sitting next to a real loon?

"Oh?" I replied with due caution, "Is this something I should be alarmed at?"

"Well, I guess not, not really. I mean, you'd probably never even know he was on the plane anyhow. But if you did, it might be...sort of...creepy."

"How so?"

"Well...he's dead. He's flying in the baggage compartment. I'm taking him home to Rockford."

Thud.

Her announcement landed like a brick and it lay there, demanding to be picked up. I was staring a hole into the upright seatback tray in front of me, trying to summon the appropriate response for such an occasion: something sincere, yet neither familiar nor cloying. I thought of "Gee, that's too bad," but I wasn't sure it *was* too bad. Maybe he'd spent the past decade in a coma, or with a wasting disease. On the other hand, "what a blessing" was most likely not the appropriate response. I settled on a noncommittal "Oh. I'm sorry," and gingerly, tentatively volunteered the invitation to the next step in the dance:

"Was it sudden?"

The plane had reached altitude and the NO SMOKING sign dinged off; we gratefully grabbed our cigarettes and each lit one.

"He had lung cancer."

Her husband had been treated for a couple months at the Vets' hospital in Seattle, but he was terminal; she took him home to Spokane because he was happier there. For months, maybe a year, she'd kept her job as a nurse in a Spokane hospital and came home to care for him. Having left the Vets' hospital, they'd incurred a $20,000 debt for private care. It seemed to me an abomination that she should be left with such a debt when the patient, after all, had died. But she said she didn't mind; it gave her something in the future to work toward.

When it finally happened, his death had been sudden; neither he nor Harriet were expecting it to come just yet. His lungs just filled up with fluid, and he died. It happened yesterday. Having explained this, she became fearful that perhaps she had contributed to his sudden death—she was a nurse, after all, and she had been with him only a couple hours before—couldn't she have anticipated that his lungs were about to drown him? She was fearful of what I might think of her, failing to save her husband.

"I doubt there was much to be done even if he were in the hospital." I was trying to reassure her; she really did know it wasn't her fault, but needed to hear it from someone else just then. "I've heard of that happening, people's lungs suddenly filling with fluid. I guess it happens pretty often to people in your husband's condition."

This seemed to relieve her; she sighed and relaxed back into her seat. She seemed to want to hear more, and so I continued, trying not to sound trite: "Sometimes it can be a blessing for it to happen suddenly. I mean, it might have saved him suffering." This is what she'd needed to hear. At that moment, a pact formed between us: we were simpatico. She rambled on through the three-hour flight, asking only brief affirmations from me. And I listened, often too close to tears to respond, trying to offer responses which would help her continue to release the tension she poured out by way of stories. Public mourning was out of the question. She needed to talk and keep talking.

"He was watching the Iran-Contra hearings. He watched all of it, right up until he died. It was keeping him happy—he really got a kick out of them going after North like that. He especially likes Inouye and Mitchell, the guy from Maine. But the day he died—yesterday—he was really excited because Proxmire was coming up that day. He got himself all set up in the easy chair in front of the TV—he's just like a kid."

She liked thinking of the pleasure he had taken in the Contra hearings; it seemed to suit a sense of humor they'd shared. Listening to her talk about it, I got a sense of them as partners and companions. She was just now learning to refer to him in past tense, after fifteen years in present and future tense. Throughout the flight she struggled with the shift, from "is" to "was," from "are" to "am," from "loves" to "loved." Sometimes she caught herself speaking as though he were still alive, and she'd correct herself; each time, she confronted it anew. It was a heartbreaking process to witness. Their lives together disintegrated into their constituent elements and she was forced to distinguish her life from his. Her mate was dead.

"I don't know if he ever got to see Proxmire; I was at work when it happened. I'll bet he's really disappointed he didn't get to stick around for the end; he wanted to see how it all came out. But then, he'll probably know what *really* happened long before the rest of us; after all, now he can go ask ol' Bill Casey himself." She laughed at this, as much as she was able, and looked my way to gauge my reaction. My hands covered my mouth to stifle more of a laugh than would have been polite, but she must have interpreted this as shock on my part.

"Oh god. You must think I'm really sick to make jokes about my husband's death. I've been told I have a morbid sense of humor. I'm sorry if I offended you. It's hard to know what to do. I've never done this before. God—I've been a widow for twenty-four hours. I mean, what can you do on an airplane? It's not exactly a good place to mourn. I don't know how to do this. Am I doing something wrong?"

"No. You're not doing anything wrong. I don't really think there's any wrong way to do it. You won't offend me; you can just go ahead and say whatever you want." I was determined to provide her a safe place to do whatever she needed to on this flight. By now I was glad she was next to me and not sitting with that cross-looking business man in front of us. She was looking forward and I peeked behind those obscuring glasses of hers. Her eyes were all puffy from a long bout of crying, and somehow this reassured me; I felt it was an accomplishment on her part, a sign of good mental health. She didn't need any help mourning with her husband's death—she just needed to get through this flight. She needed to talk, and to find ways to express what was happening without making a public display.

And Harriet did find ways to tell me what she was thinking about. It seemed every story was packed and layered with meaning, all told with a kind of back-fence humor and grace I rarely hear anymore.

"He was a bone-thrower," she said, and delighted in the befuddled look on my face. "See, a lot of the time he worked in a slaughterhouse, and what he did, his job, was he was a bone-thrower. After all the flesh was stripped off a carcass and all that was left was the bones, the cutters would throw the bones in this trough behind them, and my husband would come along and pick them up and throw them in this bin and cart them away. So he was called a bone-thrower. I just love telling people that—'Oh, my husband's a bone-thrower.' I especially liked saying that to people in the hospital."

She would be going back to work in two weeks. She looked forward to it because she dreaded living in their home alone and having too much time to brood. "I tell you, if you ever want some time off, just go into your personnel office and tell them 'my husband just died,' and they'll be falling all over themselves to give you some time off. It's real effective."

She told me about her brother, who'd be picking her up at the airport and was already making arrangements for the events to come. They'd had a somewhat odd relationship in their teens—always picking on each other and always close.

"He was a real lady-killer, and he always had a lot of girlfriends. He had this big old Buick and, you know, it was the sixties and sexual liberation and all that. Well, he sure liberated a lot of girls in that car. And then during the day he'd let me use the car, and I'd keep finding all these girls' panties in the back seat, so I'd just go and return the panties to whoever was his date the night before. But then one time I returned them to the wrong girl. Boy, was she mad. And then when he found out, and this girl told him off, he was mad at *me*. So I stopped returning his girlfriends' panties. I started throwing them in the trunk."

She started thinking about dating, and about sex. "Hell, I'd never thought I'd be a widow when I was young. I'd never thought I'd be in the dating scene again. I haven't done that since the sixties, and it was different then; I don't know how it's done now. I mean, back then we had diseases, but those diseases were just embarrassing. Nowdays you've got diseases that'll *kill* you."

It was early evening now and the plane was on its approach to Minneapolis, a much bigger airport than I'd anticipated. The stewardess suggested that everybody check the airport maps and their boarding passes to find their terminal; that's when I saw Harriet's name on her ticket. We were both flying out of the same terminal, on the other side of the airport, so I suggested we walk there together. She visibly relaxed a bit; she'd been dreading the airport crowd. So had I. As we left the plane and entered the stream of foot traffic, I found myself feeling fiercely protective of Harriet, ready to block oncoming bodies like a football player run amok. I wanted to clear a path for her. I wanted to shelter her from any critical eyes, any unkind act. I didn't want her to have to deal with any of it. I wanted to keep her safe.

We both had a short layover, so we stopped at a bar, out of the glaring lights and the obstacle course. She continued with her stories; by now she was anticipating the days ahead with her family and her husband's. They had left Illinois to get away from them. Now she worried about how she was going to pull off services and reception combining the two families: hers were hard-drinking Catholics, his were teetotaling Protestants. She wanted so much for everyone to get along, for everything to go well. She dreaded running interference between the two clans, and she felt responsible for the outcome. She expected herself to act as hostess more than grieving widow.

"Maybe you don't need to take care of them all," I said. "Maybe they can take care of themselves. You deserve a little caretaking yourself; don't run yourself ragged to please someone else."

Over Bloody Marys she recalled growing up on the farm, her father's alcoholism, and her allergy to corn, her father's staple crop. When the corn was tassled, she'd stay inside and sneeze and struggle to breathe. It was that season now.

"I just know," she said in parting, "when my brother picks me up, just as soon as I walk out of that airport, my eyes will start watering, and tears will just be streaming down my face."

I looked at her. "I'm sure they will."

Laurie Lindsay is a Seattle writer working on her doctorate in anthropology at the University of Washington who considers flying to be a private and sacred act not performed with the assistance of others. She is the former editor of a northwest trade magazine and accomplished cook.

11

R.A. Lindsey
Young Impression

Jennifer has been my fantasy and my inspiration since we were kids together. Except I'm not sure Jennifer was ever really a kid. She always seemed so much more mature than her peers (including, especially, me). I swear, at ten years old she was like a short adult. Not aloof — just different. Our friendship was a coincidence. We were neighbors, and we were both loners, and that gave us something in common. But it was funny how we made such an odd couple; her, tall and dark and wild like a predator, and me, helplessly goony-looking with my palsy, wheelchair bound, forever a prisoner of my own body. And she was a turn-on, a junior Lolita. Her skinny girlish figure, unconsciously graceful, seemed over-anxious for womanhood, and was unnervingly capable of sending pangs of lust straight to my stupid youthful genitals. In fact, I distinctly remember the first time my loins were stirred to feel anything more than the urge to pass water. I was ten years old and it was Jenny who had been responsible. And even though I hadn't understood at the time, I never forgot it. Never.

She and I are the same age. (She's an older woman by two months.) And I recall when we were thirteen years old *it* happened; Jennifer became a woman, an earth shaking event, making headline neighborhood news the day her mother proudly stocked up on "feminine needs" for her at the local grocery store. There I was, still playing around with toy soldiers and model airplanes, and Jenny had gone the distance, she was a *woman*, and the things about her that had only made her different when we were kids playing together now made her mysterious.

It was during this time that we drifted apart and she became like a stranger to me. But still, my young fantasies about her evolved into masterpieces of erotic daydreaming. It's curious now that memories of my school friends, whom I associated with daily, are all forgotten or vague, while memories of Jennifer, whom I saw less and less of as time passed, still remain sharply detailed. (Reminds me how much her friendship meant to me — and how impossible it has been to find another who could so effectively make me forget how *different* I am.)

I turned inward, leading a basically quiet existence. But the summer of my thirteenth birthday really bowled me over. In the midst of my loneliness a spring of creativity had been tapped and was happily gurgling forth, and my sketches and doodles were developing into something that was beginning to look like *art*. I preoccupied myself with my creative discoveries for most of that summer, so it was August before I noticed that a landmark event was happening — Jennifer Morrison was growing breasts! Her mother had strapped her into a training bra two years premature, and the early stages of development had gone unnoticed behind elastic-bound barriers of pure white cotton and lace. Then, one day, WHAM! Things had changed, and I was suddenly intrigued to say the least. And it immediately became a matter of artistic pride to render in drawings and sketches my young friend's recently acquired charms with all the imagined detail my budding talent could provide. I would observe her from a distance, in a crowd, shy, I wanted to assume our friendship had weathered our childhood intact, but she wasn't the same Jenny anymore. She was my inspiration and my model in absence. I remember back to that first incident when we were ten. We had been sunbathing with her older sister, Sharon, basking on towels on the patio. Nearby, a sprinkler watered a grassy area where Jenny periodically cooled off with a quick dash through the sparkling water. Once she returned on dripping tiptoes with a wet towel and doused Sharon. Sharon screamed, and, forgetting her unfastened bikini top, sprang up bare-chested. Later we dripped water on the playhouse floor and laughed about it, and Jenny asked, "Did you see how big

Sharon's boobies are?" Reaching behind her back, unfastening the top of her suit. "Mine will get big like that someday."

I may have been too naive at the time to appreciate the potential lewdness of the circumstances, but I could hardly miss the distinct difference between Sharon's budding teenaged breasts, bobbing and jiggling, crimson capped and markedly white against her sun-bronzed torso, and Jenny's skinny little-girl figure, where cosy-pink nipples lay flat on a taught-skinned chest. She pinched her nipples and pulled them into little points — it didn't appear very promising. I was relieved. Really, I had an instinctive fear of her growing up. Jenny, on the other hand, wasn't afraid of much of anything.

"Won't it be exciting when they start to grow?" she said. "I can't wait!" Then she looked at me, asked, "Won't you be excited when you become a man?"

Actually, I hadn't given it much thought. "How will I know?" I asked, puzzled.

"You know ... when you start doing ... you know, *men's* stuff ... when you get all hairy."

"Hairy?" She really had me going, now. It had honestly never occurred to me that I'd become *hairy*. My father was hairy as a monkey; but my father wasn't crippled. I mean, we were different — in every way, it seemed — so I don't remember myself ever expecting to be like him. I don't guess I ever really thought about growing up, or the future at all.

"Look," Jenny said, and before I realized what was happening, she had removed the rest of her suit and was tugging mine down around my knees. "I'll show you." She stood like a young Venus, childishly naked, and I sat open-mouthed in my wheelchair and gawked. She may have been a little girl, but the way she moved and touched herself was entirely womanly, tracing curves that were yet to appear. She said, "First thing, my breasts will start to grow." She traced the circular outlines of something not yet there on her girlish flat chest. "Then I'll have boobies like Sharon's except better." She pinched the nipples until they were red and hard as BB's, pulling and cupping her hands under imaginary flesh. "Sharon doesn't pinch hers enough," she said. "She knows she should, but I don't think she cares."

"*Pinch* them?" I was staring at her in shocked disbelief. She pinched and twisted her inflamed nipples harder and harder with her eyes closed and a smile crept on her face like she was eating homemade chocolate ice cream. "How do you know it's OK to do that?" I asked.

"When my cousin, Glen, visited in June," she said, "he told Sharon *everything* while I was hiding in the closet. And Glen told her that if she wanted to grow bigger boobies she'd have to pinch and pull on the nipples a lot. So I pull on mine all the time. Do you think it has helped?" she asked, thrusting her shoulders forward. Her assaulted nipples were blood-red and distended, but, to be honest, her chest was as flat as ever. She ran her hands across her tummy and down to her bottom, said, "I'll be glad when I start growing a lady's figure. And hair will grow here," she touched her bare mons. "Sharon has a little bit on hers," she said, "And Glen had a whole bunch all around his cock."

"Cock?" I had never heard the word before. "You don't have one yet," she assured me. "You've just got a *pecker*. Glen said you're a man when you can make it hard. *Then* it becomes a cock, and took my flaccid young member in her hand, squeezed it, said, "Yours is soft. Think you could make it hard?"

I wouldn't have even believed it was possible. But then it happened. I was scared speechless as I felt myself stiffen and grow in the palm of her warm hand. And every time she squeezed it, it grew longer and harder. She was delighted. She squealed, "Oh look! You do have a cock!" I suppose I should have been delighted to hear it. But, instead, I'd never felt so embarrassed in my life. If it had been anyone in the world but Jenny whom I had trusted since the egg I would have died of humiliation. But Jenny was so excited by the discovery that I had a cock that her excitement eventually overcame my embarrassment and we took turns holding it while she gave me a guided tour of her naked pubis, explaining what I — as a man — would one day be expected to do. She even suggested we give it a try, but my glorious young cock returned to humble peckerhood before she could convince me, so we dressed and played Rook instead. But for weeks afterward I worried, checking myself out daily, expecting to see the first sprouts of a regular forest of pubic hair (that didn't show up for three more years).

The incident had faded in my memory until that glorious thirteenth summer when I discovered that Jennifer Morrison was growing her long-awaited breasts; little ones for sure, but the real thing nonetheless. And much more exciting than the fanciful mountains of flesh my imagination had conjured for my secret artistic renderings of which there were hundreds — sketchbooks full of pencil sketches featuring Jenny connected to a variety of ample figures (mostly copied from pilfered men's magazines and art journals). It was the same year that the old shed way back on the property line became my private studio after Mom talked my father into putting a new roof on it. And I spent larger and larger volumes of my time there until it began to isolate me from my family who had always been so careful and protective of me. Helped me feel independent — something I had begun to crave; something I never could explain, but my resolve to have independence made me strong in my fortress of solitude.

There was a ladder at one end of the studio that led up to the loft and first inspired me to pull myself out of my wheelchair. That rickety old ladder probably did more than anything else to break the chains that had bound me all my life. I remember how much I craved to climb to the top of that ladder, and how much I risked every time I did, because, if I should lose my hold and fall, it would be hours before anyone would think to check on me there in my place. But it was my private goal and I worked at it daily, building my arms and chest in compensation for my unreliable legs.

Finally, one hot afternoon I made it to the top and collapsed in the dust, exhausted and ecstatic, and I was rewarded with the sight of my adolescent young life. There was a window at the top of the ladder that had a clear view of the Morrison's house, and as I was looking in that direction, Jenny entered the bathroom, and without remembering to close the curtain, she undressed, showered, and then dressed again. And as I watched shame and excitement rushed through my veins like hot synthetic adrenaline.

Later that night, perspiring under my bed covers, I masturbated while I recalled images of Jenny's budding womanhood, remembering her growing sexuality. The real thing wasn't at all like my sketched fantasies, but it was the *real* thing and therefore much more exciting. I squeezed my eyes closed and recalled the way she had massaged and lathered each budding breast — and pinched the tips, of course. Pinched them hard. No one could say Jenny Morrison didn't care; she was going to grow the finest pair of breasts in the county.

She had been too far away to see clearly through the bathroom window, but that wasn't important. I saw her sharply in my mind *to the smallest detail.* And I remembered that time in her playhouse and how little-girl flat she'd been, how she had pulled her nipples into pointed little warnings of what I presently witnessed. And I remembered the mysterious slit I'd been afraid to touch. The flower-like lips she had pulled aside to reveal the mysterious, forbidden place. I threw the bed covers back, was lying in a puddle of sweat, eyes closed, concentrating, pumping, my pulse pounded in my ears. Remembering. I saw her in my mind's eye, all of her like that day when we were ten — except Jenny was all woman now, all curves and blushes and forbidden secrets, dark and mysterious, shadowed with a woman's fleece ... waiting ...

Then release came, panting and sweating and sticky, and content at last in the humid August night.

An artist, Rod Lindsey looks at the callouses on his hands with a certain detached resentment. And he keeps waking up in the middle of a dreary pseudo-reality where he's a carpenter and works too damned hard to earn his wage, has a mortgage, votes, supports a family, etc. He writes to exorcise such demons.

12

Terence A. Loose
Eyes of Despair

Mother was arrested today. She was picked up in the middle of her living room wearing a pair of dad's old pajamas. Surrounding her were broken pieces of china, glass—anything that could be smashed against the brick fireplace. She has cuts on her feet from stepping on the remnants of her rage.

Woody, my roommate, took the message. It was from a Sergeant Anderson, asking me to call him. The news didn't exactly surprise me as much as it made me sick to my stomach. I had been through this just a year before and I knew what was involved. There would be no bail that I could pay. Oh no, it wouldn't be that easy. It would involve horrible visits that I would have to make, seeing her among people who were hiding from reality in their own little worlds, occasionally waging a war against ours in desperate "psychotic" fashion. It's hard to see a stranger lost and alone but to see your own mother give up trying is beyond feeling, it confuses your emotions to the point of numbness.

There would be that time-altering walk down the hospital hall to get to my mother's room, which they always seemed to place at the very end. Everyone would stare at me without expression knowing that I was not one of them. Looking at them I will see their loneliness but at the same time feel more alone than anyone on the planet. And then I would see her, my mom, peeking around the door of her room at me. And as I stepped closer I would see what I was dreading all along: the unbelievable humiliation in her eyes. Not the mere humiliation of the person who knows that it will be forgotten shortly, but the destruction of a soul, the look of a person who has been destroyed and discarded. The look of a person who is not thought of anymore, who knows that they are seen to be unimportant, just a burden to society. Her humiliation must be unbearable; she has undressed her mind and left it sitting naked for all to see—and they have judged it mutated, no good.

Finally, I will come to her and give her a hesitated hug. I'll ask her the ridiculous question "How's it going?" with a planned softness in my voice that just misses the mark of sincerity. She'll look up at me with wounded eyes, those eyes that are worse than death, eyes that are humble without nobility. "Fine, but what am I doing here?"

I'll try to block out the increasing despair, the shocking truth in front of me, so I can offer some kind of comfort. The words will have been in my mind for hours but they will still be almost impossible to utter, for I know that once they are said I am guilty of denying reality too and I will be forced to ride out the next forty-eight hours on the side of the illogical and unreal. But what can I do, this is my mom — the one who stuck up for me against evil high school teachers, the one who went along with pretended illnesses in grade school only to wait on me hand and foot. Yes, there is only one thing I can say and only one course I can follow. "I don't know, mom. It's all a big mistake, you shouldn't be here, they're crazy. I'll talk to them; I'll straighten this out," I'll say without being able to look her in the eyes.

And the next half hour will be filled with casual talk about a movie or my classes or even the weather; as if nothing unusual had transpired on this beautiful fall day. But all the while I will feel that pulsing reality, the horrible assurance that everything will work out—so there can be a next time. Like an impending doom that is never actually realized but always feared. She, I think, feels it too but neither one of us will face what has to be faced. Nothing will get better but nothing will get worse, it will just hover here in this limbo of denial.

Eyes of Despair

I call Sergeant Anderson, get in my car, turn toward the hospital and try not to think about the next few hours of my life.

Terence A. Loose is 24 years old and graduated last autumn from the University of California at Irvine with a degree in psychology. He finds this sadly ironic, as he still can't make any sense out of his own behavior. He has been writing for about two years, and has had work published in Surfer *magazine. Terence has been on a journey of indefinite duration through Australia, Indonesia and Malaysia since we last heard from him.*

13

T. Jackson Lyons
Between Love and Lust

The Doctor's chrome and Naugahyde office masqueraded in exposed brick drag like a new hotel in Philadelphia. From the bullet-shaped bulb in the center of the Doctor's face hung half-moon eyeglasses, the fingerprinted lenses pearled and flashed. He looked past the office cash register—his moral equivalent of a home pay phone—through the open double doors which looked and felt like old varnished oak, but moved as heavily as a cell door, clanging rather than latching, and into his household where a party gently raged. At the bullseye of his party, he watched his Friday-night guests gather like ducks running after each other in the boardwalk's duck shoot.

The Doctor wandered in, holding his stemmed glass as one holds a pistol: trigger-finger cupping the bowl, thumb and fingers gripping the stem. He peered over the eyeglasses as if to avoid the nose that might remind you of a fat brown child squatting in the mud. He was mostly bald, but, as if to make up for his head's topological bareness, his neck was a windjammer of fully rigged loose skin.

Naturally, most of the Doctor's guests looked nothing like him: they were radicals who could again afford long unfashionable hair. Radical, the Doctor wished he was, but could not be, and wished it even more when his look met the two eyes of his evening's ageless lust: the white student looked directly at the black student and if you'd thrown dust between them, light might have appeared. Their gaze was provoked by his definition of psychiatrist: "A physician who never signs death certificates." His comment came after he'd started discussing one of his cases: a family who enticed children into their suburban ranch-style home with candy, then made them engage in a family argument. After the children were convinced, either with more candy or several good strops of daddy's belt, to yell, scream and cry, they all made up. And pederasty followed reconciliation—something like couples who follow their arguments with lovemaking.

"Why don't they molest their own children?" The white boy's blue eyes showed respect for the Doctor's sublime indiscretion of discussing a current case. His bleached flax hair looked like a second opinion of his skin, the loose fitting blond pastel clothes made you understand why artists and pornographers must have nude models.

"Or each other?" questioned the black boy whose crystal white eyes blinked nervously, finally breaking their laser-like gaze.

The Doctor cleared his waiting throat, forming it around the distant, tasteful words, "Hell if I know. My pure speculation is that the other children were simply surrogates; they were, in effect, molesting their own children. It's odd how repression manifests itself in people," he concluded, his lips twitching. He went on quickly, "To help them bring out their stunted, inarticulate feelings, we conducted primal scream therapy with the whole family. Also regression therapy by baby-bottle sucking, both widely accepted therapeutic events. It seems that they screamed in whole sentences run together—as it turns out, several 99-year sentences." The Doctor guffawed, spilling his drink. "The photographs of their open mouths became exquisite with the actual scream played beside it. We have video equipment on order."

The rectangular black face moved its heavy sculpted lips. "You have a fascinating profession."

"Not profession," the Doctor growled harshly, but under his breath. Then his tentative, genial smile and half-closed indulgent eyes returned. "No, I'm nothing more than a professional amateur, if you will." He reached out to massage the black boy's elbow, physical forgiveness and flattery from the Doctor who thought that as long as the boy sounded as if he sold the world's finest items without being touched by the contaminants, the very contents, of that sensual bazaar, as long as he could look at him and bask in his mutable beauty, then he didn't have to really listen.

At the center of the whole shooting match, the Doctor felt like a sterile artist whose technique had become his art, masturbation having become his sex. The Doctor knew his party had surrendered to the infinite perfectibility of neurotic rich people when a very sick woman with large curls and much gold clanking in the cavern between her breasts rushed up to a newly arrived guest at the door: "Stanley! Darling, do come in." Then she cried, "Wait!" Her large, slightly buck teeth flashed back toward the audience, alerting them, "You can't come in unless you promise to fuck me." She spread-eagled to bar his entrance. Try this some time; it is possible to make a roomful of people who had been discussing movies roar with laughter. Poor Stanley, all dolled up in his receding hairline and light tan suit, was scandalized, but had the presence of mind to take his wedding band off.

The Doctor's mental eyes rolled toward heaven but his real ones twinkled merrily. Still twinkling, he turned to his two young charges and, barely moving his smiling lips, said, "I feel like a gadfly on the biggest flop in the galaxy. Why don't we leave these people to stare at themselves in my mirrored mantle. The fire is too warm here, I think. There's a colder fire outside—it's burning blue and friendly, let's go."

They left to walk through the damp winter cold of the woods around his house, finding their way by the light of the silvery moon. Reflecting the party lights, the snow seemed yellow instead of the usual calmly laconic blue of nightfall. From a vial he pulled out like a pistol from his pocket, the Doctor inhaled deeply. He wafted it toward the two young men, saying, "Have you ever dreamt to fly—or leap a tall building, or the Royal Gorge Bridge—and survive? Fly with this, it gives enough of the sensation of flying that you only want the dream."

They walked some distance down a gravel lane running through his acre of trees in this exclusive suburb. "Doctor," said the white 18-year-old, "there's talk that the quality of the urban geography follows a downward curve declining arithmetically with age."

"Pause. Do you think this will ever be a slum?"

"Isn't that a pretty thought," replied the Doctor, his real eyes rotating at a rate roughly equal to Malthus' underground RPMs. He shrugged his shoulders enthusiastically and with a warm smile said, "Well let me just look at you boys!" He put a hand on each of their outer elbows and pushed them toward each other until they touched.

"That's funny," the black one declared, "that's what my pop always says."

"Diet?" the Doctor snapped. "Don't you ever call him 'sir'?"

To mollify the Doctor, the white boy said, "If we were back inside we'd be talking about fucking movies—cheer up."

The Doctor brightened up. "Alright, no movies and say 'sir' every now and again."

"Have you heard any good jokes lately, sir?"

"Ah, my boys," he said, swinging them around, taking their inner elbows and walking them down the path, "this weather, it's just like heaven to touch. This cold static white, so blue it looks like flesh that dies in it; it reminds me that we are all mortal. Now why doesn't that lessen my extraordinary fear. I'm even afraid of you. Do I have good reason to be?"

"Oh no, sir," replied the black one, too quickly.

Just as quickly the Doctor said, "An Arab is walking down the street and walks into a wall. Which part of his body hits the wall first?"

The two boys gazed at each other and the black one spoke to his white friend as if the Doctor had been forgotten in the same way an audience is excluded from the action in a play: "When this is over we renegotiate terms." White friend nodded. They turned back to the Doctor and said simultaneously, "His erection."

"No!" the Doctor exulted, "His nose!"

They chuckled politely.

The white one said, "Doctor, I saw you across the room as you came in tonight. You looked very good. Sir."

"Instead of 'very good looking'? Well, no matter. Some enchanted evening, you might see a stranger, on the other side of a crowded room. Remember that boys, you'll be needing it at the lineups before long."

The black one nodded sharply down at his white friend. The Doctor had been leading them by the elbows, and at the nod, they jerked him up under the armpits and executed a 180-degree turn while the Doctor's feet spun beneath him. "I think we should go back and see if Stella and Stanley have had their fuck yet," said the black one.

The Doctor smiled bitterly for just a moment before recovering his genial, fatherly smile. Didn't he want them to see that he had the power to be bitter, or was it all trick photography like Jeckyl becoming Hyde? Doctor chuckled softly, "Well, I see you've grown up right around your old dad. You don't use 'sir' anymore because your bosses are all called by their first names. Times have changed—it's little ways like this that make us really know that times have definitely changed."

"Yes, Doctor, I think you're right."

"'Doctor'! I've heard that so often that I've forgotten my real name. But I'll bet you boys have it memorized from all those checks. 'Doctor'! An M.D. does all that to you. All I really want to be right now is ho...ho...homo—" His lips oscillated involuntarily, like a jellyfish in waves searching for its next meal.

"Easy does it, Doctor. Nothing's going to hurt you. We certainly can't."

"I know," the Doctor says warmly, faking it this time, "my boys are all right. Good strong lads. With lots of things on your minds. Like your girlfriends and future families. It's a good time to be just starting out in life—if you start from the right place."

"We certainly hope to, sir."

"Good," said the Doctor, lighting a big green cigar with large puffs and a flaming tip, "we'll go chase the sluggards out and call an end to this party."

Meanwhile, back at the ranch house, the Doctor's professional hostess had cleared away the littered glasses and floating cigarette butts. Just as the three man, elbow to elbow, crunched up the gravel and ice lane, it started snowing. "Oh! Merry Christmas every one," the Doctor said, squeezing their elbows just hard enough to cause pain.

They entered the heavy paneled front door, stepping onto the plush beige carpeting that ran to the large central stair, winding upward in a weighty white marble spiral. He gave his wrap to the hostess, "Thank you, Martha. Are Stella and Stanley still here?" he asked mischievously.

Martha, a thin black matron on the outer rim of middle age, stiffened capably, "I'm sure I wouldn't know, sir."

"Thank you, Martha. Why don't you go on home now. Come back at 8:30 tomorrow morning. I'm going to work some tonight out in the carriage house and need to get out early. I'm going to sleep over there tomorrow as well. You'll have the whole house to yourself—just what you've always wanted. When you're done, take the rest of the day off. How's that, Martha?"

"Well, sir," she said with the gulp of exploited labor, "it's terribly early and tomorrow's Saturday, too. But if I get Wednesday off, I'd really appreciate that, sir."

"Good, Martha, then we're agreed."

He walked down a hallway to the guest room and yelled, "Stelllaaaa!" He opened the door slightly, swinging it open in terrible disappointment. "They have gone. How boring." The Doctor turned to his young charges, "Well, it's a long drive in and snowing, I've got plenty of room here. You might as well stay over."

The ivory and ebony consulted with a glance, and the black one said, "Fine Doctor, we'll stay out here." He pointed down at the living room's plush brown carpet.

He accepted this, saying, "My office is through the double doors, the guest room is down that hall. It has a queen size bed," Doctor choked.

The black student smiled gently at the Doctor's little howler, "I'll sleep on the sofa, thank you."

The Doctor muttered unintelligibly, politely bowing out of the room.

The white boy walked to the guest room's bed, sitting on it as if to test its advisability, then stripped to his white shorts. He stood up and his bare arched feet mashed shadows in the plush pink carpet, like the impression guilt leaves in you mind. Guilt and humiliation leave the same sort of impression: one is a passive mortification and the other is an active one. The Doctor was a very active man. It had been a lifelong avocation for the Doctor. For instance, approaching his Chief in medical school for a charity, he was rebuffed by the Chief's large reptilian eyes. The Chief tugged his lab coat into position and demanded a statement of receipts and allocations before he would give. The young Doctor was confused, but then said, "You have every right to feel that way sir—how do we know where all the money goes anyway?" The Chief snickered, "No, I don't in fact feel that way, but I didn't want to let you get by without sharpening my needles, either." The Chief gave him a check for $15.

And thus, the Doctor's impressionable mind created, then, this narrative:

The blond boy's hair was short and swept back over his squarish head. In a kind of denunciation of his features' regularity, short blond curls popped out, rumpling the otherwise smooth plastic look of his hair, giving his entire face an aura of occasionally imbibed wildness.

His body was covered with a layer of hair so fine that even on his arms—those monstrously tan sheaths of muscle, vein, and sinew so dense that you couldn't have said whether there was a bone in them—only under the brightest light could you have seen the hair. And the Doctor liked to see it. He liked the bright lights of the third degree with its heat and vague shadowy white forms of the shouting police.

The white one walked out to the living room where his friend stretched from end to end of an enormous plush red velvet sofa. Once you've seen that big a sofa on a brown rug, the dark black youngster stretched all over it makes you come to a new sense of which colors go together. A good antidote to racism.

The squarish black face turned and because of the pillow crumpling his hair, you could see in a shock that his hair was cut to create the squarish manly appearance. His dark arm, with a pale palm up, moved to scratch his inner thigh up to the bottom of his black mesh underpants.

The white boy stroked back his hair with impatient narcissism, then said, "Want to talk?"

"About the old man?"

"Yes." Waiting.

"Harmless."

"That's not what I meant."

"We haven't argued with him yet over money to send us to Europe for our summer vacations." The black boy's shrewd voice, soft but abrupt, stopped you like a cobweb in the dark. "Or perhaps," he concluded softly, "it would be better to get our winter vacations in Jamaica now, and worry about summer on the continent later."

The white boy, showing he was no slouch when it came to opportunism, suggested, "Do we need him with us, if there is a way to get rid of him, to arrange for these things?"

"Ah not yet!" said the black one softly. "It's too soon since the last one. And we have to glide longer in between from now on."

In the Doctor's beige office with its short-napped rugs, the cash register rang tinnily. The Doctor had listened long enough; now what he meant to say was: "I won't squat in the mud anymore. I am the carpenter's son who breaks loaves and multiplies fish! There is only one revolution which will not destroy me, and that's my own." Instead, knowing that it would destroy him, he said to the young woman seated opposite him, "Go now, Sophy. Save me, my daughter."

Sweet Sophia darkened the moonlit wall, breaking it like the cheap spine of an old paperback mystery. The black boy pops off the couch when he sees his sister and the silhouette of his family. The white boy who is draped in moonlight, black shadows from erect nipples score his pale torso.

Sophia raised a gun. Her hair looked tortured and dishevelled as if by benign neglect, as if unraveled like a weighted string twisted tight, all that energy released in a brief family war. She wagged the gun meaningfully, and her brother moved with animal confidence, white muscle rippling like the coat of a black panther suddenly prey.

"Don't do that! Something's bothering you, but not this way, not now, there's someone who can help you." He smiled and glanced at his white friend. "Give me the gun."

And her hand relaxed, but it had already been too late: "Yes," the white boy said, "Doctor can help you." She snapped alert, shooting. Chips of white enamel flung from his mouth, teeth and oblongata shattered to nubs. The undertaker would have to suspend a bridge over his gums to elicit the corrupt compliments for his trade that hover like brimstone fumes over heavy American caskets. He didn't do anything for the missing oblongata.

Sophia took a deep breath, and faced her brother. Murder, like war, temporarily reduces the complexities of life.

"Stop now, I'm your brother, I can help you."

Turning toward her brother's dead lover, speech buried deeply, froths in a dark throat, "What? No complaints? No desire to join him. No begging on your hands and knees to be allowed to follow your lover? Or only distressed damsels did that? My brother," she flung out the words as one flings out used flypaper, "catching that white boy's disease. You should shame, you should get on your knees and beg forgiveness." Pronouncing it "forgiveness," as if being saved once were for all time. "I never liked Momma's kind of religion, but it sure has its uses." He moved to face her. "Don't move a muscle," she reminds him.

"Am I so horrible that you've come to this? Why can't you just idly hate like everybody else? Wait," he says, beginning to sweat, "people can learn to hate without passion. Doctor can teach yo—"

Only one shot shatters the bridge of his—what else?—aquiline nose. His body slumps from the wall that has already absorbed all the deadly force without cracking. Sophia dropped the gun, wringing blood from her hands as if to wash away the pearly fingerprints. Who'd have thought them to have had so much blood?

"No 'sucker,'" she said turning to enter the office, "you can't teach me to hate without passion."

T. Jackson Lyons says "I don't know if you're big on contributors' blurbs, but I detest them—as long as you spell my name right, who cares? The story doesn't live or die by my hand anymore."

14

James Maloney
Artichoke Art

"She was as pretty as an artichoke."—a term of admiration.

The mayonnaise was all gone. The leaves, stem and inside 'fuzz' were scraped together into a pile. The heart had been eaten. All that was left was sticky fingers and the aftertaste.

"It's really a flower, you know."—from the amateur botanist at the table.

No one else in the fruit bowl really liked the artichoke. The oranges thought him too radical. The bananas called him gangly. The pear accused him of being too aggressive. But really, they worried about him being actually worth 49 cents.

The conversation progressed like an artichoke. We peeled back the green phrases, one by one, chewing on their ends. Only to find our separateness at the heart of the matter.

Stan poked at the artichoke in the green boiling water, with a fork, as the steam clouded his glasses. "How long you suppose to boil this thing?" he asked.

Articulated Shopping List

White Bread: *toast, sandwiches, bread and butter, predominant American values.*
6 pack Pepsi Cola: *Pepsi please, with lots of ice, lots of sugar.*
Tortilla Chips: *junk food.*
Sliced Lunchmeat: *sandwiches, white bread.*
Campbell's Soup (1 can Cream of Mushroom, 1 can Beef Noodle): *lunch, rainy day. Mmmm good.*
Fryer Chicken Pieces: *articulated creature, movable parts.*
2 cans Tomato Sauce: *enough to smother any meal.*

> Sustenance.
> You are what you eat (or so they say).

Articulated Shopping List II
(organic version)

1/8 lb. Bee Pollen: *insect version of espresso.*
Sprouts: *potential for a whole pasture.*
5 lbs. Whole Wheat Flour: *nice alliteration, bad pie crust.*
Tofu (bean curd): *a test of ingenuity.*
Fresh Vegetables (cauliflower, broccoli, carrots, celery, brussel sprouts): *nature's silent creatures, looked upon with same ardor as meateaters have for sirloin.*
2 lbs. Brown Rice: *staple of China (and you know how many Chinese there are).*
1 lb. Falafel: *The hamburger of India.*
Fruit: *junk food.*
Goat's Milk: *smaller is better.*

> "Refining food takes away some of the most nutritious parts. Over the last sixty years, food has become more and more refined. It's scary to imagine the results of this trend continuing."
> Eating can become a way of life.

James Maloney has been writing for years, and occasionally gets a little recognition and a groupie or two.

15

James Maloney
The Bar

  The cops are out canvassing the bars, swinging their night sticks, walking slow and deliberate. They're looking around, letting their presence be known. It's an unspoken reminder to stay in line. The cops saunter in, friendly and familiar. Upstairs the boys are smoking reefer in the bathroom. The cops don't go that far. Here on the south side of the block authority is respected. As long as authority is respected you can do anything you want. The boys upstairs respect authority. "Everything in its proper place," they say, smiling at one another between hits. It's a nice bathroom with clean white light and very little piss on the floor. The bar is a nice bar, except that the drinks are weak unless you come here often. The waitress sometimes smiles as if she wasn't working. One of the cops tells a joke to the bartender, who nods but doesn't laugh. To him they're just two more customers. He offers them a drink and they turn it down; it's part of the ceremony. The bartender eyes the clock, twenty 'til twelve and ten minutes fast. The customers are drinking and talking to their compatriots and watching each other. What else is there for them to do? Music comes from a stereo controlled by the bartender, it is part of the mystery of his position: he knows the ingredients in a Cuba libre, he is in charge of manipulating the bottles, and he knows what brands are attached to the hose for the house liquor. "Jim Beam," he says, "Gibley's, Gordon's, and Cutty Sark." But who knows? It is only a hose that comes from the depths of the bar. The cops slowly turn around to leave. They're in no hurry. "See you around," the tall one says. They're off to spread authority elsewhere. They're just part of the ambience, like the music, like the special night air provided by the owner and circulated freely by the air conditioner even when it isn't hot out. It all goes together to give the bar that certain atmosphere, like ashtrays that are never dirty. The boys, out of the bathroom now, order another round of beers, while a middle-aged businessman takes their place and works to relieve his constipation. It is all part of the atmosphere. And the atmosphere, like authority, is always respected.

This short vignette describes the atmosphere of Jim's favorite locale: a bar, any bar, just so the beer on tap is plentiful and someone is willing to buy. He writes or 'does' art after getting up, which is usually around noon. Currently on furlough from an advertising design firm, he finds comfort in unemployment.

16

Jay Marvin
The Rag Picker

After barely surviving a slow, steamy bumper to bumper crawl home up Highway 17 from the Silicon Valley—and with his head pounding and ticking like an overheated automobile radiator—Ed Lolly determined his only salvation from an otherwise shitty day was to change into his swim trunks, position himself out on his apartment balcony, and languorously suck on an ice cold Anchor Steam Beer.

And it was while out on the balcony sprawled on an aluminum lawn chair watching the last rays of the California sun filter through an orangish-purple sky, and bounce off the dull, pink stucco buildings of his apartment complex that Ed Lolly first spotted the Rag Picker. He held his beer and stared as the old man worked his way through a battered, green metal trash dumpster which made its home right across the parking lot directly in Ed's line of sight.

From the very first, Ed's anger and frustration over having to see an old stew bum go through the garbage ran through him like a jolt of alternating current which arced back and forth between the emotional poles of resentment and envy. He *resented* the old scavenger, because he felt it was unfair to have to work, pay taxes, and shell out $800 a month for a shabby one bedroom apartment the size of a microchip thirty miles from work, only to arrive home after a hard day on the job to find his little piece of the American Dream included some old geek going through the trash.

He *envied* the Rag Picker, because unlike himself, here was a man who appeared happy and who seemed to be making it in life without having to go a job every day where the shit rained down like brown bombs. And the only refuge from the managerial meat-grinder was to use the old sick call routine.

Having killed the bottle of Anchor Steam, Ed got to his feet and went inside his apartment. After the day he had had, he didn't even want to think anymore about some old fuck going through the garbage. Instead, he made a mental note to remind himself to move to a better neighborhood as soon as he got his first big promotion from Textronics. Of course, he wouldn't move until after he bought the bright red BMW-320-I he had been looking at ever since grad school.

Two nights later, Ed Lolly was lying out on his balcony listening to Linda Ronstadt, and nursing a cold beer in an effort to rid himself of a throbbing headache (caused in part by the fact that under pressure at the office he had accidentally grounded off a gold cap from his back right molar)—when he saw the Rag Picker. The old man was dressed in dirty, grease stained, blue overalls, a pair of crusty, mud-caked combat boots, and a faded green and yellow Oakland A's baseball cap.

Ed held his beer and watched as the old man bent over the smashed up, green Dempsy dumpster and probed inside it with a long metal pole. Every time he jabbed at the trash can's insides a swirl of evil-looking black flies moved above his head like a dark funnel cloud. The sight of the Rag Picker and his flies made Ed feel sick, uneasy and, most of all, angry.

"Why doesn't somebody tell that old fuck to get lost?" Ed moaned, grabbing his stomach and grinding his teeth. "Is this what you get for 800 fucking dollars a month?"

He leaped from the lawn chair, and stomped into the apartment grinding his teeth and reaching for the phone. He started to dial before he realized he didn't even know the apartment complex manager's number. Slamming down the phone, he pulled the telephone book off the counter, almost knocking over his brand new French blender from *Neiman Marcus*, yanked open the book;

The Rag Picker

found the number; dialed it, and stood listening to the phone ring while he ground his teeth, felt his head begin to ache and his jaw start to hurt. On the fifth ring the manager's, Mel Stewart, voice came on the line.

"Wagon Wheel Apartments...the best in suburban living with a country feel! May I help you?"

"Yeah," Ed shouted into the phone. "This is Ed Lolly over in 124..."

"Yes! Edward, how may I help you?"

God, how I hate it when anybody calls me Edward, Ed thought. *No one ever calls me Edward except my mother.*

"Look, Mel, I'm sitting on my apartment balcony minding my own fucking business, when guess what I see?"

"I don't know Edward, what?"

"A fucking rag picker. Some old guy scrounging around in the trash can...that's what! Is this the best in suburban living with a country atmosphere for 800 dollars a month?" Ed yelled into the phone so loud a dull, blue vein popped up on his neck like an angry cord.

"Now Edward, calm down...I'll have Dick Splitinger, head of complex security get on it right away. Ole Sheriff Dick will handle it...And thanks for calling."

"Oh fuck you and your sheriff Dick," Ed yelled into the phone, hanging it up with such force the plastic casing cracked. "If I had wanted an apartment with a view of a fucking street scavenger, I'd of moved to Bombay."

On a Monday night following a weekend in which Ed Lolly had argued with his fiancée, Rowena, trying to tell her one just doesn't bound up the corporate ladder at Textronics like one were on a pogo stick, and after a day at work in which Ed felt sure he must remind his boss of his long-lost, first wife's obnoxious brother, the way he was being punished, Ed stood over the sink gulping a spoonful of pink stomach medicine.

When something caught his eye.

It was the Rag Picker. Swallowing the liquid with a grimace, and wiping the horrid stuff off his lips, Ed Lolly stood there spoon and bottle in hand checking the old man out. At once he felt revulsion. But even so, he felt some weird fascination with the old man like he used to feel when his father would drive him down

Spring Street in Los Angeles to look at the winos and bums standing out in front of the Rescue Mission. Ed slowly put the spoon down on top of his new deluxe microwave oven.

He had an idea.

Decked out in his new Adidas jogging shoes and shorts, and wearing a 'Disc Drive Does It Better' T-shirt, Ed was going to find out what this old freak's story was once and for all.

As soon as the Rag Picker had loaded up his day's find, and sidled off out of the complex parking lot, Ed slipped out of his apartment and started to trail the old man, making sure he was far enough behind so as not to be noticed.

The two men turned off the main boulevard that ran in front of the apartment complex, and trudged up a long, winding hill, with the Rag Picker leading the way. At the top, Ed saw the old man push his cart up the driveway of an old, rundown, pastel blue house. *The old son of a bitch has a better view than I do*, Ed thought, pausing at a four way stop sign to catch his breath, and tugging on his T-shirt to try to cool off. He noticed it was beginning to get dark, and he could not quite make out what the old man was up to. He needed to get closer to the house for a better look. Down below he saw the lights from the apartment complex and the city of Hayward. He mopped the sweat from his face with the back of his hand, and very carefully inched his way across the street. Once he was close enough, he stopped and crouched down behind one of the juniper bushes standing guard along the house's driveway.

Peeping over the top of the dark, prickly bush, he saw the old bum busy in the garage meticulously going over the day's treasures. The garage was filled with yellowing newspapers, bits of torn rags, old clothing, stacks of Bibles, and on the walls were plastered old and wrinkled pictures of Jesus that had been ripped out of religious magazines. Ed stared in horror, and amazement, as the old man pulled a half-eaten fried chicken wing out of the cart and began to gnaw on it.

Ed had been squatting for quite a while, and his back began to hurt, not to mention he was starting to develop a cramp in his right calf muscle. He desperately wanted to stand up and stretch. But was scared the Rag Picker would spot him. Finally, he couldn't bear the pain anymore and stood up, lost his footing, tried to maintain his balance by flapping his arms like an eagle on acid, and fell face first on the driveway. Jumping to his feet, he stood looking like a deer caught by the side of the road in the headlights of an oncoming car. The Rag Picker turned and eyed him, the chicken wing still in his mouth, turned and pointed at him and began to shout, "He that believeth and is baptized shall be saved; but he that believeth not shall be damned!" Then he looked up at the dark sky and mumbled something about sin and damnation.

With that, Ed spun around and ran down the driveway and kept on running until he was out of breath and at the bottom of the hill.

When he went to bed that night he couldn't sleep. Every time he shut his eyes, visions of the Rag Picker tumbled through his head. The more he tried to rid himself of the image of the old bum, the more he seemed drawn to him. He hated him, yet, there was something. Oh, hell, he turned over and squeezed his eyes shut trying to force out the old man's face.

"Shiiit!" Ed roared, stumbling from his Datsun B-210 and lurching around to the front of it. He had put a dent in the car while trying to park. Running his hand over the large crater-shaped ding, he let out a loud laugh, held his hand over his mouth and looked at the auto with a devilish grin. Fumbling for the keys, he found his front door and stood before it swaying back and forth, trying to get the key in the lock.

Once he was inside, Ed flopped down on the chair and buried his head in his hands. The whole day, shit, the whole week, had been too much for him. No one in the history of the Lolly family had ever been fired. What would his parents think? And what would their friends back East say? And what would he tell his fiancée? He had tried so hard at Textronics as a junior accountant.

Anger began to rise in Ed's throat like bad stomach acid. He grabbed a lamp and threw it against the wall. It landed with a loud crash. Then, he turned and picked up an ashtray and hurled it toward the front door. It ricocheted and slid under the couch. From there, he scooped up a handful of record albums and flung them around the room.

Next he stalked into the bedroom, lifted up his brand new home computer and heaved it through the sliding glass door leading to the balcony. Sticking out his arms, he ran the length of the bedroom wall knocking off all the pictures. Then, he ran into the kitchen, pulled a butcher knife from a drawer, crossed into the living room and, laughing hysterically, he began to slash the upholstery on his brand new couch with long, violent arcs.

By the time the Hayward Police Department arrived on the scene, Ed Lolly was sitting in the middle of a pile of rubble that had once been his apartment. The two police officers gently pulled him to his feet and led him off, while he cried and mumbled something about how the head of accounting for Textronics would burn in hell, among much wailing and mashing of his teeth.

After sixty days of observation, Ed Lolly was released from the psychiatric wing of Hayward General Hospital. It had been easy to convince the doctors that he didn't care about losing his job. And that he didn't care about breaking up with his fiancée. In fact, most of the time he felt like a TV set tuned to no particular channel—just a blank screen. He felt it must be God's will.

The sun was setting and the two men worked over the battered green Dempsy dumpster like red ants attacking a chocolate chip cookie crumb. One had a long pole. The other—the younger one—worked at loading bits of paper, clothing, and discarded beer cans into a small metal shopping cart. As they worked, the older one spouted quotes from the Bible and wiped sweat from under his faded green and yellow baseball cap.

When they were done, the old man turned and signaled to the younger one it was time to go. The old bum stuck his pole in the shopping cart and sidled off out of the apartment complex. Not far behind, Ed Lolly followed, chewing on a half-eaten baked potato and pushing a metal cart.

Jay Marvin is a former major market disc jockey who once worked in Chicago and San Francisco. He now does a daily radio show in Salt Lake City. He is also at work on a novel.

17

F.J. Matozzo
The Golden Fleece

There lived many years ago, in a distant land, a cruel and powerful tyrant named Zandor the Terrible.

His was a well-earned notoriety, gained by countless wicked actions, among them keeping his people in a state of virtual slavery. He would tax them beyond reason and execute them for the slightest protest. He stole from the countries treasures, while raping and pillaging those neighboring countries unlucky enough to border his own. He was hated and feared by everyone. Especially feared, because it was said that he possessed the magical power of invulnerability.

This was not idle rumor. It was officially recorded by Zandor's court biographer that three times he had been struck by assassin arrows; and twice more wounded by the enemies, sword in battle. Yet each time he survived, reappearing to his people after only a few days, convalescence, unscathed from wounds that would have killed most men.

It was the magic of the fleece that kept him thus, the "golden fleece" as he called it, stealing the phrase from the ancient Greek legends. The most closely guarded secret in the kingdom. Only two other people knew of this fleece: Alzira, his beautiful young wife, and Elle, the Nubian handmaiden who was Alzira's servant, confident and (it was whispered in court) her lover.

It was Alzira who actually possessed the magic, a mysterious power bestowed upon her when she was a child. A power that would remain with her for as long as she remained a virgin. This alone was the reason Zandor married her, keeping her a virtual prisoner in his own palace, denying her the tender love of a husband and secluding her from all men. The only time Zandor touched her was when the power of her fleece was needed, and then he would strip her naked, roughly, and quickly begin the healing process. He would look upon his wife's young body with mounting lust—the delicate curves of her breasts, the slender waist, the soft, pearly skin—wishing that he could consummate the marriage and knowing that he never could, for the magic would be gone forever. The magic that lay between her legs: the shimmering, golden pubis nestled between her tender young thighs, blessed by a cynical old shaman long since dead—with the power to heal.

Zandor's power led itself to many indiscretions—the Terrible One was inclined to take freely from those around him, no matter how precious or sacred the object was.

One fateful night he came to the modest quarters of Elle, who lived in the palace as did all the royal servants. He came with the sexual hunger of a wolf, lusting for her dark-skinned beauty.

He spoke not a word to her as he entered her quarters, but savagely threw himself upon her naked, sleeping body. Elle, swiftly awakened, fought back fiercely, raking her fingers down his cheeks, drawing blood.

Zandor laughed, her fury serving only to ignite his burning lust more than he would have thought possible. He raped her brutally, savoring the immense power he felt from lancing this strong, long-legged black woman; growing drunk on the sensual pleasure he stole from her. During the course of the night he raped her again, and yet a third time, taming her as one would tame a wild horse.

Not once that night did Zandor think that his actions would be the catalyst for his downfall.

Wagstaff, the tall, powerfully built Captain of the Guard, was Elle's secret lover. When he learned the next day what Zandor had done, he flew into a rage.

"If he were not invulnerable, I would kill him with my bare

hands!" he shouted, stalking his chambers as Elle told him what had transpired. She had never told anyone the secret of the King's 'invulnerability'; now she decided it was time.

"Zandor is not invulnerable," she whispered, then, breathlessly, she told him the story of Alzira's golden fleece.

Wagstaff shook his head in amazement when she was finished. "How do you know this is true? And why did you not tell me sooner?"

Elle hesitated. Should she risk losing this wonderful lover, a man that satisfied her desires as no other had, by telling him the true nature of her relationship with Alzira? Deciding that the greater sin would be to lie, she told him everything. She told of Alzira's budding, yet unrequited sexuality. Of the natural longings forbidden her by Zandor. Of her subsequent need for a lover and the fascination she always had for the tawny, silken flesh of her handmaiden. She told him finally of the endless nights of love between the two women, the Sapphic pleasure they enjoyed.

"You should have told me of this before," said Wagstaff.

"You're a man," she replied, staring into his blue eyes. "Could I hope for even you to understand this special love? To not feel disgust? Inadequacy?"

Wagstaff leaned suddenly forward and passionately kissed her thick, cinnamon lips. Gripping her hands with his own, he brought them to his crotch. To his swelling prick. "Feel my disgust," he whispered, licking her neck.

The blood pounded in Elle's veins. Together, they fell onto the bed, tearing like animals at their clothes. They fucked wildly, Wagstaff kneeling between her legs, lifting her by the hips to meet his spearing cock. Elle felt like a child in his hands, felt like her entire body was opening, becoming a soft, velvet channel for his steely rod. He lifted her, higher and higher still, his strong arms pounding her body into his cock. She began to cry, then laugh, her head thrashing from side to side, the fire in her cunt spreading through her belly, into her limbs, into the tips of her clawing fingers. They came together, Wagstaff roaring as he seeded her womb; Elle screaming in silence, her body taking on a life of its own, tearing itself away from her control, from any semblance of modesty. Tumbling and thrashing into the volcanic world of pure, exquisite release.

Later, as they held each other, they plotted their revenge.

Alzira knew that she shouldn't have allowed the tall (and yes, undeniably handsome) palace guard to enter her bed-chamber, but she felt obligated to her handmaid, Elle, who obviously had more than a passing interest in the man. Besides that, she couldn't just leave him stand there, bleeding onto the floor.

Thus, Alzira let him enter and soon found herself in the uncomfortable position of sitting on her own bed next to the wounded guard, who was stretched out on the sheets. And worse, listening to Elle, beautiful Elle, her lover — begging her to use her magic power on the man!

Had Alzira known that a carefully punctured sack of goat's blood lay hidden in Wagstaff's crotch (for indeed, it was the intrepid Captain of the Guard lying upon the bed) she undoubtly would have thrown him out. Instead, she looked dubiously at the wound and asked, "How did this happen?"

Elle commenced a wild tale of attempted assassination, and the heroic intervention on Zandor's behalf by Wagstaff. "The poor Captain," said Elle, "he took the arrow meant for your husband, the King."

"My goodness," exclaimed Alzira. "What should I do?"

"The King gave me strict instructions."

Wagstaff moaned from the bed. Elle pointed at him.

"As a reward for this man's bravery, the King said you were to take care of him as you would your husband."

Alzira frowned, her round face the very picture of innocence mixed with doubt. "Where is Zandor now?"

"Seeing to the execution of the would-be assassin."

"I suppose my husband was aware of the, um, exact locale of this courageous man's injury?"

"He was."

Alzira sighed. "So be it."

As short in stature as she was fair of skin, Alzira hopped nimbly astride the good captain and began to raise her bedclothes. As she did, Elle swiftly lowered Wagstaff's breeches — a feat in itself since the warrior, seeing the magical golden fleece slowly revealed before his eyes, was burdened with an erection worthy of a stallion — and hid the empty sack of goat's blood under the bed.

Because most of the red liquid had been absorbed by his clothes, very little could be detected on his pulsating shaft. "It looks fine to me," whispered Alzira, gently touching it with the tips of her fingers, in awe of its size. "But, truthfully, I have little experience in such matters."

"Yes, kind Lady. But I, Elle, have much. If you do not act soon this man will be a man no longer."

Alzira bit her lower lip. Raising her slender legs, she straddled the Captain, her golden fringed cunt enveloping the entire length of his hardened member. She could feel the heat emanating from it and shuddered to think of the consequences if, by a slip of fate, his throbbing lance entered her. Slowly, carefully, she began to administer treatment, sliding herself back and forth atop his shaft. An immediate change came over her, as sudden as lightening in the summer sky. A change most apparent in the pink, now wet, folds of her virgin cunt.

"I must stop!" she cried. "If I continue I will do something forbidden... I will lose my power!"

But even as she spoke her body, not to mention Wagstaff, betrayed her: the lips of her wondrously moist channel opened willingly, and by directing his prick with one hand and suddenly thrusting upwards, Wagstaff buried himself deep within her.

"Oh! Oh!" she gasped, frozen momentarily between equal halves of pain and pleasure, her long protected maidenhead finally torn asunder. Her body wanting to escape, yet not wanting to.

Elle moved onto the bed. She embraced Alzira, playfully nibbling on her ear. Her long, expert fingers cupping and kneading the young girl's breasts. She whispered lewdly in her ear—"Fuck, Alzira... slide your wet quim up and down his manly spear... feel him explode inside you!"

Alzira, having finally overcome all fear and inhibition, did what her handmaid suggested, and more. In an instant, all the sexual desire denied to her for years was released. She rode the good Captain like a hurricane until he spent, deep in her belly, triggering her own thrashing, crying orgasm. Her body, as taut as the reins of a chariot, suddenly released itself, and she drifted down from the pinnacle of sexual ecstasy, like a fallen rose in the wake of a storm.

"What have you done!"

Zandor the Terrible burst into his bedroom, trembling with rage. His black eyes jumped from Elle, to the Captain, to his no longer innocent wife. "I'll kill you!" he cried out. "Kill all of you!"

"You'll kill no one," hissed Elle. "Your secret has been exposed and your claim to invulnerability is no longer viable. If you so much as raise a finger, all the people of the kingdom shall know! All the rulers of the lands surrounding you, all your countless enemies shall know!"

Zandor felt mortal fear for the first time in his long reign as tyrant. He knew in his heart that the woman before him, this Nubian servant, issued no idle threat. Worse still, he knew that the power of the fleece had been irrevocably lost. "Please tell no one," he suddenly begged, his voice like a child's." I would be killed in an instant . . ."

"And with good reason!" shouted Wagstaff, looming naked above his cowed Ruler.

"Death would be too good for this swine," declared Elle. "You may still play ruler, Zandor, but by our rules. You will call your armies back from War! Return the treasures you've stolen! And put an immediate end to all senseless taxation and persecution!"

"Yes, yes," agreed Zandor, now on his knees. "Only please, tell no one of my secret."

Alzira, quite bored with all the talk of politics, suddenly pulled Wagstaff back onto her bed, nimble young fingers coaxing his dangling cock into life. "Can't all this talk wait?"

Elle laughed, joyously, as Zandor stared in frustration. Then she leered at him, much the same as he had looked at her the night she was raped, and produced, from Wagstaff's uniform, a riding whip. "Disrobe," she commanded the whimpering tyrant.

According to F. J. Matozzo: I've been ransacking my past for some bio material, but there's nothing much there except that I've been writing for several years and have, through laziness, lack of talent, inspiration, and time, established myself as one of the most obscure semi-amateurs in the country. Currently working on a book (why doesn't that surprise anyone?).

18

Andrew McCormick
Compassion

I was talking to these people. "Wyoming," I said, "I left Wyoming. I went to Billings. Then I left there too. I met my wife in Missoula. In a resort. I did maintenance. Grounds. I vacuumed the pool. She was a masseuse. She was lithe. One day she left for Arizona with a guy who came in all the time. A regular. They went to Tempe. He programmed computers. He liked the desert. For a month I searched for them. When I found them the guy pulled a gun on me. I'm not kidding, a gun. When she saw that kind of craziness she left with me. We got out of there. Then, later, she went somewhere else."

"You came to Seattle," Lee said. He was the Korean. His eyes were kindly.

"Not at first," I said. "First I went to Alaska. I took the ferry up. The Inside Passage. I was there four days. I couldn't afford to hang around waiting. Somebody told me Boeing was hiring. I headed back. They weren't. I was at a low point. I entered a salmon derby. I figure what the hell. There's not much I know but fishing's one thing. I caught one fish. A squawfish. It looked like a whale had disgorged it. But anyway one of the guys I fished with worked construction. He told me his crew needed a flagman. I became a flagman."

"That's what your job is," Robert asked, "signalling traffic?"

"I'm not saying it's much. I'm not pretending that. It's only

temporary. They call me when they need me. Under the table. Nonunion. But until something else comes along I've got to make do. What I'd like to find is landscape work. I like the idea of working outdoors."
"Like you did, where was it, Yellowstone?" Joni asked.
"There," I said, "and other places."
I excused myself then and stood up. I told them to think about dessert. I make my way through the darkened restaurant stumbling like a drunk. Things—elbows, chairs, waiters, coats—kept appearing in my way. I found an empty hallway and leaned against the pay phone. I smoked. I thought about what my chances were with these people. I considered the impression I was making. The strongest thing against me was my age. I was thirty-three. But I could pass for less, maybe five, six years less. Robert and Joni were going full time to the community college. They looked like students. Lee was here from Korea because his sister needed a guardian. So I was told. Being Oriental, he looked both old and young and his eyes were calm like a sailor who has seen the world. I counted him for an ally. Robert I figured was the problem. I imagined that he would hold my age and various experiences against me, because in comparison Joni might find him dull. I was just drunk enough to consider that a possibility.
The danger in what I was doing was making up a past far too glamourous for me to live up to. I had to impress them, but only enough to get the room.
The room I needed badly. They were renting it for very very cheap. The deposit was reasonable. I had been living in my van but it was getting too cold. Winter was coming on. I'd stand outside on the days I worked waving flags, sometimes in the rain, jogging in place for warmth. Then I'd get wasted and crawl into the van and sleep. There was almost no housing in that city that I could afford. There was a crisis. I knew no one to stay with in the meantime. I was alone.
Seeing the room advertised in the college paper was the first real break I'd had in a long time. When I returned to the table, Robert said, "Could you give us a few more minutes? We're deciding who we want."
"There's been a lot of applicants," Joni said, "We want to make the right choice. You're the last person we're interviewing."
"We want to settle this tonight," Lee said.
"I understand," I said.
I hunted my way to the bar, sat on a stool, and ordered bourbon

and soda. It was weak. I had another. I told the bartender to ring my tab on the dinner bill. I figured that if the decision went against me, if they decided on someone else, I'd let them help me out on the check, even though it was I who invited them in the first place. I wasn't going to spend thirty bucks to be polite.

The drinks settled me. I felt calm, composed. The story I had presented them about my past amused me. I liked all the drifting in it. And it wasn't too farfetched that I wouldn't be able to recall details of it later on, should they ask. And they would have to be the ones to bring it up; I didn't intend to speak about the past very much even when I got to know them, if I did. Especially the real past. The one that I had lived. For it was just a series of dumb and trivial losses, the bleakness and boredom of which I couldn't face honestly. Like, for example, the guy my wife ran off with was a good friend of mine who knew our marriage was on the rocks. I almost think he believed he was doing us a favor. Maybe he was. When I finally showed up in Tempe, he was all ready to give her back. Whatever I wished. She wasn't coming through. Instead of pulling a gun, he asked me if I wanted to play tennis.

The rest of it's more or less along those same lines.

Down at the service counter I noticed a small group—the bartender, a couple of regulars, the barmaid—had clustered around some guy with a deep, scratchy voice. He was telling a story. I couldn't see him so I moved closer.

"I don't know," he was saying, "you live thirty-four years with someone and then bang! one day she's gone. Vanished like smoke. Of course it's the way she went that makes it so hard to take. I came home from work and found her lying half-propped on the couch. The TV was on. Her eyes were open. There was blood all over the goddamned place. Everywhere—on the walls, on the curtains, on the carpet. Blood like you wouldn't believe. I don't talk about this but once in a while. I don't like reliving it."

"When did this happen?" somebody asked.

"Two years ago November."

The barmaid asked, "What did you feel like at first? I remember when my setter was run over I went into shock for weeks. I was spaced."

"I guess I went into shock," the man said. "I assume I did so. They gave me a sedative. But I'll tell you, I remember everything that happened like it was yesterday. I kept thinking over and over that it should have been me lying there. That I should have been the one to get it instead of her. She should have been spared. The enemies I have who would do such a thing I've made on my own. She was never involved. I don't want to sound noble here, I don't want to play heroic, but that's the way I felt at the time. Still do."

"Did they catch the killer?" the bartender asked.

"They did not," the man said. "There's lots of killings."

The barmaid whistled sadly and shook her head and took away a tray of drinks. I could see the speaker. I felt a lurch of recognition. It took me a while to positively identify him. What finally clued me in was his wildly tousled hair, and the maroon turtleneck he was wearing.

The very first few weeks I'd been in Seattle I'd worked for Manpower and they'd sent me to a warehouse to help with the inventory. The tedium was deadly and during the course of the day my supervisor and I used to look across the street to an ugly, drab apartment complex. We always watched the corner unit on the first floor because the drapes were never shut.

In this unit lived the man now speaking in the bar. He had been there as long as my supervisor—over three years. We had his routine down. He got up when we started, retrieved that paper from the porch, went somewhere for half an hour, and then, and for all day, sat in front of the TV. A Mexican-looking maid came and cleaned some afternoons. He ate fast foods and Winchell's donuts. From this schedule he never deviated. And always he was dressed in the same maroon turtleneck he now had on in the bar.

It was plain enough that his account of coming home and finding his wife murdered on the sofa could not possibly be true. For one thing, my supervisor would have noticed all the cops. For another, there would have been stories, publicity. The incident would have been living legend in the warehouse where I worked.

The man was still talking. He was now discussing the loneliness and grief of being an aged widower. I no longer listened. I was deciding whether to humiliate him with the truth. One more drink in me might have aroused viciousness. I could feel cruelness floating up within me. I considered that exposing him would be a service to the people who had had to hear his story. It was a helluva thing to be talking about murder like that.

But then I pictured him in front of that TV year in and year out. Season after season. I didn't know why he had chosen to lie in this particular way. Maybe he had his reasons. Maybe one day long ago his wife had gotten blown away and now, after so long, he had gotten the facts all mixed up. All day alone, sitting by himself, in sorry circumstances, thinking up a story to tell people later that night in a bar—he was bound to confuse himself. Even if the source of his suffering was imaginary, he was still suffering.

I also thought about what I had been telling Lee, Joni, and Robert about my own past. Who was I to be catching a guy like that out? I, who was without a steady job, whose skills were limited, whose wife had run away with my friend—what could I say? The only thing separating me from the old man was that I could fabricate my stories a little better. My tales had coherency. Only God knew the whole truth.

I left the old man in peace, to quaff down the drinks being sent his way as fast as he could manage. He appeared to be smiling a little. People were consoling him.

At the table Lee stood up and nodded to me. "You're the one," he said. "You're in."

I shook hands all the way around. I felt that happy. I think the fact that I was so obviously excited to be getting a crummy basement room must have relieved Robert a little; nobody could envy my desperation. Maybe, like I had with the old man, he felt slightly compassionate. Maybe he was just drunk. Whatever it was, they all chipped in to pay the bill.

Through a softly falling rain we then walked to where the van was parked. We passed a house with the front door slightly ajar. Somebody was playing a piano soft and dreamy-like. The music seemed to drift through the misty air and hover around us like a magic cloud. Out of nowhere the evening had become enchanted. I walked ahead a little and started humming. I was a new man. I had a room.

Andrew McCormick is a Seattle playwright and fictionist. He says he prefers drinking to writing, but adds, "Mom doesn't like drunks."

19

Ralph Robert Moore
Sex on Sheets

Mid-morning. My sheets are speckled with blood, cum, ashes, wine stains, lip prints, pubic hairs, marijuana seeds, and suntan lotion. She and I are lying in bed on top of all that, flat on our backs, all tuckered out, waiting for the sweat to dry. We didn't stop to turn off the TV in the living room, so it's still talking to the cold coffee cups, now about quiz shows instead of the morning news and weather. She's got one hand behind her head, making one breast more alluring than the other. She's talking about her childhood. I'm not listening. She has a bit of cigarette paper on the corner of her lower lip. She doesn't realize it's sticking there. I'm not going to be the one to tell her. After she finishes, we're both quiet again. She exhales a stream of smoke much too long for such a little slip of a girl up to the venetian bars on the ceiling. Thinking god only knows what other people think when they're not talking. She looks down, startled, when I point out the condition of my sheets to her. I'm going to have to get new sheets now before I get a new girl. This I don't tell her. For all I know, she may be trashing my sheets on purpose, like a dog lifting its leg at well-traveled spots. She examines some of the stains, says she's sorry, then settles back and starts talking again. I look across at her. The pretty face, pillowed, profiled; the straight vein in each upper arm; the muscles on the back of each calf. Sensing rather than seeing my appraisal, she shifts over onto her side, pointing her body at me again, her long jogger's legs curling open in a smile. "Wanna?" I raise my head enough to look down at the bag of genitalia plastered to the top of my thigh. "Let's wait a while." She reaches down over her temporary side of the bed and comes up with a can of Coke, dribbling the first mouthful onto the bed. "God, usually it's my knees that are weak afterwards." That little bit of cigarette paper jerks up and down. We kiss, and I try nibbling it off. Her long nails grope between my legs. "Let's finish the champagne first, before it goes flat." The stretch of sheet over which her goblet passes sprouts a meandering trail of rose colored asterisks. I turn over to face the ceiling, resigned, arching my spine up off the bed with a curse. Nothing gets so cold so fast as warm sperm. She moves closer. "This champagne is really good. Oops!" Her hand strikes out at the latest spill. For some reason I start getting an erection. They follow their own tide tables. She's talking to me again, now about work, but there's a change in the register of her voice. It becomes hurried and automatic, like a magician's patter, because most of her attention is on trying to fingerlessly determine if she's wet enough. I'm not listening even more than usual, because most of my attention now is on trying to assess how dependable this particular erection is going to be. Am I getting a stiff, greedy engorgement, or one that'll go dismayingly thumbs-down if I try to enter her? I want to be sure before I commit myself. I don't want to pin her arms down by her tiny wrists, taut and compact as wrenches, then have to murmur, exuding confidence and musk, that it'll get hard once it's inside her. She's looking at me, deliberately not saying anything at all, pushing her shoulders down against the mattress like a cat already arching up under an approaching hand. Her blonde limbs stretch out so the filtered sun picks up their silvery down. We start kissing, shifting our bodies during the kiss until we're both lying comfortably against each other, like a chessboard with the pawns gone. She's not fully wet but that's OK, that's the way she seems to prefer it. A soap opera starts in. Afterwards I pull it out and, like a prone bottle suddenly uncorked, my cum leaks out of her, forming a new pool on the sheet. My sheet now looks like an animal with large, moist paws has walked slowly across it. Does her husband know where she is? She shakes her caked hair. "He thinks I'm with a friend."

"Soyuri!"
"Hi, Scott."

"Come on in, Soyuri!"
"Thanks. Busy?"
"Not for ol' Soyuri. Drink?"
"Why not?"
"Scotch?"
"Perfect."
"Sit down."
"Thanks."
"So...."
"Nice place."
"Thanks."
"Do it yourself?"
"Leftovers from the divorce. Plus a few new things."
"Mind if I look around?"
"Please."
"Nice view."
"Thanks."
"Never make your bed, huh?"
"Never have the time now."
"Must be quite a life, being single again."
"Really ."
"Unusual pattern."
"Yeah."
"Where'd you get them?"
"Who knows?"
"My wife has sheets just like these."
"Does she."
"Yeah."
"I guess that means I have good taste Soyuri, huh? Ho Ho Ho."
"We cut a little square from one corner at the bottom to try to get matching curtains."
"How about that."
"Mind if I push these blankets off here for a moment?"
"You might as well since you've done it already, Soyuri."
"You have a little square missing from your corner, too."
"I honestly never knew that."
"Are these my wife's sheets, Scott?"
"Are they your wife's sheets?"
"Yeah. Are they her sheets. Our sheets."

"Well as a matter of fact, now that you mention it, I believe they are."
"They are."
"Yeah."
"..."
"..."
"Well I guess the next question is kind of obvious."
"What's that?"
"What my wife's sheets are doing here in your apartment. On your fucking bed."
"She lent them to me."
"Did she."
"Yes, as a matter of fact."
"...why would my wife loan you our sheets?"
"I needed them."
"You needed them."
"That's right."
"Here's another obvious question. How would my wife know you needed new sheets, Scott?"
"I told her."
"You told her."
"Yeah. "
"How the fuck did you get around to discussing the state of your sheets with my wife?"
"We were talking about the trouble I was having decorating the apartment, Soyuri. I got the VCR, but Sue Linda got most of the little stuff. Pots and pans, wok utensils. The radio. Sheets."
"Uh-huh. I see. Sure."
"So she offered to give me a set of her sheets. Because my sheets were such a mess."
"So are these."
"So I've been a bad widdle boy. I'll buy them from you."
"I'm angry because I stop over your place for a drink after work, and my wife's sheets are on your bed. And there're all kinds of stains on them."
"Like you said, it's quite a life. I'll buy them from you. Will you take a check? If I postdate it?"
"Cum stains."
"It's quite a life."
"..."

"..."

"So what did she do, put them on your bed herself?"

"No, I did that."

"She just watched."

"No."

"For sure. She just watched, and maybe her clothes weren't on, right?"

"She wasn't here."

"She wasn't."

"No."

"Not that time."

"What do you mean?"

"I mean she has been here."

"What's that supposed to mean?"

"It means I'm asking you if my wife as ever been here, in this apartment. Your apartment."

"..."

"..."

"I thought you were mad because I borrowed your fucking sheets. Now you're asking me if I ever slept with your wife. I invite you over here, your fucking sheets in plain view, I don't try to hide them or anything, I don't even make the fucking bed—"

"Wait a minute, wait a minute."

"You wait the minute. You're wandering around in here, a scotch I poured you in your hand, looking out my window, and never mind we've been friends for a couple of years, all you want to know is if I ever slept with your fucking wife."

"Don't call her that."

"I'll call her anything I fucking well want to call her. What are you going to do about it?"

"What am I going to do about it? Is that what you're asking me? Are you asking me what I'm going to do about it?"

"Yeah."

"I'll tell you what I'm going to do about it. I'll do anything about it that I want to do about it, and I'll tell you what that is when I feel like telling you. Get me?"

"Big fucking man, five minutes in my apartment and you think I'm fucking your wife. Big fucking friend."

"Hey!"

"Take your fucking sheets. I'll go down to the fucking store and buy my own. I'll sleep on the fucking mattress. Fuck you."
"Watch it."
"Fuck you. What the fuck do you mean, 'Watch it'? What the fuck are you going to do? Here. Here. Take your sheets and get out. And don't dare take another sip of that scotch. That's my booze. And you know what you can do?"
"Hey, listen I—"
"No. You listen. If that's all our friendship means to you, if that's how much you can trust me, then you know what you can do?"
"Scottie, listen, I --"
"You can go fuck off."
"I'm sorry. I'm really sorry, man. Honest."
"Fuck. Off."
"Listen, I —"
"Hey!"
"OKOKOK. I'm going, I'm going. But I'm sorry. I really am."
"Sure you are."
"I am, man."
"I'll bet. I'll just bet."
"Scottie, listen: I've been putting in a lot of overtime, you know I have. Here. No, here, look at it, man. See all that overtime? Eighteen point four hours, man. The strain's just been too much on me, and I come over here, I come over here, and I see the sheets—and it turns out they're here for a perfectly good reason—but I just for a second jump to the wrong conclusion. I don't value our friendship lightly. I'm sorry about what I said."
"I'll just fucking bet you are."
"I am, man."
" . . ."
" . . ."
"You think I've been fucking your wife while you're working late, is that what you think?"
"No, man, no. I don't. Honest."
" . . ."
" . . ."
"Sure? No doubts?"
"None, man. I don't think that at all now. I did for a second back there, but I don't now. It's just been the strain."

"O.K."
"O.K.?"
"..."
"..."
"O.K. Here's your drink back."
"Thanks, Scottie. And the sheets are on the house."
"...I just didn't like the idea that you thought that while you're at work, I've got it buried up to the hilt in your wife's sweet blonde honeypot, you know?"
"Yeah. I know, man. I know."
"Up to where her eyes roll back like a doll that's been put on its back, up to that fucking hilt, man."
"..."
"..."
"You've been fucking my wife!"
"..."
"..."

The arguing went back and forth into the late evening. I got tired because it wasn't going anywhere. "Want to go for a swim?" He balled his fists at his sides. "You're fucking my wife!" "Let's go for a swim, OK? I'm going to change in the bathroom. There's another pair of trunks in that second drawer." "I've got my own trunks on underneath my suit, man! I don't need any trunks from you." The street was still and cool. We walked side by side down the middle of the road, past the parked cars on either side of us, tense and careful not to accidentally brush against each other, because who knows what might flare up then. When we arrived, and I unlocked the gate and creaked it open, there was no one in the water, of course. It was so late by now that I think technically it was past the pool's curfew, but that made it better somehow. Soyuri hurried through, turning around once he got inside to make sure I wasn't planning to jump on him. I padded over, poised on the edge, and dove in. The shock of the water's coldness was so intense I had to fight not to open my mouth to let out the scream of pain while I was still underwater. By the time I had to come up for air, the temperature felt invigorating, and I was far enough away from the diving board to put my feet down on the bottom and stand up. I took an awkward, slow motion step forward, arms out, fighting the heavy sway of the water, so that I was still immersed from the chin down. Soyuri was at the shallow end, standing on the second concrete step, in the water up to mid-ankle. He was shivering. "Jump in." "I jump in here I kill myself! Good for you, maybe. Not so good for me!" I swam a little more in the deep and, then paddled over to the edge of the pool where I had left the towels. I hauled myself out, sat on the edge, and started patting myself with one of the towels. I tossed the other one to Soyuri. He started drying his feet with it. Then he held it up suddenly, high up in the air, racing with it over to the light. "My wife's towel! That one too!" I started drying my legs. He stood there under the gate's light, looking ghostly, stared at me, stared at the towel in his hands, threw the towel down, and started running towards me. I had enough time to get over to the grass. His fist hit my shoulder, and it stung more than I thought it would. I grabbed at him. He hit me in the rib cage, left side, right side. I got his head under my arm, tripped him, and we started wrestling on the wet grass. We were both about the same height, same weight, same musculature. The only obvious physical difference between us was that I was white, and he was Oriental. Every time his relatively warm body came in contact with my pool cold one he sucked in a shiver of breath, and the icy dampness of the grass was adding to his misery some too. He started trembling and muttering, "Fuck my wife! Fuck my wife!" to goad himself on, but he was losing, and we both knew it. It took a while, but I got him over onto his back, wrapped my hands around his wrists to keep his arms against the ground, and pinned his legs down with mine. Our swim-suited crotches brushed against each other, probably accidentally the first time. After awhile, he wanted to go back to my place. We dried ourselves off in the living room, using his wife's towels. He was still trembling and kept clearing his throat, not looking at me. When I was dry I tossed the towel on the sofa. Finally, he came over to where I was standing in the middle of the room. He looked at me then, a long look, the sort of look whose length neither knows, neither of us moving, and then I let him take my trunks off for me. That left me standing and him kneeling in front of me. I didn't know if I trusted his sudden passion enough to let him suck me off, so I led him into the bedroom. His breathing was so harsh it was the only sound in the apartment. He got out of his trunks. Not that it matters, but my cock was bigger. I more or less knew it would be. His wife had told me so when I asked her. I gestured for him to get on the bed. Although I didn't specify, he deliberately positioned himself, with a few quick, ardent glances, so that his cock was pressing right into the most recent stain. Right then I knew he was going to get more out of this than I was, but I put some spit on my fingers anyway and rubbed them down the shaft of my cock, lingering the fingerpads on the thick underside vein while I watched him push his slim walnut ass up at me like an animal who only gets it seasonally. Afterwards, he stayed lying face down on my bed, on his wife's sheets, crying the bitter, unfamiliar way some Orientals do, striking the stained sheets feebly with a spent fist, mumbling, "Fuck my wife. You fuck my wife."

"Could I have a drink before we start?"
"Everything alright?"
"I don't know."
"Here."
"Thanks. "
"What's up?"
"Nothing, probably. Just problems. Soyuri's cheating on me."
"Soyuri who?"
"Come on."
"How do you know he's cheating on you?"
"I just do. Oops. Sorry. He stares at the TV all night, and I know he isn't watching it, he doesn't laugh at any of the jokes. Then he gets this infuriatingly urgent look on his face, slaps his hands down on the arms of the chair, and announces he's going to take a shower. I snuck in once while the water was still going and slid the door open. He tried to make out he was just soaping himself really thoroughly like his mother taught him to, but his eyes gave him away. I've lived with him long enough to know his guilty look. I'm not putting you to sleep, am I?"
"No, let's talk about Soyuri all nonfucking morning."
"Let's not. Let's just forget it. Help me out of my bra, OK? You still want to, don't you, baby?"
"Why not?"
"Exactly. That's what it all comes down to, isn't it? What's this?"
"What's what?"
"These stains."
"Us."
"Not this one here. And here's a new one over our old one."

"Don't cry. Here."

"Thanks."

"They're all us. Honest."

"Please don't lie to me. Tell me anything, but don't lie to me, OK? I'm in my twenties, I get tired a lot more easily now, and I just don't bounce back like I used to. OK?"

"They're ours. All of them. I turned the sheet around to give us some new areas to stain."

"Really? Let's see. No, you didn't, because if you had turned the sheet around this little cut out square here would be at the top, and it's still at the bottom. Fuck."

"Don't cry."

"Don't worry, I'm not going to cry for very long, it just gets to me sometimes, and anyway I'm still horny, I guess. Thanks. So Soyuri's cheating on me, I'm cheating on Soyuri with you, and now it turns out you're cheating on me with someone else. Fuck. We're all just insects eating other insects."

"What I really meant to say is that I meant to turn the sheet around, but I got lazy."

"What's this here?"

"Where?"

"Right. Here. Look. I don't have short black hair. Who is she? Do I know her?"

"..."

"I hope I don't. I hope there isn't some girl you get in here who knows me. Somebody who might have snubbed me even before all this happened, and the two of you are lying here on this filthy bed having a good time when I'm not around. Laughing at me."

"Don't worry, baby. You don't know him. I mean, her."

"Him? You went to bed with a guy?"

"I don't know. Maybe."

"Really? You went to bed with another guy?"

"Blame it on the Bossa Nova."

"Come on! Did you?"

"Yes."

"Really?"

"Really ."

"..."

"..."

"What was it like?"
"It was pretty good."
"What was he like?"
"Japanese."
"...Japanese?"
"For sure."
"Does Soyuri know him?"
"Exactly."
"..."
"..."
"...It wasn't Soyuri, was it?"
"I suppose there's no casual way to tell you this, but as a matter of fact—"
"You went to bed with my *husband?*"
"He wasn't that good. I don't blame you for cheating on him with me."
"..."
"..."
"...are you serious? You actually went to bed with Soyuri?"
"He has a little cluster of freckles down where his spine starts, just above the cleavage. It's the nicest thing about him, as a matter of fact."
"...tell me more."
"When he gets close, he starts gibbering in Japanese."
"Like what?"
"Like what?"
"Like, *Mo tengoku no giu no kai don wa nai*. Something like that."
"What does that mean?"
"How the hell do I know? I just fuck 'em."
"This is incredible. This is really incredible. First you get me, then you get him, now next thing you know the three of us are probably going to wind up in here together."
"I did promise Soyuri I'd bring it up with you."
"...did you. And when did all this happen?"
"Well, he cried after the first time he came, but after the second he asked me for a drink, which turned into a couple of drinks, you know how that is, but we were snorting whites by then too, so neither of us got really drunk, just hornier and hornier, and it took both of us forever to get off the third time, those damn whites, but after we did he wanted me to hold him in my arms while we smoked our

cigarettes. He was real easy to break, by the by."

"...will you tell me about it?"

"Sure. Would you like me to tell you about it real slow?"

"Super slow. And how he acted, and what he did to you while you were doing things to him, OK? And touch me right here while you tell me, OK?"

"Right here?"

"Mmmmm, perfect. And put your other finger in here? And pull it out just a little, that's it, and rotate it right around the rim while you're telling me?... God. Do you really think he'd go for it? I never made him cry. I always thought he was too much of a foreigner for that. You should smell him after he's eaten at his mother's. Or have you?"

According to Ralph Robert Moore, "The facts, as adult and serious-looking as ten and twenty dollar bills, are: I was born 36 years ago in the Northeast, moved to California in my mid-twenties, where I met my wife Mary. We're living in Maine now, mostly to kill lobsters and photograph snow, but we'll be packing our boxes and getting up on the highway again in the Spring of '88, though where we'll descend next is unknown. Currently, I'm trying to market my first novel, Always Again."

Editor's Note: *The transliterated Japanese from above is from David Bowies 'Its No Game (Part 1)','from the* Scary Monsters *album and translates as "No more free steps to heaven," copyright 1980 by Bewlay Bros. Music and Fleur Music Ltd.*

20

Brenda Munroe
Lyle's Dream

I went downtown last Tuesday to visit my friend Lyle. I stood in the musty hallway and knocked on the door of his apartment. When he yelled for me to come in, I did and closed the door behind me. The room was dim like sundown, and when my eyes adjusted to the dark I saw Lyle sitting in an orange beanbag chair, stark naked. Small piles of leftover food and kitchen scraps surrounded him on a clear plastic drop cloth. Wagner's "Ride of the Valkyries" boomed out of the stereo and Lyle was smoking a little cigar.

"Oh my God, Louise! I thought you were the TV people," he said. "Please don't mind the mess. I have an appointment, and they'll be here any minute."

I looked at Lyle's round little belly and the bristly blond hairs covering his skin. He sat back in the beanbag chair, his legs extended and crossed at the knee, his little feet beating time to Wagner. The room smelled like overripe tomatoes.

"What the hell, Lyle? You don't smoke," I said.

"This is just to celebrate. I'm making my own TV show."

"Well, I guess it's ok if I smoke in the house today, then." I pulled up a chair and lit a cigarette. "Why don't you put on some clothes if the TV people are going to be here?"

"Well, normally I would, but the concept I'm introducing today requires that I be completely nude."

"Is it for cable or something?"

"Oh yes, of course. You're welcome to stay and watch. I'd love to have an audience."

We heard footsteps coming up the hall and stop. Someone was trying to ring Lyle's doorbell, which doesn't work.

"Would you please get that for me?" Lyle said, handing me the ashtray. "Do you want me to turn on the lights?" I said, ditching the ashtray in the sink and looking around the room frantically, afraid to open the door.

"No, I just want this single spot on me." There was a desk lamp on the table behind Lyle, the shade tilted to put all the light in the room on Lyle's head.

I turned off the radio and opened the door. A man wearing a brown suit, carrying a briefcase and camcorder, asked me if this were the residence of Lyle Verona.

"Yes it is," I said, "please come in."

The man sat down in the chair next to Lyle and put his briefcase on the floor.

"You must be Lyle," he said.

"Yes, I am. And you must be Tom Baird of the Creative Development Agency. I'm very happy to meet you."

Tom Baird looked at Lyle with a slight smile on his face and stood up with the camcorder.

"Yes," he said, "I imagine you are. Are you ready to get started?"

Lyle said he was, and after Tom Baird found a suitable spot from which to shoot Lyle's performance, he said action. Lyle sat up straight, keeping his legs crossed, and began.

"Hello, I'm Lyle Verona and this is Scraps of the Stars! Today we have James Caan, Connie Stevens, Elizabeth Taylor, and so very much more..."

Without looking down, Lyle scooped up a handful of stewed tomatoes and slapped them on his chest. They stuck, only trickling down a little. He rubbed them into his skin and said, in a hushed voice, that they were right off William Hurt's table.

"That's right. Imagine William Hurt eating stewed tomatoes, and serving them to guests even!"

He grabbed a paper carton of Chinese food, noodles and vegetables, and dumped it in his hand. He held it for a moment; then rubbed it all over his round hairy belly, talking the whole time of Jack Nicholson and busy folks who just don't have time to cook.

This went on for thirty minutes; Lyle spoke reverently of the stars and their food while rubbing the casserole and coffee grounds on his neck, his thighs, his chest, even his feet; back and forth, in strokes and circles. Lyle was covered with food, banana peels draped over his shoulders and red and brown and green smears of glop covering every inch of his exposed body. At this point he took up the last remaining relic, a halved cantaloupe rind and slowly brought it up to his face and kissed it.

"They say the King is dead, but what would you say if I told you that a waitress in a Kansas City truck stop sent this to me, with a letter swearing that she herself served this to the King and watched him eat it. Elvis is alive, somewhere, and he's watching his weight!"

Lyle put the hollow cantaloupe rind on his head and blew a kiss toward Tom Baird.

"That's it, my friends! See you next week with Scraps of the Stars!"

Tom Baird said cut, and turned off the camcorder. He picked up his briefcase and looked down at Lyle, still wallowing in his scraps of the stars.

"Wonderful, Lyle, really wonderful. We'll send you your copy of the tape and the bill later this week. Thank you!"

Tom Baird left and Lyle stood up. He went into the other room and I could hear the shower running. I opened up all the curtains, turned on the lights and opened the windows all the way. I felt hot and thirsty and got a diet soda out of the refrigerator.

I rubbed the cold can on my face then gulped the sharp fizzing drink until my chest hurt. I threw the orange beanbag chair in the hall closet and folded the dirty plastic into a little square which I stuffed in the trash under the sink. I hung my head out of the window and took ten deep breaths.

Lyle came out wearing clean gray sweat pants and a white T-shirt. His hair was wet and when he opened the bathroom door the clean soapy steam wafted out into the living room. I went into the bathroom and brushed my teeth and washed my face. When I came out, Lyle was sitting in the kitchen chair drinking a Diet Pepsi.

"Lyle, I feel like I just woke up from a pornographic nightmare.

What could have possessed you to humiliate yourself like that? And to pay for it?"

"What do you mean, humiliate myself? I just happened to come up with a great idea for a show so I decided to give myself a chance for once."

"A chance for a vision straight from the pit of warped emotional hellfire," I said.

Lyle didn't answer me. He strolled into the kitchen and started filling up the sink to do the dishes. He hummed to himself, washing first the glasses, then the silverware, finally the plates. I lit up a cigarette.

"No smoking in this house!"

"Excuse me all to hell, Lyle! I'm just going home if you're not even going to talk to me! An hour ago we were smoking cigars and having public humiliation and rotten food orgies in here, so just excuse me for living!"

Lyle picked up the other kitchen chair and put it directly in front of me. He sat down and put his hands right on my knees.

"Ok. I'll tell you. But you'd better not mock me."

"Please, just tell me," I begged.

"Well, why don't you give me one of your cigarettes first?"

I shook my head and gave him one. He lit it, and took a long drag.

"Well," he exhaled, "a few weeks ago I had this dream. I dreamed that I was at a fabulous dinner party in a beautiful mansion in Bel Air. You would not believe who the hostess was at this party."

"Who?"

"Marilyn Monroe. And she was wearing that white dress, you know, the famous one from when she stands on the air vent? And dripping with diamonds. She was sitting at the head of the table."

"Who were the guests?"

"Well, me of course. And James Dean, and Elizabeth Taylor, and Montgomery Clift, and Judy Garland and Fred Astaire. And they were all young. They were all beautiful and funny and charming."

"So what happened?"

Lyle shot me a look and shook his cigarette at me.

"First let me tell you about the food! The table was absolutely groaning with food. All of it delicious and beautiful. There was baked Alaska, chocolate mousse, strawberry shortcake, apple pie, gooey Tollhouse cookies..."

"That's all dessert."

"Will you please let me finish? Yes, it's all dessert. But it's my dream. Do you mind? Anyway, here's what happened. I was sitting at one end of the table and Marilyn was sitting at the other end. I got up from my chair and took off my tie. We were all in formal attire of course, the men in tuxedoes...so I took off my tie and walked over to Judy's seat, the first on my left. I took a piece of cake off her plate and ate it. Then I went to Fred's, then Liz's, and so on, until I got to Marilyn. She was looking at me in the gushy way she does, her lips parted, breathing hard. When I got to Marilyn's place at the table, I was completely undressed. And I slowly took a handful of her baked Alaska and rubbed it on my chest; and the mousse and the shortcake, all over my body. Oh my God, it was the most incredible dream. I had such an erection when I woke up."

I quickly lit another cigarette.

"Do you understand?" he asked me.

"I understand the dream, but why the show?"

"Because eating and touching the stars' food is like having sex with the stars."

"I know that. But why did you actually have to do it?"

"Because it was a great idea."

"God, Lyle, it was so cheesy the way you actually did it. Your dream is so much better."

"You just don't have a taste for real porn," he said.

"But it wasn't even erotic! It was so cheap and real."

"See what I mean? It's cheap and it's real and it's shameful and that's why it's hot!"

"Lyle, no one is going to put your show on TV," I said quietly.

"I know that, you silly goose," he said.

"Why did you pay those people to film it, then?"

"Because I wanted it to be realistic!"

"So this was just for you?"

"Who else?"

Brenda Munroe primps vegetables and sells soy milk to healthy people at a natural foods store in Eugene, Oregon. She's working on what appears to be a novel which features biscuits and gravy, but no rich desserts.

21

Kim Pearson
Weirdos Sleep Till Noon

Judith and Gretl are roommates but not especially friends. They met when Judith answered Gretl's ad for a roommate. That they feel no special affinity for each other pleases rather than disturbs them. They are both self-contained people.

They live in the top half of an old duplex in a chic but crumbling part of the city by Mr. and Mrs. Sandhorst, who own the whole house. Mr. and Mrs. Sandhorst are old, and Mrs. Sandhorst is an invalid of some kind. Neither Judith nor Gretl has ever seen her, but they can hear her laughing. Mrs. Sandhorst watches TV every evening and laughs through the programs. She laughs in a monotonous low chuckle. Huh-a-huh-a-huh-a. But she doesn't laugh at the commercials. The chuckle pauses for three minutes at twelve minute intervals. Judith has timed it. Judith pictures Mrs. Sandhorst sitting in a wheelchair with a blanket over her knees and a shawl over her shoulders. (The house is cold because Mr. Sandhorst is cheap.) Mrs. Sandhorst folds her hands on her knees as she listens to the commercials in reverent silence, but her wrinkled cheeks jiggle when she laughs at the programs. Judith pictures Mrs. Sandhorst as wispy and withered despite her fat healthy chuckle. The contradiction pleases her. Judith calls Mrs. Sandhorst a weirdo.

Judith is a connoisseur of misfits. "I hate weirdos," she says often, with dark enjoyment. Her hatred drives her to seek them constantly. She gloats over deformities and revels in stupidities. Judith is addicted to contempt. It has a rich and bitter flavor.

Hers is a secret vice. To herself she calls it her "collection"; but it is not on display. With most people Judith is quiet and withdrawn. She listens and observes. Only the faint contraction of muscles about her mouth and flatness of her eyes hint that Judith is adding to her collection.

Judith drinks pickle juice and olive juice, another addiction. Once a week she buys a jumbo can of olives and a king size jar of dill pickles. She sits in the living room in the overstuffed easy chair with the saggy cushion and the threadbare armrests, the pickle jar on one armrest and the olive can on the other. She eats the olives first, balancing them one by one on her lips and sucking them in with sudden soft plops. She fishes the pickles out of the jar and stuffs them beneath the cushion, and she drinks the pickle juice in one long swallow, tipping the jar above her mouth so the translucent green fluid flows in a graceful arc. Last of all she drinks the olive juice. She forgets the pickles. They are usually found by Gretl the next day. Gretl wraps them in paper towels and throws them away. Gretl never sits in the easy chair because she doesn't like the smell of pickles.

For the next three days Judith has diarrhea. The diarrhea smells bad even to her; an acrid brown smell so pungent it has a taste, and clogs her throat. She leaves the bathroom gasping for air, sometimes forgetting in her hurry to flush the toilet. Gretl does it for her and does not complain.

Gretl is not German or Scandinavian despite her name. She is Heinz 57 American. Gretl is vague, almost bland; but, mysteriously, forceful. She absorbs mannerisms and gestures from other people and regurgitates them as expressions of her own; they appear foreign yet somehow Gretl. Gretl does not drink pickle juice, or olive either. When she sees Judith doing so, she mock gags, her shoulders jerking inward in a peculiar mannerism borrowed from Judith. Thus it seems that Judith disgusts herself. Possibly this is Gretl's intention.

Gretl and Judith see Mr. Sandhorst regularly. Mr. Sandhorst is tiny and bent, with slithery pale eyes. Gretl sees him when she pays the rent, which he insists be paid weekly, every Monday at noon. In person. Gretl pays the rent because she has a regular salary. Gretl works for the city as a middle level administrator. She is forced to make a special trip home every Monday at noon to comply with Mr. Sandhorst's demand. For some reason she does not resent this. On Mondays Gretl's eyes slither like Mr. Sandhorst's.

Wierdos Sleep Till Noon

Judith buys the food, which can be bought anytime. Judith's money comes in drips and spurts. Judith works three afternoons a week as a counselor in a battered women's shelter, and other times as a free-lance photographer. She is good at her jobs even though she says she hates them both. She sees a lot of wierdos.

When Gretl comes home Judith tells her about her day. She describes the new wierdos she has found, dissecting them with relish, making Gretl a present of her contempt. Judith feels that her collection is somehow safe with Gretl. Gretl absorbs Judith's corrosive ramblings in silence. Judith is not sure she is listening; Gretl never comments. Her eyes are flat and blank.

At night in bed Judith relives her day and savors the new additions to her collection. She sees again the man she saw on the bus that day. He was reading the *National Enquirer,* nodding with approval. His pants were brown polyester and his shirt had come partially untucked, showing his jockey shorts. (Judith knew they would have skid marks.) He had pimples on his face that he had picked, shiny red. He had missed one pimple; it was a plump white globule of pus underneath his nose. How had he missed it? It was the most noticeable one on his face. Right under his nose, in fact.

Alone in her bed Judith chuckles, sounding like Mrs. Sandhorst. She pictures this nerd, this wierdo, coming into her bedroom, fumbling at his fly. In the semi-darkness his pimple glistens, white and shiny like a black man's teeth. She sees him take his prick out of his fly, not taking his pants off. His limp prick is silhouetted against brown polyester. He leans down to her, lying on the bed. Her eyes are bright and flat, a lizard's eyes, watching him. His prick stiffens suddenly and goes off a second later. It spurts greenish white semen onto her breasts. At the same time the pimple under his nose erupts and pus dribbles onto her face. Her orgasm courses sluggishly through her. Her skin is damp and sticky. She falls asleep.

Judith sees Mr. Sandhorst regularly too. She sees him every night around 2 a.m. when he sneaks upstairs to search through Judith and Gretl's garbage. His wispy footsteps sound like scattering mice. They wake Judith up. She steals quietly into the bathroom which is next to the kitchen and watches him through the partially opened door. Mr. Sandhorst kneels painfully on the kitchen floor and opens the cupboard under the sink, inching it open stealthily. He has a large flashlight beside him. His eyes slither over his shoulder from time to time as he slides the bag of garbage onto the floor.

Judith enjoys watching as the finicky little man carefully extracts each morsel of garbage from the bag and arranges them on the floor. He shines his flashlight to examine them one by one. He flicks his fingers lightly over them while he makes delicate moos of distaste. Judith doesn't know what, if anything, he is looking for. She doesn't care.

Judith hides little surprises for Mr. Sandhorst in the kitchen garbage. Erotic photographs, used Tampax, cat shit, even once a voodoo doll one of her clients gave her. She observes Mr. Sandhorst's expression change in subtle ways that probably only Judith would recognize. His mouth opens slightly and his fingers flick faster through the garbage, betraying his excitement.

Mr. Sandhorst always puts everything back into the bag, carefully and in the same order that he took them out. Even the coffee grounds and cigarette ashes are swept up into his hand and placed delicately back into the garbage bag. He slides the bag back into the cupboard and creeps out of the kitchen. Judith goes back to bed and dreams of Mr. Sandhorst among her garbage.

One night Judith has a special surprise for Mr. Sandhorst. Just before two o'clock she sneaks into the kitchen and hides in the cupboard under the sink. It is an uncomfortably tight fit; Judith is not a small woman. She manages it by sitting cross-legged, hunching her head and shoulders over as far as she can, her arms circling the bag of garbage which she holds on her lap. Luckily she doesn't have to wait long.

Judith hears Mr. Sandhorst shuffle into the kitchen. Her mouth curls in anticipation. She hears him kneeling slowly outside the cupboard. His knees creak; Judith can hear the tiny popping sounds. Mr. Sandhorst opens the cupboard and sees Judith. His mouth falls open and his eyes dart rapidly away. Judith flicks an onion skin at him, hitting him on the nose.

Mr. Sandhorst reaches into the cupboard. His fingers are pale and thin; they look like the bones of some small bird. Mr. Sandhorst gently clutches Judith's arms. She can feel his fingers trembling. Mr. Sandhorst tries to slide Judith out of the cupboard. Judith has to help. Judith and Mr. Sandhorst sit facing each other on the kitchen floor. She still holds the bag of garbage on her lap.

Mr. Sandhorst takes a butter wrapper out of the bag. He sticks it on Judith's arm. Judith reaches into the bag and pulls out a Coke can. She pours the last drops of Coke over Mr. Sandhorst's head. He smears day old gravy on her chin. She puts carrot gratings in his ear.

They decorate each other. Mr. Sandhorst's mouth hangs loosely open. Judith's eyes are feverishly bright and her upper lip twitches on one side.

When the bag is empty they begin to rub the garbage into their skins. They caress each other through the garbage. Mr. Sandhorst's tiny white fingers flit furiously over Judith's body. She begins to pant. A soft whine escapes Mr. Sandhorst's lips.

At last they lie entangled, dripping with slime, on the kitchen floor. Exhausted, they fall asleep.

Gretl is the only person in the house who ever gets up before noon.

When she goes into the kitchen she finds Mr. Sandhorst and Judith asleep in the garbage. Mr. Sandhorst's head is flung back, his mouth wide open. A lettuce leaf, oozing green juice, hangs partially in his mouth and flaps with his breath. Judith's head is pillowed on Mr. Sandhorst's lap; she is drooling in her sleep. Gretl cleans up the mess.

She works efficiently, rapidly flicking the garbage off Judith and Mr. Sandhorst, who do not wake up. Gretl leads Judith, semiconscious back to bed. She carries Mr. Sandhorst downstairs and places him gently outside his door. Mr. Sandhorst curls into a ball and goes on sleeping. Gretl goes back into the kitchen, sweeps up all the garbage, puts it into a new bag, and places the bag under the sink.

Gretl leaves the house to go to work. She looks placid and satisfied. She is smiling with one corner of her mouth. She notices some coffee grounds still adhering to her skirt. She lightly brushes them off with her plump fingers. She doesn't notice the stain of olive juice on her sleeve. When she does she will clean it.

According to Kim Pearson fiction is much easier to write than bios, but here goes anyway. "Although I have been writing all my life, until recently I have been struggling through the jungles of the electronic industry in pursuit of the almighty silicon dollar, and writing on the side. I have had some success in the latter; my short stories have appeared in literary and regional magazines. Currently I am on sabbatical from `real work' (my mother's term) and am in the process of completing my first novel. How's that?"

22

Patrick Quinn
The Hitchhiker and the Doctor

The Mojave Desert. Southern California. Early November, 1984. Fifteen minutes before midnight.

"What's that light ahead?" Tommy Travis asked the Hispanic truckdriver.

The driver looked ahead as he spoke. "That's the Braden Lodge. It never closes. It's a gas station, tiny grocery store, motel and cafe."

"It sure looks lonely."

"Yeah—it is. There's no building within thirty miles of there."

"You turn off in a few miles?"

"Yeah—I'm going to Barstow."

"Would you let me off there?"

The driver nodded. When he reached the Braden Lodge he pulled the old flatbed Chev truck onto the unpaved parking lot in front of the cafe.

"The next time we meet the favor is on me," Tommy said.

"Gracias."

There was an old battered light pole in the parking lot. Tommy zippered his blue wool sweater and walked up the eight wobbly, wooden steps leading to the little all-night cafe.

There were three truck drivers and an elderly man in a blue business suit seated at the six-stool counter. No patrons at the tables.

The tiny, red-haired waitress handed him the little one-page, plastic-covered menu. Tommy reached for the menu and at the same time glanced at the sandwich she had just placed in front of the old gentleman.

"That looks good," Tommy said. "I'll have the same and coffee."

The old man had gobs of white hair on the sides of his head but not a hair on the pate. He took a bite of the ham sandwich on rye and turned to Tommy.

"It is good," he said. He had a flash smile. A split second and the smile was history.

Tommy Travis was 26. Dark-haired and good-looking. Average size.

"You just get off that truck?" the old man said.

"Yes."

"You hitchhiking?"

Tommy sipped his coffee. "Yes. I left my hometown—Philly—three weeks ago."

"Headed for Los Angeles?"

"Yes."

"What's there for you?" the old gentleman asked.

"A job—I hope. And a new start."

The old man had a fast laugh. Like his smile, it took just a split second. "Not too easy," he said, "to get a ride out here—at this time of night."

Tommy had a bite of sandwich in his mouth. He swallowed some and looked at the old man. "No—it might take me a couple of hours—this time of night and no traffic."

"I'm going to Banning," the old man said.

"Banning?"

"That's over a hundred miles from here—and a hundred from Los Angeles."

"You mean."

"Yes—you're welcome."

"Thank you. I'm Tommy Travis."

"Doctor Klosky."

"Medical doctor."

"Yes. Psychiatrist."

"Oh—psychoanalyst?"

"Yes."

Tommy put down his coffee cup. "Freud once gave a lecture at my college."

"Oh—where?"

"Clark University."

"Worcester."

"Yes."

"That's quite a school. They stress talent above raw intelligence."

Tommy laughed softly. "Yes. They seem to think the world was built by nuts."

Dr. Klosky gave one of his fast smiles and fast laughs. "I wonder what the so-called normal people do?"

"I guess they just hang around to keep score."

"You graduate?"

"Yes."

When Tommy finished his sandwich he handed the check and a five dollar bill to the waitress. The waitress shook her head. "He paid it," she said.

Tommy looked over at Dr. Klosky and slowly put his bill back in his wallet. "Thank you, Doctor."

Dr. Klosky was a small man. Almost tiny. He had the six-way seat in his big Oldsmobile sedan up as high as it would go. He slowly pulled the car onto the old one-lane blacktop highway and stepped his speed up to 55 miles an hour.

Dr. Klosky kept his speed steady. They spoke little for the first 30 miles. Just courtesy talk.

"I wanted—at first—to become a psychiatrist," Tommy said.

Dr. Klosky gave Tommy one of his flash smiles. He said nothing.

"I wasted four long years," Tommy said.

"On what?"

"An experiment."

"Tell me about it, Tommy."

"I don't know—it might shock you."

"Psychiatrists are shock proof," Dr. Klosky said.

"Remember early in Freud's career when he cured the pianist with the crippled fingers?"

"Yes—he crippled himself because he didn't want to play."

"Correct. Freud found his hiding place. The unconscious mind." Tommy looked out at the barren desert as he spoke. "In most of the advanced countries of the world today the educated people find it difficult to hide the reasons behind psychosomatic illness."

"Yes—Freud found the hiding place for that type of illness."

"That created my experiment," Tommy said. "When people of the world lose their hiding place they look for another."

Dr. Klosky gave another of his flash smiles. "Did you find another one?"

"No."

"What did you find?"

"I don't know the meaning of what I found."

"Tell me about it."

"What I found is now my problem. That's why I'm going to Los Angeles."

Dr. Klosky nodded.

"When a scientist does basic research he never knows what he'll find," Tommy said. "He rarely finds what he's looking for."

"I guess that's what I found."

They approached the desert town of Twenty Nine Palms. Dr. Klosky slowed down until they cleared the town. Tommy said nothing until they were once again on open highway.

"It seemed to me that the only place left to conceal a secret would be in the orgasm—during sex. Coitus."

Dr. Klosky looked over at Tommy. "But there is no thought during coitus. The sensation is physical. There's a mental blackout."

"Correct. That's the way men and women have been having orgasms for—well—since our species began."

"How else could they have them?"

"I wondered what would happen if I kept my eyes open during the ejaculation."

"You mean think through it—rather than surrender?"

"Yes."

"But the biological reason for coitus—other than procreation—is total release of tension—if one doesn't surrender to it—well—that would be quite dangerous—I would think."

"It is. I did it for four miserable years."

"Your health was severely affected?"

"I went from one hundred and sixty-four pounds to one

hundred and forty-one."

Dr. Klosky slowed down as he eased the big Oldsmobile through the little desert village of Joshua Tree. They continued talking after again hitting the open road.

"I was going on a theory," Tommy continued, "that it had never been done before."

"It probably hasn't—I've never heard it mentioned by Freudians—or any other school of psychiatry."

"I know—I've read everything Freud wrote—even selected letters of his."

Dr. Klosky turned off the soft playing stereo.

"Yes—I went through five girlfriends and four jobs."

"And what did you find?"

"The first year I didn't understand anything I saw—just images that had no meaningful shapes. So I took up drawing at night school. And I began to draw the images—or pictures—that I saw."

"You couldn't relate them to dream interpretation?"

"No—the symbols are different."

"You had to break the hieroglyphics?"

"Exactly. Freud said that in the ancient Egyptian language many words had opposite meanings—such as the word 'cold'—it also meant 'hot'—the word 'down' also meant 'up.'"

Klosky nodded. "Yes. If they wanted to use the Egyptian word for 'cold' to mean 'hot' they put something indicating heat above the word—such as a hot kettle."

"Yes. And in speech they did something similar—if they wanted to use the Egyptian word for 'down' but meant 'up' they merely pointed up."

Dr. Klosky again gave Tommy one of his flash smiles. "They still do it today—among most ethnic groups. Some use their hands as much as their mouths."

"That was what gave me the strength to carry on. I began to draw pictures. Hundreds of them. Thousands of them. And comparing them. They had to mean something."

Dr. Klosky slowed down to get through the desert town of Yucca Valley. They quit talking. As they again hit the open road Tommy turned to the doctor.

"I found that there is no such thing as mental junk. Everything has a meaning. I found that long lines meant one thing. Circles meant something else. It was something like the Rorschach test."

"You could read them?"

"No—not exactly. When I put my findings together they didn't—well—it didn't become a whole."

"The meanings weren't related."

"No."

"Go on."

"It took me another year to solve that. I found that the relation is not in the same orgasm. It's in previous orgasms and future ones."

"Then it became cohesive?"

"It did—yes—but only once. I could never do it again."

"And what did the hieroglyphs tell you?"

They eased through the little town of Merengo Valley. And then once again out on the open road.

"When I finally got a completed sentence I gave up the experiment. I was physically and mentally exhausted."

Dr. Klosky said nothing. Just looked over at Tommy—waiting for him to continue.

"This is the hard part, Doctor. You're going to think I'm psychotic."

"You're not psychotic"

"Thank you."

"Have you ever told this to anyone—other than me?"

"No—no one knows it—except the two of us. How could I tell something like this to a layman?"

Dr. Klosky said nothing.

"I put the words together so that they would form a sentence," Tommy said. "Three words came up—and then more. I kept transposing them until they made sense."

"The words."

"Giggle Creek, Little Pauline's, murder, seven-forty at night."

"Where is Giggle Creek?"

"It's a little town a few hundred miles north of Los Angeles—at the foot of the High Sierras. Little Pauline's is a restaurant. It took a lot of research—to find what the words represented."

"That's why you're going to Los Angeles."

"Yes—to get a job for a couple of months before going up to Giggle Creek."

"And the murder—man—woman?"
"It didn't say. Just gave the time."
"And date?"
"January thirty-first—Thursday."
"Do you have any idea—at all—of what you might have done?" Dr. Klosky asked.
"Done?"
"I mean it does seem difficult to relate to reality."
"That's the problem, Doctor—it does. I think I intercepted what we call 'fate.'"There is probably an equation for fate. There's a reason for everything. 'Fate' is certainly a planned event."

They passed within a couple of miles of the town of Desert Hot Springs. Neither spoke until they reached the San Bernadino Freeway.

"How far is Banning?" Tommy asked.
"Fifteen miles."

Dr. Klosky pulled the big car onto the freeway. He drove in the slow lane even at 55 miles and hour.

Tommy looked over at him. "Doctor."
"Yes."
"What do you think?"
"I don't know."
"Do you believe me?"
"You—yes."
"But you don't know about my interpretation?"
"Exactly."
"I feel the same way. I do wonder."

They talked little more until they reached Banning. Dr. Klosky Pulled the Oldsmobile off the freeway and drove about a mile through town. He stopped at the curb to let Tommy off near an on-ramp.

"Here's my card, Tommy. I don't practice much anymore—just an occasional emergency at the hospital."

Tommy glanced at the card as he opened the door. He put it in his wallet. "Thanks for the ride—and the breakfast, Doctor."

"Tommy."
"Yes?"
"Call me if your plans change?"
"Change?"

"Yes—I'll be up there with you on the thirty-first—at Giggle Creek."

"You really do believe me—don't you?"

"Yes."

"Doctor, have you thought of something else?"

"Else."

"The person that gets killed—if there is a killing—might be me."

"Or me. But if we stayed away and there was no killing—then what?"

"We would never know for sure—would we?" Tommy said.

"Yes," Doctor Klosky said. "To test your experiment we'll both have to go."

Giggle Creek in January is a gorgeous little town. Calendar pretty. Cozy. Little Pauline's was the only posh supper club in town. The patrons were, for the most part, skiers and sportsmen.

Dr. Klosky and Tommy sat in a small booth from which they could see the entire dining room. They couldn't see the cocktail lounge or the vestibule. They had driven up in separate cars.

It was seven-thirty. Time for murder was seven-forty.

They were both sipping on a before-dinner drink of scotch and water. There were about 30 persons in the dining room. Almost all of them appeared to be skiers, sportsmen and tourists.

Doctor Klosky looked at his watch—seven thirty-nine. He looked at Tommy. Tommy nodded. "Any second now—or not at all."

A middle-aged, jockey-sized man wearing a cowboy outfit walked into the dining room. He looked the patrons over quickly and walked to a small table where a blond, fortyish woman sat alone.

"This is it," Tommy said.

The man pulled a hand-gun and fired three bullets into the woman. There was no conversation. He walked out—slowly and calmly.

Dr. Klosky did what he could while waiting for the medics to arrive. The woman died while being placed on a stretcher. It was almost 20 minutes before Dr. Klosky was able to get back to the table after helping the medics and the police. Tommy never left the booth.

Dr. Klosky sat down slowly. Neither spoke for almost a minute. The waiter brought their soup but neither touched it.

"What do we do now, Tommy?" the doctor asked.

"Do?"

"Yes. I'm worried about you."

"My problem is over. The experiment is over. I'll never look back. I'm going to lead a normal life."

"You might have found a continent."

"Don't name it after me, Doctor."

"Do you mind if I report your findings in the psychoanalytic journal?"

"Not at all. As long as you keep me out of it."

But no one can read the hieroglyphs but you. It took you four years to figure it out."

"Other men will just have to do it the way I did it—alone."

Dr. Klosky nodded.

"Doctor."

"Yes."

"I suspect something."

"Yes?"

"After the article is published it will lead to a cult."

"It could."

"Doctor."

"Yes?"

"Poor bastards—I'll cry for them."

Patrick Quinn has been writing for over six years—only short stories. He has had eighteen accepted for publication. According to Patrick, "The first three years, however, of my writing career were quite lean. Now I seem to be able to sell everything I write—although not the first time out...or the second."

23

Patrick Quinn
The Secret

She was a mildly attractive woman on the soft side of 50. Her husband called her Vera. He was her age. A largish man with commendable good looks and a splendid speaking voice. She called him Ernie.

Ernie drove the five-year-old Ford across the lonely desert of southern Nevada. The scorching heat had softened the blacktop and the car's tires hummed as they rolled over the sticky asphalt.

Ernie was a professor of physical sciences at a small liberal arts college in New Mexico.

A few hundred yards ahead they saw the little complex that suddenly appeared as they came to the top of a long dip in the highway.

Ernie pulled the car into the service station bay. Vera walked ahead to the coffee shop as Ernie waited for the teenage girl to fill the tank.

They sat in a small booth in the refreshingly cool little coffee shop. Vera sipped on her iced tea and then slowly put the glass down. "I've been here before," she said.

He laughed politely. They had always been quite close. Their 30-year marriage had been one of enviable solidity. "Unh-uh."

The waitress brought two ham-and-cheese sandwiches. His

sandwich was so large that he fumbled with it trying to find a corner small enough for his first bite. "Deja vu," he said, replying to Vera's remark.

"But is deja vu that strong? she said. "I always thought it was a sort of mild passing moment in one's life."

"Mostly—yes. But not always. Sometimes—so strong that it actually causes panic."

"Oh."

"What did you do the last time you were here?" he asked.

"I bet on a horse called Red Bucket. In the casino."

"He win?"

"No. A horse called Black Tears won."

"When was this?"

Vera spilled some iced tea. She spoke as she wiped up the wet spot with her napkin. "I don't know. Maybe two weeks ago—maybe two years ago."

"Forget it. You've never bet on a horse in your life."

They finished their sandwiches and once more drove across the blistering highway toward their destination.

"Ernie."

"Uh-huh?"

"What causes deja vu?"

"Causes it?"

"I mean its origin. What brings it on?"

"Oh. It takes a person back to the time when she—or he—was leaving the womb. The moment of birth."

"It what...?"

"That's correct."

An isolated gust of wind, on the otherwise windless day, blew a couple of tumbleweeds across the highway. Ernie braked softly to avoid hitting the larger one.

"But how could there possibly be any connection between the two scenes?"

"The womb is the *one* place that everyone has been."

"Oh god. Now who figured that one out?"

"Freud."

"Who...?

"Freud."

"And you actually think he was right."

"Vera."
"Yes?"
"Freud was always right."
"But why—was he that smart?"
"He did his homework."
"And homework is *that* important?"
"Homework is *everything*."

Neither spoke as Ernie waited for a chance to pass a slow-moving old camper. After he had passed safely Vera looked at Ernie as she spoke: "Ernie, let's go back there."

"Do what?"
"Please—I'm serious."
"But why?"
"I don't know why—it's such a strong pull."

Ernie hunched his shoulders. "Okay." He continued to drive for a couple of miles until he came to a cut-out alongside the road. After waiting for two oncoming cars to go by he made a U-turn. A little prairie dog scooted across the highway as Ernie spoke: "It's probably better that we go back," he said.

"Oh?"

"I mean that if we didn't go back the scene would be nagging you for a long time."

Ernie made a left turn into the complex and parked in front of the coffee shop entrance which also led into the casino. "Let's go to the bookie," he said, as they walked up the steps to the big entrance door.

"Why?"
"See what happens."
"What is supposed to happen, Ernie?"

He put his arm around her. "I really don't know. But I suspect it has something to do with the horses—the illusion you had of having bet on Red Bucket."

"And Black Tears won." she said.

The entries of the thoroughbreds at the many different tracks were posted on the wall of the sports-betting room.

Vera refused to enter the bookie room—as if it were a bit beneath most people of reasonably good character. But Ernie walked up to the bookie in the cashier's cage. "Is there a horse running somewhere today called Black Tears?"

"Yeah. I saw his name somewhere. Look at the entries on the wall—you'll find him."

Ernie found Black Tears in the second race at Saratoga. "Odd," he said, as he walked up to Vera.

"Odd?"

"I think I've found why you wanted to come back here."

"Oh?"

"There *is* a horse called Black Tears. And he *is* running—at Saratoga."

"He's going to win."

"Sure?"

"Positive—absolutely."

"How much do you want to bet?"

"I don't know."

"A hundred?"

"Too much."

"How about twenty dollars?"

She nodded. "Okay."

"It will be at least an hour before the race goes off," he said. "We can kill time—somewhere."

Ernie played a little pool and Vera killed time in the coffee shop over another glass of iced tea.

Over an hour later.

Black Tears lost by over 10 lengths.

Once more they hit the highway toward the small Nevada college where Ernie was going to give a series of summer lectures.

There was little noise inside the car other than the healthy hum of the big V-8 motor and the soft swishing-sound of the air-conditioner.

"Ernie."

"Yeah?"

"You know how much I love you."

Ernie slowly raised his right eyebrow. He looked over after he had rounded a rather mild curve. "What brought that on?"

"I *hate* confessions."

"Confessions?"

They were now coming to little dips in the highway. A hundred yards ahead of the dips, which crossed the desert washes,

The Secret

road signs read: Beware Of Flash Floods.
"I'm going to join Gamblers Anonymous."
"You?"
"I've been a gambling addict for years."
"What kind?"
"Just the horses. Nothing else."
"You are serious?"
"All the way."
"Then the whole scene back at the casino was staged?"
"Completely."
"Oh."

Ernie edged a bit onto the left side of the road to avoid a young hitchhiker who was too far out onto the highway.
"I'll *never—never—*gamble again."
"I do like that."

Vera seemed exhausted from the effort of her confession. Neither spoke for several minutes.
"Ernie."
"Uh-huh?"
"Say something—please."
"I've been thinking..."
"About what?"
"I've also got a confession to make."
She very slowly looked over at him. "Go on."
"I've known about your problem for years."
"Oh?"
"Almost since you started—over three years ago."
"Who told you?"
"Your first bookie—the old man—Augie."
"Why did Augie tell you?"
"I was suspicious. I called him."
"Why didn't you let me know?"
"You weren't ready to quit."
"You think I'm ready now?"
"I do."
"Why?"
"A successful rehabilitation always starts with a voluntary confession."

She nodded. "Ernie—what made you suspicious?"

"Little things. Tiny things."

"Can you give me an example?" she asked.

"Back at the casino you refused to go into the bookie room—as if it were beneath you."

"A bit too sanctimonious?"

"Uh-huh. If I hadn't already known you were a horseplayer it would have captured my fancy."

"It's like Freud said...," Ernie began.

"Are we back to him?"

"Just *one* more time?"

"Let's have it."

"Freud said there probably isn't anything that one person can actually hide from another person."

"And you think he was right?"

"I do."

"So do I."

Patrick Quinn has been writing short stories for a decade now. This is his 49th published story. In the past three years he's been able to sell his work to "large circulation slicks such as Gambling Times, Dialogue, Senior Life, Art Times, *etc." Some of his own favorite pieces have been sold to the smaller literary magazines, where he seems to be much happier. His work first appeared in* SOTT *in 1986.*

24

Richard Rabicoff
The Chair of Privilege

"You got to agree," Jesse Barr said, "if it hadn't been for Ruby, there wouldn't even be a hotel to raid. You got to admit that."

"And I'm saying we would all be better off if they'd gone ahead and dynamited that place the way they wanted to fifteen years ago," said Wylie Perch. "Maybe put the new school there, or a dime store, or something useful. Instead of an eyesore and a den of iniquity besides."

"That's enough, folks, let's come to order," said Artemus Crum, rapping the table with his brassbound bookend in the shape of a stag's head. "This is the Fenton City Council, not some hog-calling contest at Saw Mill. I know we all harbor some pretty strong feelings about Ruby, and Ruby's hotel. And we all have to be upset about last week's goings-on there. Lord knows, I am. But this is not the time or place to put that subject at the forefront. There's three pretty important resolutions on the docket this morning, and I think this body owes it to the people of this town to give a just and due deliberation."

"Artemus is right," said C.L. Karriker, and the other members of the Council chimed in yes, you bet, and ditto, because C.L. always spoke with some authority (his wife Marjorie was only half-joking when she called him the "First Authority of Fenton"), but his words carried special weight today, because he occupied the Chair of

Privilege. That meant C.L., from where he sat, looked up squarely into the huge portrait of Agnes Crum, late wife of Artemus, which hovered over the mantelpiece. It was, to all eyes, the most godawful picture of a woman who, as C.L. remembered her, had only been mildly plainfaced. Artemus had paid a bunch of money for a well-known artist to fly down from St. Louis to paint Agnes, and a bunch more for the black taffeta gown with the ruffled shoulders and lace bosom that Agnes posed in. The dress was about the best thing in the picture. Even if Agnes was no Miss America, she was no Old Gray Mare either. But in the picture the face sagged like it was made of slowly dripping honey; the head was tilted back so you looked right up into big black rectangular nostrils. The eyes, which C.L. remembered as warm and lively, displayed a shade of apricot he'd never seen before. The mouth flashed a menacing grimace, as if Agnes were counting to ten deciding whether or not to take a strap to Ben or Sally. It hurt to look at this picture. But if you happened to sit on the north side of the poker table Artemus Crum set up for Council meetings, you had better be prepared to gaze at Agnes for the better part of a Monday morning. Of course, Artemus loved the portrait, maybe because it cost him so much, or maybe he really thought Agnes looked beautiful this way. At any rate, you couldn't tell Artemus you didn't want to sit in the chair facing the portrait because his dead wife's apricot eyeballs nearly gave you a migraine. So there arose an unspoken agreement among C.L. Karriker and the other members of the Fenton City Council—Wylie Perch, Jesse Barr, and Dolly Dreher—that they would take turns occupying this seat at the Monday morning meetings. And it came to be understood, although nobody was fully conscious of it, that the person who sat in that seat deserved extra sympathy and consideration from the others. He or she could speak a little more unbuttoned and be sure of a fair hearing, even if what came out was nonsense. It became a Chair of Privilege. And today C.L. Karriker sat in that chair.

"Ladies and gentlemen, please turn to Bill Number Seventy-Nine, which you got in front of you," said Artemus Crum. "Will the Council Secretary now please read Bill Number Seventy-Nine as it's written?"

Dolly Dreher quickly gulped down a piece of caramel candy, stuffed the cellophane wrapper in her purse, licked her fingers, and read off her mimeo copy. Bill Number Seventy-Nine provided that the license for altered dogs should be one-half the price for unaltered dogs. It was known that Mayor Welch was partial to this bill and expected it to pass.

Jesse Barr tittered and related the old story about Walter, the Messmers' dachshund. Walter was vicious and every day would attack Jesse as he made his postal rounds. By Friday, Jesse's shin would look like a barber's pole with all the bites and claw marks. And the Messmers wouldn't do a thing about it. Said it was natural for a dog to protect the house, and why else have a dog. Jesse even took to carrying a stick with him, to fend Walter off. But one day Walter bit off more than he could chew. He got into a tussle with two of those opossums that nested back of the Messmers', and they took a chunk out of Walter where it hurts most. I guess you might call that Nature's way of altering a dog, concluded Jesse.

Wylie Perch whacked Jesse on the shoulder. "Hush up, Jesse Barr," she said. "Lord, but you have a crude way about you, sometimes."

The stag's head came down on the table with such force that C.L. had to grip the water pitcher with both hands to keep it from toppling over the side. "Now are we going to vote on this bill or aren't we?" thundered Artemus. And when they had voted, five for and aught against, to raise the price of a license for unaltered dogs to $15.00, while the license for altered dogs would remain at $7.50, Artemus thanked them all and called a ten-minute recess so they could all cool off.

As the others moved away, Dolly Dreher edged closer to C.L. "I knew that hotel was ruined the day Ruby painted it bright red," she said. "Destroyed all the dignity of the place." Dolly unwrapped a caramel and daintily held it between two fingers before flicking it into her mouth. C.L. wondered how anyone could eat caramels at ten in the morning. "You know what Lucille calls it, C.L.? Red as Sin Red, and I agree with Lucille." Lucille was Dolly's lifelong friend, housemate and business partner. For forty years the ladies had run Heavenly Freeze, by common consent the best homemade ice cream parlor east of Sidalia. Only vanilla and chocolate, and Dolly and Lucille wouldn't mix the flavors in a cup or cone. If you wanted them mixed, you'd have to take them home. There were still old diehards in Fenton who remained loyal to Dolly and Lucille and refused to patronize the Baskin-Robbins at the Plankton Mall, which offered thirty-one earthly flavors instead of two heavenly ones.

"I suppose even painting that place Red as Sin Red would have been okay, if only Ruby hadn't put in all those weird things. People coming into the Freeze have told me about it. Black commodes, black toothpaste. Sick. Very sick." The caramel clucked in Dolly's jaws as she said those last words. "And I even heard there's this one suite there, with a row of torn off dolls' arms bolted to the wall for a towel rack and...what is so darn funny, Mr. Cecil Lamont Karriker?"

"I beg your pardon, Miss Dreher," said C.L. "But those dolls' arms are a hoot, really they are. You have to have some sense of humor about Ruby's, that's all. Now, I certainly don't habituate the place. But I was there once, my senior year at Fenton High, when some friends and I spent a night there. Just to see what it was like. Disneyland is all I can compare it to. Everything at Ruby's is a surprise. Even a towel rack isn't a towel rack. I bought a little necklace in the gift shop Ruby had in the lobby. It was made of olive pits strung together, cost about fifty cents. My seven year old is wearing it now. I remember buying it to wear with my Nehru jacket."

"Well, you're a different generation from us old folks," Artemus said, placing a refilled pitcher of ice water on the table. He wiped the sweat off the pitcher with his palms. Jesse Barr and Wylie Perch took their places again; all the members were back. "But I bet even you, C.L., were pretty shocked about what happened at Ruby's the other night."

"Sure C.L. was shocked," said Wylie Perch. "Any decent person would be, at such...such...poor deportment." Miss Perch, a retired high school geometry teacher, had a way of sounding like a report card, on occasion.

"Too bad, pretty young thing like that," Jesse Barr said.

"Your mean Mary Don Hawkes? She's not so young, anymore, two kids in school," said Dolly Dreher.

"Not so pretty anymore, either, not like she was," said Artemus Crum. C.L. looked up at Agnes, whose portrait called into question Artemus's credentials as a judge of beauty.

"Mary Don's husband was supposedly involved in this too, you know. She wasn't alone," Wylie Perch said.

"Yeah, but you know Harvey Hawkes," said Jesse Barr. "You'd expect those shenanigans from a guy who can bowl with either hand."

"I didn't know that about Harvey," Dolly Dreher muttered, as if to herself. "I wonder if Lucille knows that."

C.L. Karriker put up his hand and all turned to the Chair of Privilege. "With all due respect, I think we should wait until we have the details of what happened at Ruby's. All we know is that the place was raided. That's all we know for sure, and until the grand jury has its turn, all we've got is hearsay evidence. Certainly nothing that would hold up in court."

"The hearsay I heard would hold up, all right," Jesse Barr said.

"I declare, C.L.," Wylie Perch said, "you're not still sweet on Mary Don, after all these years? You're not careful, I'll tattle on you to Marjorie."

"Don't be ridiculous," said C.L.

But Wylie Perch was not the sort of geometry teacher to let a pair of flirting pupils break her concentration. Not Wylie Perch, who used to rhapsodize about scalenes and isosceles as if they were compelling characters on *Love of Life*; who could go through three class periods with chalkdust on the frames of her glasses and never notice it or take the time to wipe it off.

In fact, she paid little attention to any of her pupils, except those she had to discipline, and those who were her pets. Her pets were always boys, and there were always two in each class. No matter what they did, whether it was prove a difficult theorem or simply dust off the erasers, Miss Perch would announce to the class, "Now you just watch Tom (or Ike, or Will, or Renny). That boy works hard. That boy's going to get someplace, someday." C.L. was not one of Miss Perch's favorites. Sometimes he wondered what she must think of him now, now that he was a successful lawyer and had got "someplace."

Why couldn't C.L. Karriker take his eyes, or at least the corner of his eye, off Mary Don? It wasn't that he particularly hated geometry class, or could so easily tune out Miss Perch's dramatic recitations about scalenes and isosceles. It was just that he never knew what Mary Don might do next. He might catch Mary Don leaning forward, both elbows resting on her desk, pressing her fingertips together to form a steeple, rolling a number two pencil between her lips as if it were a tube of lipstick. When she did that, C.L.'s bow-wow stood right up to attention. To be that eraser, for just three minutes, prayed C.L.

But what sent C.L. the most was when Mary Don clenched her

hands behind her head like you do for a sit-up, and then arched her body way back, curling her spine against the back of the seat, so far back the ends of her ponytail almost touched the seat. It was like a huge, silent yawn of the body. Even the chair didn't creak. Mary Don's majestic breasts would press against the buttons of her Girl Scout shirt, just the way C.L.'s perpendicular bow-wow was pressing against the zipper on his bluejeans. Then suddenly, as if nothing important had happened, Mary Don would spring back to regard Miss Perch with full concentration, as if the mating of angles and sides were her purple passion.

Margaret White, who sat behind C.L., leaned forward and breathed against the nape of his neck, "Don't be a dope, C.L. Mary Don did that all last year in Civics, to get Danny Fifer's attention." "Did what?" whispered C.L. over his shoulder, as innocently as guilt could make him. Margaret slugged him right on the backbone, to make C.L. turn around. "You know what I mean. This," said Margaret, and she began to imitate a Mary Don type stretch, except she kept her arms folded across her chest. Margaret had no tits to speak of. She wasn't in a class with Mary Don. Geometry class, but not tits class.

Margaret White just had it in for Mary Don. She spread the story that Mary Don wasn't really all that stacked, that it was a kind of optical illusion. "It's the way she stands, is all," Margaret would say. "It's her posture. If I stood with my shoulders way back and my chest way out, like Mary Don, I'd look big, too. But I have too much self-respect to do that."

That's a bunch of bull roar, thought C.L. Nobody else believed Margaret's theory either, and if they did, all they had to see was Mary Don at Lake Wakitan that summer, leaping over the hull of a canoe in her flaming orange two-piece bathing suit with the black tiger stripes. The deep, glistening gulch between her breasts told you they could possibly go all the way to her navel if she let them hang free. Tufts of bosom overflowed the underside of the bra cups, despite the wiring put in by the manufacturer. Seeing her in that two-piece nearly knocked the wind out of C.L. There could be no doubt that they were real, but C.L. still heard umpteen opinions, many of them based on very sound reasoning (if not experience), about what they would feel like if you stroked or squeezed them. It was all a wonder to C.L. He had no opinions, only questions. Were they shiny and rock-hard like the girls in *Playboy*? Was the area around the nipple dark like a prune or light like a peach? C.L. knew plenty of guys who had tried with Mary Don, but nobody had had any luck until Darryl Hantover took the matter into his own hands, so to speak, the night of Cherry Chesbro's hayride at the Atchity Stables.

For months Cherry had been talking about celebrating her sweet sixteen birthday with a "momentous" hayride around the outskirts of Fenton. Her Uncle Zeb was coming all the way from North Chanutesville to drive the team, and Cherry was quick to point out how Uncle Zeb had it all over Ed Retrum, Atchity's resident driver for most normal hayrides. Uncle Zeb was such a famous expert on wagons and horses that the people who made *Wagon Train* begged him to serve as their Technical Advisor. He would usually charge about twenty dollars an hour to do a hayride engagement, but as Cherry was his favorite niece and she'd showered him with pretty pleases, he was doing it for nothing. The ultimate special sixteenth birthday present.

C.L. Karriker was there, with Nancy Mulvehill. When Nancy had asked C.L. if he had a date to Cherry's yet he said no, and then there was a pause, and it occurred to C.L. that the only polite thing to do was to ask Nancy. (He'd been thinking of asking Laura Smeyne, but what the heck.) Nancy was okay, but her mouth was way too small. It looked like a keyhole turned sideways. Tonight Nancy looked pretty good to C.L. All the girls did, better in this summer moonlight than they looked in winter, under the unkind glare of the fluorescents at school.

Nancy looked good to C.L. but something about her, her perfume or hair spray, smelled awful, like a mistake with phosphorus in the chemistry lab. "What's that you got on?" asked C.L., sniffing deeply.

"Crepe de Chine," Nancy said. "My mom's. You like it?"

"Yeah. Great."

"Quick, C.L., we've got to be first," Nancy said, and when C.L. had pulled her up on the wagon with him, she rasped into his ear, "Guess what I've got with me?"

Perfume remover, I hope, thought C.L.

It was a little red flashlight, no more than five inches long. As the kids tumbled onto the haywagon, with Uncle Zeb hoisting the girls up by their armpits, Nancy beamed the light into each one's eyes, saying "Lookee, lookee. Lookee, lookee."

When they first set out there was lots of jostling and tossing of hay. Girls gossiped with girls and the boys jawed intensely about MGs and the Cardinals. The gang grew quieter as the road darkened. For a spell, all you heard were crickets, the clop of Duke and Daisy's hooves, a rustle of hay and whispers, and Uncle Zeb humming "On the Wings of a Snow White Dove." C.L. wasn't sure what to do with Nancy. She shivered and burrowed into his neck, her head butting his Adam's apple back into his throat. My, it's getting chilly out here, she said. C.L. felt perfectly warm. He painstakingly traced with his index finger, just for Nancy, the Big and Little Dippers, and made some educated guesses about other constellations and planets. A gasping sound arose amid the crunch of hay.

"Let's spot them, C.L.," Nancy said. She fished the little flashlight out of her purse. By its feeble luster, and through a dense mesh of shoulders, arms and legs, they could make out Mary Don Waldron and Darryl Hantover, kissing so deep they looked like Siamese twins joined at the lower lip. It was Mary Don who had gasped, and she continued to make little sniffly noises, like somebody fighting back a sneeze. The other girls on the haywagon were a bit more still, but C.L. could hear the soft smacking of lips and gusts of rapid breathing; a sweep of the flashlight revealed a dozen clashing bodies in silhouette. The wagon halted for a moment so Daisy could take a dump. Uncle Zeb hummed "Please Help Me I'm Falling" and then went into "Primrose Lane" without a pause, as if they were the same song. Nancy heaved a deep sigh, then another, and nuzzled into C.L.'s neck again. She wanted to be kissed, obviously; but the fumes from her Crepe de Chine gave C.L. a headache. He felt like a mosquito that's been blasted by insect repellent.

Nancy wanted to lie back, like most of the others, but C.L. froze into a sitting position. His eyes were riveted on Mary Don and Darryl. Darryl kept sliding his hand over Mary Don's shoulder blade and onto her huge breast. Each time Mary Don, without unlocking her lips from Darryl's would push his hand away. She didn't say please stop, but it was clear from her struggling and her murmured uh uh, uh uh, how far Mary Don would and wouldn't go. Blades of brown hay clung to her blonde hair. Closing his eyes, C.L. could listen to Mary Don's sweet sounds and imagine it was he, and not Darryl, caressing and exciting her. It made his bow-wow stand bolt upright, the sound and the picture. Duke took a dump. The stopping of the wagon jolted

C.L.'s eyes open. He saw that almost all the girls were going farther than Mary Don. Even Margaret White, who was flat as a home plate, was letting Bucky Bierbower pet her chest, and inside the blouse, too. Nancy Mulvehill lay sleeping with her hands folded over her belly. The flashlight was wedged tightly between her hands, with the thumb pressed to the "on" button; a speck of a ray peeped through her fingers.

The next morning C.L. received a breathless phone call from Billy Deacon. "Is it really true about Mary Don, C.L.? That she let Darryl do all those things?" Billy was laid up with the flu and had to miss out on the hayride.

"What things?" C.L. said.

"What do you mean, what things? Just about everything, to hear people talk. You know, inside the bra. Even down the pants, a certain person told me."

"Well, I don't..."

"Darryl's saying he got it bare. That Mary Don begged him for it. Says she was moaning and squirming like she had a toad in her drawers. You see all that?" Billy was shouting at the top of his voice. C.L. hoped for sure Billy's mom wasn't within hearing distance.

"Well, Billy, she did make an awful lot of noise. But..."

"Geez, I wish I'd been there. Gotta go, C.L.," and Billy hung up. C.L. felt his stomach knot, like when he told a lie. He very seldom told a lie, except to spare somebody's feelings (usually his mom's, about her cooking). He hadn't said right out that Mary Don had shoved her tits in Darryl's face, or plunged Darryl's hand down the front of her slacks, or cooed more, more, more. That would have been...an exaggeration. But who knew what he missed during that time he had his eyes closed? Mary Don could have done anything. The phone rang again.

"Forgot to ask you, C.L. How'd you do with Nancy Mulvehill?" asked Billy.

"Oh, we got along just fine," C.L. said.

"I got you," Billy said. And he hung up.

Everybody was buzzing about Mary Don. Nancy Mulvehill said she saw it all because she had the flashlight trained on Mary Don and Darryl the whole time (and what else would she have been doing, with that "cold potato" C.L. Karriker for a date?). Margaret White declared it was shameful to go *that* far in front of everyone; it made the other girls, your everyday good girls, feel cheap just being on the same wagon, and their boyfriends would think they were prudes, because they wouldn't dare go as far as Mary Don. Cherry Chesbro was heartbroken that, thanks to Mary Don, her sweet sixteen hayride would be remembered not for the great fun everybody had, or for how handsome Uncle Zeb was, but for that wild boy and girl who set some kind of all-time record for a public display of affection. Cherry vowed she would never speak to Mary Don again.

After Cherry's hayride the boys seemed to lose their curiosity about Mary Don. Their parents instructed them to avoid her because she was "fast," which meant you could get into deep trouble, and she could, too. C.L. noticed a change in Mary Don once school started again. She no longer smiled at him when they passed in the halls; she never lingered at her locker. She dropped out of Hestia, the homemakers' club, even though she was a great seamstress and a shoo-in for club president. Now she went out with boys from Rubidoux College in Saw Mill, beer-bellied guys who would speed around with the top down and one arm curled around Mary Don. Somebody told C.L. that one night Mary Don got drunk on beer and took on the whole pledge class of Pi Kappa Alpha. Bull roar, said C.L. He still liked Mary Don.

C.L. should not have been surprised that, by the time the Senior Prom rolled around, nobody wanted to ask Mary Don. But he was. After all, Mary Don was still a doll, even with that heavy eye shadow, and the guys from Rubidoux. If only for old time's sake somebody should ask her, thought C.L. He took it upon himself. He had nobody else to ask; he didn't even want to go to a damned Prom, but his mom kept pushing him, said it would be the most romantic night of his life, till he got married.

Mary Don was surprised to hear from C.L. He had never talked to her on the phone before, and her voice, separated from her gorgeous body, sounded deep and strong, kind of businesslike. I'd be happy to go with you, Mary Don said. One thing, though, you mind very much if we leave early, say eleven? I've kind of got a date with Rob, he's from Rubidoux, for his frat party. I made that date a long time ago. Okay?

That was fine with C.L. It might be exciting for people to see him leave early with Mary Don. They'd think...well, they'd think *something*. Mrs. Karriker's face sagged when he told her whom he was taking to the Prom. C.L. assured her he would be home before midnight, and that eased her mind.

The kids at the Prom shied away from C.L. and Mary Don. The girls looked resentful, as if they wanted to call out to C.L. the names of the girls he could have asked, who were staying home miserable this night. Some of the guys were snickering, and he caught his supposedly good friend Benny Crum making obscene gestures in his direction.

Nothing mattered to C.L. but Mary Don. She looked beautiful. Her blonde hair was tightly braided and piled on top of her head. Her satiny pink gown was cut low to expose the crests of her breasts, which were as white and perfectly formed as two giant scoops from the Heavenly Freeze. With all the other girls made up, Mary Don's mascara and eye shadow didn't seem cheap at all. She didn't seem like a fast girl, either. C.L. had forgotten how nice Mary Don was to talk to, once you got your mind off those tits, and saw how close she listened. As if she cared.

Did she care that C.L. was going to Plankton Junior College next year, and wanted to be a lawyer someday? Like Perry Mason? asked Mary Don. Sure, C.L. said. Mary Don was taking a job as cashier at Pemberton's, the stationery store. No more school for her. Mary Don didn't want to dance the fast dances, because of the dress. She would bounce too much. They danced the slow ones. At five minutes to eleven they danced to what Mary Don said was her favorite song and, with her breasts quaking just inches from his chin, C.L. felt her jaw moving as she mouthed the words "To know know know him is to love love love him, and I do." C.L. knew she was probably thinking of this Rob, not him. He knew he would be taking her to Rob in less than five minutes. But C.L. felt happy. His bow-wow nestled calmly in his pants, complacent and unpressured. For the first time this century, his mom was right about something. This was the most romantic night of his life. At least till he got married.

Maybe Wylie Perch had watched C.L. dancing with Mary Don that night and noticed how sublimely happy he was. Maybe that's where she got the idea he was sweet on Mary Don, way back then. At any rate, it was the voice of Wylie Perch that snapped C.L. out of his revery. "I don't think you can entirely blame Mary Don for what happened at Ruby's. It's Ruby's hotel. A proprietor is the one responsible for propriety, eh?"

"You're right, Wylie," said Dolly Dreher. "That hotel's been jinxed ever since Ruby took it over and redid it. The wonderful old Blackstone. Remember she brought all those hippies here? Bad seeds, all of them. Smelled bad and did bad things. "Smellpots,' Lucille used to call them, and I agreed with her."

"Uppity Negroes, too," Jesse Barr said. "In those jungle get-ups, dancing those native dances and smoking dope, right on the steps of the hotel where Teddy told us to make the world safe for democracy."

"That was Woodrow Wilson, Jesse." C.L. had corrected Jesse Barr on this point at least seven times. "Teddy Roosevelt was never here. It was Wilson who did a stopover at the Blackstone, so they say."

"What aggravates me," said Artemus Crum, "is the clientele Ruby caters to nowadays. Any decent folk will pass us by and go to the Ramada Inn in East Carpenter. It's these ads Ruby puts in those East and West coast papers, that draws all the weirdos here. And then they look at us as though we were weird. Remember that skinny old fellow, a year or so ago, carrying around that cardboard sign of Laurel and Hardy, lifesize? Said he was toting it all over the USA to take photos of it in weird places, and Fenton was one of them. I bet he wouldn't have even heard of this town, if Ruby's fame hadn't spread far and wide."

"But isn't that a good thing, Artemus?" asked C.L. "How many towns in Missouri with only 2100 people can attract visitors from all over the country?"

"You've missed my point, boy, but we're getting behind schedule. Dolly, what's the next item on the official Council agenda?"

It was an ordinance concerning parking meter rates for the purpose of increasing the meters to forty cents an hour on Market Street and twenty cents an hour on the east side of Parkview Lane. Jesse Barr had opposed it through all the Council's lengthy debates the past few months, and he opposed it now. Bad for Fenton business, he argued. Folks will drive to the Plankton Mall to shop and park free. You'll see. But Jesse was overruled and the ordinance was enacted.

"Here's one we can all agree on," Dolly Dreher said. "Resolution Number Four hundred seventy-one: Congratulating Benjamin and Ernestine Rayl on the occasion of their sixtieth wedding anniversary, July 22."

"Hear hear," said Jesse Barr, and the members of the Fenton City Council all rose as one to clink their glasses in tribute to the Rayls.

Chair of Privilege

As they seated themselves, Wylie Perch said, "I feel that we on the Council ought to go on record as condemning the kind of deportment that went on at Ruby's last week. I hereby propose a resolution to that effect."

"I'd second that, Wylie. I bet Lucille would, too," said Dolly Dreher.

"Hear hear," said Jesse Barr, raising his glass. Jesse seemed to be getting tight, although all he'd had to drink was ice water.

"Wait, we don't really know for sure what happened there yet," C.L. muttered, so softly that Dolly Dreher had to say, "Come again?"

But Wylie Perch had heard him, and pointing her finger at C.L. as if he were one of her unruly geometry pupils, she said, "Now look here, young man, we all know what Sergeant Willoughby saw them doing at..."

"Well, Willoughby's lying," shouted C.L. To everybody's amazement, he stood up suddenly, knocking the Chair of Privilege hindwards, his face red with a rage that seemed to come out of nowhere. Leaning with both hands flat on the table, his eyes scathed the Council members and even the overhead presence of Agnes Crum.

"She didn't do it, I tell you. She didn't do a damn thing," C.L. kept repeating, until the stag's head came crashing down just inches from his fingertips.

Mr. Rabicoff spent his buoyant childhood and Era of Non-stop Potency in Kansas City, Missouri. He poached a diploma from Washington University, then moved on to 13 years in plenitudinous New York City, earning various graduate degrees and ending up in public relations. He now lives in Baltimore with his wife, cat, PCjr and (at this writing) a 5-month old fetus named Fortunoff.

25

Diane M. Rebel
The Hunt

The forest is beautiful. I have always loved it. Even with gunshots ringing through the hills, echoing off the straight gray tree trunks, it is still heaven. The hunters in their square red plaids disturb our serenity for a short while, but then everything is as it was, watching birds, waiting trees, the living forest. For eternity I have been close to the woods. My husband brought me even closer last year. I thank him for it, though he does not know it.

Every hunting season he would go, bow in hand, hoping to kill, his face shining, not with lust for death, but with lust for life. The movements of his rock-like body would reveal his mounting excitement. He would walk into the forest, carrying his bow, relishing the clean coldness, anticipating adventure. He would never return disappointed, even when empty-handed, because walking the hills in itself was a joy to him.

Last year he begged me to come along. He said if I came, for luck, he would surely find a kill. We had been unhappy with each other for a while, so I agreed, hoping the aloneness would draw us closer together. The beauty of the forest and mountains would surely make us forget our differences. The camaraderie of the hunt might give us unity again.

The day before the hunt we left laden with our packs. Our hikes in the past were pleasant experiences. I would lead, being slower. We would take time to look at new plants and insects, wondering at their strangeness or enjoying their beauty. My Eagle Scout would teach me his woodslore.

But this day we hiked with a purpose. My husband led. I struggled behind him up the narrow path, tripping over roots and rocks. All was still except our marching boots through the silent trees, and the hushed objections of an occasional small bird.

We hiked many miles from the road and made camp for the night. On past nights in the woods we would make camp leisurely, now and then stopping to sigh in the coolness. Sometimes we would stop to climb a small rise and enjoy the feeling of lightness that shedding a heavy pack brings. After pitching our tent and building a fire, we would play, Showing the forest and each other the beauty of bodies. We would keep each other warm, not needing a fire, only each other.

But that day, last year, we made camp quickly. After tent and fire came more work, almost endless target practice. The zip and pop of flying arrows echoed through the hills until the animals quieted in apprehension. My arms shook from exertion beyond their limits. My left breast and forearm burned from the friction of the bowstring scraping across them when I fired. We stopped only when the light of our fire made a bright spot in the gathering blackness. Then my husband's desire for dinner and sleeping bag seemed almost urgent—but he ate with strange detachment. The low monotone of his few words seemed to make the darkness press closer around us, as if trying to eavesdrop on a closely guarded secret. When we finally slid into our sleeping bags, the silence and the night crouched outside our tent like waiting cougars, breathing quietly next to me. Sleeping with a stranger would have been more satisfying .

On the day of the hunt we dressed carefully. The mixed grays, greens, browns and yellows of our clothes blended us with the foliage. We were nearly invisible. If we put our hoods over our faces and sat extremely still, we disappeared.

With quartered apples in our pockets to hide our scents, and our daypacks on our backs, we left the camp. At dawn we were in the gray mist a mile upwind. My husband asked if I would mind separating, insisting we would have more success if we did.

Although knowing I couldn't kill a beautiful animal, I agreed. Argument would defeat the purpose of my coming.

My husband disappeared through a green wall nearby. I listened to his footsteps rustle away—then silence. I sat stock still as he'd shown me, against the mottled bark of a tall pine. With my shaded hood over my face and my bow parallel to the trunk, I looked like a giant burl at the base of the tree. I waited. An eternity passed without a sound. My mind wandered. I remembered back to our first year together. We loved each other very much and the extra we gave to the world. How righteous we were in our new love! It always starts passionately, joyfully, and so sweetly. But time changes a love, like wine into vinegar.

A sound woke me from my reverie. I waited. Rustling, closer this time. More waiting. The rustling drew steadily toward me. Muscle by muscle, moving one at a time, I slowly tucked like a stalking cat. As the rustling approached I rose to my feet, bow poised, arrow drawn, mind boring into the sound. I stood ready to kill, not feeling like a hunter. As the rustling drew closer, I felt hunted.

I stood tingling, legions of dark green sentries around me, silently watching as I waited for my target to show itself. My shaking arm charged the bow with mounting energy, increasing tension. All sound stopped, except the rustling. I stared in the direction of the sound.

As I watched a green giant rose from the bushes. It was my husband. I relaxed my bow and closed my eyes in relief. Then I heard the zip of an arrow and with the impact of a splitting-maul, something hit me in the chest. It knocked me back against the tree. My body began working by its own command. I felt it trying to stand. My eyes saw only shapes without detail, except for the sharp image of a straight green stem with a feather flower on the end. It sprouted from my left breast. I thought how delicate the blossom looked and how smooth the stem. I wondered how it grew there. A shape appeared dimly before me. It watched my body make secret little signs that denied the arrow and the fluid legs. The shape spoke muffled sounds that grew even fainter, like the echo of a voice shouted down a well.

When my body finally ceased functioning, I watched my husband pick it up. He threw it across his shoulders and walked in the direction of the camp. I followed.

As I moved I heard new sounds. The trees whispered to me when I passed, welcoming me to the world. I noticed chipmunks and squirrels chattering to each other about me. My attention changed from the retreating man and his load to the darks and lights of the forest, to the green beneath and the blue above. I wandered and joined the forest. It knew me and was glad of my existence. I discovered the forest had always loved me.

The last time I saw Diane Rebel was on a ferry ride to Winslow on my way to the Last Resort. She was houseboat shopping. This is the first issue of Sign of the Times *that Diane has appeared in. We hope she contributes again.*

26

Red Onion
Beating the TV

Oh no, I didn't ask for it. I was just sweeping up a little in front of my fish store. It gets pretty trashed most days. Some of the punkers like to hang out in front of my window. There's a little ledge there they sit on, or else they just bag out on the sidewalk. I don't mind: they remind me of the fish. Some of their haircuts look like fins. And the wild colors—I bet they wish they could get their hair to shine like the bettas. It's like they're in a tank of their own out there. They never seem to go anywhere. Like I said, I don't mind, except I always have to sweep up the cigarette butts at the end of the day.

When I'm done I usually go back inside and flip the "closed" sign over. Then what I like to do is turn off all the lights except the fluorescents behind the tanks. I never get a chance to watch the fish during the day. Too busy. Anyway, I pick a tank and just sit and watch it for a while. It's relaxing, I suppose. Those fish, they're pretty lively as long as the lights are on. Still, they're graceful, even when they're darting around. Some people might think I'm weird. But I don't think it's any weirder than watching TV. And maybe that's why the guy picked me out.

They figure there's over five billion people in the world now, and he picked me. He said he wanted to look at the fish. I flipped the sign over anyway, so he'd be the last customer. He seemed kind of frantic,

Red Onion

like he'd been drinking coffee all day. But he was friendly enough. He was talking about the fish and what an easy life they had. He called it "an honest existence." I thought at first he was an insurance salesman. Then he asked me if he could tell me a story, and I figured what the hell. He seemed like he really needed to talk and he looked harmless enough, even if he was a bit wigged out. Around this neighborhood you get used to making that kind of judgment the minute you see someone. So we pulled a couple of chairs up to a scalare tank and he started telling his story:

"It is a horrible thing to admit, but my wife and I have become creatures of habit. Every night we go to bed at nine, read until ten, and fall asleep by ten thirty. Every night, regardless of rain or snow, we open the window a crack. If we don't open the window we tend to toss and turn and dream of smoke filled rooms, hot humid days and chemical warfare.

"Our bedroom window looks out on a blank brick wall. We have no idea what those bricks house. Perhaps that is where they make the chemicals. In any case, it is a brick wall, and very good at reflecting sound. If you have ever played pool you will know that a ball leaves the bumper at the same angle with which it hit. If you know anything about sound waves, you will know that they can emanate at many different angles from a single source. Knowing these things, you can see how easy it would be for the sound from the neighbor's television upstairs to bounce off the brick wall and into our sleeping ears.

"Evidently we are not the only ones with habits. Many is the night at precisely eleven o'clock that I have sat up in bed like a mouse trap going off. Since I refuse to close the window and dream about chemical warfare, I dream instead that I wake in the middle of a large extended family not my own. There is a mother-in-law, a husband and wife (both twice divorced, once from each other), one son, many aunts, uncles, cousins, friends and friends of friends. The source of people is inexhaustible. I know none of these people. They are nothing like the people with whom I was raised. They argue all the time, almost inevitably because they misunderstand each other so routinely. They argue about the most inconsequential things; they argue about who left the faucet dripping, who carved the turkey last Thanksgiving, whether Fred Freidrich is a second cousin, a cousin twice removed, or both. They argue at top speed and with tantamount sound. There is never anything I can do to stop them. Sometimes I try, sometimes I don't. Both tacks are equally frustrating. Then, as I sit there in bed I wake, slowly, and realize that the TV is on upstairs.

"It is the latest thing in evening soaps, I guess. And they use the latest marketing tool—they run it every single night of the week. I say 'I guess' because I don't own a television and I don't know what goes on these days. But even if I did have a TV it would be the last thing on my agenda to turn it on at eleven o' clock in the evening just to find out what the upstairs neighbors were watching. One does not hide in the closet to escape solitary confinement. One does not beat one's own head to cure a headache. One does not dive into the water to avoid a shark.

"I have tried ear plugs and discovered that the problem is not the noise level, even though the creatures upstairs must be deaf as rocks to turn the volume so high. No, it is not the decibels themselves but the nature of the sounds. It is the quarreling, the alternately whiney and angry tones. Their accusations sound like a chain saw cutting through a Quonset hut. Their denials are like glass carboys being catapulted into mountains of cinder blocks. The soft sound of argument, the apology, never comes from their television. There is never a mumbling sound that could be taken to mean 'I'm sorry.' There is only argument and the tortuous reprieves where the commercials are silenced—tortuous because they are always temporary.

"When you are first asleep, any string of words no matter how softly it is whispered in your ear can wake you and keep you awake. The other night they were recalling this chain of events: The wife had cheated on the husband with a fifteen-year-old circus worker. The husband had discovered them behind the tattooed man's tent. He had pulled his handgun out of the breast pocket of his suit jacket and shot each of them in the left knee. Instantly regretting that action (or not, that being the argument) he had called an ambulance, which was good fortune for the wife since she broke her water at the instant he hung up the phone. It was years later when their boy took ill that they discovered the wife to be a carrier of that new virus (the television's euphemism, not mine). Amazingly the husband showed no signs of the virus, although perhaps not so amazingly after all, because since that day at the circus he had not touched his wife. The boy, being seven by this point and surly for his age, tried to take revenge for his one-kneed mother. He snuck up to his father as he lay sleeping in his recliner and bit him on the ankle. This did not accomplish much, however, since he hadn't sharp enough teeth to break through his father's argyle sock, and the two became fast friends.

"After this argument was dropped they went on to discuss whose turn it was to be the family kleptomaniac, whose the hypochondriac, whose the bulimic and whose the amnesiac. I tolerated months of this kind of arguing before I gathered together enough stray courage to go upstairs. Some might find my hesitation spineless or at least lame, but I am normally a quiet man and not used to nonchalantly strolling into the enemy encampment.

"One of their arguments was having a rerun. The mother was asserting that it made no difference if the boy did have the virus, it was his turn to be the hypochondriac and there was no excuse for his slacking in his duties. I found as much of a pause as I could and knocked on the door. There was immediate silence. Well, I reasoned, at least they know enough to turn off the TV when unexpected guests arrive. But the door opened as quickly as the set had gone off, and the handsomely flushed face in front of me was not at all what I had expected. I had thought perhaps a potbelly and a can of cheap beer would open the door—as dispassionate a man as there could be, having seen it all on TV. Instead the face snapped at me, 'What!' He hadn't even the time to elaborate on which 'what' he wanted.

" 'I thought perhaps you could turn down your television a bit.'

"'Don't be a smart ass,' he said, punctuating his comment with the slam of the door.

"When I thought about it later I decided that I should have expected as much. It was obvious that with people who loved television as much as they did one could not take such an ordinary approach. Interpreting this maxim to its fullest, I went down to the marina and bought a sturdy and barbless flying gaff hook and a length of nylon rope. I felt fairly confident that with the aid of a series of strategically placed knots I could climb my way to their window.

"To what purpose? Well, I suppose I was desperate. I told myself that somehow I could rig the set so that it couldn't run at night. Maybe a piece of bubble gum in just the right place. Or foil, perhaps. But in the back of my mind I knew that I had nowhere near the knowledge to effect such a repair and that I would probably just poke some holes in the speaker or sever the cable connection. As I say, this was in the back of my head. I considered myself not at all that destructive of a person, and to avoid coming face to face with this part of myself I busied my mind with the logistics of getting through the window.

"It was really much simpler than even I had thought. The window was open all day, being on the second floor and the season being the height of summer. The faceless brick wall shielded me from all views except up and down the alley. The streets were vacant in the middle of the day for the same reason that the apartment would be empty; everybody was at work. This was the surest thing of all. In those days it was more likely that my brand new rope would break than it was that somebody would play hooky from work, walk down the street, look down the alley, notice a man climbing on a rope up the side of the building, care enough to take a second look and get excited enough to do anything at all to stop him.

"A flying gaffhook, as you might know, was so perfect for my purposes that one might have suspected it was designed for me. Its handle was long enough so that by stretching most of my arm out my window I could just hook the neighbor's sill. With a simple tug I could disengage the hook from the handle, leaving only the rope trailing down the wall. With a little finesse I could repeat the process in reverse and retrieve my hook when I was done. I needed only to dull the point a bit with a file—to reduce damage to the sill and make the hook easier to recover—and I was in business.

"I have never been much of an athlete. That is why I enjoy fishing. A base hit, a goal, la touche, they never seemed enough reward for the exertion, not when you could have a nice ocean perch instead.

"You know, sometimes I wonder if you can't offend a fish, sitting here talking about gaff hooks and nice ocean perch. I'm not one of these crude sportsmen who has no respect for his opponent. Some men will kill an animal for the pleasure of killing and call it sport, much in the same way that they might hire a whore and call it making love. But look at these fish here. Look at how they dart around and chase each other. Some of that motion, I realize, is jockeying for territory, but some of it is downright fun and games. Some of that motion is what we would call hide and seek or follow the leader. No matter how subconsciously it is done, I think you have to wonder about an animal that has the capacity to play. I think you have to wonder what else they feel inside those tiny brains.

"In any case, I made the climb, and there was no question that my heart raced when I looked down from two floors up. But I must admit that I enjoyed it just a bit. Just a bit. The apartment was done completely in fifties art deco as nearly as I could tell, which was not very near. There could have been some twenties pieces thrown in. The effect was complete, to the dishes in the cupboard and the shaving mug in the medicine cabinet. You may think me overly snoopy, and I am, but imagine my chagrin when I could find a television nowhere in the place. I got a bit frantic, I suppose, and searched in places that weren't likely to hold one.

"I suppose I was a bit frantic about the decor, too. Was it in homage to the period of history in which the television came into its own? Was it in homage to the mindless way of life that period represents? Finally I consoled myself with these speculations: the deco stuff was pure eighties and merely a sound investment, the television was out being repaired. Well and good enough. I would have at least one night's good sleep, and probably a couple weeks'.

"We went to bed that night as usual, I promising my mate peace without admitting how I could predict such a thing. Ten thirty came and went and I was drifting into other lands when the voices came on in my head. At first I thought I was dreaming that I was watching a boxing match (a thing I never do), but then I awoke in full and realized the horror of my situation. The television that did not exist was on again, and running at top volume. There was an argument in progress about the boy, who had come to love his father (or had he?) and how in the progress of a friendly wrestling match the boy had accidentally poked his father's eye out.

"I did not sleep a bit that night. I was busy at my desk with pencil and paper, drawing up some special plans. I took a small nap in the early hours but was anxious to get to the hardware store as soon as it opened so as to buy some lengths of PVC pipe, one of them two inches in diameter and one of them two and a quarter, with elbows for each. Next I hit the drugstore and had some difficulty locating the little oval pocket mirrors that women always carry in their purses. It seems oval had gone out of style in favor of square with beveled corners. In any case I eventually found them and wasted no time at all in assembling my periscope. I glued a mirror into the crook of each elbow and threaded the elbows into their respective pipes. The smaller piece of pipe fit into the other quite nicely, with plenty of room to swivel them about. And of course the whole thing was designed to reach from a comfortable resting position on my window sill to the very bottom of the sill above, so that by simply grasping the lower elbow with one hand and the outer sleeve with the other I could telescope the midsection and have a full and leisurely view of the happenings upstairs.

"As tired as I was, I was not tempted to sleep. The closer the digits of my clock counted toward ten thirty the more active I became; pacing, chewing gum, rubbing the glue off my fingers, looking into the refrigerator. I thought perhaps my wife would shoot me on the spot — or, not having a gun, something worse. As much as she disagreed with my spying on the neighbors it was nothing to the way she disagreed with my nervous activity. Each time I opened the refrigerator door I could feel the prick other eyes as she steadied their aim over the top of her book. You can't know how deeply I regret that I cannot create the precise effect for you. It is one of her best tricks. I am certain there is no one who can do it as well as she.

"Finally the hour came, and caution was advised. The last thing I wanted was to wave the head of my periscope about and attract their attention. Slowly I extended my contraption up the wall, pausing at the sill, waiting, waiting for the TV to go on and for their dull stares to be fixed to it.

"What I saw, when the sound came on, was a thing I had hoped I would never see again. Years ago when my son was first starting college and young and foolish as all freshmen are (he has remained so) he invited me to visit him and attend classes with him for a day. To my horror our very first class of the day was an acting class. In the dim basement below the main stage I watched as the instructor had the students raise their arms like the branches of a tree and wave them in the wind, then crawl about on all fours and lift a leg to an imaginary hydrant, then wrestle around with each other like orangutans gone mad. And for the closing act they all gathered their dignity and departed with all aloofness, doing their very best 'sophomores.' As frightening as that was, what I saw through my periscope was worse.

"The man and the woman would stand still until they imagined that a cue was given and then they would both begin to argue as vehemently as they knew how. They would shake fingers, spit, point, scowl, feign surprise, feign shock, feign disgust, feign rage, feign ennui, threaten to throw things, threaten to leave the room, threaten to tell so and so and threaten to die on the spot. They would bang doors, bang on tables, slam the telephone, kick, pinch, poke, gouge and bawl with all their might. It was a horrible spectacle, a thing from which I could not turn my eye though it was the thing I most wanted to do. And then, as if a silent voice from nowhere had called 'cut' they would halt the action, wipe the sweat from their brows, smile at each other and congratulate in whispers, gather themselves into new positions in the living room now instead of the kitchen and wait for the new cue. These last were the silent spots I had always assumed were commercials hushed by the swift hand of remote control.

"My wife and I have started to take midnight walks. We know it is not always safe, but it is better than the torture of being dead tired and unable to sleep. The sound of television is everywhere, but nowhere do we see the blue glows in the windows like we used to. I was already dreadfully close to driving my wife over the brink, but I insisted on spending a whole Saturday afternoon going around to various electronics and department stores. Sure enough, there was not a television to be bought in the whole of the city. Then at the end of the day, just when my wife was in the height of one of the most beautifully withheld rages I think I have ever seen I demanded that we drive all the way out to the land fill. And just as I had thought, there was a separate pit devoted entirely to televisions.

"Of course we took the matter straight to the police, but we found them playing. One of them was acting the corrupt cop, one the worried police chief, one the greasy undercover, and the rest were slicked up members of the vice squad. They promised to take the matter on at once and went right out and arrested fifteen whores. The whores were having a wonderful time, playing at kicking and screaming and spitting. It looked a good setup for them, because of course there are things you simply cannot show on TV.

"We took the matter on up the line to the mayor and city council, but all of the politicians were still watching television. In fact, it was all they were doing. They had no idea what was going on. They were busy trying to adjust their video images to meet with what their pollsters had told them the public wanted. It was absurd. It was impossible to keep their attention for any longer than thirty seconds.

"The neighbors don't even go to work now. They just lay about the house all day, sleeping mostly, and then as evening wears on they apply makeup and do their little warm-up routines in preparation for their business. My wife and I don't work either. There is really no need to — we are pretending to play a retired couple. We don't go out much anymore, but we do have to go to the bank once in a while. It's nice that they don't keep the accounts any more. Still, we don't pull out too much money. It would be a shame to get caught up in the role of a millionaire or a drug dealer. And we get out of the bank as quickly as possible, because you never know when the bank robbers will come. We get off the streets quickly too. The streets are simply not safe at all, what with all the car chases. Still and all, it is an easy life.

"But you can understand my excitement when I saw you there with your broom and realized what you were doing. Surely you must know that nobody is an extra anymore. It could be dangerous, you know, drawing attention to yourself in this way. But I suppose that is your business.

"I hope that you can forgive me. It is hard these days. There is no one to talk to, no one who will listen to a story. As easy as life is, I am not sure I can stand it much more. Perhaps today I would have lost my composure had I not found you. I hope that goes a little way to make up for my inconveniencing you, to know that you have helped a man through a tough moment."

And then he left, just like that. He went walking off down the street with his head down, like all he wanted to see was the sidewalk. I heard a siren, and then the cops pulled up and put him in the car. He didn't seem the least bit surprised. He didn't try to run or anything. Thinking back on it, I'm sure he was convinced it was just part of the program. I'm sure he thought he'd go through some pretty tough questioning, the hot lights and the cigarette smoke and all, and then just take off when the scene was shot. And maybe he was right.

The bio from Red Onion: "I read The Guardian, but I don't believe everything I read. I have never owned a television, although I don't persecute those who do. I enjoy eating. I believe that Ronald Reagan has been the worst thing to hit the shelves since prefilled disposable diapers. I think that is about all you need to know about me."

27

Ben Satterfield
Everybody Talks About Reality But Nobody Does Anything About It

My life smoothed out the day I stopped knuckling under. I'd had enough. Fuck it, I said. I walked off my job right in the middle of a rush-up on an English bulldog (I worked for a taxidermist, a saturnine old man whose single pleasure seemed to be in making dead things look more or less alive). A Shih Tzu was waiting, and the old man had promised to stuff a kinkajou and a Shetland pony the next day for some blue-haired crone who had more money than sense, but I couldn't deal with the dead things that looked as alive as their owners anymore. That sad-faced bulldog with its nose shaved and its belly open as we packed it full of unnatural things—different kinds of space-age acetates and foam rubber—suddenly reminded me of myself: stuffed full of somebody else's crap. It was a powerful flash. So I went home, got a beer out of the fridge, flopped on the couch and watched television for the rest of the afternoon.

I didn't enjoy it much because it reminded me of taxidermy.

By the time my wife came home, I had emptied a sixpack and was feeling fuzzy, not to mention a little blank from the TV, which sort of drycleans the lobes.

"What are you doing home?" Wanda asked first thing. Women love order, routine, schedules; it has to do with their being on a cycle themselves.

"I live here," I said. "I'm watching TV. I'm drinking beer." That should cover it, I thought.

"You're unraveling," she said, plopping in a recliner chair across from me. She stared at me and sighed. "I'm not surprised."

Women are like that. You could all of a sudden shave your head and paint it fuchsia, they'd say "I knew it, I've been expecting it."

I ignored her. I was about ready to decide that she didn't exist when she sighed again. Wanda was an Olympic sigher and hard to ignore. I sang what I could remember of a Bob Dylan song, and on the line, "When you ain' t got nothin', you got nothin' to lose," she interrupted.

"Do you think you could be a little reasonable?" she asked.

"Not by your definition." I thought a moment, then added, "Not by anybody else's definition."

"I shudder to think what yours might be." Sarcastic, not the least bit interested in anything different.

"It's a matter of perspective. I no longer have a vested interest in..." I waved my arm in a wide semi-circle to indicate as much as possible.

"Oh boy," she said.

After a while she sighed again a world-class exhalation then left the room. Marriage is a broken door, its hinge always creaking.

I tried to remember the last time we'd made love, but I couldn't. I'll bet she couldn't either. Marriage. Why can't we see that for the working population it's a snare, a device for social control.

When Wanda came back into the room, she had two packed suitcases. "I'm leaving," she announced. So conventional.

I waved good-bye.

She left.

I drank beer and watched TV.

After a week or so I had to go out for groceries. At the supermarket I loaded up and waited until the boxboy had put all the sacks into a shopping cart and the checker had announced the total for the third time. "Fifty-two-eighty-seven," he repeated, frowning, a bit curious but not yet apprehensive; his lines had always worked before, so he trusted his script, and kept giving me my cue.

I smiled and started pushing the cart out of the store.

"Hey!" the cashier yelled. Improvising now, no script, but he knew his role. "You can't do that."

The world has too many people saying things like that. Don't you agree?

I kept going.

I got through the doors before the cashier and a manager stopped me. The checker was holding the cash register receipt in front of him like a dead snake.

"Nice catch," I said.

They both scowled. The manager, a pudgy guy around forty with a sagging face, thinning hair, and a defeat in his eyes, said, "You didn't pay for your groceries."

"Don't be absurd." Denial invites confrontation.

The manager looked at the checker, who was still clutching his paper snake.

"He didn't."

I started to move the cart away. Nonchalantly.

"Wait," the manager said, sounding uncertain. "We've got to get this straightened out."

"Do as you please," I said, and pushed the cart to my car. They looked confused by my freaky advice. Sort of an alien concept, and not one to be dealt with in a supermarket parking lot.

They came to the car and watched me load the sacks into it. "He says you didn't pay," the manager whined.

"I've paid all my life," I said, getting into the car. I looked at him, at his sad, defeated eyes that reminded me of that bulldog. "Just as you are paying." I started the engine. They stood still as statues and watched me drive out of the lot.

There are ways to get by.

On weekends I would dress up and drive to the well-to-do neighborhoods, those exclusive residential areas of the privileged, and cruise around until I spotted a party. Sometimes I would just walk in, grab a drink and head for the buffet table. Other times I would ring the bell, depending on how I felt. Whoever came to the door would look at me with an ambiguous smile, and I'd say something like, "I couldn't get here before now hang-up at the office," and barge right in. Only twice was I asked who I was, and I made up a phony name and said, "I'm a friend of Mike's." At a big party—or maybe even a small one—there's always a Mike. Sure. Americans love Mike.

Food, booze, cocaine and even invitations to other parties.

Once I came home with three fine joints of blooddancing weed that came from the District Attorney's office, another time with half a gram of pharmaceutical coke, and always with food and hootch. I spent only enough money to keep the electricity and water coming in and to avoid eviction.

At one of those parties I met a wild-eyed woman on the upside of thirty who told me about certain things she wanted to try before she got married and settled down, both of which she was planning to do in a few months. Her name was Samantha. I took her home with me and we spent a couple of months in uninhibited revelry, carnal ventures, exploration of slippery boundaries. We devoured the sensual like amorous birds of prey. We did as we pleased. Why not?

She paid the bills, and would have stayed longer, but the wedding date had been announced.

There are lots of ways to get by.

I drew unemployment for six months. Many papers involved, nearly all meaningless since each document is designed to serve as evidence in case of fraud, which is rare-very few people lie about being out of work, a disgrace in this country. Nevertheless, the State is suspicious and resentful. For my first payment I had to wait an extra two weeks as a penalty for quitting (the State dislikes any voluntary act), but I told the petty bureaucrats that I had developed an allergy to dead things and they accepted that. It was the truth, and something the paper pushers could understand. Most of them were dead, too, all the light gone out of their eyes, zombies going through the motions, doing their jobs.

God bless America. Land of the free.

After nineteen weeks in succession of being the uninvited guest at parties, I got booted out of a house. The hostess caught me stuffing sandwiches in my jacket.

I have to admit, I was getting a little loose.

Cops came to the door two or three times, but I didn't answer, even though they knew I was home. They made threats through the door, irritated that they couldn't exercise their authority, but they were rookies, hadn't learned to lie well yet. A direct correlation exists between authority and lying: the more authority one has, the more he lies. The president? He tells only enough of the truth to give some credence to all the lies.

Shine, perishing republic.

One day Wanda showed up, said she was filing for a divorce. More papers.

"Do as you please," I said, remembering that when she cooked, she always followed the recipe *exactly*. Good soldier.

Wanda works for a monolithic insurance company. She believes in actuarial tables, statistics, order. She knows that every day so many people die and so many are born. She has the figures.

Millions of years of evolution and what do we have? Statistics.

Wanda stared at me and didn't sigh. "I'm worried about you, Jack," she said. "I'm frightened."

"Considering how dangerous everything is nothing is really very frightening," I replied quoting Gertrude Stein. Do you think Gertie would say the same thing if she could see the world today? Probably. After so much, there's no point in worrying any more.

She claimed her lawyer had sent me papers to sign and I hadn't returned them. I invited her to go through what was in three large pasteboard boxes by the front door.

"Jesus," she said, plowing through all the flyers, bulkrate mail, solicitations, bills, threats whatever the carrier left in the box. She found seven letters addressed to neighbors and one to another person several streets over.

"Close," I said, remembering the haggard looking postman and his bulging shoulder bag. I felt sorry for the guy, slogging his route day after day like Sisyphus to make sure everyone knew about the Publisher's Clearing House Sweepstakes. "We shouldn't expect too much."

Wanda shook her head and kept digging until she found the letter from her lawyer. She opened it and asked me if I would sign the form inside.

"Sure," I said.

Quite legibly but with a flourish at the end, I signed *Gerald Nixon Reagan.*

Wanda sighed.

So predictable.

The reason people love conformity is that everything is predictable, and as long as people act in a predictable fashion, we can delude ourselves into thinking that everything's under control.

But it's not.

"Aberrant behavior," the judge intoned, reading from a sheaf of papers, looking as though he took everything seriously, especially himself and aberrant behavior. Wanda had filed some real red-line papers, not just the fill-in-the-blanks form to unlock the fetters of marriage. In my best interests, she claimed, and that got my attention. When anybody does something in someone else's interest, that other person is likely to get pokered something fierce.

She was going to have me "put away" unless I could provide the court with satisfactory reasons for my nonconformity.

How could I explain anything to that judge, a red-faced man sitting at a desk elevated like a throne and wearing reading glasses with strings attached to the temples and looped around his neck so that he would never misplace them. A careful man, has never taken a chance in his life, keeps his money pinned to an inside pocket, votes straight Republican. Aberrant behavior? Well, I guess so.

He shuffled his papers. If it weren't for the invention or the microchip, I was thinking, the human race would sooner or later bury itself under paper, its own records. Praise be to silicon.

Holding up the document with *Gerald Nixon Reagan* on it, the judge asked me, "Why did you do this?"

"She asked me to sign it," I said.

The judge frowned. Somewhere behind me I heard Wanda sigh. She was in good form.

"What do you take seriously?" the judge asked.

That was a hard one. Anyway, what could I say that would make sense to a man wearing a dress?

Naturally I couldn't come up with anything and the judge acted in my best interests. Have you ever noticed that the State has no interest in you whatever unless you cause a problem? You could beg for help day and night, and get nothing but stony silence and indifference; however, if you fail to give up your money or in any way screw with the system, you're in trouble.

I was in trouble.

But I wasn't worried. Worry is for the accountant who has to get his numbers right. Worry is for the salesman (or traffic cop) who has to make his quota. Worry is for the bill-paying citizen whose life, like a highway paved with paper, is mortgaged to his grave. Figures. Worry and figures go together. Statistics. Ah, Wanda, no wonder you learned to sigh so expertly.

What could they do to me that would be worse than marriage, wage slavery, and generally living life between the lines and following the *arrows?* I couldn't think of anything. Can you?

After some cursory examination by psychiatrists, who asked their textbook questions in rote order, and another psuedosomber and mechanical hearing, I was committed to an institution and gotten out of the way. The *status quo* was safely *quo.* Hail Columbia.

What did you expect? That I'd be permitted to run loose, snubbing my nose at the culture and giving the finger to expectations? Not a chance. I had to be put where the rule followers couldn't see me. They might get ideas. So they threw me in the briar patch. And here I am, certified abnormal. Hah.

Some of the people who are "institutionalized" here, believe it or not, are well-adjusted. More than anything else, they enjoy putting the wig-warpers on, which shows that they love to act, they just don't like the scripts they were given. To be sure, we have some zombied-out shells, just as you have out there; only these no longer bother going through lock-step motions to please others.

I talk to a psychiatrist every week, sometimes twice a week if he needs it. Initially he played games with me, but I've cured him of such nonsense. The first time I went in, he sat and stared at me without saying anything. Shrinks go to school for twenty years and all learn the same thing. They think if they sit and stare silently at you so that you will get spooked and blurt out that you wanted to kill your father or something. Not me.

It was quiet and I enjoyed the rest. He didn't like that at all.

Now, he asks me questions and I tell him the truth. He is, of course, fascinated by my answers, thinks he's discovered a new kind of socio-psychoimbalance, one that perhaps will be named after him. He's writing an article and thinking about a book. His name is Scheicker and he calls my "problem" (which is really his problem) the Scheicker Shirker Syndrome. It's an awful misnomer, but he's so hungry for recognition that he can't bring himself to remove his own name from the label. Poor fellow, he has a lot of trouble getting his needs met.

At least he has forgotten about trying to "help" me, and I'm glad. He could be dangerous.

The wig-warpers know about various and sundry kinds of craziness, delusions, hallucinations, but they know nothing about sanity. Which means that I'll be a permanent resident. I'm secure. The shrink, however, could get fired.

It's safe here, much safer than living in any city could be. The vast majority of mental patients are not criminals and, as a matter of fact, have never harmed anyone unlike most politicians, say, or manufacturers, or just about any other group of people who in some way dominate others.

The inmates are rather pacifistic, not aggressive, and I like that. They lack power or they wouldn't be here in the first place, and now they are kept powerless. But it seems to me that, in a subtle but very real way, we have control. Like those who rule outside, we do nothing to keep all the machines going, whereas the people who watch over us have to run the treadmill. They *are* slaves.

Life is smooth now. I have nothing to worry about. Don't need a retirement plan, don't care about the stock market, don't worry about insurance, inflation, taxes, trade deficits, IRS-not even the FBI. And I never have to say "Have a nice day." Or hear it either, a blessing in itself.

Oh you may object, "What about the Bomb, Star Wars, thermonuclear devastation, the environment?" I, like you, have no control over the future of the planet, which is, as you know, dependant upon madmen. Worrying about the future could drive you crazy. Not worrying about it means you are crazy. It's your decision. Do as you please.

I'm content, the food here could be better (a little too starchy for my taste, so I exercise regularly to burn it off—mens sand in corpore sano, right?) but I can't complain. The orderlies have all kinds of dope—which they use a lot themselves—and for the most part we're living co-ed. I've got a girl friend who is like Samantha except that this one isn't going no settle down, and the TV is on cable. It still reminds me of taxidermy, but then so do most people, especially the ones who take care of us.

Oh well. Nothing's perfect.

Ben Satterfield has never served, done hard time, or been a deep-sea diver, but he still has devoted his life to making good dust jacket copy by working at a number of jobs that would disaffect anyone close to normal, whatever that might be. His fiction, poetry and articles have appeared in scores of magazines, and a novel, Junkman,*will be published in 1989.*

28

Ben Satterfield
The Naked Facts

In Rockbottom you can kill a man and get away with it, as many have done over the years, but you cannot buy a copy of *Playboy* magazine. Apparently, few things are more threatening than exposed flesh.

So it was no surprise that the townspeople were discountenanced, as some of the more articulate put it, by the nakedness of Calla May Winslow, whose exposed flesh could corrupt St. Peter himself, to hear them tell it. Malvin Goodroe, the undertaker, claims that he had just rolled Old Man Studstill into the front viewing room when she strolled by outside, and the Old Man, dead as a dartboard and with his veins full of methanol, groaned and nearly put a dent in the top of his casket. Other men merely told of ripping their pants or popping their zippers, and if you were to believe the stories that people told, Calla May had every cock on Main Street at rigid attention. Tenpenny swore on the Bible that the statue of General Jethro T. Harlan (C.S.A.) moved six inches when she passed by.

But nobody stopped her.

At least not right away.

It was the second Saturday in June, about two o'clock in the afternoon when Calla May, naked as the day she was born but looking a lot healthier, drove to the corner of Third and Main, parked her red

Mustang in front of the funeral parlor and walked the two blocks to the poolroom, attracting the undivided attention of every person in town with the least amount of eyesight. Old Blind George kept pounding his cane on the floor of the Dixie Grill and shouting, "Tell me again, tell me again!"

And the telephone began ringing in the office of the sheriff, Homer Barlow, a heavy-gutted easygoing man of fifty who was dozing in his cushioned chair behind a large oak desk whose edges were fluted with cigarette burns made by a dozen former sheriffs, dating back to 1896. The sheriff's office was in the front part of the county jail, downstairs, and was usually quiet this early on a Saturday afternoon. Homer had closed his eyes and laced his fingers over his large belly a half hour earlier, thinking of a rainbow trout, yellow perch, and suchlike. In his dream he had just hooked a largemouth bass and was reeling it in when he heard the telephone ring in the cabin nestled in the pine trees behind him. He continued reeling in until the noise roused him and he let the fish escape. The cabin in the pines disappeared too as he lurched for the phone.

The first call was from Agnes Stritchfield, cashier at the Paradise Theater (where only G and PG pictures were shown), always quickest to report any wrongdoing on Main Street. She screamed like a banshee and nearly addled the sheriff, who wasn't quite awake and was still thinking of fish. This uproar, he managed to discern, was occasioned by a naked woman *walking the street plain as sin and in broad daylight!* As soon as the sheriff put the telephone down, it rang again, allowing him no time to think. When Beulah House confirmed Agnes Stritchfield's hysterical complaint, the sheriff said he would "get right on it" — immediately regretting his choice of words. Before he got to the door, hat in hand, the telephone rang again. He picked it up and without identifying himself or his office said, "I'm on my way," broke the connection, then left the receiver off its hook. He opened the door to the jail behind his office and yelled down the solemn row of cells. "Hey, Rubbydub, you doing anything?"

A mild ironic voice answered from one of the barred rooms. "Nothing important—just *time*."

"How 'bout answering the phone for me while I'm out?"

"Shore." A lean angular septuagenarian of six feet threw open a cell door and shuffled toward the sheriff, grinning toothlessly. "Be a nice break in the routine."

The Naked Facts

Rubert Leggit Croft, known to everyone as Rubbydub, was serving a ten day sentence for public intoxication and disorderly conduct. He was often drunk, but seldom disorderly; harmless, but easily influenced. Some of the local pranksters had put him up to taking a leak on the mayor's new Cadillac just as the mayor and his missus came out of the Bar-B-Q House licking their chops and patting their tummies. The magistrate, a small portly man who took himself and his office with a seriousness bordering on the fanatical, was outraged and demanded that Rubbydub be arrested. Tenpenny was there, of course, he being one of the instigators, telling the mayor that Rubbydub thought he was a hound dog and was just being natural. Then some of the others tried to get the old man to howl, but he was too drunk to do more than groan and croak.

"We'll take him back to the kennel, mayor," Tenpenny said, but the mayor was too incensed for levity, although his wife cracked a horsey smile when Tenpenny told them Rub needed worming and a distemper shot. "His honor don't like jokes," she drawled.

Normally the sheriff would take the old man home and tell him to sleep it off, not giving a thought to arrest. In this case, however, he had no choice, because the mayor, irate as a harridan with boils — "He pissed on my car!" — insisted on pressing charges. The indictment itself posed a problem: nobody knew of a law that specifically prohibited peeing on automobiles, a discovery that irked the mayor, who seemed to think there was a law against showing disrespect for public officials. The closest thing the law had to offer was an injunction against urinating in public, one of the many indecorous breeches of custom under the broad category of Disorderly Conduct. Unmollified, the mayor—who favored public stocks—said he guessed that would have to do, after being persuaded to accept the fact that disrespect *per se* wasn't an amerciable offense and that Vandalism wasn't a valid charge because no actual damage had been done.

The mayor carped about the sentence too, claiming that ten days wasn't nearly enough.

"Just tell whoever calls that I've got it covered," the sheriff said.

Rubbydub nodded and perched on the edge of the chair behind the sheriff's desk. He put the receiver back on and watched the instrument as though it were magical, waiting for it to ring. He was as alert as a cat stalking a bird.

The sheriff strode to his car, shaking his head as he heard the jangle of the telephone behind him.

He remembered the Saturday afternoon Johnny Shine had gotten drunk, staggered out into the middle of Main Street, and started shooting at traffic lights and neon signs with an ivory-handled .38 revolver, causing all vehicles to stop and Minnie Waters to miss her period. Only two calls had come in then, one from Ida Slote at the Western Auto store and the other from Agnes Stritchfield, who was angry but far from hysterical as she crouched in the Paradise ticket cage, her Window on a World of Irritants. He wondered how Agnes kept her blood pressure down.

The sheriff got to the poolroom right behind Calla May. Her husband, Eban Winslow, spotted her at the door, threw down his cue and dashed out the back like a sprinter at the tri-county track meet.

"Eb!" Calla May called to his fleeing back, but it was no use. She might just as well have been trying to halt the flow of the river or the falling of rain.

All the others in the pool hall stopped dead still and gawked at the naked woman as if frozen in their tracks like rabbits in the glare of headlights.

"Calla May," the sheriff said, "what are you doing?"

She turned around and looked him straight in the eye, her arms akimbo. "I came to get my husband."

The sheriff frowned. "You ain't got no clothes on, Calla May."

The men at the tables sniggered and Tenpenny said, "Ol' Homer's got a sharp eye, ain't he?" and someone else said, "Cain't put *nothin'* past him," but the lawman ignored them.

"My idea was to shame him into coming home," Calla May said.

The sheriff shook his head and fought to keep his eyes from wandering. "I don't get it."

"I came to see what's so fascinating down here—and to let everybody see what he's got at home."

"And we sure appreciate *that!*" Tenpenny declared.

The sheriff took off his hat and scratched his head, his eyes falling, then closing quickly like a book slammed shut. When he opened them again, he gazed at the bridge of her nose, which he noticed had a few tiny freckles that were just lovely. "I don't understand."

"Ever since I was twelve years old," Calla May explained, "men been trying to get at me."

"I believe it."

The Naked Facts

"But my husband's *got* me and he don't even try."

This news seemed to pain the sheriff, and he expressed his wonderment with a deep sigh.

"And I'm in my prime. Wouldn't you say I'm in my prime, sheriff?"

"Oh yes," he moaned.

"Every night in the week he's too tired, says he works so hard. All he wants to do is watch TV and go to sleep. Sunday he claims is the day of rest, and so that only leaves Saturday. And what does he do on Saturday? Gets out of the house quick as he can and hangs around here all day. It's not right."

The sheriff put his hat back on. His face was red and he kept taking deep breaths and pulling at his collar as if he couldn't get enough air.

"All day he hangs around down here and leaves me home alone. Why does he do it? Why doesn't he stay home with me?"

"Lord help me," the sheriff said, "I don't know."

"Make him come home."

"I got no right," the sheriff said. "He's not breaking any law." He paused and took another deep breath. "But you are."

"You gonna arrest me?"

"Now, I don't wanta do that, but I can't let you go around town nekked."

"Then you gonna have to arrest me."

Tenpenny started tearing off his clothes. "Arrest me too, sheriff!" he yelled. "Lock us both up and throw away the key."

"Shut that up," the sheriff ordered, "right now," then looked back at Calla May, his face pleading for understanding. "See what a mess you're causing? Now, be reasonable."

She shook her head. "I ain't gonna be reasonable."

The sheriff looked stricken. He closed his eyes, then took out his bandana and wiped his forehead. "Calla May," he said forlornly.

"Nope."

He patted his forehead, tugged at his collar, and hitched up his belt. Then he put the bandana back in his hip pocket and yanked at his collar again. "Well," he said at last, "come on and get in the car."

"You taking me to jail?"

"Naw, I'm gonna take you home."

"I don't wanta go home till Eban goes with me."

"Maybe he's already gone home."

"Ha."

"Well, I'll go look for him then," the sheriff said. "But you gotta get out of public."

Calla May chewed on her bottom lip. "You'll make him come home?"

"I got to find him first."

"Okay, you can take me back to the funeral parlor."

As they left the poolroom, Tenpenny, who always has to have the last word, yelled, "Watch out your gun don't go off, sheriff!"

Homer put Calla May in the back seat of his car, then took off down the street in the opposite direction from the funeral home. He made a turn at the red light and drove to the jail. "I'll be right back," he told her, and pattered into his office. Rubbydub jumped up at once, like a jack-in-the-box, beaming at the sheriff. "Is it true?" he asked, his voice quavering. "They all said—"

"It's true," Homer replied, marching past him and into the supply closet. Half a minute later when he came out with a sheet for a single bed draped over his arm, the front door to his office was open and Rubbydub was gone. Homer started to yell for him, then changed his mind when he saw the old man bent over the rear window of the sheriff's car, staring at Calla May, who was smiling and saying something to him. With a trembling hand, Rubbydub opened the door—and she stepped out.

The sheriff chugged up to them. "You're not supposed to be out," he said, not sure which of the two he was addressing.

"Everybody else in town's seen it," Calla May said nonchalantly, striking a pose. "I'd hate to deprive Rubbydub."

The old man's mouth hung open and his eyes were big as plums. He was making a noise — "Huh, huh, huh" — as he breathed, and he was breathing faster by the moment.

The sheriff handed Calla May the sheet. "You put that over you," he told her, "'fore he has a stroke. I keep a blanket in the trunk but it's kinda rough—this'll be more comfortable."

"Why, thank you, sheriff," she said, wrapping the sheet around her and pulling it close. "That's very considerate."

Rubbydub looked as though he were going to cry. Homer put a gentle hand on his shoulder and guided him back toward the jail. "You take care of things while I'm gone."

"Huh, huh, huh," the old man wheezed, trudging back to the office like a condemned man approaching the gallows. When he reached the door, he turned and waved to Calla May. "Thank you, honey," he said. "You're a real sweet girl." Calla May was so moved that she opened the sheet wide and gave him a final treat before slithering into the back seat, saying to the sheriff that it was getting real easy, a statement he found less that comforting. The old man stood in the doorway, his mouth gaping, his head bobbing loosely, like a cork on the river.

The sheriff returned to the funeral home by going down Jefferson Davis Street and cutting back on Third, avoiding Main Street until the last. He parked beside Calla May's car and she got out of his vehicle and into hers. She wadded up the sheet and tossed it through his open window. "You bring him right home, you hear?"

The sheriff nodded. "And you go straight home, *you hear*?"

She smiled and started the engine.

For the next hour Homer drove up and down the streets of Rockbottom, looking for Eban. He didn't know what he was going to say if he found the man, for Calla May's behavior had been so embarrassing—no, it was worse than that, it was humiliating, and the sheriff wasn't one to add to another's misery if he could help it. But he had promised Calla May that he would look, and look he did.

She had married Eban Winslow about three years before. Eb was born and reared in Hampton, but he wanted to get away from there and the domineering influence of his father, who owned the Winslow Canning Company and one of the largest homes in the county. Success had not made Winslow *pere* an easy man to live with. He saw himself as having the mien of a nobleman and the wisdom of a sachem, neither of which was true. His wife and son saw him as a petty tyrant who would never understand why people didn't love him.

Eban got a job in Rockbottom as the manager of the combination machine shop and garage owned by "Tool" McKenzie, his second cousin, and had worked there successfully for three years. He was generally well-liked and especially admired by most of the men because he was married to Calla May. They would roll their eyes and grab their crotches, saying, "If I had that in my bed, I wouldn't *never* want to leave!"

But the sheriff thought that being married to Calla May must be a hell of a burden to Eb. He was beginning to feel burdened himself. Shortly after three o'clock he gave up his search and drove to Eban's house, a small bungalow set back from the street and canopied by huge pecan and pink-bloomed mimosa trees. Calla May's Mustang was in the driveway and he thanked his luck for that, at least.

After he knocked twice, Calla May opened the door and smiled shyly. Her face was flushed, her hair was rumpled like a bed sheet after a restless night, and the robe she had on was unbuttoned. "He's here, sheriff," she said, "and everything's fine."

"I'm glad to hear it," he answered. "Mighty glad."

"Sorry for your trouble." As though in a terrible hurry, she gave him a half smile and started closing the door, so the sheriff just nodded and touched the brim of his hat.

"And I thank you," she added, quickly shutting the door and scurrying back to the bedroom where the shades were pulled all the way down.

The sheriff drove around the outskirts of the city, trying to scour the image of Calla May's nakedness that was in his mind like a brand in cowhide. Failing, he drove home and wrapped his arms around his fat wife, who had just put a cake into the oven and was so surprised by his attention that she assumed he had been drinking and was afraid he'd lose his job. "Your color's up," she said, sniffing his breath suspiciously.

"I ain't been drinking," he told her. "And can't you get it through your head that I'm *elected*? Or that I just might be trying to show you some affection?" He stomped out of the house without saying another word to his bemused wife, a woman of sober habits who had made a routine for her life as fixed as the movement of the planets. She sat at the kitchen table and pondered her husband's words for several minutes, finally resolving that she would be real nice to Homer when he came back.

However, that was not the way things turned out.

Before returning to his office, Homer made two more stops: one was for the affection he had missed at home and the other was for a bottle of muscatel wine, which he would give to Rubbydub after supper to settle him down. At least on Saturday night the old man would have a little musky-doodle, if nothing else.

It was one of the quietest Saturday nights in history. The sheriff ended up breaking open a quart of whiskey, and he and Rubbydub, after a long but inconclusive discussion of the mystery of women, got knee-crawling drunk and spent the night in jail.

Nobody saw Calla May or Eban in Rockbottom again. Sunday they spent packing and Monday they moved into the Winslow house in Hampton, where they still live today. People say that Calla May so shamed Eban that he couldn't show his face in Rockbottom, that he just had to leave.

But all sorts of stories began popping up about Eban after that Saturday. Cecil Hardaway, a grinder in the machine shop, said he once caught Eban whacking off in the john, and was so flabbergasted by what he'd seen that he couldn't believe it, at least not until that Saturday afternoon. "Why in the world," Cecil wondered, sucking his breath in over clenched teeth and shaking his head in disbelief, "would a grown man beat his own meat when he had a bee-yo-tee-fool girl like Calla May?" It was more than he could comprehend.

Others began to speculate that Eban was "funny," that he didn't really like girls, which was why he had a job that surrounded him with men and why he chose to spend his leisure time in an all-male hangout like the poolroom. That story didn't have much currency, though, because the men who hung around the poolroom didn't like what it suggested, and the others simply could not believe that a man—any man—married to a sexy girl like Calla May could *prefer*—. No, it was unthinkable, a perversity beyond belief.

Tenpenny says that when Calla May got home, Eb was waiting for her. Enraged, he began slapping her around— "really whippin' her fine ass" —and in the process of venting his anger he discovered that he was excited in more than one way—and so was Calla May. "It was just a matter of establishing his dominance," Tenpenny explains like a professor of psychology, "which is what they both needed. So he threw her down on the living room floor and plowed into her with a plow hardened by powerful feelings he hadn't had in a long time. And from then on, it was 'Me Tarzan, you Jane' all the way."

Nobody ever asks Tenpenny how he knows these intimate details, but he swears they are the naked facts.

"You can drive to Hampton right now," Tenpenny assures the skeptical, "and you'll find Calla May with a big smile on her face and Eban rushing to get home from his day's work—" here he inserts a wink and a leer—"which he often cuts short."

Others say Calla May has taken to drink and letting herself go, so that you wouldn't recognize her now if she walked down the street in broad daylight clothed or naked.

But what happened to her and Eban after they left Rockbottom is another story.

That warm afternoon in June gave the people of Rockbottom more than a perennial topic of conversation. What nobody mentions is the fact that over three times as many babies as usual were delivered at the new city hospital the following March. Forty-two, the paper said, was a record for that or any month. Nineteen of those babies were female, and not one was named after Calla May.

And you still can't buy a copy of *Playboy*, even from under the counter.

Ben's novel, Junkman, *will be published in paperback by Avon Books this summer. It's a killer novel, so don't miss it. Should be in fine supermarkets everywhere. This story originally appeared in Volume Four, Number Four.*

29

Gary Smith
A Lady Not Quite of Quality

Elmira Wilkinson became a hooker when she was sixteen. Men had offered her money before; she'd started taking it was all. She claimed it was like crossing the state line: if you didn't see the sign that said WELCOME TO OUR STATE, you'd never know a boundary had been crossed. Of course, money hadn't been that important then. Sometimes she had spent the entire night with a man and never charged extra.

Now that she was older—fifty-six next month—things were different. Most of the men who picked her up were coarse and smelled of alcohol and cigarette smoke. She missed the sweet fragrance and smooth skin of her past customers. That's why the money had become important.

Elmira leaned closer to the mirror and stretched her mouth to paint on a set of lush red lips that extended beyond the line of her own thin ones. The radio blared on the dressing table beside her. She hummed along as Tammy Wynette sang, "Stand By Your Man." One more year, she thought, and I'll have saved enough to move to Australia.

Elmira knew all about Australia from the dog-eared copy of National Geographic that she kept on her bedside table. Australia was filled with young cowboys and handsome shepherds. The article said that men out-numbered women ten to one. They were bound to be lonesome with so few women around. She had heard somewhere that men in such predicaments did things with sheep. Well, she was better than a sheep any day! They'd want her even if she didn't still have her looks, which she did if you didn't look too close and the lights weren't too bright. She had long legs, too. Men liked women with long legs.

Elmira adjusted the light over the mirror. When she'd had those teeth pulled to save the expense of root canal, the dentist hadn't told her that her face would cave in when the gums shrank. She added more light-colored pancake to the little hollow under each cheekbone to compensate for the shadow, then leaned back to survey her face. Satisfied, she wiped the make-up off her fingers, adjusted her wig, and inhaled deeply. The new red lace brassiere she had on worked just as the saleslady said it would, holding her breasts high so they squeezed out of the low cut dress and lay against her chest like two quarter moons. Still humming, she switched off the radio, grabbed her purse, and headed for the streets. I'll make a mint, she thought.

That was the night she met Dennis: the night she first wore the red lace brassiere. It was an unusual evening, the first one of the year with no chill on the air. After a long winter, people were glad to be out again. A festive, almost carnival, atmosphere permeated the neighborhood. Laughter and loud music from inside the bars drifted through open doors onto the crowded sidewalk. Liquor flowed freely. Even the neon beer signs in tavern windows seemed to shine with a gaudier intensity, snapping and buzzing with an electricity not unlike that which filled the streets.

Elmira knew immediately that she'd made a mistake coming out so early. Expectations were running too high. Men who would have normally gone with her—their eyes darting about even as she stood before them—held out in anticipation of the night's vague promises. Elmira had been through other evenings like this. She knew that the only thing to do was bide her time. Walking over to the brick-paved mall that surrounded the old Lincoln courthouse, she sat on a stone bench to wait for what she called the Cinderella hour: the point that came about as the evening wore on, and the booze took effect, and people tired. Dreams turned to pumpkins then, and men were willing to take what they could get and call it a night. Around twelve-thirty, Elmira began to score.

Her last encounter was with two men who had circled the block several times before pulling over to the curb; and when they did, Elmira could hardly believe her luck. One was a good-looking Italian in his late twenties; the other a shy, blond boy of about eighteen. The older man made the arrangements. When they got to the hotel room, he insisted that the boy go first while he stood behind and watched. When he reached that point of excitement to where he was oblivious of all but the sensations, the man pressed himself against the boy's back and began caressing him. Elmira had thought it most peculiar.

As she headed home—down the silent, pre-dawn street—she wished she had a girlfriend that she could sit with over a cup of coffee in Jack Robinson's all night restaurant. She would tell her about the Italian man and the boy; and the friend, elbows on table, would listen eagerly. A nagging loneliness—the vague longing for one person instead of many—threatened to spoil the happy mood Elmira had been in. She tried to rid herself of the feeling by concentrating on the young boy she had just left .

She was almost home when she heard the moan from the alley that ran behind the delicatessen. She bent over awkwardly on her spike heels and peered into the semi-darkness. As her vision adjusted, she inched her way in, tripped over Dennis, and almost fell. He was sitting on the ground, dressed in women's clothes. He'd been beaten up, she found out later, by someone who thought he was a girl and had found out differently. If the wig hadn't been knocked off his head, Elmira wouldn't have known he was a man. He looked like a high fashion mannequin all set for a show window display except for the hair being added. When he refused to let Elmira call the police, she helped him to her apartment and tended his wounds herself.

"My mother will kill me," he moaned. "These are her furs...And now just look at them. Blood all over. It'll never come out."

Elmira, dodging his wild gestures, dabbed at the bruises and cuts with a damp cloth. "Honey, them furs are the least of your worries. You can fool some of the people some of the time, but there's some things you can't fool nobody about none of the time."

A half-sly, half-pleased look crossed Dennis' face. "I have before. Look." He pulled open his blouse to reveal two huge breasts. He smiled at Elmira's surprise. "They're real. Go ahead, feel them."

Astounded, Elmira reached over and gingerly squeezed a boob. "Well, if that don't beat all. They're bigger than mine."

"Thank you." Dennis buttoned his blouse. "It's the hormone shots, you know."

Elmira was totally confused. "What about the rest of you?"

The smile faded. "That part has to be done yet. I have to have an operation. That's why I got beat up tonight," he said angrily. "He was no gentleman, or he would never have found out. Usually I can keep them from going that far, or the ones I can't don't care by the time they get there."

Still shaking her head, Elmira went down the hall to put clean sheets on the bed in the spare room.

Two weeks passed and, during that time, nothing was said about Dennis leaving. When Elmira came home one day and found him unpacking boxes of his belongings, brought from his parents' house, she knew he was there to stay. He rearranged the furniture, painted the walls a baby blue, and hung brightly colored gold framed pictures. He washed windows, scrubbed floors, and sprayed for cockroaches. For dinner, he fixed tasty dishes with fancy French sauces; and at night, after they had both come home, they sat in the living room and sipped wines with names that Elmira couldn't pronounce.

Elmira had never lived in such luxury. The only problem was that all this cost her more than she meant to spend, even with Dennis helping on the expenses. It especially irritated her that he bought good liquor to serve to the men he brought to his room. Sometimes they drank so much that Elmira was sure what he made from the man wasn't enough to cover the cost of the alcohol. Dennis wouldn't admit that he was just as much a hooker as Elmira was. The men were "gentlemen callers," he said, and the money "a gift from my beaux."

"Honey, I don't mean to yell. It's just that I'm trying to save as much as I can for Australia," Elmira tried to explain. She showed him the article in the National Geographic. "Look at that. The plains are full of sagebrush and young men. You can drive for miles and miles and never see a woman. We'll be the only ones." Her eyes took on a faraway look and her voice grew low and dreamy. A smile played about the corners of her mouth. "Why, they have things there like you can't find nowhere else in the world: live teddy bears you can make pets of, and kangaroos with pockets in their bellies to carry their babies in, and whole tribes of little midget colored people—I forget what they call them—so cute you just want to run up and hug them."

"Those are aborigines," Dennis said, thumbing through the magazine, "and they're not midgets. You're thinking of the Pygmies in Africa. There's an article on them in here, too."

But that made no difference to Elmira. What bothered her was that Dennis refused to share the dream with her.

"Not until I get my operation," he said.

"But, honey, you'll never get it, spending money like you do."

"A lady of quality must maintain standards," Dennis said primly. "After all, we do have gentlemen callers coming here."

Elmira groaned. "Aw, honey, those're just *tricks*. Don'cha see, going with a guy is no different than having dinner. It can be real quick, just to hush the hunger pains, like grabbing a MacDonald's hamburger when you're too busy to do anything else. Or nice and slow, leisurely-like, simply because the food's good. And sometimes maybe even special, with someone you really like, in a nice romantic atmosphere. But you *gotta* learn which is which. You just don't bring out the wine and turn on the music and light the candles every time you have a Big Mac."

But it didn't do any good. Elmira had to admit, though, Dennis did have class. Why, just let a roach run across the floor! He acted like it was the end of the world. One day she had noticed him scratching and made him lie down on a sheet so she could search his skin with a pair of tweezers.

"Yep!" she cried triumphantly, holding one aloft. "It's crabs!"

Dennis began to tremble. Elmira had to slap his face to keep him from getting hysterical. She hurried into the bathroom and made him rub on the oily liquid she poured into his hand from a bottle of A-200 pesticide. After he had showered and dressed in clean clothes, Elmira reached over and squeezed his hand. "It's an occupational hazard, honey. Why sometimes I've had them for weeks before I found out."

The next morning, while Dennis did the laundry to keep from

getting reinfested, Elmira went to a drugstore to replenish her supply of pesticide. She waited patiently until several customers moved away from the counter, then asked the woman clerk for a bottle of A-200.

"Do we have any A-200?" the woman yelled to the druggist at the other end of the store.

The druggist, a little bald man, came running, his face red. "I'll take care of this," he told the woman quietly.

"And then he waited on me," Elmira told Dennis later, "just as if I were a respectable person."

It pleased Elmira to take care of things like this for Dennis. It made her feel needed. She'd never been needed by anyone before. She smiled to herself and tears filled her eyes. She know she could never go to Australia and leave Dennis behind. They had been together too long now, and she loved him too much. There was really only one thing to do: withdraw the money out of her savings account and give it to him for his operation.

"We'll just watch our budget," she said. "In a year or two, with both of us working—that is, with me working and tips from your gentlemen callers—we'll have enough saved again so we can both go to Australia."

Dennis was ecstatic. "Just imagine," he bawled, "I'll be a twenty-two year old virgin."

Elmira accompanied Dennis to Chicago, where the operation was performed, and stayed with him until he was well enough to come home. She insisted he stay in bed while she served his meals to him on a tray until, finally, he convinced her that the healing process required a certain amount of exercise. Even then, she followed him about, ready to clutch his arm should he start to fall. It was only after he had managed to sneak his first gentleman caller into the apartment and lose his new virginity that Elmira would believe he was well.

That's when the trouble began. Before the operation, when Dennis was Dennis and not Denise, Elmira had had the advantage. She was a real woman. But now Dennis—Denise—had the advantage, being a real woman and several years younger too. When they went out together, Denise seemed to be embarrassed by her. She constantly criticized Elmira for using too much make-up and wearing flashy clothes. Once, when they went to Jack Robinson's for a late night snack of onion rings, Elmira made a quick dash into an alley to relieve herself. Denise was offended.

"It's not very lady-like squatting there with your knees stuck up in the air like some—some cypress tree," she complained.

Nor did Denise save money as she'd promised. Elmira began to doubt that they'd ever get to Australia. And then something happened that made her forget all about Australia: she found a boyfriend.

One night a transient hotel down the block caught on fire and eleven people died. The police found the ledger, but the names in it were all aliases and families could not be notified. None of the bodies were claimed. After the fire, the city sent inspectors around to check the other buildings in the neighborhood, mostly old two-storied brick structures with laundries, porno bookstores, bars and pawn shops on the first floors and apartments on the top floors.

Elmira was alone when her inspector arrived: a young blond boy just out of college, smelling of soap and new clothes. He eyed Elmira appreciatively, and when she took him into her apartment to inspect it, it was a long time before he came out again.

His name was Rick, and he came back the next night and the night after that.

"I like older women," he told her.

Elmira was happier than she had ever been in her life. She stopped working the streets and got a job tending bar during the afternoon at one of the neighborhood taverns. Denise said very little when Elmira talked to her about Rick. Elmira thought it was because Denise didn't have a special beau of her own or because she was worried that Elmira might want to live with Rick. She assured Denise that there was no reason the three of them couldn't get along together. She started making a special effort to include her when Rick was around.

She and Rick had been going together for three months when Denise surprised them by fixing an anniversary dinner complete with cake and candles. After eating, the three of them moved to the living room. Wine flowed freely. Elmira grew sleepy. Rick and Denise were discussing politics. All Elmira knew about politics was that she had to be more careful about plainclothesmen before elections. She leaned back and smiled as she listened to the two of them. She dozed off, thinking how very happy she was.

When she awoke, the lights had been dimmed and she heard whispering behind her, near Denise's bedroom door. She closed her eyes and listened.

"Do you think we ought to right now?" Rick said. "What if she wakes up?"

"Oh, she won't. She's had a long day. She's older than you think. When she falls asleep, nothing can wake her. Sometimes she snores so loudly, I swear, the room trembles from the very vibrations."

Elmira swallowed several times to hold back the expensive wine that seeped sourly into her throat. Acrid tears burned her eyes as she leapt to her feet and turned to face them. She weaved unsteadily, trying to keep her balance. "I don't sleep so sound that I don't feel a knife when it's stuck in my back by my best friend," she bellowed between sobs.

Denise clasped her blouse where it had been unbuttoned to reveal her full breasts. Her face was white with fear.

Rick grinned foolishly. "Aw, hey, maybe I better go. Why don't we talk about this tomorrow when we're all cooled off a bit?"

Elmira ignored him. "If you want him so bad, take him," she screamed at Denise. "Take him and get out of my apartment."

"It's not what you think," Denise whispered, unable to look her in the eye. "It's not."

"Have you told him about your little secret?" Elmira asked quietly, her voice deadly.

Denise looked up, her eyes wide. "You said you'd never mention that. You promised you'd never tell."

"Then get out."

Their eyes held for a long moment. Finally, taking Rick's arm, Denise led him out of the apartment. "What secret?" Elmira heard him ask as she slammed the door after them and sank to the floor sobbing.

For the next few weeks, Elmira stayed inside. She had to force herself to eat and bathe. She didn't bother doing the dishes or putting on make-up. When she closed her eyes and tried to see Rick's face, nothing appeared. It was Denise she mourned. Rick didn't matter.

For a while, she listened to the footfalls in the hall, hoping that Denise would come back. Then she gave up listening. Her pain, like the deep ache of a festered tooth, blocked out all other thoughts. She moved listlessly about the apartment, pausing only to caress some object that had belonged to Denise: a ceramic bird found in the Goodwill Thrift Store, a sweater draped over the back of a kitchen chair, the hairbrush on the vanity. At night, she lay on Denise's bed and smelled the scent of her perfume in the pillows.

A month had gone by before the knock on the door came. Denise stood there, her head bowed. Elmira felt a brief surge of hope, followed by despair. Denise had probably come for her things, was all. She figured it was safe now.

"I'll make some coffee," Elmira said.

Denise stepped inside and closed the door behind her. She sat on the sofa and waited until Elmira carried the two mugs into the living room and placed them on the coffee table.

"The apartment is kinda messy," Elmira said. "The roaches came back after you left."

Denise sipped the coffee. Her hand trembled as she put the cup on the table. "He kicked me out the night after we left here," she said. "I was afraid to come back." She looked at Elmira pleadingly. "I guess you never know how much someone means to you until you betray them."

Elmira held her arms out and Denise went to her. They cried for a long time.

"I promise I'll never steal another beau from you ever again," Denise said when they finally separated and began drying their eyes.

Elmira got up and went into the bathroom for a wad of toilet paper. She blew her nose loudly. "We won't have to worry about stealing each other's beaux," she said happily, "We'll have so many we won't know what to do with them. You haven't forgotten about Australia, have you, honey?"

Gary Smith spends all his time away from an eight-hour-a-day office job almost exclusively at his typewriter.

30

Gary Smith
Fergus' Closet

Characters

Fergus	A sixty year old homosexual, part Negro. He is slightly effeminate and speaks with a hint of dialect. His clothes are drab: baggy pants and white shirt, wrinkled and rather faded looking.
Miss Leona	A very rich, very elegant, very blond, seventy-two year old virgin.
Jamie	Eleven years old, fair, large boned and clumsy. He is quite innocent and can be easily led.
Fete	Same age as Jamie, or maybe a little older, but smaller. He has dark hair and is very handsome. He tries to act tough, but is almost as innocent as Jamie.
Driver	A good looking dark haired man.

Setting

The play is set in Mr. Fergus' antique shop, which is also his home. It is a quaint, neat house in any small Midwestern town with painted clapboard, a green shingled roof, and gingerbread trim. This is only indicated since the walls, except for the side entrance on which hangs a handpainted shingle proclaiming FERGUS' CLOSET, is lifted to reveal a room. There is a round oak table and chairs, an overstuffed wingback chair, a smaller chair, and an assortment of tables and cupboards full of antiques in the room. A large Jesus picture hangs on the wall and a birdcage stands by a window. At the rear is a staircase. The space beneath the steps is enclosed to form a storage closet. In contrast to the sunny exterior, the room is dark and cavelike.

To the right of this is an outdoor setting with trees, grass, perhaps an indication of sheds. It is bright and airy, yet also a place where one would feel secluded and protected from the view of others. This area should have the feeling of fitting in with the house, almost as though it could be physically next to it, although in reality it may be a block or so away.

Scene One

Open with Fergus on his knees rummaging through the closet. He pulls out several items (an old feather boa, lace shawl, etc.) which have been concealing a medium sized cardboard box. He takes a stack of magazines from the box and stands up with some difficulty.

Fergus Jesus, I'm getting old. It gets harder all the time to get up off my knees.

He sits at the table, catches his breath, and begins to thumb through the magazines. They are male nude magazines. He holds one up sideways and peers at the centerfold.

Outside, Miss Leona, assisted by her driver, approaches the door, tries the handle, and knocks. Fergus panics and hurriedly begins to gather up the magazines.

Miss Leona It is Leona Summers, Mr. Fergus. Open the door.

Fergus relaxes, puts the magazines down on the table, and goes to open the door. The driver exits.

Fergus (Genuinely pleased) Why, Miss Leona. This is certainly a pleasure. Just last week I got in a walnut sideboard that I was sure you'd be interested in.

Miss Leona Mr. Fergus, when will you abandon the fiction that I come to look at antiques? (She hugs him.) Face the truth. I come here because your company is the only company in this town worth having.

Fergus One can never be too careful in a small town. You *are* a white lady and I *am* a black man.

Miss Leona I am a seventy-two year old virgin dying of cancer and you are a sixty year old homosexual — with a heart

	condition. Really, Mr. Fergus! Oh! I see why you had the door locked. (She picks up one of the magazines and looks admiringly at it.)
Fergus	Yes, if they ever found out about those, I'd be run out of town. (He begins to prepare the tea.)
Miss Leona	They certainly have no shame nowadays, do they? Look at that. Photographed right out on the beach.
Fergus	I always dreamed of sex in the open. By the sea, with waves eating the sand from beneath my body like little nibbling fish. Instead, I've had to settle for back alleys and dark rooms and magazines that come in the mail with brown paper wrapping around them.
Miss Leona	(Lays the magazine down and sits in the wingback chair.) Good. I see you're going to be talkative today. With my ever-failing health, I would have considered the trip a waste of energy were you not.
Fergus	Dear lady, you will outlive us all. (He hands her a cup of tea an sits down in a chair across from her.)
Miss Leona	I hope you never sell this chair.
Fergus	Why don't you buy it?
Miss Leona	Because then I couldn't sit here in such comfort and listen to your stories. (She sips the tea and nods her approval.)
Fergus	When you knocked I thought it might be one of the local boys.
Miss Leona	Have they been harassing you?
Fergus	No, no, no. I've seen a few of them cut through the yard from time to time. It's a shortcut they use. Still, there's always the possibility. I *worry*.
Miss Leona	You should shoo them away.
Fergus	I should drag them inside and (laughs)...no, not really.
Miss Leona	You are truly degenerate. That's why I love you so.
Fergus	Oh, I was *doomed* from the beginning! From the day I was born.
Miss Leona	In New Orleans, I know. Your grandmother, Black Bessie, delivered you in the little shack on Burgundy Street.
Fergus	Yes. She laid me in my dead mama's arms and leaned her tired old body against the window to catch whatever breeze was stirring. The scent of blood and bougain-

villea hung in the humid air. It was beginning to get light and only the morning star, next to the moon, remained in the sky. She named me Morning Star, said it aloud several times to test the sound of it, pronounced it "Moanin'" like the sounds of pain or sexual ecstasy. "Tha's what ah'll call you," she said, "Moanin' Star." When she died, they sent me to live with relatives in St. Louis who said it wasn't fittin' for a boy to be called Morning Star. They called me Fergus instead.

Miss Leona (After a long pause) I never tire of hearing that story. You *have* led a fascinating life: funny at times, sordid, often sad, and always, like blood, colorful.

Fergus Your own experiences haven't been exactly what I would call dull: born to riches, traveling about the world, China ... Africa ...

Miss Leona Yes, a missionary's daughter does get around. On Papa's fortune. Money wheedled out of the poor and ignorant. We all believed his lies—at least I did—until it was too late. We all believed, except for Papa himself. Maybe he did too, once, but he died in terror, not knowing if there was *really* any life after death, or maybe believing that there was and regretting the fact that he made life miserable for so many poor souls. I remember how he made the Africans cover their nakedness: the bare-breasted women in all their glory, the men so— viril — in their nudity. They looked clownlike in the clothes. One time I saw a young boy and girl, playing in the forest. They peeled off their clothes and threw them to the ground as they ran, laughing. I wished then I could shed my—primness—with such ease. They made love. I stood behind a baobab tree and watched. Their skin was like black silk. It was beautiful, like the earth, renewing itself. You'd have thought that somewhere during all that travel and all those years that I'd have found a man, for a night, even an hour. But I was afraid.

Fergus Well, Lord knows, I've had my share, when I was working the club in St. Louis. But those days are long past. I've been here for almost forty years now. Oh, I've had my visitors during that time: young men from the coal mines, married men who had fought with their wives. Sometimes I sit and think about them. Memories come back like the flash of lightning bugs' tails and then are gone—lost to the dark—as I will be too someday. But the flashes are nice: a smooth blond face—the work callused thumb that's so gentle—bellies rigid and warm and after a while a little moist and salty tasting. Yes, I've had my visitors. In those days, they climbed flagpoles and ate goldfish and came to visit me. (Light begins to fade until it is dark at the end of the scene.) I'd sell my soul to relive one of those days.

Miss Leona   Well, we won't be young again in this world. Maybe in the next one. We ought to go to Europe is what we ought to do. Just the two of us with the little time we have left. Get one of those handsome gondoliers to row us about. When I die, I would like to die in Venice.

Scene Two

Later, the same day. The light rises gradually on the outdoor set. Jamie and Fete run in, breathless, laughing. Fete pulls a pack of cigarettes out of his pocket, opens it, and lights one.

Fete   See, I told you it would be easy as pie.
Jamie   (Nervously) I never stole anything before. Are you sure she don't know who we are?
Fete   I told you, Old Lady Collins is blind as a bat. I've put one comic book inside another one and she just charges for one because she can't see how thick it is. Fete hands the cigarette to Jamie. Jamie takes a puff and coughs. Fete laughs benevolently.
Fete   Kid, you have to learn to do four things to be a man: smoke, drink, fight, and fuck. (He halfway shocks himself with his language.) That's what my dad says.
Jamie   Have you ever done it with a girl, Fete?
Fete   (Debating whether he should tell the truth or spin a wild tale.) Nah, but I will soon as I get the chance.
Jamie   I wonder what it feels like.
Fete   Good, I'll bet.
Jamie   Annabelle Avery wanted me to kiss her. Have you ever kissed a girl?

Fete	Sure.
Jamie	I never have. I wanted to kiss Annabelle, but I was afraid I'd do it wrong and she would laugh at me. She's kissed all kinds of boys.
Fete	Aw, that part's easy. All you do is put your lips together and stick your tongue in each other's mouth.
Jamie	Ugh, that sounds awful.
Fete	Well, you don't have to touch tongues. You can do it without that part.
Jamie	Will you show me how?
Fete	That's queer!
Jamie	No it's not, not if you just show me. You're the only one I can ask that won't laugh at me. If you show me how, I won't be afraid to kiss Annabelle.
Fete	Okay, but let's do it fast. (He leans over to Jamie and grabs his head in both hands.) Close your eyes.
Jamie	(Closes his eyes, then pulls away suddenly) Don't do the tongue part. (Closes his eyes again and puckers his lips)
Fete	No, just leave your mouth normal. (Kisses him quickly)
Jamie	You mean that's all? That wasn't much.
Fete	(Slightly offended) That's 'cause we're both guys, dummy. It's different when you kiss a girl. You can feel her tits against you and smell her perfume and everything.
Jamie	Annabelle doesn't have tits and she smells like milk.
Fete	You'd better not tell anybody we did that or they'll think we're like old Fergus that runs the antique shop.
Jamie	My parents said I shouldn't ever go around him.
Fete	(Confidentially) My big brother and his buddy went there. Long time ago. Before they went into the army. I heard them talking about it. (He leans over and whispers in Jamie's ear. As he does so, Jamie's face shows a mixture of shock and surprise.)
Jamie	Honest?
Fete	(Snickers) Yah! But don't ask me to show you how to do that.
Jamie	I'd be afraid to let somebody do that. I'd be afraid they'd bite it off.
Fete	They said it was good as a girl. Maybe better.

Jamie	Really?
Fete	Yah. (Cautiously) Why? Do you want to go there?
Jamie	Do you?
Fete	I asked you first.
Jamie	I will if you will.

The light fades.

Scene Three

Several minutes later. Fergus is at the table going through his magazines as the boys approach the door and ring the bell. He grabs the magazines, runs to the closet, and puts them back in the box. The boys ring a second time. Fergus unlocks the door and opens it.

Fergus   Come in. I'm open.

The boys enter and look about the shop. Fergus closes the door.

Fergus	For your mother?
Fete	Yah.
Fergus	I have a nice print here for only two dollars. Or maybe she'd like this carnival glass. It's five.
Fete	We'll just look.

The boys make an effort to browse.

Fergus   Take your time.

Jamie elbows Fete, motioning with his head and other gestures for him to ask Fergus. Fergus watches them, half amused, half suspicious, knowing they're building up their courage for something, but unsure of what.

Fete	My big brother was here before. Him and his friend. A long time ago.
Fergus	Oh.
Fete	Yeh, oh, they said you, oh...
Fergus	(He begins to realize what the boys are there for. He moves to the armchair and sits down.) They said I what?
Fete	They said you did some things to them. Some ... naked things.
Fergus	They told you this?
Fete	I heard them talking.
Jamie	(Helpfully) My parents said we shouldn't ever go around you 'cause you... did things.
Fete	Queer things.

Fergus beckons Fete to him. Fete stands before Fergus, blocking Fergus from the audience's view.

Fergus   Your brother. Did he say he had a good time?
Fete   (Weakly) Yah.
Fergus   That's what you and your friend are here for? To have a good time?

Fete nods his head up and down. Fergus loosens Fete's belt and pulls his trousers down. He is wearing loud baggy boxer underwear with some type of story book design. These also come down and Fete's backside is bared to the audience. Fergus moves suddenly then, grabs Fete, pulls him across his knees, and smacks his bare bottom.

Fergus   Here's a good time for you (smack), and one for your friend (smack), and one for your brother (smack)...

Fete pulls away, manages to yank up his trousers, and he and Jamie run out the door.

Fergus   (Yells from the door) And one for the whole damned town.
Fete   (From off stage) You son-of-a-bitch You'll be sorry!

Light fades as Fergus sits and takes a nitroglycerin.

Indistinct voices and rustlings can be heard outside the house.

Fergus   Miss Leona? Did you get the sheriff? Did he say how long it would take him to get here? (The headlights of a car shine through the window and sweep across the walls.) I don't know how many. A whole mob. Another car just pulled up. I'm not sure. Grown men, I think.
Voice   Come on out!
Fergus   They'll be breaking in if he doesn't get here soon.

There are sounds of glass breaking. A hand holding a flashlight appears through the window, shines the light around the room, and withdraws.

Voice   We know you're in there.
Fergus   No, I'm all right. Someone was shining a flashlight around the room. (A red light flashes outside.) He's here. I see the red light. (There is the sound of running feet, car doors slamming, and vehicles roaring off.) They're going now.
Sheriff   (Knocking at the door) Are you all right in there?

Fergus	(To the sheriff) Y-yes. Thank you. (To the phone.) You're sure he'll stay all night, in case they come back? Wait. Hold on. (He gets up, turns on a lamp, pours a drink, and tries to compose himself.) I'm back. No, they're all gone. It's over for now. How old is he? The sheriff. Oh, well, it doesn't matter. I don't guess I'd stand much chance, after this, of luring him inside anyway. (His attempt at humor fails and he stifles a sob.) No, no. I'm all right. I'm sorry I put you through this. I wasn't sure the sheriff would come if I called him myself. Go back to bed now and try to get some sleep. Europe? Are you serious? All right. Yes, I'll go. I don't have much choice now, do I? Of course, you'll have to promise not to die on me in Venice. Yes. Yes, tomorrow. (He hands up the phone and lights dim.)

Scene Five

The next day. Fergus stands in the room, packing a small valise. He is dressed in a suit. Several pieces of luggage are in the middle of the floor. Miss Leona sits in the wingback chair. She is wearing a travelling suit and a hat. The driver lounges against the entrance outside.

Fergus	All this time and I thought no one knew about me, but everyone did. You knew they knew.
Miss Leona	You were discreet, so they let you get away with it.
Fergus	If it had not been for those boys and their lies, I would have stayed here for the rest of my life.
Miss Leona	You still can. I've taken care of the parents and their friends. I'm not without *some* influence, you know. I threatened to sue them for all they had if they bothered you again. By the time you return from our trip, the whole affair will have been forgotten. Although I imagine that once you see Europe, you won't want to come back here.
Fergus	I would have died here, probably at this very table. It might have been weeks before someone found the body. The plants would have shriveled and turned brown from lack of water. The canary would have starved and fallen to the bottom of the cage.

Miss Leona   I've given my driver explicit instructions about the bird.
Fergus   They would have gone through the closet and found my magazines and the clothes I sometimes wore. They would have laughed and made jokes about me. Even — especially — the ones who visited me from time to time. (He goes to the closet and pulls out the old boa. He drapes it over his shoulders. Light dims except for the spot on Fergus.) I wore this at the club in St. Louis. (Bumps and grinds music starts up.)
Offstage voice: (Deep and thickly accented) God damn, don't that Moanin' Star look like the real things. (Whistles accompany the voice.)
Fergus   Thugs followed me one night. Called me names.
Offstage voices: Faggot! Nigger!
Fergus   They threw rocks through the window where I lived. One night they shot at me. (Sound of a gun being fired. Fergus jumps, startled. The spot goes off and light comes up.)
Miss Leona   I've taken care of everything. No one will bother you.
Fergus   They always bother. They never leave you alone. For a little while maybe, but eventually — they bother. I remember once, in St. Louis, there was a girl. Her name was Rosie. We were totally opposite in personality, and perhaps these friendships are the best, for there is so much more to give and receive. But people would not allow a good thing to develop unmolested. Women smiled and hinted knowingly of romance; men expressed approval through the most crude jokes and slapped me heartily on the back; all agreed that I was finally becoming a man. This sudden acceptance surprised, then pleased me, for I had never belonged before, you see. I began looking at our relationship in a new light and one evening — well, one evening I tried to kiss her. She never forgave me, and left soon afterwards to join the WACS. But that was — many years ago...
Miss Leona   (Stifling a sob) We'll see Rome, Paris, Venice. I want to die in Venice.
Fergus   I let them scare me away from the life that was right for me. I came here and hid in my closet. They found me anyway.

Miss Leona It *wasn't* your fault.
Fergus I was afraid. They brainwash us from the time we're children with fairy tales and boogeyman stories: stay on the walk, don't stray from the path. I saw the flowers and wanted to smell them. I wanted to pull off my shoes and run in the grass. But I was afraid I'd cut my feet on broken glass. I was afraid the wolf would get me. So I hide in my closet.

Miss Leona has leaned forward during this speech, one arm holding her stomach, the other gripping the arm of the chair.

Fergus (Alarmed, hastens to her) Are you all right?
Miss Leona Yes, it's the excitement of the trip. Oh, I wish we'd gone years ago. I don't know why I didn't think of it before. It's the excitement. Feel my heart. (She places Fergus' hand on her breast.) It's like a bird. Fluttering. Oh, yes. Yes, that's better now. (She holds Fergus' hand to her breast for a long while.) Yes. I'm fine now.

Fergus helps her to her feet and out the door where the driver takes her arm. Fergus returns for the suitcases. The light begins to fade. He pauses at the door and looks about the room.

A chorus of offstage voices: (God damned queers.) (Come to yo' ole granny, Moaning' Star. Give yo' ole granny a kiss.) (Man, ain't that Moanin' Star som'pin. Who-whee!)

Fergus goes out and closes the door. He puts a CLOSED sign across the shingle and exits with Miss Leona and the driver. The light fades except for a spot on the sign.

Gory Smith is an Illinois writer whose story 'Consuelo and the Red Dress' appeared in the last issue of SOTT. For his bio "I've been sitting at this typewriter for damned near an hour trying to think of something interesting to say for my bio. If I persist, I'm afraid its going to take longer to do a half page bio than it did to do the entire one act play. So I'll just say thanks for publishing this play, and, thereby, opening the door to Fergus' closet."

31

Willie Smith
The Wild West

Joey and me were watching the Lone Ranger on tv. Joey sat playing with himself. "Better stop that," I kept saying. "You'll go blind."

The Lone Ranger was one of our favorites. He was romantic as hell. He wore tight white shirts, gloves and pants. His boots were shiny, creaky and jangly with spurs. He was handsome, well-proportioned.

He wore a kind of black nylon stocking across his eyes. That really icinged the cake.

But he had one defect — he never killed anybody. Oh, now and then he'd shoot a bandit in the hand; maybe once or twice in the ass or foot. Never anything serious. And these guys were *gunning* for him. In fact, sometimes it seemed well over half the town, desert mountain states were dedicated to the elimination by violence of the Lone Ranger. This left me in the cold, when it came to identifying with his lack of passion.

On the other hand, Peter Gunn had no qualms about death. He'd plug guys in the gut, blow their eyes out. Pop 'em in the heart so they'd pop off right in your face; ice 'em in the street; stop 'em dead in a crowded bar.

He didn't strap any sexy underwear over his eyes; wore a

business suit and looked like a man selling real estate; but the girls he knew more than compensated for that. They dressed in nylons and heels and were all built like birthday cakes. I wanted to blow on 'em till their candles went out, then lick the icing, slice 'em up and dig in.

Once I had even seen him shoot a girl. It was in her bedroom and she had it coming. Because she'd poisoned his whisky and was waiting for him to drink it and drop dead. So she could escape The Law.

I wasn't supposed to watch Peter Gunn. He came on late, and was bad and dirty. But I saw ten minutes here, two minutes there, and pieced together enough to know that even though he wore a suit and tie like that big dip Daddy he was more my kind of guy.

Especially when it came to killing. The Ranger kind of resembled Jesus, Santa Claus and the Easter Bunny — I couldn't get a grip on him. He was just a little too much of an insubstantial fairy.

I sighed, wishing it was late at night and not early afternoon. Then we could sit up and watch Dragnet, maybe get a minute or two of Peter Gunn. The screen eased back into focus. "Don't do that, Joey," I muttered. "You'll go blind."

The Lone Ranger and Tonto sank to their haunches to investigate a trail outlaws had left. Tonto was a stupid Indian who probably had bad breath and tarred a lot. He never said anything. But he spotted clues the Ranger was quick to pick up on. This was why they kept him around, despite his lousy acting.

The Ranger removed his glove and outlined a hoofprint.

"Yes, Tonto," he said, tight-lipped, from under his black stocking. "They passed here less than an hour ago. Chances are, we'll find them camped at the end of that box canyon up ahead."

Suddenly, gasping for breath, Panty burst into the room. He fell on the rug beside the tv and writhed like a razored worm. His face went purple. His eyes bulged. He tried to tell us something.

"Okay, Panty," I looked back at the screen. "What's wrong now?"

"I... I... I..."

"Spit it out, c'mon! Joe and me are keeping an eye on things and might have to shoot a thief or an Indian *any minute*. What is it — did you swallow a piece of hard candy and catch it in your throat? Vision go black and syrupy like you're gonna die? C'mon cough it up!"

"You're right, Tonto! " the Ranger snapped his fingers. "They'll post a lookout. They saw our dust—I'm sure of it."

Black nyloned eyes filled the screen. Joey played with himself furiously. Then a closeup of the Ranger's hand as he snuggled it back into his white glove.

Next: outlaws thundering into the box canyon.

Suddenly I knew what it was.

"*Joey!*" I broke out: "Stop playing with yourself—it's making Panty choke... cut it out... he might upchuck!"

I floated up into the air, the better to comprehend the situation. Joey, eyes stuck to the tube, persisted in whacking his dummy. Couldn't blame him. Staring at the Wild West two feet before your nose works up *energy*. And the only logical outlet for that, since Joey didn't smoke or drink, was...

"Make him stop!" Panty finally got out. "I'm gonna explode. I can feel my heart bombing inside my head and also my *penis!*" He grabbed his shorts compulsively, as if protecting a baby squirrel. He doubled over, gnashed his teeth and fell to kicking and squirming.

The Ranger loaded up with silver bullets, mounted his horse, reared in front of the sky... and flashed into a commercial.

I zoomed off the ceiling into myself and groped for a gun. Whatever it was they were selling, I wanted it shot...

Cheerios. Already had holes in 'em. Okay, I'd get the little kid. Next time he came back on, grinning over his cereal...

Cocked. Aimed. Waited. Cocked again... re-cocked

Cheerios kept falling. Billions of 'em. Hole after hole after hole — tumbling across the tube like bluegray froth. Invisible children sang a jingle about good health and happiness... could wait no longer... opened up, firing repeatedly, fanning the hammer fast as mom chopping carrots... heaven? Were all three of us now united on the Roof of the Sky?

I glanced over at Panty. He was sitting up with a smile, calmly taking his hands off his shorts.

Still staring at the Cheerios, Joey cleared his throat; buttoned his fly. He wasn't smiling. But, unlike usual, he didn't look constipated. He put his hands on the floor behind him and leaned back, eyes half closed the way a cowboy daydreams around a campfire.

The kid came on. I was out of ammo. His perfect teeth gleamed above a bowl of cold milk heaped with Cheerios. I hated cereal. No, we were still on earth, home, in the living room.

A bandit on the edge of a cliff was about to shoot a rifle into the air. Tonto grabbed him by the neck before he could.

"Good work," the Ranger walked up. Then drew his gun and glared puritanically down into the box canyon. "Now we can round up the rest."

"Good," sighed Panty. "I'm ready to rest, too." And he curled up on the rug beside the TV.

Decided to take a nap.

Mom looked in and startled me: "What's going on in here?"

"Huh?" I jerked awake. "Oh... nothing."

"But I heard voices—like you were talking to somebody."

"Oh," I said, as the Lone Ranger trotted onto a hill and hi-ho-silvered away, "it's okay. I was just *playing* with myself."

The William Tell Overture erupted, horning into a frenzy, but was cut short by a commercial.

Willie Smith, a Seattle writer, has this to say about that. "Shit, man, I already sent you a bio, when you accepted that story about the kid who sucks his Dad's cock, whatever that piece of trash is called you still gonna publish it? I wouldn't blame you for one morning deciding to wipe your ass with it and flush the evidence down the crapper. However, here's my latest bio: 'Willie Smith is just another quiet guy with a big dick.'"

32

Willie Smith
Essay on the Vacuum

You remember the Electrolux of the Fifties. Gray. Red 'n silver logo. Built like a mortar parallel to the floor. Steel runners. Elephant trunk hose.

Attachments for: under the couch; behind the china closet; top of the cocktail table; the carpet; the ceiling.

If you pulled the cord, like you wanted to tell a cat you loved its ass, and not really wanted to torture it, the card snapped back inside the machine. It was a good feeling. Tugging that cord several times a day almost equal one orgasm.

The bag was the bomb — the shitcan, the graveyard, the entropy where everything wound up.

I hated changing the bag. Groping to release the two-foot rubbery tube crammed with debris. Trotting it out back. Kicking open the ashcan. Twisting the lid off the bag. Cascading filth, hair feather, lint, grit, sand, soot, scunge into the galvanized can I always seemed to miss with half the load.

Dusting off my shoes, coughing, sniffling, clearing my throat, eyes stung, I'd make my way inside with the reuseable bag. Stuff it back inside the vacuum.

Otherwise, we got along fine. Like a good wife, Lux kept the joint clean. Stayed out of sight. Didn't mind if I drank. Many is the time she sucked up a shattered beer bottle. Never said a word; just the tinkling her hose made, while rocketing shards into her gorge.

I loved her noises. They disguised my wails. When I clean house, I adlib dirty jingles. The lyrics never get far, the tunes clichés. It's not something I think about. Keeps my mind off the work. And Lux's motor whine, her vacuum whoosh and her hissing-sucking-farting conveniently drowned out my vocalizations. I felt at ease, unable to hear my own bawdries, knowing no one else could.

Then came that afternoon, harvesting dust bunnies behind the furniture, when my relationship with Lux inexorably changed.

I was on my knees, angling the bristly attachment between the wall and the couch. I hadn't cleaned there in months. A lot of spiders had set up residence, profiting by the neglect.

Then to better twist the bristles after an especially obese arachnid, I sprawled across the machine, pressing my crotch against the carrying strap that fell into a slot on the body of the machine. Say what you want about Lux, she was streamlined.

One thing led to another. I got excited; disgusting.

Dreamily I drew the hose from behind the couch. Ripped off the attachment. Found myself contemplating sodomy.

Freed of the attachment's resistance, the motor accelerated. Higher and higher she sucked, like an angel needing it bad.

Before I knew what was what, I unzipped. This was an experiment. A scientific adventure. Christ—you blew up in front of your class! Like a fool. Burned in your own fuel. But here I stood, fist around yang, ready to strike a blow for peace between man and machine.

I shoved it in.

Lux make squeaky french noises. Inside the metal sleeve at the end of her hose, my tool swelled. I rocked, bumped, ground, boogied. She sucked and farted, jittering my shaft.

I saw every woman I had ever known. The *Bible* slapped me in the face. I knew it was wrong. But it was fun. And who gave a fuck? I was getting it on!

That was our first session. Month after month it went on like that. I started vacuuming twice daily. The apartment stayed clean as a whistle. The lest mote of dust drifting onto the carpet became a signal to haul out the machine. Stretch the cord. Plug her in. Make a quick foray without any attachment whatsoever. Then fall on Lux with desperation born of passion abused.

Essay on the Vacuum

But one morning, my perversion betrayed me.

I had breakfast. Brushed my teeth. Brought Lux out. Whisked a nit off the bookcase. Got engorged with the usual suction. But decided —maybe it was too much coffee, or bad dreams the night before—I had to have more.

Detached the hose. Screwed it in her back. Where exhaust bled around the rear of her bag.

Cranked the motor. Inserted her hose anally. And into my rectum vomited eight months of dust. Thought I'd only get air. In the frenzy of my desire, I'd forgotten physics.

I was sick for a week. Crapping ash. Tasting death.

As soon as I could stand, I broke into the closet. Yanked out Lux. Bundled her into the ashcan.

Last I ever saw of that sucker. I got better. But, well, you know, I never had better.

Willie Smith is a struggling Seattle writer who has been called a "modern day Bukowski'." Others have asked whether we need another. This is Willie's third contribution to SOTT over the last three issues.

33

Dale L. Sproule
On the Punko Beat, Beat, Beat

This whole horror show started a week ago, Tuesday. I was bopping down Davies Street to the beat of The Brash's anti-anthem "Pillory the Power Mongers." Then, in a series of events about as likely as Ronnie Raygun copping to a charge of male pattern baldness (complete with cover-up), I was strong-armed by a pair of goons in blue and given a free ride to the local Waldorf Alcatraz.

Joey Snotface was dead.

They needed a goat. And since Joey had been plugged into one of my headphone/hairdriers at the moment he'd shuffled off to the House of Blue Lips, they fingered Yours Truly as *the* major suspect.

"Electrocution," they called it. "Criminal negligence. Unsafe product...probably custom-rigged."

"Finding a patsy," I called it. And I should know. I was in the dick schtick for three years before throwing off the mantle of capitalist totalitarianism and going underground.

Joey'd run a store called Dead Fly Video. Off the cuff? Yes. Sick? Perhaps—but that corporate moniker wasn't as dumb as it sounded. In 18 months, Dead Fly had gone Number 1 with a bullet in the city and had started picking up partners for the National Franchise Tango. Going great guns...until that recent wet December night, when J.S. was 'electrocuted' while watching the *Crude Boys* video on the Fly's

giant screen—with the audio apparently jacked through one of my Stereo-Blowers.
 CHAPTER TWO—The Inquisition. I was David Jannsen in *The Fugitive*. "Look for a one-armed man," I told them.
 "Huh?" They replied.
 "I'm innocent, you dips! These hairdriers I invented work on C cell batteries...not enough juice to kill a fly."
 They even missed my clever play on words. "Have your lab boys check it out," I demanded.
 They looked at each other—Herod and Pilate. Then they turned back to me, pockets bulging with nails.
 Obviously, I couldn't sit there on my rattailed comb and wait for these Bozos to clear me. When I was finally released on my own recognizance, I swung straight downtown and hung a 'closed' shingle on the door of *Waves & Shaves*—that's the name of my salon—then I went home and dug the old private eye license out of a drawer. Like it or not, CherryJack was back on the track.
 CherryJack—that's me. The name on the license is John Walker, but I picked up the nom de plume while beating the skins for a nouveau combo fondly dubbed The Radiation Blisters.
 This was my kind of case (except that my own neck was on the line)—just enough unexplained clues to give me a head start on the badges. Like the video cassette, reduced to a pile of plastic fragments on the floor. Either the homicide boys know something I don't about the kinky things people do in the throes of electrocution—or some foot *other* than Joey's did the Demolition Stomp on the video tape. And WHO but someone with heavy duty hate-on for the new wave culture would destroy a pricey tape any self-respecting punker would've stolen? Besides, the cash float wasn't touched, nor were the assorted other goodies they found around the store: a kilo of pot, packet of coke (half a gram and change), page and a half of blotter acid, chunk of hash, cookie jar full of mixed delights (mostly reds and 'ludes), plus a tank of laughing gas and a big bag of Ritz crackers they found beside the body. It looked like the murderer I was after was someone straighter then Hitler's hair.
 But I couldn't go back to the cop shop armed with mere suspicions, no matter how valid. I needed the Bad Guy(s) himself, hopefully complete with written confession. Even then, they'd probably think I'd conned a phony plea out of some junkie, because as soon as

they see my startling pink mohawk and the earring though my nostril, their red complexions start creeping out from under their collars to discolor various other parts of their anatomies and they become blind to life's subtleties. Little things like deductive reasoning and common sense.

So I was in 7th Heaven when I discovered Joey had a girlfriend. This might be the ally I needed. PUNKS-1...AUTHORITIES-ZIP.

She lived in a small stucco block with no lights in the corridor. After 20 minutes in the hall, I decided that one of the two apartments numbered "6" had to be a "9" with the top nail missing. But the door between apartments "8" and "10" was rattling on its hinges under the assault of a ponderous bass beat that was no more Romeo Void or the Sex Pistols than it was Perry Como of Doris Day. It sounded like...NAH! Joey was a punker. Why would he live with some burnt out babe from the age of Dinosaur rock? But it sure sounded like Motorhead or Deep Purple or some other head-banging darling of the Hell's Angels and the manual laborers of the world. There was only one way to find out.

I knocked. LOUDLY. After a while, the volume subsided and the door swung slowly open.

"What is it man?"

I couldn't believe it. She was wearing a poncho! I hadn't even seen one since high school. Her black hair hung down in a limp imitation of a string mop and her bloodshot eyes squinted out through the tangle.

"You Yvonne Simpson??"

"If you're delivering another token handful of plastic flowers, take'em down to the morgue. I'm not into funerals." She began to close the door.

"Wait!" I implored, "I have to talk to you."

With a shrug, she motioned me inside. Her living room was littered with floor cushions and bedecked in black light posters. I began to reconsider my need for an ally. I was dangerously close to losing my lunch.

My nerves must have been on edge, because the explanation came out in a torrent. I told her that getting a fatal zap from one of my hairdriers was about as likely as getting fried by a transistor radio and that the cops were going to nail me for it anyways and how I used to be a private detective but became disillusioned and lastly why I was sure Joey had been murdered.

"Wanna blow a doob?" She proposed, extracting a marijuana cigarette from the fringed rawhide bag concealed beneath her poncho.

"I wanted to make sure you understood about the hairdrier."

"I knew the pigs were full of it when they told me how he died," she said as she inserted the entire joint into her mouth, pursed her lips and pushed it slowly back out—like sucking spaghetti backwards. Shrugging, she passed me the joint, its still flaming tip glowing white under the black light, and wheezed, "So whatcha gonna do about it?"

I interrupted my toke, "Find the killer. But I need your help."

She got up and put a record on the turntable. "Ozzy Osbourne." She shouted over the din of an extended primal scream entitled *Howl at the Moon*. Howling along with the chorus, she flopped down on the pillow beside me, leaned over till our faces were only inches apart and brushed her hair out of her face. "What exactly can I do for you?"

The hot smoke burst from my lungs as I coughed at her full in the face. I glanced down in embarrassment and discovered that despite her weirdness, she had a great set of melons. I stuttered, "I n-n-need to put together a list of all Joey's uncool contacts. You know...creditors, competitors, relatives, customers...even friends."

"Is that...all?" She breathed, almost inaudibly

I nodded.

"Yeah, okay man," she said, turning and leaning back against the wall. "I can get that together. By the way, your mascara's smearing."

When I got back from the bathroom, she was sitting at the kitchen table, already working on the list. I stood beside her chair, watching silently. When she finally passed it up to me, I didn't know how to respond to the expectant look in her eyes, but she quickly solved it for me. Quite matter-of-factly, she said, "I haven't been laid in a week."

As I worked out of her place over the next few days, the motivating forces behind the strange union of Joey and Yvonne became quite clear to me.

CHAPTER 3—The List. There must have been 100 names! I mean, she even included Joey's dentist! I'm all for turning over stones, but this was one daunting sucker of a list. Yvonne helped me boil it down to a short list; then I got started.

CHAPTER 4—The Search. Joey and his 250 pound shipper-receiver had locked horns in a violent argument only days before the murder. His name was Bert, the type who always seems to have a tool in his hands. Hammer, pipe wrench, screwdriver. He told me he'd been a professional wrestler, a butcher and a truck driver before settling down to work for Joey. I steered the conversation back to the night of the murder. Bert got touchy, evasive and turned redder than a traffic light and I thought I was onto something. But it turned that Bert had been dancing that night at a club called "Poof's." Who would've guessed he was the type to dress up like Ziggy Stardust and hang around in gay bars? He didn't have the figure for it. But his alibi checked out.

As soon as Joey's mother opened the door to her little brown-shingle bungalow, I guessed that there had been no love lost between her and her son.

"You Mrs. Snotface?" I confirmed.

I thought she was gonna slug me. "Snoteyvko," she said coldly. "You gotta be one of Joey's friends."

She hesitantly let me in and was soon reminiscing fondly about Joey's childhood. When she reached the teens, her smile disappeared. "Had I known he'd grow up into a green haired pervert, he'd a never seen the light of day." The anger seemed to flare from her eyes until all that was left were the ashes of sadness and she looked at me and asked, "When was the last time you visited your mother?"

Her camouflage fell away like leaves in a rainstorm. There was love concealed under the cover of sniper fire. This hardbitten trooper was revealed as still just a mother in search of her lost child.

"My mother's dead," I said.

Her head snapped back like she'd been shot in the forehead. "No wonder she's dead...seeing you like that, she musta had a heart attack!" Pausing, she eyed her own reflection in the oven door. "Get outta here. You remind me too much." Heaving her tiny boxlike figure out of the wooden chair, she beelined for the living room and I backed discreetly out the screen door, careful not to slam it behind me.

Next was Joey's biggest competitor in the vid-biz, a smalltime sleazeball named Branca who owned a chain called Triple XXX Video. But I didn't make it halfway up the back stairs to Branca's office before being bounced back down by two of the toughest hoods who ever hefted an Uzi. Little did they know how co-operative they were being—who needed Branca, when these guys answered all my questions? Electrocution was wayyy too subtle for these boys. After a run-in with them, the cops would still be scraping Joey's body parts off whatever walls were left standing.

I propped myself against the bottom step and fidgeted with my busted Walkman headphones while considering my next move. Then I moved my right leg, gasped from the pain, and spent five minutes pondering the maneuver to follow. It took me an hour to reach a standing position and another 20 minutes to reach the bus stop. The bus driver took one look at me, with my pink mohawk and the blood covering the front of my snazzy mauve check sports jacket, and kept going. With sudden total recall, I remembered all my non-political reasons for getting out of the private eye racket.

I found a booth, made a phone call and an hour later, Yvonne arrived to pick me up. I hadn't given her any details of my situation—like the broken tailbone I strongly suspected—because at the time, I didn't know she drove a Harley Chopper. This was not my day.

Despite her offer to droop me over the seat, cowboy style, I insisted on making other arrangements. After lending me ten bucks, *she* insisted on wiping the blood off my face while we waited for the cab. The rag was so oily that I'm sure the cabbie thought she'd run over my face.

Once back at Yvonne's apartment, I laid my stiffening body on the couch and mumbled something about the onset of rigor mortis.

Smiling, she said, "I have just the thing," and flitted out of the room. I laid there listening to the distant breathing—plus a sound like a corpse being dragged across the carpet. Yvonne was lugging a large metal tank into the living room. At the end of the hose trailing from the tank was a war surplus gas mask.

"I don't think mercy killing is called for quite yet," I whispered. Even my voice hurt.

Yvonne giggled.

"Hey! My pain isn't all that funny."

The laughter continued till she ran out of breath. Then she tapped her fingers on the side of the tank. "Laughing gas," she managed to spit out before crumbling under another outbreak of hilarity.

Something clicked deep inside my pain-shrouded mind, just as she passed me the mask.

It was like the deep breath I sucked in contained the very insight I was looking for. A second stray thought flashed through my mind in the same instant. I hadn't fed my dog in three days. I found this so hilarious, I almost forgot about the first thing.

"Nitrous oxide? Didn't Joey have this tank in the shop the night he died?"

"That was a different tank," Yvonne laughed.

"Do you grow them, or what?"

She shrugged. "There's two more under the sink."

It was all coming clear. Unfortunately, I chose that moment to pass out.

The dentist, Dr. Winfield, had been crossed off Yvonne's list. As soon as I was able to get up off the couch I decided to pay him a visit. His house was up in the Properties. It took me three busses to get there.

Mrs. Winfield's flaring nostrils reminded me of the business end of a double barreled shotgun. Aiming down the full length of that hooter, the old girl let loose with a snort which miraculously stopped short of dislodging her delicate, gold-rimmed bifocals. "Preposterous! My Harvey is a respected dental surgeon. Not likely to associate with human trash of your ilk, let alone be involved in a murder! I suggest you return to searching the sewers from which you so obviously sprung!"

Calling on my latent suburban guerilla reflexes, I executed an admittedly salesmanlike gesture. Stuck my foot in the door. But my inexperience showed. I was unprepared for the umbrella handle which descended with shattering impact on my right shin. As I struggled to free my genuine, early '60s, patent leather, pointy-toed shoes from the vise grip of the door, I came to a terrible realization. She'd scuffed them! Mint condition pre-Beatles relics, and this bourgeois old bat had scuffed them! My blade chunked deeply into the doorframe. Her terrified scream, which accompanied my instant freedom, demonstrated a prime tenet of the new wave culture: SHOCK WORKS. Reaching into my encyclopaedic memory of upper-middle class mannerisms, I anticipated her phone call to the cops and ran like hell back to the bus stop.

Another tack was evidently called for. If I could trace the tank of nitrous oxide from the supplier, I should at least be able to confirm the connection between Joey and the dentist.

I searched the thin metal tank for a lot number, thinking I might be able to prove that this one came directly from Winfield's inventory.

Came up blank on the lot number, but hit a BINGO on my phone call to the supplier. Bravo Laboratories like to brag about their extensive client list. Turned out that Winfield was a 50 tank a week man—more of the stuff in a week than most clinics used in a month.

All I had to do was confront him with a bit more evidence than I actually had, and hope to force his hand. And since I didn't dare risk another run-in with his wife, I decided to catch him at work. The best way to see a dentist is to make an appointment. My recently rearranged dental work (courtesy of the Triple XXX Orthodontics Team) was the perfect excuse. The receptionist informed me I was in luck. The doctor could see me at 3:45...just over an hour. With a busy schedule like that, it was no wonder Winfield had to resort to selling drugs to support himself. I'd talked Yvonne into feeding my dog, so I left her a note and headed for the bus stop.

Posh office! For a loser, Winfield was doing alright. I settled into the chair uncomfortably. I hate dentists, but I permitted the pudgy, balding dentist to examine my mouth, planning to let him get comfortable before springing any surprises on him.

"Pretty bad, eh, Doc?"

"MMMMMMMM," he replied enthusiastically.

"Think it'll take more than one visit?"

"My, my, my," he muttered, as though he just discovered it was terminal.

"I imagine you'll just do X-rays today."

"Tch, tch, tch. X-rays won't do you any good, young man."

"If you're gonna do any work, I want you to know, I'm allergic to Novocaine."

"Allergic?"

"Yeah, I was wondering if you could use Nitrous Oxide..."

"Never use the stuff," he muttered, still shaking his head, "well, we'd better get started."

"Just a sec! I wanna know mmmphll gllyph gag mmfgnng..."

The last thing I remember is the mask descending over my face.

CHAPTER 5—The Ending. Light was filtering in from somewhere in the distance. "damned Harvey...let us take care of him until he'd fixed his teeth...find out what he knows...too much...take care of him..."

My surroundings slowly came into focus. I was in some sort of a warehouse, its shelves brimming with gas tanks and boxes. I must have moaned or something, because I felt a sudden stabbing sensation at the base of my throat and looked up to see the grim, furry countenance of Mrs. Winfield, holding my own blade to my neck. She sneered down at me.

"We simply cannot tolerate meddlers."

I forced a smile and the white-gloved hand holding the knife pressed the instrument down more firmly.

"I'd advise you to...spill the beans...immediately, before we decide to terminate your worthless existence right here and now."

I licked my lips—sandpaper on concrete—and croaked, "whattdya wanna know?"

"Everything you know. Who's in this with you? She turned the blade, without lifting it from my throat. "I appreciate your delivery of the weapon, right at my *door*. Your fingerprints are the only ones on it. Now...if you don't..." She coughed politely, "start singing, you'll end up as another suicide statistic."

Wondering how long I could drag this out, I answered, "I know all about how your husband was supplying..."

"Husband, schmusband. All Harvey cares about are bicuspids. If I hadn't...persuaded his instructors, he wouldn't have made it through dental college."

So! *That* explained the throbbing pain which emanated from every nerve in my mouth!

There was a clunk from across the room, and a voice I recognized as the one which had been conversing with the old hit-woman when I'd come to shouted, "Got another order!"

Mrs. Winfield turned her head and I took advantage of the distraction, bringing my fist up under her elbow and almost giving myself an instant tracheotomy in the process. The handle of the blade bounced off my ear and the weapon clattered to the floor. I rolled off the table I'd been laying on and dumped my assailant with a shoulder block. Then I got my first glimpse of her partner. At a rough guess, I'd say he was 6 foot 8 and 340 pounds. He made the toughs at Triple XXX look like munchkins. Hoisting a tank over his head, he prepared to launch it like a torpedo at my retreating stern. My tongue and hands were tingling and my field of vision washed over with darkness. I dropped like a depth charge.

A familiar voice sounded in the background. "Hey, man...get up against the wall before I blow your bloody head off!"

Yvonne! Wondering if she'd arrived in time, I groped for my backside and confirmed the absence of a giant steel suppository.

Then I wondered how she found me. *I didn't even know where I was!*

CHAPTER 6—The Epilogue (Ephram Zimbalist always had one). Turned out that Yvonne had read my note and come after me. She'd arrived at the dentist's office just in time to see them carting me out. She thought for sure they'd catch her. "Ever try following somebody discreetly on a chopper?" she explained.

The boys down at homo-cide were in hot water, too. Apparently, they'd been told to lay off me until they received the forensics report. But they were so sure the blue lips were a sign of electrocution, they thought they had me cold. Actual cause of death was asphyxiation. The nitrous oxide had been replaced with carbon monoxide or something, and when Joey sat down to suck up some happiness, he got the old skull and crossbones instead. The bruises on his forehead had come from heavyhanded help in putting on the gas mask, not a hairdrier.

These days, Yvonne comes by the shop almost daily. Ruins my rep by flashing that hairstyle of hers in the front window, while she tries to convince me I should get back into the Cops and Robbers game—with her as a partner.

The hairdriers aren't moving too well (the badges would've had a dandy time proving someone was electrocuted by a unit that can't put out enough power to dry hair). And the temporary shutdown hadn't done any great shakes for business. In fact, Yvonne's proposal is looking better and better every day.

Dale Sproule is 32 years old, married, with a really nifty infant daughter. He's Creative Director at a Victoria, British Columbia radio station, a chronic University of Victoria creative writing student (another couple years and he may even have a degree), and writer of stories which have appeared in Waves, Ellery Queen's *and* Dark Visions.

34

C.P. Stancich
The Heterosexualization of a Catamite

  I don't care if I can't do innocence anymore, the whole thing is stupid and I don't want to do it or talk about it and that's it. I know it happens to everyone and it's something you have to face, but I've heard enough from all the guys who thought I was plenty innocent to know that even if you have to change there are plenty of different ways to do it. And it's funny, but I always thought Carlisle had it on the ball before this.
  I mean I know he's been at this for a long time and I know he's got my best interests at heart, and he's thinking of the harem—like Smith says—but he's just blown it...the call I mean. I just hope Smith comes through with something. That's the one nice thing about the old Honorary Eunuch; if Smith or I can come up with something that'll work instead, he'll let me try—at least as long as I don't "bring down the quality." God! That took nerve. Quality my ass! Quality's underneath the innocence or whatever you use, and I wouldn't be here unless I was prime.
  Not that the package isn't important. Take away the packages and we're all just nice boys with bad habits. Okay, I'm getting too old for the "I didn't know *that* was what it was!" routine. Not that I wasn't good; over the last two years I've become one of the best virgins the harem's ever had—even Carlisle said that (though you'd expect him

to be complimentary, considering when he said it). And of course you get a better variety when you're set up for hunters (at least that's how they see themselves). You get seducers from all walks, and of course, because they think they've got to finish the job the old H.E. only started, they've got to get you interested in them and that means sooner or later you've got to talk about what they do. And of course since they think you're almost ready but have to be handled carefully (only of course you're not) it's real easy to satisfy them and still not be bored. I've heard from some of the older dears that it's not like when you have to specialize.

My problem is my face, or at least that's what H.E. says is fast becoming my problem. It's not that the old kisser is going to turn men off, it's just that it's going to be perfect for those women—or so says Carlisle. I guess it's flattering—to be too perfect for one thing to waste myself on another—but it's still out of the question. Carlisle can be awfully single-minded at times, so I've just got to have dear Smith arrange for me to meet some of those in-house visitors to get some experience. It won't be the same as getting out into the community of course, but as one of my archaeologist patrons once pointed out, field work is only the beginning.

You can't tell me that my nose is going to be so perfect for women that it's not going to have the same masculine draw for our regulars. The trick of course, is to get a good sampling in before Honorary pressures me again. I have to be able to show him rave reviews or he'll introduce me to Mrs. John Q. saying "give it a try" like it's no big deal. That Carlisle takes a lot for granted.

I've always wanted to do leather, and I'm a little ashamed I *am* so innocent about that. I mean that's supposed to be part of the job. Smitty keeps us young ones so sheltered! A little bondage wouldn't spoil the naive show, would it? Of course when we got holidays a few of the rest of the virgins and me used to raid the latex and leather wardrobe and try to generate something. But to tell you the truth either the clothes were so good we couldn't wait for the chains and other goodies, or else the damned things were so confusing we were out of the mood by the time we were dressed. Of course Smith is very good at bondage himself: muscular and hairy with arms and thighs just made to ooze out of a gladiator's tunic. The trouble with S&M is that all of your clients turn out to be lawyers and judges and they never want to talk about their work unless they have a whip in their hand. Smith loves to joke with our staff of "happy captives" by cracking his riding crop and shouting "Justice? I'll give you justice!" I honestly don't think it's a specialty I'd want to stay in for long; for me acting can only be so much of the job.

You get a good variety in the Greek racket, and you can work in-house or in the field—and of course there's some innocence involved. It all depends whether you've got some 45-year-old who's turned on by guys sweating and straining their muscles or a younger guy who's into man-boy athletics as foreplay. I could do okay with that sort of thing as long as it wasn't too heavy. I like exercise as much as the next fellow and it's healthy and all that, and I can even see the thrill in it; but sticky sex is tricky sex, as Smith says. It's never been easy for me to change from Spartan youth-in-training to close-order drill convincingly. And god! if I ever have to do it on one of those gym mats I'll lose the customer for sure. If I hear that sound of sticky skin peeling off the mat I just know I'll burst out laughing.

I suppose I'm well-suited for the "pals." Of course they're really just seducers looking for older boys. But it's all above-board with pals; they just like you to pretend you look up to them. I don't mind that; I really do get a kick out of extracurricular education, and I've heard of pals popping for trips to Fiji and Europe and stuff like that. Not that they're like the campers; they're all businessmen who never got summer camp out of their systems and like the challenges of skinny dipping and sleeping bags. Pals are a lot more concerned with the individual; you really can get to know some neat stuff if you play it right—I've seen a bunch of palsy guys as a virgin. You get a lot of GPs and cops as pals—and of course teachers. The trouble is you can't afford to get your head messed up with romance and that's exactly what most of them would like. I've heard a lot of weepy pals crying on Smith or Carlisle trying to see their regulars—and of course it's easy to get all caught up in the game, even when you're a pro.

Straight-shooters are safe as far as that goes, and they're usually in-house, although I've heard you can get some nice weekends. But you have to like politicians, bureaucrats and actors and they can be really demanding—and for god-knows-what reason. I hear quite a bit of bitching from the boys in that closet. "Might as well be a common whore," they say, while Carlisle answers back that there's nothing common about them and if there is, they should pack. But it *is* sort of petty, I think, and it's all too regular for me. It's like enrolling in Future

Bitchy Gigolos of America. Of course that's another thing that bugs me about Carlisle's designs on me.

But the main thing is, you've got to have a very open mind or some kind of drive to switch to dames. It's a whole different kind of seduction. And then what are you? Just a toy. Okay, that's not it either—not all of it. The thought of women...older women, sort of gets the muscles in my neck tightening up and my head gives this sudden shake. The same thing happens whenever I remember swallowing castor oil. I mean alright, it's only natural and all that. I remember when I was really new, "heavily into hormones," as one of the other guys put it. I'd see one of the girls, really nice girls, mind you, from the other side of the harem, and I'd get all hot and bothered. Of course the girls of my own gender were already putting that brand of hot-and-bothered to shame. Yes, the female body is a nice thing to look at; yes, a 25-year-old woman dressed just right can give me the same kind of delicious sensation in the pit of my stomach as Smitty in his tunic. But the difference is that if it ain't Smith it's still something I can handle, while if it isn't some receptionist (and for the trade Honorary has picked out for me it won't be) it's somebody's aunt with blue hair, an udder and a Pomeranian named Flu-Flu. It makes me squirm.

But Smith says there's hope. He says that if I just let things blow over, Carlisle might defer "what's best for my career" in favor of what I want. And anyway, maybe I'm not going to keep growing that type of face; maybe I'll cross the frontier and be a man's burgeoning jock. I can't figure out how the H.E. can be so damned sure just by looking at me. But Smith says he doesn't miss often. Smith says he's the best in the business and nobody argues with that.

It was a mistake. It was a good idea but it was a mistake. Good old Smith was only trying to help and I was tickled, really, but it just sort of backfired. "Babe," he said, "you want to play with the big boys, you still got to flaunt what you've got. And when you stand with the futurestuds, your best asset is being a kid." It was sort of defeating the purpose, me supposed to be a veteran and all—that's what I was supposed to be proving anyway—but you don't argue with Smith about orgies. No, he calls them something else: "Never doubt me about aesthetics, love," he said to me as he was putting on his sandals.

It was a hell of an honor and he did go out on a limb. The house only has a *Satyricon* Night twice a year and there's always a fuss about who gets to play Giton. It doesn't matter what type you are, twice a year you walk around trying to look like an effeminate 16-year-old. Of course I can look 16 and because I'm not quite, it comes off a little campy. What I have trouble with is the looking knowledgeable. There's that innocence popping up again. Quiet sodomy with anticipating clients is one thing; a bawdy orgy is another. I was actually nervous for real.

But I have to admit, if the profits are in virginity, the ego grows on exhibition. There was everybody in their skimpy little tunics stretched out all over the couches and cots, waiting for those sluts to bring in the sweet and sour, and I got to make an entrance in a G-string and cape. There was everybody else in their whites and pale yellows and their cute little plastic-leaf chaplets, all looking at me. My headgear was the same, but the rest...gold lamé and a real gold chain instead of elastic. I remember thinking, "what the hell have I been missing?" I was kind of giddy as I stood there with old Smitty's arm around me. He got me all trembly with a saintly little kiss on the neck (for a real man he can be such a tease) and then left me with one of the county councilmen; I don't remember his name but one of the other lads said he was suffering from second term syndrome—confidence and power. Anyway, he was too young yet to be reallymatter of fact so we both played the spectator while some of the younger vets got all sweaty trying to do pagan dances.

Then the food came in and somebody started a row because the sweet and sour had been changed to drumettes and all the snacks that were supposed to look like Roman delicacies were really dry. But Smith said that Carlisle said that he wasn't going to have anything that dripped or stained, not with all those rented costumes. Then somebody bitched that they could be careful and Smitty snapped back to the bitchy guy that he'd been there last time and was one of the group that camped it up in the prawns and camped out in the sweet and sour spareribs.

Then old H.E. came in dressed in an entire toga. He was looking stern and really wicked and one of the other guys whispered to me that he always came into period pieces like a vice squad cop; otherwise things got too damned casual and the customers would start taking it for granted. Carlisle thought it was a miracle that he allowed an extra West Point night this year. Well, anyway, I hadn't thought that Carlisle would show up—me and my ignorance. Well, I see by the way he looks at me that Smith didn't tell him I was going to play Giton and right away I get this picture of a horny frustrated den mother offering me cookies, milk and a look at how her bra unfastens. So I turned and started rubbing thighs with the councilman and then of course we had to hurry and pick up all the drumettes he spilled before the grease stained the satin sheets.

Well Honorary went on and mingled, and Smith gathered me up and took me on the pre-orgy rounds and I got my first introductions to some of the more affluent and less self-conscious regulars; that's one thing I learned right away about the orgy crowd—hang-ups and inhibitions get left at home and it's kind of refreshing. Anyway, I looked for a pal and settled for one of the coach types, only I didn't know the whole idea of Giton was to spread yourself around. So Smith gets to grabbing me in those nylon-pile arms of his and plops me down here and there. It was delightful, but I wasn't used to the wine. When you're innocent, you don't do naughty things like booze and dope unless you specialize in truant officers or evangelists. At least I managed to keep going until most of the group was zonked. Then I managed to steal away and joined this portly John in the john; he'd only made it as far as the sink, so I got to puke in the toilet.

Well the next thing I know, somebody's got my forehead and keeps saying "watch yourself, easy." But I'm making so much noise myself that I can't tell exactly who's talking. It turned out to be Carlisle. The old guy must have seen me shuffle off to the little boys room, because he's got a washcloth already and a minute later in comes Thor, one of the really cute muscle boys, with my cape. Well you know, after something like that I have to admit that the guy cares about me, but it also reminded him that he thinks I'm primo for the other trade.

So he says to me that my face has still got that perfect hint of hetero ruggedness that drives forty-year-old broads wild and that he really had to arrange something. Well, what can I do? I have to go along and hope I'm either a flop (which I doubt) or I get used to it (which I doubt even more). I've got a week maybe, before my first date with the wrong gender, and Smith says in the meantime he'll work me up with some one-nighters *àla* pals and otherwise I can work in-house. There's an off chance I can save myself from my fate with a few rave reviews from the respected regular band members, but I'm afraid I'm going to have to bluff it out in the end. I don't want Carlisle mad at me, after all; not when he's got everybody's best interests at heart.

I warned him it would happen. I don't care what he *says* he thinks, I think he knows I didn't do it on purpose. He's only being stubborn about it. If he makes me try again the same thing's liable to happen; that ought to give him cause to think. I mean I'm damned sure the house has lost one customer...poor old gal. Still, I warned them both.

Smitty! Smitty was a big help, urging me on like that, trying to get me to make the best of it—as if they were thinking I wasn't going to try my best. But it's not the same as bluffing it out with somebody who's ugly or bulky or smelly. A woman, for God's sake! Castor oil! Such a pity too; I thought I was handling it so well. And she was surprisingly up front as well, which was pleasant. I thought I was going to have to struggle with heavy virginity on top of everything else, but she told me she thought I knew what had been arranged and so I got to say, yeah, that I knew and she wasn't going to have to seduce me or talk me into anything (should have known H.E. wouldn't give me an out like that).

And at least I didn't have to act embarrassed—*that* was real enough. I felt more naked with just my shirt off that first minute in her apartment than I ever had in two years in the harem. And then the rest! Oh, she must have ate it up, and I never got the satisfaction of knowing it was my acting skill that was behind it. She set her hand on my chest and I trembled—shit, if I could bottle that tremble! Then I stood in my cute jockey shorts while she carefully undressed in front of me. Boy, that was tense. I was hoping for a miracle, maybe that I'd start to get horny before she got to anything physical. Then I might get some control, might make the whole thing like with men. Her excitement wasn't going to be a problem, I could see that. In fact it was going to take an awful lot to screw up her mood. I guess you can say I came up with an awful lot.

Actually, I think overconfidence finally caught up with me. Just as we were both in the buff, I began to feel comfortable and in control of myself. I stupidly began to believe all the things I was telling myself about how I was feeling toward her...toward her. It wasn't a bad body, not for a woman her age I suppose, and certainly not in comparison to my fears; though I suppose Carlisle wasn't out to give me a hardcase right at first. So anyway, she put her head on my shoulder and gave me a seductive little rub. I thought to myself, "alright, you're going to come through it okay." Then she asked me to hold her breast and so I did and then I puked all over her.

She gave me cookies and pop and had me play her son's Atari while the cab made its way to the house. I don't know if I put her off for good; I never got to know how strong her bent was. Pity if I did queer it for her though; she was a nice guy and close, I think, to finding what she wanted.

Well Carlisle was a little miffed, and let his emotions get out before his usual logic. He accused me of being too sensitive for someone in my profession and even of deliberately screwing the deal. I looked real hurt, which worked until he remembered that hurt is one of my bread-and-butter expressions. At least he calmed down. Still, he's not ready to give up. He let me go with a "well, then, if it wasn't deliberate we shall have to let you try again." That was three days ago, and my stomach's still queasy. I'm worried, because I know Carlisle's looking for somebody else for me—somebody who's not so easily put off, someone who'll let me retch and keep right on going. Smith says he'll see reason eventually, but we need to buy time.

That Smitty, he's a dear. He took me down for vaccinations and passport pictures today. There is this nice young guy I've been with a couple of times since *Satyricon* night; he was looking for a "nephew" to take on a trip to a conference in Brussels. We hit if off and plans sort of snowballed into a three-week walking tour of England. I've heard that trips don't pay much more than house commission, and I don't know about this walking; but that guy *is* kinda cute and I really do have to get away.

C. P. Stancich is a freelancer and freeloader from Gig Harbor, the Scranton of the Northwest. For a really good time he sits alone in a dark room and thinks dirty thoughts.

35

C.P. Stancich
The Belch of Midge Besselman's Husband

In modest rooms in the great city of High Gotham, there lived a woman named Midge Besselman. She was a kind woman, but of the variety that occasionally demands the right of feeling ill-used for that kindness. She lived with her husband, Vernon, a peaceful soul who went to work each day hoping to dispatch cases of portable folding charcoal grills to retail outlets but usually got distracted helping the boss's son learn the ropes. Midge had raised two children who had grown and learned and left. She had friends and just enough of a job to keep home from being depressing — doing the books for her friend Roxanne's brother-in-law's deli.

Thus, though she complained to Vernon once in a while for practice, Midge's life was contented enough: except for one thing. Midge loved music. Not any music, nor especially the music she and Vernon had grown up with (which was what Vernon thought *was* music). Midge loved classical music. She enjoyed the sound, but that was only part of it. As the music would play she would see the glitter of the city in the evening, here the bustle of cultured people, and smell the romantic smell of rain on asphalt. Her dream was of the symphony, of Vernon in formal attire, of casual glances around the concert hall, of all the musicians playing just for her. This was one thing she longed for — to be "The Besselmans ... going to the symphony."

But Vernon was difficult. He went with her to Citrus City every February; he took her to visit the kids; he even went dancing with her. But he avoided the symphony. She would ask and he would pretend not to hear. She would ask again and he would say he wasn't interested. She would press and he would say it was too expensive, or that she should go with one of her friends. She did not want to go with one of her friends; when she heard the music and dreamed the dream it was Vernon sitting beside her, not Roxanne.

One day it happened that she remembered her niece Phyllis's birthday was approaching just as she passed an on-line sign for the lottery; so she chose numbers based on Phyllis's birthday; she won $565, before taxes. This emboldened her, and Vernon found himself in fancy clothes, heading out to the symphony to make Midge's dream come true. They were going to the symphony — with the great Tookus Fotz as guest soloist, no less.

Now Vernon was an agreeable fellow, and now understood how important it was to his wife, so he had given in. But he was also mischievous, and when Midge took too long fussing over her dress and didn't leave enough time to sit down at a nice restaurant, he teased her and took her to a street vendor for hot dogs. She was embarrassed at first, but the sight of Vernon in dapper formal wear holding a frank smothered in onions made her laugh, and she realized it didn't matter where they ate, so long as they were on time.

Everything was as she dreamed. The people were breathtaking. Vernon was lovely. And the orchestra seemed to tune up with a special flair. The program began with Mozart's Overture to *Cosi fan Tutti*, and quickly proceeded to Saint-Seans' *Dane Macabre*. Then the great Fotz appeared. It was not often that the violin virtuoso performed in High Gotham, and Midge felt her dream expanding to hold more joy than she thought possible. Through the first movement of Mozart's *Sinfonia for Violin and Viola (K. 364)*, Midge fancied herself in heaven.

Beside her, Vernon was wondering why he had put up such a fuss, when the onion-laden hot dog within him began to make its presence felt. Vernon rarely worried about such things, and he knew he could tease his wife, because she would be the only one to hear the impending burp and would grow all red from embarrassment. He let a strong, healthy belch escape, expecting it to be drowned out by the *Sinfonia for Violin and Viola (K. 364)*. But as luck would have it, the first movement ended just at that very moment, and Vernon's belch rose above the smattering of coughs and throat-clearings to dominate the otherwise silent pause. The trauma was so surprising that Midge emitted a long bleat, a noise only partially covered by the opening of the second movement.

Though people in the audience were so polite as to take no notice, Midge felt as if she must be consumed by the fire of her embarrassment at any moment ... and hoped very much that she might be. Vernon listened on blithely, still surprised at how pleasant a classical concert was, all things considered. His happy oblivious expression didn't help his wife's mood, though even without it, the concert would have been just as ruined. First there was the shame, and then there was the dream shattered.

And yet, strangely, by the end of the evening the music had soothed her a little, and she hoped she might forget that horrible moment. After all, no one there knew them, and no one she knew would know of the incident.

But the next day she learned just how amusing Vernon thought the whole thing was, when Roxanne and her husband, Mac, came over for a drink. "I thought Midge would strangle me," Vernon said after recalling the incident. Then he recalled it a second time, and seeing his wife's reddened face added: "See? Still fit to be tied!"

All Midge could do was deny this accusation, and then try to ignore the whole thing — which did nothing to discourage Vernon, who managed to tell all their friends (and no doubt the boss's son at the portable charcoal grill warehouse, though Midge couldn't be sure of this and didn't ask). Her outlook grew bleak and her interest in things diminished, especially in music.

But as the story aged it grew less interesting to Vernon, and Midge was allowed to forget the incident as much as she could. She listened to her music again, and even entertained the idea of going to the symphony again sometime (though she did not mention this to Vernon).

Then one day Vernon came home with a new LP. The jacket was filled with titles and subtitles mentioning the great Tookus Fotz and the fact that the program was recorded live at the High Gotham Concert Hall. Midge put the record on and began to read the literature on the jacket when Vernon, who was pouring himself a highball, asked: "Do you think we might be on it?"

Midge realized they were listening to Mozart's *Sinfonia for Violin and Viola (K. 364)*. She checked the liner for the date of the recording and gave a bleat of anguish.

"No, no," said Vernon appraisingly. "It was a little higher," he added just as the first movement came to a close.

Midge Besselman stepped to the stereo, pulled the LP off the turntable and never listened to classical music again.

C. P. Stancich is a P.R. hack at Tacoma Community College and Director of the Tacoma Writers Conference. His prose has appeared here and there—most recently in Sou'wester, Sign of the Times *and* Kingfisher.

36

Dave Swartout
Tutelary Angels

I needed a hero and Sol came to me. Sol needed a community, and we moved to Heron Flats. The ad in the *Seattle Post-Intelligencer* read: *Live full lives. Peculiar people wanted. For sale: Grocery/gas stn/frn frmhs/cheap...*

I was sitting on the toilet, tangled in the newspaper with the intention of both the obvious and finding the sports section so I could say something intelligent, or at least current, when Sol came home from Fetus Fighting that night. Instead, I found the strange ad in the classifieds.

The telephone number was in the 509 area code, which meant eastern Washington; the wrong side of the Cascades for most western urbanites. I had lived with and loved Sol for most of two years, and had progressed so far from my abject self-esteemlessness that I was given to larks. Me! I still couldn't speak face-to-face with strangers, but I could use the telephone.

When Sol came home we hooked up the conference line and called.

"Heron Flats can be likened to a traveling circus that don't go nowhere," Marguarite Weatherby said. She had placed the ad and was eager to sell. Her voice placed her between eighty-five and centennial. "It's peopled peculiarly—not with what you'd call freaks—no, by big city standards they're average. The business takes in about $25,000 a year, so you're best to be a selling artist or handy on the side if you want to make more. Summer's hot—desert Washington. Winter's no good if you're over seventy-four—glacial Washington.

"Got a dime store owned by some sort of squaw, but I made a peace pact with her so we don't compete for business; there's a tavern owned by a youngish married couple who can't or won't have offspring." She laughed like a cluster of leaves before they fall to the ground. "We got a whorehouse run by the Taggart triplets if your balls itch, but stay away from Rowena and Ranger 'cause they're a pair. Then there's Rox and Liz that have the boardinghouse, but Rox was left with a small fortune in land and dollars, so they usually room and board the occasional overnighter for free. Look on a map; Heron Flats is about five miles east of the Hanford Nuclear Reservation and thirty miles north of those Tri-Cities. Are you peculiar?"

"I'm a research librarian."

"Funny," the old woman said, choking on a dry leaf laugh for at least a minute, "you sound like a man."

"Sol was a pro football player, but went bad—started dating men."

"You'll do then if you got cash. I will see you this weekend. Good-bye."

Sol and I were running from the law—not in the sense of threatening penal institutions—like Kennedy and Monroe, but less suicidal than plain tired.

Seattle liberates farm kids but oppresses lifers and I was a lifer in an ant farm; a troubled insect that doesn't dig and tunnel for the pleasure of its viewing public, but digs and tunnels to get the hell out of its narrow confines.

Sol landed in Seattle with the Seahawks, but was let go after three years. I believed him for our first year together when he told me that faggots were the first to be cut if a franchise has to pull in its draw play and money is tight. (Aghast, and not yet keen on sports, I asked him if since fags were *cut*, then were lesbian athletes *hysterectomized* when they didn't meet par? No.)

When Sol was certain that I loved him, he admitted that it was his knee. His contract had been bought, an extravagant insurance policy cashed, and he had more than a few pennies in the bank.

I knew about the pennies, liked the frowning crease across his solar plexus above his navel, and didn't deserve his love, but to this day, I don't see why he couldn't still play football. The flesh on his knee looks like a couple of blind Doctors Frankenstein worked on it, but he doesn't limp.

Professional football players, I have been told, are not masochists. Sol was. He came home from Fetus Fighting wracked (as in dungeons of fundamental torture) with pain. He bled often and didn't have a team doctor to repair him. His solace was my progress. "The most heroic man I know, Mitch," he would lie. I got stronger.

Another reason I was ready to run, was because I was tired of explaining the democratic institution of sex and love between two men. Sol's friends (I had none) could imagine only one position between a librarian and an ex-football player.

No. I had not over-indulged in steroids.

Yes. Even as a librarian, I had good penetration. (Sol had been a tight end for the Seahawks.)

It was, in fact, tight ends and good penetration that convinced me to watch and enjoy Sunday and Monday Night Football with Sol and his friends while drinking and belching beer that tasted great and was less filling.

We bought the Heron Flats grocery and gas station that weekend.

During the days, the desert surrounding Heron Flats is animated with tension. The sun pounds the grit, the purple and pink phlox, the sagebrush, and the occasional balsam root until they become fatigued and wobble in the shimmer of reflected heat as though the earth itself is about to topple with exhaustion.

Marguarite Weatherby died two days after we moved into her home and place of business, which made the population of Heron Flats seventeen, if Sol and I were included. I had read few horror stories, but knew Heron Flats already had the necessary devices: Death and a pair of innocent strangers in a drowsy rural town.

"With angry superstition," Sol warned as a fan of horror, "the townsfolk will band together and do something really weird to either scare us out of town, thinking we're a bad omen; fearing failed crops, stillbirths, and *National Enquirer* reporters, or seduce us into some heathen fertility land rite—maybe sacrifice us to the sun."

The sun. Sol. Christ, my lover was doomed.

"Wait a minute," I said, feigning terror. I have never intentionally faked an orgasm, but faking terror, since I was genuinely terrified of everything, was fun for once. "You picked me from among the mass of meek librarians only to seduce me and groom me for the day you and your conspirators in Heron Flats demand I copulate with terra firma. Help!"

"Ooh." Sol's 'oohs' are often salacious and inviting. "Leave it to my lover to come up with something better than mud between the toes."

It turned out, we were told later, that Marguarite Weatherby was the local equivalent to what genteel people call, A Fucking Bitch. Neither Sol nor I queried as to what less genteel people called her.

In Seattle I once saw two national and overly franchised convenience stores not only on the same block, but next-door neighbors in business. We wanted a Mom's and Pop's, or rather a Pop's and Pop's, but unfortunately, our new store was a rural reproduction of late twentieth century convenience. It looked, smelled, and felt like a bunch of chrome with digital numbers that a mad computer salvage company had thrown together—devoid of passion. Sol's first improvement was to unplug the electronic clerk. Sol's mechanical.

I was washing the front windows when I saw our first taste of indigene crossing the Main Street and carrying a pie. The streets of Heron Flats are paved, but the slightest breeze from any of the four corners coughs up a layer of gritty soil stuff that isn't exactly sand, but not quite dirt. I fell in love when I saw the approaching woman close her eyes and turn her face into the breeze for a moment, allowing the grit and wind to blush her cheeks. I suspected that she was the 'squaw' since she had come from the dime store.

"Sol..."

"Blink, Mitch. Your eyes are as big as the windows you're streaking."

She was legs. Long, beautiful appendages hooked to slender and flattering hips on top; sunk into scuffed snakeskin cowboy boots on bottom. (We found out that religious grounds demanded simulated snakeskin.) Her eyes were black, not dark brown. I tried to look away, examine one of the scars I was streaking on the window. "Sol," stunned, I knew I was drooling my words, "look at her hair." Like a good stretch minus the yawn, it ran the length of her spine. "It's as black and glossy as dress shoes."

"Not very poetic, Mitch. But, yeah..."

She stepped onto the wooden sidewalk and smiled at us. We were gaping.

"Twenty dollars says she has a voice that sounds like an electronic pinball machine and a personality to match," Sol said as the woman reached for the doorknob. Her fingers were those of a concert pianist. "New place, new start Mitch, so start new."

This was Sol's cue of support. He expected me to talk. Talk! to a stranger. I was just recently a librarian for Christ's sake; I researched and I talked to myself.

In the store, she smiled like a friendly woman in faded jeans and a tan blouse filled with darker colored breasts. Her skin was the color that stodgy men's club Colonels, usually from England, call exotic—darker than olive, but neither black nor sunworn Native American. I smiled (because Sol stood between us) and escaped to the canned vegetables across the store.

I didn't see any string beans, baby potatoes, honeyed carrots, onion pearls, mushrooms, olives, or any stock canned goods. In front of me were cans and cans and cans of creamed corn and water chestnuts. I blinked and cursed. My lips were sealed. I could never talk to this woman.

"And this is Mitch," I heard Sol say. "Mitch, this is Nia."

"Nice to meet you, Mitch."

She was an alto, maybe a bass. There was nothing soprano or electronic about her voice. Low. Rich, like garden loam. If I had been a better student of patriarchy, I would have lusted when I looked into her eyes. Instead, I appreciated. Loved. I wanted to walk on her as do people who trust the solidity of earth.

"I baked a wild blackberry pie for you and Sol. I'm not certain where the berries were roaming in their feral state, but they were jumping around in my freezer this morning begging to be baked."

I think I laughed (out loud). Sol did, and took the pie, thanking Nia and placing it on the counter.

I oozed unglamorously with sweat. The sun yelled through the windows and made the store feel like someone had turned the thermostat to broil. "Could we offer you a cold drink?" I asked.

I instantly bragged to myself with a smile and laughed at Sol who was fast approaching. He bore a high-five as though it were a priestly blessing—Christ—a distant deity is the only one who may know why I slammed my open palm into his over the vegetable counter, but I did.

"Con-fucking-great-undulations, Mitch!" Sol's sense of histrionics is too Spartan for some. "You did it!" He turned to Nia, "Or maybe you did!" He beamed and grinned like a lunatic and scowled good riddance to another part of my past. Nia appeared frightened; Sol was oblivious at the time, which forced me to do it again.

Speak. "I, uh, don't talk to strangers," I said. "Uh, you see. You know, unless they're on the phone or, ummm, transmitting electronically. Ummm, or if I've met them three times."

Nia smiled fearlessly at the wretched and servile beast I knew I was. I felt some strength through Sol's pleasure, and wanted to tell Nia that it wasn't exclusively women that I feared, but men and children, also.

She pulled herself onto the counter and said, "Really." This was not a question. It was a boastful pair of syllables before she broiled with laughter. "Then fuck-your-great-congregation!"

"Close, Nia," Sol laughed. "Soda, wine, or beer?" he asked, walking over to the cooler.

I don't remember which she requested. There on the counter, next to the pie, I laughed at Nia and myself. Even in my less than heterosexual mind, I associated Nia with cherry pastry. Sol was rubbing off on me, leaving curiously masculine thoughts like caked splotches of his come on my belly. I didn't know if this was good or bad, fair or unscrupulous. It was funny.

Nia told us she was Indian. "As in Bhopal, where people were chemically rendered into puddles, years back," she said with exaggerated neutrality, lending new meaning to the old saw about raining cats and dogs. She was in the United States when her family was obliterated, and she was not a titled American. "Dr. Nia We'll-stop-there-because-the-rest-is-too-hard-to-pronounce Grey, PhD." Grey was her English mother; the hard to pronounce name was that of her ex-husband who was an American-Soviet, who had been married to a second generation Japanese-Hawaiian, but divorced her to marry Nia so she could expedite her citizenship and later divorce him. "Soap Opera U.N.-stye." Her doctorate was in medical ethics, but since there were none, she moved to Heron Flats and opened the boarded dime store. "Like a woman who still had the right to her own hymen or womb."

Hi, men? Nia and Sol were like-minded, and for once, I didn't fear for Sol's safety as a retired but devout Fetus Fighter.

The three of us laughed and talked like old friends for most of the afternoon. Nia told us that she was neither frigid nor a lesbian, but she believed reverently in the ownership of orgasms. Thus far, she was the only person she willingly and gladly gave them to. "My ex-husband's sexual intrusions," she gaily said, legitimately without pain, I think, "gave me just that much more time to mentally organize my dissertation."

Without the standard degradation, I told Nia about my childhood and my maimed parents who didn't keep mirrors in the house. They told me that I was the ugly one, and the shards of glass would hurt when the mirror repulsed against my image. I warned her that Sol consistently lied about my virtues while he rescued me from my parents, so she should take what he says about me with a grain of sawdust. Sol went into his autobiographical ditty that revealed nothing.

"You two are the most normal things to succumb to Heron Flats since I've been here," Nia said. This did not bode well. "Let's meet back at my store in an hour or so, and I'll take you to the Truncated Heron for a Saturday night out." This boded worse.

Handsome but irritating, Sol went into his I-love-a-party mode. "Sure, let's meet the locals, Mitch."

I looked at Sol, the pie that had sunk some, and Nia. "Why don't we just ask Nia and her pie home for a barbecue?"

"Great," Sol said. "And then we'll go to the Truncated Heron." I think he saw that option as a compromise. We locked the store and left. I pouted, but it didn't work.

With Nia, our first entertaining at the farmhouse was fun. I decided other than Sol, there was at least one person of the four-billion-plus worth knowing.

"Sol, go in," Nia said.

We had walked down Main Street and met no humans. Two jack rabbits ran across the road, but had no reason to fear cars. Six stores mirrored another six down the road; one was a bookstore that was closed in the fifties, still stocked with its original inventory. Nia had always wanted to break in, but was afraid. "Too many unread books surrounding me." She cringed without a coquettish chromosome in her body, at least toward us, and leaned into Sol while we passed the building.

Sol concurred. "*Un*read books are the dangerous ones."

With newfound valor, I said, "Since I can read, I guess I could become a book-tamer with you, Nia." Both she and Sol applauded my courage.

"Now," Nia said to me after Sol went into the Truncated Heron, sat at the bar, and ordered three beers, "we'll salamander in and see what happens."

I backed away and stepped into the street. "Uh, you meant we'd sashay in, or meander in?" I had never entered a public place for social purposes, and I was stalling.

Nia shriveled her lips like prunes. "I meant salamander. You know, those lizards that can go anyplace, even through a fire and survive, because they are always themselves and don't have to rely on others to protect them?"

"I'm a chameleon at best."

Shaking her head, Nia took my arm like a date and we walked into the tavern.

"Hi, Mitch!" came a collective salutation. I ran.

Outside, Nia grabbed me more like a date rape than a friend and pulled me back into the tavern.

"Hi, Mitch!"

Nia pushed me out the door faster than I could run. A reverberation in the back of my mind saw people look up from their conversations, pool play, and bartending to say, 'hi.'

Without force, because I had none, I tried to sting Nia with hatred. "You are not..."

"I am." She fanned her long hair away from her neck to cool.

I looked through the tavern window and saw Sol drinking at his beer. I mimed to him that I was homeward bound. He laughed.

"This will be your third entry, Mitch." Nia twinkled, and sparkled, and shouted at me with a confident grin. "Only a

Christian fundamentalist is spent by his third entry. If the strangers in the Heron don't say 'hi' again, then you can do whatever it is you do when you panic."

"You are a bona fide bitch."

"As sure as Sol is Sol."

It took a shove from Nia, but there I was, inside the Truncated Heron—neither hiving nor heaving.

"Hi, Mitch!" everyone said before they again went back to their Saturday night business.

I felt vaguely comfortable. Nia and I walked over to Sol and I offered the stool at the bar next to him so Nia could sit between us. Sol read my desperate look that was painted with a stroke of confidence, and winked.

Try trusting.

The bartender extended his hand and I shook it.

"Nia says you're not fond of talking to people until you've met them three times. Name's O'Brian, and you have every right to be distrustful of some. This is my wife," O'Brian said with a tilt of his head to the woman behind the bar, "she's trustworthy."

"Kara," she said, shaking my hand quickly before she filled an order.

I looked to Sol and Nia, who nodded at my curious glance. O'Brian and Kara didn't intimidate me, I guess, because they were featureless. The type of people who would make consummate criminals because in a police lineup all the witness or victim would see was the height chart behind the two tavern owners. They were plain to the point of uncertainty; able to blend into crowds and fixtures. And O'Brian was the first to explain the reason they had no children. He could have gallantly claimed gonads as do many husbands, but he said, "We fear that we wouldn't know we had them if our featurelessness was passed on."

Nia suspected the two to be a CIA couple who found a God. Sol suspected they were relocated witnesses of some heinous crime. I couldn't see a difference.

Even though I felt like I had been highlighted by Nia with a fluorescent yellow marker, I stole some looks around the tavern. It was authentically old English in decor. The mahogany bar, which was a monstrous display of English woodcraftmanship, came from England, via an old tavern in Seattle, after a cruise and a brief stint in a hotel in the Falklands. Kara and O'Brian polished it in spare moments as though it were a child with features.

The billiards table was the webbed-pocket variety; the dart board didn't light up when people threw real darts, and each wooden and cushionless booth had a table with a chess-backgammon-checker board inlaid.

Perched in one of the high straight-backed booths playing chess, was a duplication of the same woman. Two-thirds of the Taggart triplets, I was told.

"That's Tina and Sheena over there, and along with Rowena, they run the local bordello," Nia said.

The two women were so deep in astute contemplation, that they did not fit my image of rural whores. They looked like bespeckled and bunned biochemists.

A woman who looked like she was three Manhattans beyond Staten Island was sitting in the far corner booth. She was old. Her face was powdered white with perfect circles of rouge in the dell of each cheek. Her eyes were outlined with heavy black mascara, and her silver-gray boa matched her hair and sequined dress.

"Celeste Swanson," Nia told us. "She claims to be Gloria's bastard, and in tribute to her mother and the days of silent romance, Celeste seldom speaks. Her silence is a vow of love for the days before talkies when people used their bodies to communicate more than anonymous lust."

Sol nodded in Celeste's direction and she smiled her reply.

I drank my beer, the whole schooner without tasting it, but I'm sure it was bad. I cringed at Sol's composure, and Nia's biographies. Sol ordered me another beer. His days as a Fetus Fighter, among his many peculiarities, equipped him to comfortably accept the townsfolk as our new neighbors. My distressed shyness equipped me for nothing.

"At the billiards table are Rox and Liz, that's Rox taking a shot. They own the boardinghouse," Nia said between pulls of her beer. "They have twin eight-year-old boys named Kick and Ass."

Sol ate an egg out of a jar of greenish-brown liquid.

Rox was a wholesome and handsome woman busting out with a sense of Indian Summer. She looked like what my grandmother used to call prairie-bred (desert-bred in Rox's case); equipped by nature and character to fight the elements, feed the cattle in subzero weather and demand rain when mercury peaks in thermometers; bake six loaves of bread in the morning to distribute among hungry neighbors, and sling the fully hung bull with the farmhands before she put on her Sunday best to entertain the Mayor and his wife with aplomb. (The plum bothered me as a child. I always thought it rather stingy to serve only one, or that these women didn't particularly care for mayors.) In other words, Rox looked like an indispensable person.

"Your Gramma knew Rox in a previous life," Nia said, after my description. "Except for our lack of mayoral rule, that's Rox."

Liz, Rox's lover, was the prototype of the beautiful woman of current favor—tall, blonde and fair, green-eyed, high-cheeked, full-lipped, and coated with mundane elegance like a piece of wood is coated with polyurethane. A few days later, after witnessing her work and intellect, my preconceptions of Liz were stripped away.

"Liz is artistically reclined," Nia said.

"Inclined?" Sol asked, suspecting, I'm sure, that some of Nia's English-as-a-second language thwarted her description of Liz.

I huffed, because I knew Nia probably meant what she said, and because I felt good huffing about something.

Nia huffed at Sol, and said, "No, *re*clined. She paints frescoes on ceilings. Liz is very talented, and you should see their boardinghouse. She's been reproducing the Sistine work, but somewhat altered. God is a chesty blonde with plum fingernails, slightly chipped, and realistically sagging breasts that show she spent a great deal of time nurturing. Moses is castrated, and Christ, although passionate, is a hermaphrodite. All very unusual, but well executed."

"Executed," Sol repeated. I could tell by the hard swallow and bob of his Adam's apple that he was thinking about his balls and the fate of Moses in Liz's hands.

While the women were shooting their game, they talked about the Great Douche God sent after She told Noêl to build the ark, which was one of the few nonphallic constructions of the Old Testament, I discovered while eavesdropping.

"Didn't quite take," Liz said to Rox. "The good..." Liz finally made a shot and yelped, "There is a good!" Exultant with her luck, she missed her next shot that seemed easy. "Are the sperms and eggs of the world, none of this salt shit."

"Some odiferous bacteria got left behind," Rox agreed. She looked up briefly to Sol and me before she took her shot and sank her intended balls. "Neither of you strike me an odiferous bacterium," she said, lining up her next shot.

Sol smiled and thanked her.

After Nia made the official introductions, Liz said, "How about dinner at the boardinghouse this Monday? Rox can serve her desert fare specialty, and in the name of good hosting and homosexual pedophilia we'll offer up our eight-year-old boys."

I waited briefly for Sol to reply, but accidentally spoke instead. "I'm not used to kids, but I think I might like them." I blushed. "I mean as kids, not dinner."

All but Celeste (who supplied us with a silly grin) howled, and Sol accepted the invitation.

We were also introduced to Bram Hubble, who liked to be called Old Man (which he was) and poured his schooners of beer into the planter box next to his reserved stool at the end of the long wooden bar.

"But he seems to get some drink in him anyway," Kara assured us.

"The ozone layer has been damaged," he said after disposing of another beer, "by the passion that has been sucked from otherwise strong men and women like the mist from a damaging aerosol spray."

OK. After one Saturday night in the local tavern, I was ready to plead with Sol for a quick retreat back to Seattle. Skedaddle. But I could see in Sol's eyes that no amount of pleading would dislocate us from our new home in desert central Washington.

The third of the Taggart sisters walked into the Truncated Heron wearing a resplendent glow, which neither of her contemplative sisters shared. She tossed me a wink and splashed Sol with a smile as she walked through the tavern to join Tina and Sheena at their chess game. A magnificent black Labrador retriever came in with her, but jumped up on one of the bar stools near me and whined.

"That's Rowena Taggart," Nia quietly said, "and the dog's name is Ranger. He has been given full citizenship in Heron Flats, but he's just a trainable dog—nothing eerie or mysterious." Nia looked as though she were about to spontaneously combust into a conflagration of laughter when she saw my confused face. "He has been trained to do special tricks."

Tricks, clinked in what was left of my mind.

O'Brian served Ranger a bowl of Okanogan Ale and took a glass of wine over to Rowena, refilling Tina's and Sheena's glasses while he was at the table. Sol looked at me through a cocked eye and I knew what he was thinking; that old Marguarite Weatherby had mentioned Rowena and Ranger.

Delicately smiling, Nia took what she must have thought was a suspense-filled draw on her beer. "I'm not passing judgment, but due to a lack of suitable men in Heron Flats, Rowena has taken up with Ranger."

"A casual dalliance, I'm sure," Sol said, matching Nia's animated effort to restrain laughter.

I glanced over at the big dog lapping his beer just two stools away from me. I had seen enough of Heron Flats for one night. "Ranger is a dog." I said this to Sol and Nia as though they may not have known, which broke their fettered laughter.

Not wanting to be added to Rox's list of odiferous human bacteria, I tried not to turn green, squirm, or show any of the standard signs of revulsion.

When Liz mentioned something more about the need for another Great Douche, Sol and Nia laughed hysterically and the three of us ran for the door—I was blank with wonder.

On Sunday, while Sol and I were deconstructing the store, Nia crashed through the door like a runaway car. "Bib is on her way!"

Over pie, after beer the night before, Nia apologized for our blatant introduction to Heron Flats. When I accepted her apology, suggesting that we would do our entertaining at home from then on, Sol became polemic. He scolded me for my narrow mind, reminding me that it was the size of a triple-A shoe, which was government issue for the spiritual lynch mob we had run from.

Sol grinned at Nia's concern over the Bib person and while I reeled with disdain (I think because I was meeting people more peculiar than I), I was determined to try on a pair of sensible mental shoes that didn't pinch.

"Bib is really very nice. If she were Catholic, her future would be filled with stigmatas, canonization, and sainthood." Nia looked over her shoulder through the window and down the street. "She is just a little backward. I should have told you last night, but..."

"Calm down, Nia. We don't have anything against country folk," Sol said. Still grinning, he added, "Hell, one of our best friends is from Heron Flats."

"No," Nia protested, shaking her beautiful head of hair, "I mean Bib is truly backward."

She didn't have time to elucidate before Bib walked into the store. She was a short, young woman, wearing overalls, and looking like someone's country mouse cousin. Her sandy hair was jaggedly cropped short—maybe with lawn edging shears—her smile seemed genuine, and one of her hands was shoved in a front pocket while the other held a small bouquet of pink phlox. A desert Joan of Arc.

She looked preadolescent and soft, neither male nor female, but forming, which is why I saw a genuine smile crease her frecklepunctuated face. She reminded me of a person who lost the owner's manual at puberty and hence, the gender specific instructions for future use. Either that, or she knew exactly what she was doing without the manual.

"Nia, hi," she said, tentatively pushing herself more deeply into the store. She mustered courage through a deep breath and handed Sol the bouquet as though she were entreating the mercies of a rabid lion.

"Thank you." Sol stepped back submissively. "I'm Sol and that's Mitch. We're the new owners of the store."

"And delightful. Good men," Nia said. "But, I haven't told them about you yet, Bib. They met Rowena and Ranger last night."

Bib rolled her eyes and shook her head, apparently knowledgeable of the woman's and dog's relationship. She didn't speak to us at first, but I decided she was simple—not backward— uncontrived. That would be a relief, since so far, no one in Heron Flats could be considered uncontrived.

"We have been moving things around," Sol said gently. "So just yell if you can't find what you want."

Bib smiled at both of us and then turned to Nia. "?then freely speak I Can" Nia nodded, and when the younger woman turned back to us, Nia shrugged another apology. ".condom a wear

Ranger makes she and sweet is Rowena"

Bib's statement could not pinch my mind since it had come from her mouth, yet Sol and I had no difficulty understanding what Nia meant by backward. What surprised both Nia and me, was Sol's reply.

".reverse in speaks who sister a have I"

Bib swooned. Nia and Sol were closest and caught her before she made a nosedive into the Hershey Kisses.

I knew that jocks have imaginations as big as they think their pricks are, and I knew that Sol didn't have a sister, but I didn't know he could speak conversational reverse.

Nia and I retreated to the counter while Bib and Sol carried on their colloquial widdershins.

Nia sighed and pulled up and onto the counter, turning her back to us with me rounding the counter for a private conversation. Every movement of her body was the core of enchantment and grace. "Like an American, Bib has screwed with my hometown religion." Nia was kind in tone, but exasperated. "She believes she was reincarnated, which is fine and fundamental to the caste of characters back home, but Bib is certain that in her most previous life, she was a vain goddess who died in, or on, a mirror."

I would have said something appropriately incredulous had I not been the only one facing the front of the store, and witness to what was walking in, brandishing a brace of dead birds.

It—he—was no less than six-feet-six-inches tall, wearing a long duster jacket that was so dirty the Marlboro Man wouldn't have considered it authentic. He boasted a red mustache that flanged to either side of his mouth, but streaked like red slashes of wounded skin down his chin, his neck, and beneath his collar to his chest. It didn't hang like excess handlebars—it was attached to his flesh, and for all I knew, it Fu Manchued all the way down to his toes.

His hands were probably rough and calloused, but they appeared downy soft because of the feathers attached to the encrusted black blood that covered them.

The terror on my face was enough to panic Sol, Nia, and Bib. They began to run with me to the back door of the store before they turned and looked at the material of my fright. Nia and Bib abruptly stopped. Sol slowed. I mentally packed my bags for the move back to Seattle.

"!Mitch" Bib yelled. "!worry Don't" I turned in time to see Bib pat the man on his stomach. Both were smiling. Nia looked sorry—agian. Sol looked as though he was wearing a pair of shoes that pinched. ".syrup of bottle a as sweet as he's and, Granger is This"

To hell with Seattle, I began to consider an Afrikaan ashram on a breezy little veld in fascist South Africa. The man did not look sweet. His belt was made of silver coins, his boots were spurred at the heel where chicken shit clung, and chew was crusted at the corners of his mouth.

Again, Nia made the official introductions, but added, "Granger, you look like bloody shit with feathers attached, and you have frightened my friends." Nia's jaws were gracefully clenched, but she looked frightening.

Granger was not enchanted. He laughed like a crazed chain gang murderer (unfortunately without the chains) until Bib said, ".Granger, you like just—too friends my are They"

With his hands full of dead birds, Granger began to sob. "Don't have many new people in Heron Flats, and I like scaring them. I like selling dead chickens, too."

Like the bitch I wished I could be, I wanted to say, "As though you have had a stampede of fools other than Sol and me cross your town for years."

Sol remained pinched, which was unusual, because he could find likable qualities in ptomaine.

Safely the furthest away, I reminded myself that Heron Flats was a new place, presenting *us* with a new start.

Like a man who was test-driving confidence (emphasis on *con*), I said to Granger, "Cc-clean yourself up, and c-come back with better plucked and drrrained, or whatever, birds, and we'll talk about buying them."

"Well curse my basil and make it grow! You spose if I cleaned up sixteen years earlier, Weatherby would have bought some?" He ran out the door with his birds, presumably to clean up, with Bib following.

Sol appeared less pinched and recovered from the shock of his sense of prejudice. Before we celebrated my outspokenness, he said, "Mitch, I promise you, we will move away from Heron Flats as soon as something weird happens."

Nia couldn't speak, she was kissing me with fresh accolades.

Sol had found his community, but even he didn't know that we had spent the past two days meeting the heroes of Heron Flats—our guardian angels.

I would have never guessed that I would become Sol's hero within the year.

Dave Swartout has written "Tutelary Angels" as a condensed character sketch of his work in progress, The Offending Angel of Heron Flats *(for which he holds no hope of receiving an NEA grant). He has a Master's Degree in Political Science:* Conflict Resolution, Peacekeeping, and Mediation *from the University of Hawaii, and is a full-time freelance writer with credits ranging from* In Touch For Men *to* Ranger Rick. *He writes and lives out of a garage in Ephrata, Washington, and enjoys bouts of writer's bliss when he sees courageous and deaf ears turned toward such inestimably qualified art critics as Senator Jesse Helms.*

37

Dave Swartout
Lupine

"My name is Josh."

Josh's howl of satisfaction would have echoed through the Cascades had there not been such a heavy cloud cover and so much rain. The torrent sheet bent saplings and moved large rocks. His violent constrictions, his body, thighs, arms, lips that blanketed Ken so completely, rigidly beat out—thrust his tremendous orgasm into Ken, echoed in Ken's ears, even after Josh relaxed, slowed, smoothly moved, and licked at the back of Ken's neck.

Carefully withdrawing, softer than the rain and lighter than the dark clouds outside, Josh licked away any pain Ken may have endured because of him.

Excited, prone against the nylon of his sleeping bag, sheltered in his rain-beat one-man tent, with Josh on top of him, Ken didn't know what would happen next. He didn't think he would be hurt. But he didn't think the old man, Josh, was the type to sexually sate Ken—a mere kid of thirty compared to Josh's, what, sixty, seventy years?

When Josh rolled Ken onto his back and straddled him, Ken was startled. His orgasm came with Josh's third drop towards him. Ken felt foolish. Good. And shuddered.

Josh remained with Ken inside, and smiled into the younger

man's face. "Thank you for offering me the shelter of your tent."

Ken felt vague. Very concretely, he knew that a strong man—a man who reminded him of a Swiss grandfather that climbed the Alps before breakfast, chased goats along the rocks before noon, ate lunch and then cross-country skied twenty miles for groceries before dining with his grandchildren, kissing them a lot, and blessing them with kind words before they slept—had just pulled from him an extraordinary orgasm.

He vaguely remembered pitching his tent on the rise of the meadow, where he would wait out the storm under cover. He certainly remembered the wolves romp across the vernal green sponge of the meadow, playing, not paying much attention to Ken. When he saw the man, Josh, at the far side of the wild field, Ken was afraid he was breached from his grandfamily, by about ten steep miles up; a tough climb for Ken. The wolves played across the meadow again, jumping over and nipping one another. Ken waved the man to him, offering his tent as shelter against the rain.

Once inside the small tent, Josh pulled off Ken's clothes and entered him without pretense. It wasn't rape, Ken knew before and while it was happening, but he didn't know what it was.

There was something about the old man, more than age and more than his pleasure-giving, that made Ken say Sir, a word he despised. "Uh, thank you, Sir."

Josh winked a dark amber-flecked eye and laughed. "My name is Josh."

The rain beat the tent so low that it clung to Josh's broad, thick back. "If we lie side by side, Josh, we can both fit in here, and you won't get wet."

Josh accepted the suggestion and moved, hugging the length of Kent's body into his length, covering their nakedness with the dry flannel liner of Kent's sleeping bag. He kissed Ken as though Ken were a child and Josh an infatuated lover.

Used to his own company when he hiked, Ken didn't mind when a timber wolf howled across the meadow. He nearly shrieked when another howled just outside the tent.

"Pets. Well, friends," Josh assured, kissing Ken softly on his biceps.

Another howl, this one from outside the entrance.

"I don't like this."

Ken pulled as far away as one man can from another in a one-man tent. Josh looked angry. Ken was afraid. The storm wasn't passing, if anything, worsening. Ken felt like the lost kids he searched for—alone and frightened.

Another wolf, wolves, howled from the foot of the tent. Sides. Entrance. Across the meadow.

Josh laughed.

The wind was a howl. The rain beat the tent.

Josh's laughter wasn't one of a crazed lunatic howling at the moon. Odd, but lovely. Surprising Ken with calm.

"I've seen you work," Josh said. "More than a few times. You're very good." He moved, filling the void Ken had made between their bodies. "Don't be frightened."

"Me?" Ken stupidly said, as though he were frightened. "Do you live up here?"

"Yes. But I'd rather you keep that to yourself. Mine is a..." Josh looked sad? Careful. "natural life. Do you remember the night, almost as stormy as this, that you stayed when the rest of the team returned to camp; crawled down the rocks that you shouldn't have alone, and cuddled that lost eight-year-old, Sarah, for a day-and-a-half?"

Ken remembered. It wasn't fun.

"And the ten-year-old boy who scratched at your face for the two days you were confined in that snow shelter you made for him?"

Ken touched his cheeks, and the scars. Josh kissed them.

"What about the rapist who thought he should penetrate the earth with his illegal mine? Stuck, wiry and thinner than the others, you allowed your legs tied together, one of your worst fears, and descended head first down the narrow shaft, saving him."

"How?" Ken didn't like publicity, and the forestry department never released his name to the papers.

Another howl, but the bite, some of the fright was missing.

"Sweet, sweet, Ken. When you were afraid that timber wolf was going to eat you and little Sarah—rather than shoot her with that damn revolver you carry, you told the wolf to go get help: she did. She follows you. Indeed, she has a crush on you. After you sheltered that boy, you cooked dehydrated eggs for her."

"She didn't look well."

"She wasn't. Thank you for melting the snow so she could drink."

"I didn't know she was the same one."

"Shhh." Josh chuckled deeply, and whispered, "Don't tell her, she'll be crushed."

Which was better? The extraordinary orgasm, or the exhilarating sense of fright Josh pulled out. Ken had to go to the bathroom, but the wolves were howling at the dark gray dusk descending the mountains.

"I'm not that brave, Josh. Really.. Uh, I have to go, ummm, outside..."

Josh played his lips across Ken's chest as he laughed and licked a nipple to attention. "I will make love to you, and kiss you, comfort and watch out for you—but I will not hold your hand while you piss. Go on, they won't bother you."

Outside, Ken was bothered. He squatted near an Oregon grape just blooming yellow, when two wolves approached.

"Josh?"

One, a large male, mottled, having shed only parts of his winter coat, sniffed Kent's chest and snarled quietly in his face.

"Josh," Ken whispered. Panic, like an urge or hunger, crawled in the pit of his stomach.

"Just do your business," Josh said, sticking his head out the tent. "Damn, it's wet out here!" Back inside, he yelled, "They smell me on you."

Ken considered fainting. He leaned his back against the rough bark of a fir and tried to pull his eyes from the drooling mouth of the wolf. He almost reached out to pet the beast, but tremors of mythical fear shot a warning through his hand. Would he have been as frightened had he been clothed?

The cold, wet muzzle of the other brushed against his buttocks. Shards of fear pricked out of his skin and coursed down his spine, causing his backside to pimple like goose flesh. If he moved, they would eat him.

Dusk would soon be murdered by full night. Under the tree, the rain couldn't pound him with its vehement force, but an annoying drip, drip, drip-drip, played his forehead in water torture fashion.

When the male sniffed at, and then licked Ken's genitals, he

had had enough.
"Josh! Please!"
As though they sympathized with Ken's fear, the wolves submissively backed off and sat, like mere pit bulls when ordered by their master.
"Count yourself loved!" Josh yelled. Ken heard his deep chuckle pulled along on the wind as though the wind and rain couldn't dull the old man.
Awe pushed away Ken's fright. Wonder. "Uh, can I pet you? I mean, may I shake your hand?" he asked of the big male just two feet away. The wolf nuzzled into Ken's chest and licked. Two, three, five, more—a family of wolves jumped Ken and wrestled with him. He giggled, and wrestled.
"Ouch!" A pup bit his ear and a bitch growled. "Oh, it didn't hurt much," he assured her. He liked the tackle of warm, wet fur—he'd lecture them on hygiene later.
"Josh, come here!" Ken was cheering. "Look! I'm playing with timber wolves. A whole family!"
Josh poked out his head, not minding the rain, and matched Ken's childish giggles. He laughed hard when a pup humped at Ken's naked thigh and Ken said to Mom, laughing, "Please don't think I'm a bad influence."
Ken was nuzzled and licked, sometimes nipped, but playfully, humped and wrestled, and kissed by the family until he was so exhausted he just lay on his back in the soggy meadow, arms and legs spread, bathed by the rough tongues of the licking wolves. One of the pups folded into Ken's armpit and licked his cheek.
It wasn't long before Ken's sex erectly stood, accepting the feral sensation of the pack's attention.
When he returned to the tent, reluctant to leave the wolves, but excited by Josh's call for him, the older man sniffed Ken and folded him into his dry arms. The scent of beast aroused Josh's aggression.
Pinned on his back, Ken was not frightened by the aggressive mouth, lips, and tongue of Josh's caresses.
His sounds were those of need and determination, not violence.
His mouth was gentle; Ken feared nothing when Josh filled his mouth with Ken's scrotum, then fingers, then nose, ears, erection—marking the younger man like territory.

Rolled onto his stomach, Ken winced briefly, but smiled at the whispers of praise Josh offered as he pressed himself into him. Words from a man—rapid, frightening thrusts, and deep, like an animal. Outside, the wolves howled a clarion praise for Ken. Inside, Josh's fingernails clawed into Ken's shoulders. Praise whispered. "Chosen like mates." Rapid. Faster. A low snarl. Faster. On his knees, Josh thrust hard, hard and fast. His knees squeezed Ken's legs tightly together.

"Josh you're..."

"Shhh."

Slowing, but pushing as deeply as he could into Ken, his feet searching for support, leverage, Josh shuddered. Quivered. And he was done.

They laughed and shared Ken's jerky, nuts, and dried fruit before they snuggled closely together in the sleeping bag, finding it difficult to keep their lips from one another's flesh.

There was an electric shock, mostly static, and then an immediate jangling, fierce pound of thunder—Ken had felt it that close before—and then the pup yelped, screamed outside the tent.

"Jesus!"

Josh pulled Ken back into the tent by an ankle. "It was easily a mile away. No one was hit, lovely Ken. And his Dad and Mom are with him."

Never afraid of Cascade storms, but worried for the pup, Ken fell into Josh's arms and the wrap of his embrace. "It's not much of a story, Josh said, finally giving in to Ken's interrogation. "Oh certainly, I have many tales I can tell you, and would like to tell you in the future."

Ken smiled, pushed himself closer to Josh and bit at his chin. He savored the thought of the two together in one another's company. Josh's aggression held no malice, and Ken would gladly accept his way of making love.

"I was nineteen in the early thirties when I joined Roosevelt's Civilian Conservation Corps and escaped into the freedom of these mountains. One taste of wilderness, after just a week up here, and I knew I would never descend again.

"Yes, it was hard work. That first summer was unusually hot—in the 90's by sunup—sunstroke killed two men that first month. There was about fifty of us at the camp below. Well, you know the

CCC barracks behind the ranger's station.

"I was a lead man, worked by myself, mostly because I wanted to. A lot like you, Ken. And I scouted for trails. Actually, I scouted for beauty that would mark a trail's end and give it purpose. Oh, those were the days—silly days of ignorance. You could climb, hike, through woods and forest, swim rivers and lakes, and know: KNOW you were the first man to step foot on that fresh piece of earth."

"It took me years to get used to a pack of wolves devouring a mule deer, squirrel, rabbit, old bear, lame elk."

"Oh."

"But it was the wolves you asked about. Dripping with sweat, I tore off my saturated clothes and was pulled into the lake. Diving in, I understood that I had no choice, I was compelled to bathe in its beauty. I swam for hours, laughed and swam. Rocked and floated gently on my back staring at the stark blue sky framed with snow-capped mountains. Heaven would be a crass comparison.

"Prepared to make camp, the wolves were there when I returned to my clothes. They were larger then, much larger than these children outside." Josh tilted his head toward the family Ken had played with.

"They showed anger. Teeth, and anger with me for trespassing. I froze naturally, darting my eyes about for a route of escape. To my right was a jagged cliff, steep but not too steep for a man to climb to its ledge, about ten feet up.

"With the standoff complete, I ran when the two wolves charged. I fell, got up and ran for the cliff. With little effort, I was halfway up the rock wall before one of the pair lunged and snatched a mawful of my butt, dragging me to ground level feet first. Scraped the hell out of my cock.

"The moment my feet hit the ground I sprang back up, clawing for a handhold. But the rock slipped away.

"I was trapped, stuck. My knees and feet hurt, but my hands searched for a higher rock. My body was sprawled over a lower boulder—one more boulder up and they couldn't get me.

"But if I were still. Still. Maybe they wouldn't think of me as prey.

"Oh but they could smell me. I sweat and my ankle bled from the fall when I first ran. Oddly, the flesh of my buttocks hadn't torn—it hadn't sunk its teeth into me. My nose was in my armpit and I knew I smelled of fear.

"The rock and precarious position, my right knee lifted and pressed against a slight outcropping, exposed not just my butt, but my scrotum and cock to the pair. Immobile, scared, I knew being mauled was going to hurt terribly: I envisioned my balls snatched away in one bite. I prayed they would pull me down by my bleeding ankle—then I could roll into a ball before they killed me.

"I closed my eyes to their snarling. Their scent was as discouraging as their sound. Then one screamed like a baby and sounded like death. The other ran for the cover of the brush.

"Safe. I thought I was safe. I didn't know what scared them away, but I was thankful. Until I heard a deeper growling snarl.

"A third one, larger, approached me. I thought about moving. One fingernail in the rock above, and I was sure I could lift myself to safety. There was a whimper and I thought it was me, but I was too frightened to make any sound.

"Just as I was putting power into my finger, the one I hoped to be my savior, the lead wolf, the one that chased the others away, lunged.

"Its fetid, blood-wet muzzle cradled between my left cheek and shoulder. But it wasn't snapping.

"I couldn't move. Sharp claws gripped my shoulders and slashed my skin. Its wet and warm body covered my back and it howled. It humped at me. Hit my lower back, a thigh, each of my buttocks with its wet organ. It slid the length of my butt, up to my lower back a couple of times.

"I trembled. It licked the back of my neck, I smelled blood left on my skin, but it wasn't killing me. One of its humps found its need. Once in, it was like a machine, humping rapidly, slipping out occasionally but repenetrating with its next thrust.

"Still terrified, I felt— I don't know, I never will. Not love, but a melding of sorts. Except for its claws in my flesh, I was in little pain. Its part inside me didn't hurt much, but it whined each time its furry balls hit the boulder between my legs. It snarled ownership.

"Damn, would it kill me if I moved? I tempted the beast and pushed my hand between me and the rock, between my legs, so its testicles hit my hand rather than batter painfully against the rocks.

"It was no less aggressive, but maybe it would spare my life when it finished with me.

"When it was done, and left what it wanted to leave inside of me, it remained, pinning me to the rock. I had never had a man, haven't until you, Ken, and was surprised to feel the warmth it left inside.

"Its heart beat rapidly into my back. My frightened pulse matched the pulse of its satisfaction. Its dank coat made me smell, the smell made me want to vomit. When it dismounted me, it licked my back, my legs, my butt. Its tongue was rough, cleansing. When I tried to move, it snarled like the powerful and deadly animal it was, and I froze again. It made another sound—a gentler sound. The sound of communion with me and the lupine seed it left within me.

"The other two wolves returned, apparently permitted by their lead to mount me. One of them smelled me first, smelling the first, and mounted, having no trouble with its aim. He dug more deeply into my shoulders, pushed more deeply into me. He ways quickly finished and I was quickly remounted by the third.

"When I awoke, I was on my back at the foot of the rock wall staring up at the black sky filled with stars and a perfectly round full moon, framed with mountains. The three were curled around me, warming my naked body against the cool night.

"I never returned to the CCC camp, and have lived with my family ever since."

Josh had tears in his eyes. Ken didn't know why he had been chosen, but he was thankful. He kissed softly at the ancient scars on Josh's shoulders, and the two men slept—warmed by their naked bodies against the storm outside.

Dave Swartout is currently dabbling in environmental erotica—in literary form.

38

Uncle River
The Drunk

One evening Mr. Bannister heard a loud crash in front of his house. On going out to investigate he discovered a drunk had run smack into a stone wall.

Luckily for the drunk, he was not going very fast. He was only moderately bruised in the wreck. His car, however, was inoperable.

The drunk was in no condition to get himself home. Mr. Bannister thought someone ought to keep an eye on him anyhow in case he was hurt worse than he appeared to be. Mr. Bannister brought the drunk in the house and settled him on the couch for the night.

The drunk was sort of awake by the time Mr. Bannister had to leave for work the next morning, if sore and hung over.

"Help yourself to breakfast," Mr. Bannister said. "I'll take you home later if you need."

When Mr. Bannister got home, the drunk was gone. The front door was open, and it was obvious the neighborhood dogs had been in the house. Several containers of food the drunk had gotten out were still on the counter. The weather was quite warm. Most of the food was spoiled.

By the phone, Mr. Bannister discovered the names of several wrecking services written all over a book. It was not a particularly valuable book. It was not scratch paper either though.

Mr. Bannister was quite annoyed, but he cleaned up and settled down for the evening. When he went to go to bed, however, he found the bedroom smelled of shit. This was most unpleasant, but try as he might, he could not find the source of the smell. Eventually Mr. Bannister just gave up looking and got into bed. When he did, he felt something which, upon examination, he discovered to be a pile of shit.

Disgusted and enraged, Mr. Bannister cleaned himself and the bed and then went to sleep on a foam pad on the floor in another room. In the morning he went looking for the drunk.

"And on top of everything else," said Mr. Bannister, "One of the dogs shat in my bed."

"Oh no, that was me," said the drunk.

"What!"

"I couldn't find the bathroom."

Mr. Bannister was speechless.

"I don't see what you're being so petty about," said the drunk. "It was really a very small turd."

Uncle River is currently feuding with his nearest neighbor in one of New Mexico's most spectacular and remote ghost towns. His "Mongollon News" has been a popular weekly radio and newspaper feature since 1986. His other writing has attracted lots of encouragement lately, some publication, but not much money.

39

Vava Pussy
Vavadoo

my desk is pile high with shit it looks like pauls desk. maybe it is pauls desk. i cant wait to sell this desk. once i had a large dining room wood table as my desk. it was in the living room with a couch and the fireplace with built in book shelves. there were frenchy doors that went out to the enclosed porch that held an old three speed bike that robert rode down clark st. sitting up like a prairie dog wearing a plaid cap. there were two larger than life awful paintings with xmas tree lights strung over them that robert did. they were in the dining room. one was of amber, the he she that he fucked in atlanta..the other was ambers companion. some doe boy. there was a big moon behind each of them. they were bad but they were o.k. that was the room robert painted in. my bedroom was off of it. it was the only room in the apartment that didnt have wood floors. it had a large white sheet of linoleum in it. i slept on blankets over it and there were a few necklaces hanging off the three rung radiator in that room. a tin mess dish on top of the radiator with birds wings in it. on the far end of the room my suede jacket hung on the wall the arms ripped to shreds by the wolfdog zeb that lived with us. LUNCH was written on the back of the jacket in black el marko. there were six radiators in that apartment and only half of the one in the kitchen worked. meechee the landlord one day was up tinkering but not doing shit to fix the heat scene. he was teasing zeb and zeb bit into his calf fast. the police came up to fill out a report but wouldnt enter the apartment until zeb was locked in roberts room. roberts room was on the other side of the diningroompaintingroom. at night time robert and i would call zeb from each of our beds trying to convince the dog to sleep with one of us. i think zeb would lick cum off roberts dick lovingly. i just wanted him for his coat warmth. zeb never was one of the dogs i fucked. robert picked up some guy at manscountry one night. his name was jeffrey big cock and he came by our place a few times..northwestern u. curly blond jew boy big cock. robert thinks thats who gave him aids. one day juan came by to see me. he wanted cash. i gave him 100 bucks from the lawsuit i had just won involving my skull fracture. the next morning he was back for more money. i gave him one dollar and told him never to ask me for money again. he was staying on the couch in the livingroom some nights. i didnt want him sleeping with me. he was having trouble with bert basically he wasnt working for cash. we went to the voodoo graveyard two blocks away with zeb who was chasing rabbits and showing us where all the headless chickens were. that was the first time i heardsaw a woodpecker. i wanted to fuck juan there. we hardly ever talked. we went home and fucked and then he right away decided to get on the clark st. bus and head back to pilsen to go and see bert. i went out on a walk and i was across the street from the wilson avenue fire department cruising along with zeb when a fireman yelled at me/wheres your mustache you fucking dyke?/ i pulled down my jeans exposing my black pubes to him and yelled back/right here..ya wanna try it on?/ i buttoned up and kept walking. there was arzel myles the next block up. arzel the blackest hunk of a bull terrier face on top of locomotive body. he was ready with the usual hey baby i be telling you true arzel is made for you baby arzel knows how to make you feel goooood i be telling you true. all summer long arzel be telling me true. robert wanted arzel bad but arzel was homophobe stud. robert told me to never fuck arzel unless robert was home. he wanted to film it on high contrast b & w so i wouldnt show up. robert wasnt home. i was horny and had heard enough of that be telling you true stuff. i invited him up pretending we were going to get some pot to take on a walk down by the lake with us. we sat at the kitchen table smoking a joint shooting the shit. he got up and stood behind me slipping my tits out of my fathers shortsleeved shirt that i was wearing. he bent down and started sucking on my neck licking down to my tits sucking on my nipples and i got up and he followed to the blankets on the floor in my bedroom. here finally was mister arzel i be telling you true baby stud man blacker than black myles in my bedroom. we stripped each other naked and i began to suck on his uncircumcised cock but he pushed me off it and forced me onto my back stuck his dick in my cunt. 12 strokes and he came immediately rolled off fell asleep. i lay there looking at the ceiling listening to him snore/ looking at that body. i got up and smoked some more pot and arzel woke up. he said/oh baby you must be the best i ever had i never fell asleep before you really did it to me baby i be telling you true

Vava Pussy leads an exagerated life in Knoxville, Tennessee. It is her biggest hope to get the hell out of there ... take the kids, take the husband, take the dog. Rumor has it that she/he/them/it may be moving to the Puget Sound in the near future.

40

Gary Wiener
Six Inches Up

Jeffry Kent had a problem. He was the only boy in the tenth grade—make that the only boy in school, or the western hemisphere, or the galaxy!—who didn't know about sex. And he knew it. He knew it day, and he knew it night. Ignorance haunted him like the monster haunted Dr. Frankenstein. Ignorance climbed up his legs like a great hairy tarantula that could sting at any time. It could sting anytime anyone else got an inkling that Jeffry knew nothing about sex.

He could have ended this hassle simply by asking his friends Milman or Pearlstein, quietly, discreetly, one or the other in private, to fill him in on the facts. But he didn't want to get laughed off the planet.

So Jeffry had to face the sting of occasional taunts and tests.

Like in English class, with Mrs. Green, the world's oldest teacher. She had wrinkled facial flesh that hung down to the floor. Jeffry sat in the first row on the right, fourth seat back. Across from Jeff sat Reggie Hunter, and behind Reggie, Dirk Maris. They would talk back and forth almost non-stop for the entire forty-five minutes of class, while Jeffry sat working diligently on the prepositional phrase. Mrs. Green was stone deaf, or so it seemed, and never noticed their conversations that often caused titters from students seated clear across the room.

From these conversations it was apparent that Reggie and Dirk were great lovers of literature, and had read myriad works. Perhaps Mrs. Green would have encouraged their literary critiques, had she heard them, Jeffry thought.

"You read *The Harrad Experiment*?" Reggie has asked Dirk during class one day.

"No. Any good?" Dirk asked, stretching his six-foot-three inches of gangly adolescence so that his feet angled across the aisle and came to rest underneath Jeffry's chair.

"Un-fucking-believable. Sixty-nine and everything."

Dirk began to breathe heavily, and Jeffry couldn't help releasing a chuckle. Looking back he would have suffered less embarrassment had he released a fart.

"What're you guffawing about?" Dirk immediately attacked.

"Hell of a guy, Jeffry thought. He pretended he didn't hear the question. He'd heard about *The Harrad Experiment*, all right. Hadn't read it maybe, but heard about it. College kids getting credit for screwing, or something like that. Sure he'd heard about the book. And that was why he'd laughed. After all, he may not have known anything about sex, but he wasn't stupid. Everyone knew about *The Harrad Experiment*.

"Little bastard's laughing at me," Dirk said.

"Geezus, does he have to shout it out, Jeffry thought. He knew he was in trouble. Couldn't that old bag up front hear? But Mrs. Green was absorbed in a book, a Silhouette romance novel, it appeared, while she assumed the class was hard at work on pages 36-40 of *Warriner's*.

"Thinks he knows everything, doesn't he," the demon-in-student's-clothes continued. He turned now to poor Jeffry. "Bet you don't. You probably don't even know what sixty-nine is." Jeff buried his head in his book. Go away, he thought. Go away.

"Well, what does it mean?"

To Jeffry it seemed as if the entire class (including Mrs. Green, who put down her romance, the title of which suddenly appeared to Jeffry as *Sixty-Nine Steps to Heaven*), rose as one, and began to chant, "What does it mean? What does it mean?" He shook the cobwebs of prepositional phrase diagrams from his brain and looked around. A few heads around the class were surreptitiously looking his way, but Mrs. Green was still buried in her novel, *Cytheria's Summer*.

"What does it mean?" Dirk insisted. Despite the awkwardness

that was an inevitable by product of a series of growth-spurts, Dirk had been kept on the basketball team as what the coach called a "project." Jeffry wished he were Project Apollo, and that he'd been launched into orbit. Oh God, you s.o.b., at least stop shouting. Were more heads now looking his way? Cindy Lawler and Mary Rita Canard? He had to ignore this guy. It was the only way out. But he couldn't. Besides, maybe he could bluff his way out and shut the moron up. He took a deep breath and said to himself, I'll bite.

"Shhh!" Jeffry said. Wrong opener. Dirk looked pissed. He lifted the metal bookrack under Jeffry's desk, elevating the entire seat several inches, and with it, Jeffry. Dirk may have been awkward, but compared to five-foot-six inch, one-thirty pound Jeffry, he could have been Arnold Schwartzenegger.

"What the hell does it mean, know it all?"

Jeffry cleared his throat. Reggie's ears perked up like a cocker spaniel who hears his master at the door. The fool was going to speak!

"I know what it is," said the fool. If he was lucky, Dirk would let it drop there, or at least lower his feet and let Jeffry drop.

"So, what is it?"

"Well... er... ugh... ummm... ah..."

"Well?"

"I've... err... heard... umm... ah...."

"Well," Dirk and Reggie chorused. Jeffry was sure the whole class was watching by now.

"I've... er... heard two versions." There, it was out. He brushed his forehead with his palm and it came back damp.

"Two versions!" Reggie was delighted. "Well?"

Which one should he choose?

"The first is... is... *six* inches up, and *nine* months to go," he blurted in one blast of fetid air.

"Six inches up?" Dirk repeated.

"Nine months to go?" Reggie squealed.

"Well, there's another version," Jeffry cried. Heads were bobbing up and down everywhere in the classroom, it seemed to him. He was sure Terri Davis and Sid Dickson were listening in, at the very least. God, why hadn't he called and asked Dr. Ruth the other night?

"Well, it's a double blow job."

Jeffry's desk hit the floor with a thud. He could see his words hanging in the air in calligraphic lettering.

Mrs. Green looked up. "Jeffry," she said sternly.

Oh Lord, take me now, he thought. The entire class was now, definitely, unquestionably gazing straight at Jeffry, as if he were wearing a plastic penis on his nose.

"Yes Mrs. Green?" Call the hangman. Strap him in the chair. Was there a razor blade in the knapsack underneath his desk? At that moment, he would have swallowed a hand grenade.

"Did I get your grammar homework from last night?" the teacher asked.

"No, Mrs. Green. I'll turn it in now."

"No problem, so long as you have it. I'll take it after class." She returned to her planbook, having evidently discarded the novel, while Jeffry was busily explaining the birds and bees. The classroom was quiet once more. He was saved. God, I'll never doubt you again, he apostrophized.

"What's a double blow job?" Dirk said, and Jeffry's desk was suddenly back in the air again. "I'll bet you don't even know."

Later, on the way out of class, Dirk sidled up to his partner in persecution.

"Did you ever hear of that first one before?" he asked Reggie.

"No, did you?"

"No...."

"Damn, six inches up and nine months to go. Do you think he was right about that?"

Gary Wiener's story, "A February of Underwear," appeared in the Summer '88 issue of SOTT. "Six Inches Up" is an excerpt from his work-in-progress, Sex: A Novel.